I0674101

GOT
TO BE A
HERO

CruiserPublications

Got To Be A Hero

Copyright © 2017 Paul Duffau

All rights reserved.

This book, or parts thereof, may not be reproduced
in any form without written permission.

Published 2017 by Cruiser Publications

Book design by Logotecture

ISBN 13- 978-0- 9889479-7- 9

This book is licensed for your personal enjoyment only.

All rights reserved.

This is a work of fiction. All characters and events portrayed in this book are
fictional,and any resemblance to real people or incidents is purely coincidental.

For Dori Whitford and the creative writing class
at Meade High School, Spokane

GOT
TO BE A
HERO

PAUL DUFFAU

CHAPTER ONE

Kenzie circled to her left and stayed two inches within his reach, to tempt the man into a mistake. Her sweat soaked the T-shirt she wore under her *dobok,* but she didn't care. A quick flip of her head cleared the droplets that threatened to slip into her eyes. She focused on the knot in the green belt of the lanky man opposite her, her peripheral vision sufficient to monitor his hands and feet. He feinted, she glided away.

The only sounds that reached through Kenzie's concentration came from her feet gliding over the cushioned floor and her opponent's breathing.

Her sparring partner was a newcomer to the martial arts studio. He moved smoothly, despite being old—more than twice her age. Around the edge of the sparring ring, the advanced students of the *dojang* knelt and watched in silent assessment. She faked a front kick with her left foot, designed to pull his block to the left and open his body. Instead, he slipped closer, switching to a left-handed fighting stance, and his lead fist, encased in a heavyweight sparring glove, flashed toward her.

Without thinking, Kenzie reacted with her left arm, technique perfect with the hand rotating as her whole forearm swept across her body. She stepped back with her right foot to accelerate the block with a snap of her slender hips. The impact through her glove jarred her and, at the edge of her vision, she noted surprise briefly light the man's eyes. A roundhouse kick followed the punch, but the man delivered it too slowly; she retreated to safety.

Mr. Green Belt dropped his hands a fraction of an inch, then his shoulders raised. She recognized the signs of the impending attack, his shifting of weight to the rear leg. In the same instant, Kenzie seized the opportunity to slip past his guard, get inside his defense where his length would work against him.

Kenzie sensed Green Belt shifting his weight for a kick and attacked first. She knifed in and launched a roundhouse kick of her own, leg arcing high over his fists, toes pulled back.

At the last instant, she realized that the man, not anticipating that she would aim for his head, had moved into the kick instead of evading. Too late, she tried to stop her kick, but it had a momentum of its own. She felt the ball of her foot crunch into her sparring partner's head with a sick thud, behind the ear, below the protective headgear. Mr. Green Belt snorted as his head snapped sideways, and his eyes glazed.

"Break!" The command from Jules, the *sabomnim* who owned the studio, came over the shocked murmur of the other students.

Mortified at breaking the cardinal rule of the *dojang*, Kenzie began to drop her gloves, but the man, still dazed, launched a hard straight left jab. She jerked her head back, and his fist passed close enough that she felt the snapping of the man's crisp white jacket, heard the crack that accompanied the snap.

Wide-eyed, she tried to retreat, but the man launched another attack, the slowness from the sparring drill gone. Her gaze darted up to his face. A nervous chill touched the base of her spine, and she backed out of the sparring ring. Students scattered to get out of the way, several of the older boys rising to their feet, uncertain on how to intervene.

"*Break!*"

The blows came fast, and he used both hands and both feet, in combinations. It was like fighting a well-trained but berserk octopus, blows arriving from every direction. The touch contact from the drill disappeared. These attacks were meant to harm.

She swept her right arm down to block a low round kick. The block arrived in time to stop the strike, her forearm slamming into his shin bone. Pain radiated up her arm, and the force knocked her sideways.

He's so frackin' strong, she thought as she ducked away from a whistling back fist attack that would have shattered her jaw if it landed. She pivoted low to spin away, to find some space, to escape.

"BREAK!"

Jules's strong hands grasped the man from behind. The fourth-*dan* black belt in the traditional Korean style of Tang Soo Do, a powerful woman who stood an inch shorter than Kenzie's opponent, did not try to control the man's body when he whirled to face this new threat. Instead, Kenzie saw Jules clasp the fleshy part of his shoulders to make contact through the fog in his head.

"Break, Robert." Jules's voice dropped in volume but carried the iron authority of the master. She stared into Robert's face. After an initial surge against her hands, he leaned back, giving his head a hard shake as though attempting to settle the various interior pieces of a mixed-up jigsaw into the proper spaces.

"Sit."

Robert melted down to his knee. Jules knelt beside him.

"All the way down, Robert. Sit."

He did as instructed, letting out a faint groan. He squeezed his eyelids shut, then opened them and locked on Kenzie.

"You 'kay?" His words slurred, and he still did not possess a natural perceptiveness, but at least somebody was home now.

Nervous tremors racked Kenzie's arms and legs, but she nodded. He nodded back with an expression of relief.

"McKenzie."

Kenzie faced Jules, her body still reacting to the adrenaline surging through her veins.

Jules didn't shout. Her voice held an icy neutrality. "Go to my office." She pointed. "Wait."

Kenzie shook her head. "Yes, ma'am," she said, trying without success to keep anger out of her voice.

She got a stern nod from Jules as the woman turned to administer aid to Robert.

She turned, then stomped across the mats to the gap in the low wall that split the studio from the practice floor. The other students averted their heads. Kenzie strode through the loose circle, chin up and lips pursed, her features rigid as a mannequin's. From the corner of her eye, Kenzie could see the image of an angry teenager—herself—stalking beside her, sharply delineated in the full-length mirrors that lined the front wall. She could also feel the pressure of all the students surreptitiously tracking her progress like a weight at her back.

Only when she stepped into the office, behind the protection of a wall, did she let her guard down. Flopping into a straight-backed chair, she closed her eyes, envisioning the hard strike again. In hindsight, she knew that in stepping into attack mode, she'd committed one hundred percent. In the replay version, she prayed for a way to stop it, but it was done. There was no way to change the course of the past.

She drew a deep breath, and her head dropped. She put both hands up to her face and pressed her fingertips hard on her eyeballs until red bled into her vision. The acrid stink of her own fearful sweat wrinkled her nose.

The final instant before impact refused to fade, even as the red behind her eyelids turned into white-hot sparks.

Crunch.

Kenzie waited in a stony silence while the class did form drills instead of sparring. Her muscular twitches slowly dissolved into a simmering resentment and the body odor faded to a faint reminder as her sweat dried. On her arms, dull red weals rose. She rubbed them gingerly.

A shadow passed the doorway, and she glanced over her shoulder to see Robert, changed into street clothes, leaving with his gear bag hanging heavy in his hand.

He regarded her with a combination of sympathy and embarrassment. "Sorry."

"Me too," she said. Her voice cracked. She heard the door open, the sound of the street traffic invading the quiet of the studio before it faded back to calm when the door swung shut.

Me, too.

With a start, she realized from the outburst of chatter that Jules had ended the lesson. The voices mixed together, subdued compared to the ordinary energetic cheerfulness that infected the karate kids as they got ready to leave.

Some left, still dressed in their martial arts uniforms, talking with friends until they got beside the doorway to the office, then falling silent until they left the building. Most refused to acknowledge her.

Jules's voice carried over the hubbub, reminding them to practice, saying good-byes, as she always did.

Kenzie didn't budge.

Deep silence dropped into the studio. Rustling sounds reached her ears as she tried to track Jules, but she kept her eyes fixated on the pictures that the instructor had on the walls. Amongst the usual pictures of tournaments hung a black-and-white photo of Jules sitting cross-legged in a meditative pose. The woman in the photograph was a much younger version of her instructor. That Jules was pretty, despite the severe lines of the uniform, maybe in her twenties. Instead of a feeling of peacefulness, Kenzie sensed subtle anger emanating from the image. Deep inside her, a matching anger echoed.

And something else, something unfamiliar . . .

The "something else" sent shivers down her spine, so Kenzie averted her gaze from the picture.

That's better, she thought, but her breathing stayed fast and shallow.

She had her eyes closed when the faintest rustle of cotton informed her that she wasn't alone. Her head jerked up as she located the source of the sound.

Jules settled into the rolling chair behind the desk, resting her elbows on the black armrests, hands folded in front of her. The chair barely creaked.

Kenzie focused on the hands. They were thicker than average but not unusually so. She had watched those same hands shatter concrete paving blocks. While her thoughts swirled about in her head, she noted that Jules wore clear polish on her nails. A buildup of calluses at the knuckles provided the only clue to the force her instructor could unleash.

Kenzie could feel the weight of the older woman's gaze on her, filled with reproach. Kenzie peeked up. Jules's features were composed in neutral planes. Darting glances performed an inspection of the angry red marks on Kenzie's skin. Satisfied there wasn't major harm, the woman nodded and brought her attention to Kenzie's face.

Kenzie lifted her head and blinked at meeting Jules's gaze, at the implicit disappointment. She lost control of her features, her brows knitting and lips twisting into a grimace that she tried to stifle.

Jules spoke first.

"You could have been very badly hurt." She said the words quietly, and waited.

Kenzie gave a hard shake of her head, ponytail swinging. She searched the surface of the desk, flicking back and forth as she squirmed. "Robert is okay?"

Jules leaned forward in the chair, the loose cuffs of her sleeves falling open as she shifted her elbows to the top of the desk. "Look at me."

Kenzie switched her gaze from the neat piles on the desk to Jules.

"You stunned him a bit, but there's no sign of a concussion."

Her astute gaze sharpened. Kenzie saw the assessment of the bruises forming on her arms.

"You could have been badly hurt," Jules repeated.

Like she couldn't restrain them anymore, the words spilled from Kenzie.

"I could have hurt him." Her chest tightened into a painful heartache, and her eyes grew bright and liquid. "He moved, and I tried to pull back," she said, her voice pleading, "but I couldn't stop and then I hit him and his eyes—"

"You could have killed him," Jules said, interrupting the torrent from Kenzie. Her tone was blunt, her voice soft but filled with irresistible conviction.

Kenzie's eyes widened as she stared at Jules. Shame and fear fought for supremacy; fear won. Her hands began to shake again. She was riveted on her instructor. "I'm sorry."

Jules's countenance showed a hardness, but also concern.

"Your technique is solid, Kenzie." Jules paused, considering her words. "What you lack is control. You get lost in your emotions." Jules's pointer finger moved a fraction of an inch. "Control isn't only being able to stop a kick an eighth of an inch from somebody's nose. You've done a good job of training your body, you've worked hard. Physically, you are gifted with good reflexes and coordination, and, for a small woman, you are powerful."

Kenzie sat, confused at the compliment, and uncomfortable but pleased at being called a woman. Most adults assumed that a small-statured fifteen-year-old was still a child, and treated Kenzie that way. It pissed her off.

Jules studied her, a sharp going-over that pinned Kenzie down in her chair, mute and unmoving.

"That's actually too bad."

Kenzie's eyelids fluttered at the sudden sting of the words.

Too bad?

She clenched her jaw tight as Jules got blurry. She turned her head and blinked rapidly until her vision cleared.

A frown crossed Jules's face, smoothed over in an instant. Her instructor's voice became hesitant, as though she was unsure how much to reveal.

"You have a tremendous . . . ," Jules started, before tapering off. She took a deep breath, tilting her head to peer at Kenzie. Her voice took on a confiding tone. "You've trusted me to teach you how to defend yourself. There's more to the martial arts than the movements and self-defense." She tapped her forehead with a finger. "Will you trust me now when I say I can teach you how to tap into your strengths *here?*"

Kenzie nodded once, mostly to say that she'd heard the words even if she didn't quite understand what Jules was suggesting.

"You're not mad?"

"I'm furious," Jules replied, "mostly with myself. I should have had better control of the exercise. I saw you baiting him. I didn't realize how aggressive Robert was to press an advantage. Two quick people out of control is dangerous."

Kenzie listened with embarrassment. She hadn't realized she had been so obvious about enticing the attack so she could take advantage of her speed. It also stung that Jules was taking responsibility for her actions. She didn't trust her voice not to crack, but spoke up anyway.

"I was the one that screwed up."

Jules sighed. "It was a team effort, Kenzie." She took a deep breath and made a decision.

"A man that is hurt and wounded is far more dangerous than an overconfident man. When you hit Robert, you triggered his fighting reflexes." She stopped to make sure that Kenzie understood. "He wasn't sparring. He was in survival mode, fighting mode. We can't have that happen again, ever."

They sat in silence for a minute, letting the words sink in. The door to the studio opened with an inrush of traffic noise as the first student in the next class entered.

"Hi there, Eric," Jules said, acknowledging the young boy coming in.

Kenzie swallowed. Without thinking, she reached up to rub a particularly painful bruise on her upper arm.

Jules saw it. "Call your dad," she said, standing up. "I don't want you running home today, okay?"

Kenzie stood but didn't agree. She turned to leave the office, but Jules glided forward and intercepted her, blocking the doorway.

She put a hand on Kenzie's shoulder, then pulled her into a brief hug.

"I'm sorry," Kenzie mumbled into the folds of Jules's jacket. The smell of the cotton was comforting. It had been years since she'd hugged Jules, outgrowing it somewhere between being a little kid and a confused teenager.

"I know."

They separated, and Jules left the office. Kenzie followed her out, but instead of going back onto the training floor, she headed for the open shelves where the students threw their bags. She had two bags on the lowest shelf, one for her school books, one for her clothes. She dug through the second bag. Buried under her running shoes, Kenzie finally found her phone.

She checked the display. A dozen or more texts, and a couple of Instagrams. She hesitated, feeling anxious. Her body, already on chemical overload, wanted a hit of endorphins, the kind that came fifteen minutes into an easy lope, not so slow to be jogging but nowhere near racing.

I need to run.

She glanced at Jules. The instructor was watching her in the mirrors that lined the length of the wall. She frowned when Kenzie put the phone back in her bag. Kenzie sidled away. Dropping into a low crouch, she pulled out her running gear, then slipped into a changing room. She was careful not to face Jules again. A scant two minutes later, she stuffed her uniform into the clothes bag, picked up both bags, and placed them by the door.

She was ready.

She had one hand on the door when Jules spoke.

"Kenzie."

I could split, she thought, but turned around.

Jules stood by the thigh-high wall. Understanding filled the woman's face, and concern. "Did you call your father?"

Kenzie shook her head but held on to Jules's gaze.

The black belt sighed. "Be careful. I'll let your father know what happened."

Kenzie winced, already envisioning the coming lecture. She gave Jules an acknowledging nod, then she slid out the door, onto the sidewalk. Instead of the famous Seattle gray, she was greeted by a brilliant blue with sharp white clouds decorating the sunlit skies.

In three steps, Kenzie was running, but the expression on Robert's shell-shocked face pursued her no matter how fast she fled.

CHAPTER TWO

Mitch cussed as the bolt slipped from his grease-covered fingers, clinking and clanking as it dropped into the engine compartment of the Camaro.

He waited for the metallic sound of steel on concrete, but there was no ringing sound.

Crap, thought Mitch. If it didn't land on the garage floor, it must have lodged somewhere in the compartment. He peered into the dim recesses around the motor and below the partially installed fuel pump. He didn't see where it could have landed.

He gave an irritated sigh and, with both hands, threw the full weight of his lanky body onto the front fender of the car, rocking it on the worn-out suspension. Decades-old dust rose to mix with the smell of oil and grease. He wrinkled his nose.

Nothing.

He kept rocking the car, staying with the same type of rhythm he'd used as a kid on a swing. The hood squeaked, and Mitch checked it. The latch held. Then, he gave the muscle car an extra-hard shove at the bottom of the oscillation. The car bounced, and at the back came the sound of plastic hitting the concrete and shattering—and the *tink* of the bolt, dislodged by the violent rocking, falling free to the concrete slab.

He got down on his elbows and knees and ducked his head sideways to scrutinize the area underneath the frame.

How did it get there? he thought, spotting the bolt. It sat on the far side of the car, throwing a shadow from the light spilling in from the open garage door.

Mitch had the dented metal door run up, savoring the unexpectedly bright sunshine, so unusual for Seattle in the early spring. As a bonus, the sun warmed his back as he strained to get the wayward part.

He stretched to the full extent of his long arms. Three inches out of reach.

Naturally.

He withdrew his arm, and in a graceful movement, swung his legs up at the same time he pushed off with his hands, landing in a crouch, then rose up to his full height. He took two steps and curled around the passenger side of the car. From here, it took only a second to retrieve the bolt.

As he stood, a glimpse of hot pink caught his eye. His attention shifted from his project car to a girl running down the flight of steps at the far end of the narrow cul-de-sac. Her feet flicked at the concrete treads, landing just long enough to get the next leg down, like she was skipping. His assessment shifted upward from the feet, past the hot pink shorts, the loose baby blue shirt, to her face.

She's cute.

And, noticing the motion under her shirt, he realized she wasn't twelve, as she appeared at first. The girl reached the bottom of the steps and smoothed out to a lope.

Next door, Mrs. McFurkin's yappy dog yipped at the intruder, interrupting Mitch's appreciative thoughts. Mitch glanced sideways across the yard, annoyance crossing his face. The mutt, a designer dog— three-quarters fuzzy Pomeranian, the remainder the annoying bits of a Chihuahua—who answered to Muffles, was bouncing in excitement and trying to back out of his collar.

Not a real dog, he thought as a distant memory tugged at him. *Labs don't bounce when they bark!*

Mitch stepped back into the garage before the girl could see him and mark him down as a perv. He put a hip against the car. From the relative shadows inside, he continued to watch the girl as she came down the sidewalk on the far side of the street.

A sleek low-slung black car silently slid into the driveway of the older, decrepit two-story house across the street, the rear bumper blocking the sidewalk.

The girl, closing fast, started to dodge when she was five yards from the car. At the same time as she left the walk for the grassy planter strip, the driver and passenger doors of the car sprung open and two men, dressed identically and incongruously in dark clothes and sunglasses, jumped out.

The passenger ran around the back of the car, into the street, like a defensive end cutting off a running back on a sweep. The other man closed on the other side of the girl, who skidded to a stop at the pincer attack.

Mitch watched it happen. It took a fraction of a second for the shock to wear off, and he launched off the Camaro.

"Hey!"

Muffles barked at them all.

Mitch sprinted into the street, chasing the car's passenger.

In front of him, the helpless girl shied away from the driver and evaluated the other guy. Mitch saw her glance at him, dismiss him. Chest rising and falling, she backed diagonally away.

The assailants didn't say anything as they stalked her. Mitch saw that the goon closest to him had something in his hand, saw the arm swing up. With relief, he realized it wasn't a gun.

Without warning, the girl darted toward the driver. Mitch watched as her bare left leg lashed out, straight and fast, while her tiny hands came up into a defensive position. The ball of her foot snapped into the driver's groin, the sole leaving a waffle pattern on his black trousers.

Sprinting, Mitch still managed to wince.

The driver let out a guttural *"unnn"* as his body collapsed into a fetal position, his eyes showing white all the way around.

One down.

Mitch got a clear picture of the second one as he barreled toward the assailant.

A mean-ass dude with a stun gun and a crappy crew cut. Big.

Mitch's gut twisted.

"Run!"

The girl spared a glance at him and, discounting him, reset her feet. The soles of her running shoes gripped the grass and didn't let her pivot to meet the new threat. Fear and anger flared on her face as the second man closed fast, but with caution, heeding the lesson his buddy learned the hard way.

Everything moved *soooo* slowly.

As the seconds stretched, Mitch estimated the time to close the last ten yards.

How long it would take for the mean-ass kidnappers—they had to be kidnappers, nothing else made sense—to zap the girl?

The time for the runner to finish her turn.

The math didn't work; he was going to be too late.

At the last moment, he sensed rather than saw Muffles. The pom-chi-pom-pom that Mrs. McFurkin doted over had successfully slipped his collar and chased him into the street. The next instant, Muffles attached himself to Mitch's pant leg, *grrrring* ferociously, as though it made any sort of difference. Mitch pitched head-first into the air.

Why do I only crash and burn when I have an audience, he thought irrelevantly, then straightened and swung his leg out to avoid kicking the stupid frickin' fur ball.

The world turned topsy-turvy, but Mitch could see the passenger pause at the sounds of the dog behind him. The math changed. Mitch's body rotated like a dart headed for a bull's-eye. He was on the way down and, from instinct born of frequent practice, he braced for the impact with the ground.

He hit the side of the man's leg below the knee. The fabric of the pants abraded his cheek as Mitch managed to get his head out of the way.

Always protect the brain bucket.

His shoulder took the brunt of the collision. White pain flared in his brain, a double crack echoing in his ears as the dude's knee gave way at the same time as Mitch's left collarbone. The man started to topple as Mitch's momentum carried him under the man, then he was sliding on the damp, fragrant grass on his back.

The stun gun flew from the man's hands, falling under the girl's leg, already raised in attack position. Mitch saw the leg extend, catch the guy in the lower ribs, and expected to hear another crack. Instead, the ribs folded in as the man's fall robbed the side kick of its effectiveness.

The stun gun clattered on the sidewalk and slid into the overgrown shrubbery, and Mitch slid faceup and headfirst into the bottom of a maple tree. His skull exploded in red waves of pain as skin peeled away on the bark, the back of his head riding up the trunk until his neck buckled sideways. He came to a stop when his broken shoulder arrested his movement.

Time reverted to normal speed, and with it, pain engulfed his body. He tried to lift his head, but shock waves from his shoulder caused his whole body to shudder. A moan escaped his lips before he clamped them shut.

The girl, is she okay?

He lifted his head again, suppressing the wracking signals sent by the nerve endings in his shoulder, his scalp.

He saw her standing, hands raised, eyes narrowed. Like a startled doe, she stood poised to take flight. The sunlight framed her body with a faint halo, and when she took stock of him, he saw the same golden light in her irises.

He stared at her as she took one reflexive step toward him. Her small fists opened, and one hand went to her mouth. He tried smiling as she took an inventory of the damage, flitting from head to shoulder, down his long, lanky body.

"You're hurt," she said. Her voice held dispassionate calm. The glow seemed to increase.

Thanks for noting the obvious, he thought. He didn't say it out loud, though—no sense in offending pretty girls.

"Hi," he said, easing away from the damaged side as he struggled to sit up. If he folded his left arm over and used his right elbow for leverage . . .

His vision went dark around the images, and he had to take several deep breaths. He managed to get disentangled from the maple, crushing red blooming tulips in the process. Damaged petals added their scent to the air.

While he moved, she moved, too. He saw her legs slip into his narrowed field of vision, femininely fit and muscular, as she dropped to a knee next to him. He looked up to her face, and the curve of her lips, the captivating eyes, pulled him in. When was the last time he was this close to a girl other than in a physics lab?

"I'm okay." He forced the words out and smiled. His face felt twisted and, based on the disbelieving shake of her head, he gathered the girl disagreed.

She reached out a hand, tentatively. On her arm, he saw fresh bruises. The welts sparked an unreasoning anger inside as he remembered another arm that bore similar marks.

She didn't speak.

The hand touched his chest, fingertips first. With gentle pressure, she forced him back down, prone on the grass.

Mitch let her.

She leaned over him, the pressure on his chest from her hand grew, and he found it hard to breathe. The aura around her returned, and Mitch saw small hairs, loose from her ponytail, moving on a breeze that he couldn't feel.

Warmth flowed outward from her hand, from his chest, filling his core, extending to the shoulder. At the base of his neck, a tingle started and grew.

She spoke with quiet force. One word, one that he didn't recognize.

"Æsculapium."

The tingle turned into a torrent, white light filled his brain, streaks of rising fireworks into the darkness of the pain. He clutched at the hand on his chest.

The skyrockets split and burst, recombined, and he heard himself moan, except it wasn't him.

The pressure from his chest disappeared before he could capture the hand, fingers grasping at air. The world around him went gauzy, and he blinked. The girl stood over him, staring, and backed away.

"Rest."

His last sight was the girl bounding away as his arms fell across his chest.

CHAPTER THREE

Mitch awoke to blue skies and Muffles's atrocious breath. Silhouetted against the heavens, and blocking out most of his view of them, was Mrs. McFurkin. He turned his head to get away from the flicking, slobbery tongue and the smell of week-old tuna.

What the hell does she feed that dog?

"Why'dja let my dog off the leash?"

Mitch leaned onto his elbow to lift himself off the ground, then paused, eyebrows encroaching on his forehead as he realized that nothing hurt. An ache maybe in the shoulder. He grimaced at the memory of his shoulder hitting the tree. He finished swinging over to stand, going to hands and knees before recovering his feet.

A spell of light-headedness hit him, and he held on to a tree branch for support.

"You . . . drinkin'?" McFurkin's voice sounded perpetually suspicious. "Or smokin'?" The undercurrent of her words carried the conviction that he must have been up to something.

He glanced at her as she leaned forward to sniff at him, like she could smell anything. She struck him as pickled and pissed. Mitch tried to lean back away from the woman. Her breath washed over him, and his nostrils flared. Vaguely, he wondered what would happen if he held a match up to her mouth. Visions of a flamethrower flashed through his mind, and the corners of his lips curled up.

Muffles jumped against his leg, and he unconsciously lifted it to block the mutt.

"Don' you kick my dog!" McFurkin yelled. She stooped at the waist to scoop Muffles off the ground, pressing the little animal close to her bosom. "Ought to call the cops, you causin' trouble like this, and tryin' to hurt Mr. Muffles." As she said his name, she buried her face in the dog's fur. Muffles lips curled up, supremely happy with the course of events.

At the mention of cops, Mitch's stomach had flopped.

He should be calling the cops. He scanned the scene in front of him, then over to the open garage door of his house.

Nothing.

No goons, no car, no girl.

He rubbed his chest in the same spot that the girl had touched.

No girl.

Doubts assaulted him, and he wondered if any of it had happened. His hand drifted up, touched his scalp. No scrape. He searched at the base of the tree in disbelief. He had hit that tree, hard, with his head, felt the skin tear.

A discoloration caught his attention. He knelt, touched it, came away with tacky red on his fingers.

Blood, he thought. His blood. A shiver went through him, and he swallowed.

He stood again, peered at the grass. A faint divot and a general flattening of the grass where he had slid.

McFurkin's whiny voice penetrated. She was still chattering at him, an angry squirrel trapped in the body of a walrus.

He focused on her.

". . . are you lissenin' to me?"

"No." The word slipped out, and he mentally cussed himself in the abrupt silence.

McFurkin sputtered, and her face reddened. The mouth worked, and indignant sounds emerged, accompanied by flecks of spittle. She drew herself up, and her hands squeezed together, pulling them even closer to her chest. Muffles's eyes bulged, and Mitch worried that she'd accidentally strangle the mutt.

Mitch stepped past the woman and headed back to his house. The light-headed feeling persisted all the way back.

McFurkin rediscovered her voice as he reached the driveway to his house, shouting slurred obscenities at him. Trouble sat on the near horizon, and he shook his head. Disrespecting adults was sure to raise his uncle's ire, and Mrs. McFurkin was sure to tell.

The curses faded to angry mumbles. Mitch glanced over his shoulder to McFurkin, watched her waddle into the street and carry Muffles home.

Mitch reached the garage and retreated into its safe, dark recesses, to a battered workbench. He leaned against the bench, the vise digging into his hip. He shifted his weight to the other hip.

Call the cops.

He stood and patted his pockets. No phone. Shoulders slumping, he gazed out to the street. Sunlight flashed off something shiny. His phone must have fallen out of his pocket during his acrobatics. He paused at the edge of the garage and scrutinized the neighbor's yard.

Muffles was inside. Good.

He hustled across the street. Halfway there, he saw the flat rectangle of plastic, way too small to be a phone. Mitch frowned. He stooped, and identified the card when he picked it up.

McKenzie Graham.

The picture on the learner's permit didn't capture that glow she wore. He could return it, try to explain that he'd tried to help. . . .

His throat tightened as the address below her name registered.

Lake Washington Boulevard.

Nothing on the lake went for less than a million bucks. It explained the goons, but he'd look like an idiot showing up on her doorstep— assuming they didn't have a big-ass gate keeping the ordinary folk out— to return the permit. What would he say to her? *Hey, here's your ID. You must of dropped it when you were kicking ass. Sorry I got in the way. And, dude, what the hell did you do to my shoulder and head?*

Did rich girls say "dude"?

Nervous shivers made it hard to breathe. He wasn't too sure he wanted an answer about his shoulder.

He put the thought out of his head and checked his pockets for his phone instead. Not on the ground, or in the gutter. He shrugged, frustrated, then remembered that he'd taken it out of his pocket when he went to work on the Camaro. He unconsciously did a second pat-down of his pockets as if to confirm it to himself, and slipped the permit into his back pocket.

He had half-turned to head back when another thought collided with his intention to call the cops. He kept turning, making a full circle until he faced the shrubbery. He glanced up and down the street, crossed the verge of grass. Mitch dropped to all fours, searching under the bushes.

No way they'd be dumb enough to leave it behind, but there it was, propped up like it was on display, the silvery electrodes bright on the black body.

Mitch stretched out and grabbed the woven black hand strap, dragging the device closer. He cupped it in one hand, careful not to touch the contact points. Nonchalantly, he stood and walked back to his house, eyeballs darting to see if anybody was watching.

Once he got into the garage, he quickly ran the door down, plunging the interior into darkness. By feel, he made his way to the door to the kitchen, opened it, and stepped inside.

His phone sat on the counter, right where he'd left it. He grabbed it as he headed to his room. With a thumb, he unlocked the screen. He went to dial 911—and stopped.

What was he going to say?

He tried to rehearse the conversation in his head.

How did you report an abduction when the "victim" ran away after kicking one of the attackers in the jewels?

"*Yeah, she was about five foot two, glowed, and took down a guy twice her size while I tripped and fell into the dude with the stun gun. She left a driver's permit. How do I know? I found it in the street after I came to from smashing my head into a tree. One of the kidnappers left a stun gun. The stun gun? Yeah, got that, too. Fingerprints? Uh, probably not.*" He inspected the rectangular shape clutched in his left hand. "*Definitely not. Do I need medical assistance? Naw, the glowing girl fixed me before she left. . . .*"

Mitch's thumb hovered over the Send button, jerking back and forth as he tried to decide whether to complete the call. The screen eventually went blank.

He swung his bedroom door shut with an angry shove and dropped the phone on the cluttered end table. He flopped onto the disorganized sheets of his bed, drawing his knees up as he leaned his shoulders against the painted wall. In the dim light that filtered through the curtains, he inspected the weapon he had liberated.

It was built with a hand grip reminiscent of a pistol grip, but where the trigger would be, there was a small red toggle switch. A slider switch sat under his thumb. He slid it over to the ON position, expecting something: a sound, a whine.

It sat there, like a brick in his hand, quiescent.

Mitch put the pointy silver prongs against the soft flesh of his inner arm. The chilly tips dug in.

How much could it hurt?

Reluctantly, he decided that finding out would have to wait until he had help.

Mitch's lips twitched into a smile. *Hunter will help.*

He hit the red toggle. The wicked crackle that resulted almost made him drop the stun gun as his eyebrows climbed his forehead.

Maybe Hunter will help.

Mitch's smile faded as he put the stun gun down.

Flashes of the girl's face as she leaned over him, along with a sense of her touch still on his skin, made him rub his chest. An odd pain resided there, deep. In his back pocket, he could feel the hard plastic of the permit.

He ought to return it, but that idea made the hurt in his chest worse.

CHAPTER FOUR

Kenzie heard the commotion as her father came in, the garage door opening, closing, the muffled sounds of movement as he moved into the kitchen. She stayed in her room, huddled into the corner with a comforter drawn tight around her body. Ice still filled her core, but the shakes had stopped while a deep fatigue settled into her mind, numbing her. The heavy curtains were drawn, blocking the brilliance of the day. Swirling motes drifted on a beam of light that stabbed past the edge of the drapery, illuminating the red oak floor. She stared mindlessly at the rosy grain in the wood, the darker redness of a lonely knot.

She heard the electronic beeps as he deactivated the security alarm in the laundry room of their Tudor-style home. Then she felt the wards go down, and relaxed infinitesimally. New wards went up, more intricate and powerful than the incantations she had used.

A minute later, her father entered her room without knocking. Raymond Graham inspected Kenzie from the doorway. She shot a glance up, saw creases emerge above his brows, felt the burden of intrusive probing. Instead of speaking, Kenzie held on to her knees, wrapping her arms around them and pulling the fabric snug to her skin. A toe of her shoe peeked out from the bottom, and she focused on a blade of grass captured between the fabric upper and the rubber.

"I swung by the studio. Jules said you had a rough time today."

Kenzie didn't look up but started rocking forward and backward. She had fled the scene of the attack, fled from the boy that broke himself trying to help her. His eyes were blue; not light blue, richer. She had felt the pain coursing through his wiry body, held the connection long enough for the healing energy to bind his wounds and repair the physical damage. Deep inside him, she'd felt a deep pain. That she couldn't heal, hadn't tried.

"McKenzie?"

Her father wouldn't go away, she knew that. She should say something, make him leave.

She should tell him what happened.

She opened her mouth, still facing down to the shoe, made a rasping sound like the air was passing over vocal cords frozen with novocaine.

Her father crossed the room with short, efficient steps. He knelt beside her. His hand dropped on her shoulder hesitantly, as though unsure of whether to touch her. His hand felt alien to her and, for a second, she was afraid that he would try to hug her, since that's what fathers were supposed to do when their little girls got hurt.

"I was attacked." Her voice was muffled by the comforter in front of her mouth.

"Jules told me—"

Kenzie interrupted, "No, on the way home." An angry shake of her head.

She waited for him to say something. Instead he stood, took two strides away, and then spoke with his back turned. What little warmth his voice possessed disappeared. Lieutenant Graham of the Seattle PD replaced Raymond Graham, father.

"Details. Start with where."

Kenzie blinked away moisture. Her lips pressed into a wavering, thin line, and she drew in a shuddering breath. She couldn't get warm.

He stood there waiting.

She started to talk, told him the route she used to run home, even though he already knew it, the cul-de-sac at the bottom of the steps, about the car sweeping into the driveway, blocking the sidewalk. . . .

"What kind?"

"I don't know. Black. Newer."

He had her describe her attackers. She did, eyes closed to picture them, while she pulled her legs up into her torso with her arms. The pace of her rocking increased when she told him about the car doors flying open, the men emerging, the shock of recognition that they were actually hunting her.

Her father didn't speak, not even in approval for doing what she was trained to do, when Kenzie described disabling the first attacker with a kick, pivoting back to meet the second one. Her voice fell silent in the dim light of her room. Her breath came herky-jerky, and her teeth started to chatter. In her imagination she could see the outreaching arm, feel the foot grab grass, her pivot too slow.

The boy tackling the man, clipping him at the knees.

"The rest." Raymond sounded impatient. "You said there were two of them."

Again, her lips flattened out. She clenched her teeth, and the chattering stopped.

"I couldn't turn fast enough," she began, unclenching her jaws and estimating how much to tell. At the back of her mind, a warning sounded. Not everything should be shared.

"It's not like at the studio; my feet got caught up, and this boy came flying in. . . ."

"One of them?"

She shook her head. "No, he was trying to help. He tackled the second man."

"Why?"

"I don't know!"

Her father *hmmm*ed as he considered this.

"Fine. A Good Samaritan, perhaps. We'll check it out, though."

The boy's face, apologetic through the haze of pain, floated up again. Raymond's voice pierced through the memory.

"Your attackers, did they use any magic? Or were they Meat?"

Kenzie stared up at him, her cheeks reddening at the sneering slang for the non-magical. He met her gaze with impassive features, waiting for her answer.

"They were people . . . ordinary."

"Can you remember anything else? Did they speak at all?" His hands began to weave together in an intricate pattern as he spoke.

Kenzie felt the subtle pull of the compulsion spell he was building.

"Why don't you just inject me with truth serum?"

His hands stopped moving.

"It's important that I know everything if I am going to protect our Family." There was no apology in his voice for his violation of her privacy, but the magical power bled away like a dark tide receding.

Her jaws clenched tight. She forced them to relax, pulling in a deep breath before she spoke.

"More important than me?" Below the hurt, a hot anger burst, fueled by the sparring, the attack, the indifference.

"Aren't I *Family*, Father? I know, I'm only one part of the *Family*, aren't I, it's not like I'm more important to you because we're actually freaking"—a hint of hesitation at the near-swear word before she plunged on—"related.

"No, someone attacks me, tries to grab me off the street, and all you can do is treat me like a suspect in one of your lineups. Just the facts, isn't that how you do it? Don't get too emotionally involved with the victim? Remain objective? Investigate all the facts, find the perps, and lock them up?"

She grabbed more air. Her voice rose in pitch.

"I'm the victim this time, Dad. Me, your daughter, and all you can do is put me through the inquisition and worry about the Family?"

Silence hung in the air like the dust motes in the beam of sunlight, swirling on the undercurrents in the room. Her father stood apart from her, his guarded expression measuring twice to cut once.

"You did what you were expected to do. You defended yourself—"

"You never asked if I was okay!"

He appeared surprised at the accusation as much by the fact that she was shouting at him.

"You're in shock." He paused, took note of the blanket wrapped around her, nodded. "I'll get you something to counteract the effects."

He nodded to himself again and walked to the door. He turned at the threshold, left hand resting lightly on the doorknob.

"We'll finish with this later, when you feel better."

The door swung shut soundlessly on the oiled hinges. As the latch snicked closed, Kenzie found her voice.

"Your compulsion spell sucked."

She had meant to shout it, but the sound didn't carry past the comforter, which soaked up the sound, the bitterness, the wetness from her cheeks.

CHAPTER FIVE

Mitch saw his bedroom door bang open, and the shadow of Uncle Henry, a sloppier version of his father, blocking the light from the hall.

"Get out here."

Mitch's lips curled with disgust, but he didn't turn his head to acknowledge his uncle.

"Why? I did the chores. . . ."

"Cop's at my goddamn door. He's askin' for you. Now get your ass out here."

At the mention of the police, Mitch winced. Either McFurkin or the girl must have called. His mind raced ahead, and he decided it must be the girl. The cops wouldn't have bothered if McFurkin called and told them that he was baked. As long as he wasn't disturbing anyone, they'd ignore it.

So, it had to be the girl, he thought, and a wave of guilt washed over him. He should have made the call. Then another thought chilled him. *What if she never made it home? What if this was the last place she was seen?*

"Coming," he said as he shoved the calculus book off his lap and swung his legs to the floor. His hands shook as he brushed crumbs off his jeans.

The gray-suited cop was standing inside the small entryway at the door. While Uncle Henry glared at him and settled back in front of the television, Mitch crossed the living room, hurrying to avoid blocking the big flat screen.

The cop's presence made Mitch's stomach turn over, and sinewy bands bound his chest. He reminded himself to breathe.

"Hello, Mitch."

Of course, he would already know my name, thought Mitch, stopping four feet from the man, avoiding eye contact.

The man studied him, letting the silence between them build.

Mitch knew how to play this game, too, and silence was a comfortable friend. The cop stood a few inches shorter than him. His gray suit looked like a refugee from Goodwill and didn't fit him across the shoulders. His face didn't seem right, either. Mitch expected the hard, suspicious lines of a cop. Thin lines of worry creased the corners of this man's eyes and lined his forehead, giving him an air more like a priest. A shock of unruly gray-white hair framed his face. Mitch went numb when he met the cop's eyes. They were steady, the eyes of a man who could see a thousand leagues. Not gray like the rest of him, but vibrant green, like the green of a new spring in a deep, dappled forest, with secrets hidden in the shadows.

"Let's step outside, Mitch," said the older man.

Mitch glanced over his shoulder. His uncle stared at the screen, slouched into his chair. Mitch turned back and shrugged.

"Whatever."

They stepped into the falling night, Mitch pulling the door shut behind him. The shadows slipped up the street while the tops of the pines glowed with the last light of the ruddy sunset.

The detective turned and held out his hand. "My name is Mercury."

Mitch squinted at the hand, then his gaze retraced the journey to the man's face. He held his facial muscles indifferent, and his arms by his sides.

"I suspect you can trust me enough to shake my hand."

Feeling his thoughts violated, Mitch recoiled and fell back a step, nearly tripping on the stoop. A firm hand gripped his shoulder, righting his balance, then let go as Mercury retreated a step to open up space between them again. The cop's jacket flapped open with the movement.

"Thanks," said Mitch. He felt the quavering in his throat as he spoke, and coughed to clear his voice.

The frickin' man can read minds.

"Uncle Henry said you're a cop?"

"I have a few questions for you, Mitch." Mercury paused. "It would be easiest if you would describe what happened, as it happened, and I can ask questions to fill in any blanks."

Maybe he doesn't know, thought Mitch, sensing the vagueness of Mercury's request.

"Or you can lie to me, and we'll waste each other's time."

He held his stare on Mitch, waiting.

"You don't have a gun."

"I don't like them."

Me neither, thought Mitch.

"The story."

"I don't know what you're talking about," said Mitch.

"That's okay," replied Mercury, "we'll get to it eventually. Personally, I've got all night, and I enjoy a good chase. So let's start with the girl. Have you seen her before?"

Crap.

"Aren't you going to take notes or something?"

Mercury's lips curled up in a sardonic grin at Mitch's surrender.

"I have a good memory and long practice at using it. So, where have you seen the girl?"

Mitch shook his head. "Occasionally around here. She runs by sometimes in the afternoon."

"So tell me about this afternoon, starting with the first thing that was different."

Mitch thought. "The car."

"What about the car?"

"It didn't make any noise."

Mercury sighed. "I take it back. I don't have all evening. Pretend I'm a friend and talk, everything you can remember."

Annoyance crept into Mitch's voice. "It was a Tesla, an electric car. It didn't make any noise. The only reason I noticed it is the stupid mutt next door started barking and wouldn't shut up."

"Keep going."

Mitch pointed across the street. "It pulled into the driveway, kinda blocking the sidewalk, and I didn't think anything of it until the doors popped open and these two goons jumped out. . . ."

"Describe them."

Mitch did, adding details when Mercury prodded.

"Then what?"

The rest of the story unfolded: the girl defending herself, Mitch running to help. He left out tripping, giving credit to the girl for dropping both assailants.

"Then, she . . . ran off," Mitch finished. The words sounded lame to his own ears, and he saw Mercury's features narrow.

"Now," he said, "tell me the part that you're leaving out."

Mitch got the uncomfortable impression that this was the part of the story Mercury had been waiting for, the unbelievable bit.

The man pointed to Mitch's scalp, confirming his fear. "I want to know about the part that might explain a very faint but new scar."

Mitch shoved his hands deep into his pockets, half-turning away from his inquisitor. His thoughts jumbled together in a mush, flashes of flying through the air, the girl over him whispering "*Rest,*" followed by blankness. His chin jutted out as he finished turning his back to Mercury.

From behind him, the cop spoke. "How badly were you hurt?"

How the hell could he know that?

Cops were skeptical and cynical. Tell them about a magic healing, and you'd be assuming the position while they searched for your stash.

"Who are you?"

"Just an investigator, doing his job." Mercury's tone was firm, but not threatening. "What did the girl do? I need to know every detail, Mitch."

"You're not a cop."

Silence. Through the open curtains of the window, he could see his uncle yelling at the television, but none of the sounds made it past the walls.

Finally, Mercury talked, the first to break the barrier Mitch had imposed between them.

"I can show you a badge that says otherwise."

How the hell could Mitch explain what happened? He didn't know himself—nothing that made any sort of sense.

"You got hurt trying to help," Mercury said, goading him to talk. "Which means that the girl wasn't the only one in the fight. Correct?"

"I'm done." Mitch stepped to the door and found his right arm restrained in Mercury's powerful grip. He twisted against the pressure of the enclosing fingers, but they tightened on his bicep. Mitch reversed direction, turning into the grip and then sweeping his arm up and around to force the hand loose. The hand came free, only to slide down to Mitch's chest. Mercury leaned, and Mitch's back slammed into the house. He tried to push back but found himself pinned between the wall and hands of granite.

"Don't," warned Mercury as Mitch drew back a fist.

"Let go of me. . . ."

"I will, but first I need you to listen."

Mercury's eyes seemed to catch the light of the dying sun with a glow that reminded Mitch of the girl before she touched him. A pit opened in Mitch's gut.

"Since you won't tell me, I'll tell you what I can reasonably guess. You nod when I get it right. Got it?"

Air sucked out of him, Mitch nodded, slowly lowering his upraised fist. "Good man."

The hands relaxed slightly, but the pressure stayed on center mass and held him.

"The men attacked, you saw it, you ran to help. Nod."

Mitch bounced his chin a half inch.

"You fought with at least one man, probably the second, got hurt. Nod."

He hesitated this time, then replied. "I fricking tripped and fell into the guy's legs."

Mercury nodded this time, acknowledging the bitterness in the words. "You gave her time to escape."

Mitch blinked, but nodded.

"You got hurt in the attack. Not a little scrape, either. Nod."

He glared, but his head dipped.

"And the girl, she did something you can't explain. She made the wounds disappear, didn't she." A pause. "Did she speak?"

"Some foreign word." The words came reluctantly, as though he were betraying a secret, something private between himself and McKenzie. His face warmed, and he looked away from Mercury. From the corner of his eye, Mitch observed the cop as vexation crossed his face.

The pressure on Mitch's chest relaxed.

"Thank you." Mercury let go completely and stepped away from Mitch. The cop let loose a long sigh.

"I suppose you know that you can't tell anyone about this, right?"

The corners of Mitch's mouth turned down as his nostrils flared.

Mercury saw the expression and shook his head. "Go ahead, then. If you're lucky, whoever you tell will believe that you're crazy."

"I'm never lucky."

Mercury turned his head fractionally to the side, leaning into Mitch's face to make eye contact. Mitch stood taller, peering over the top of the white-haired man. He shoved off the wall with his shoulder blades, thrusting his chest into Mercury's. Mercury backed off, and Mitch slid sideways into the space created, easing toward the door.

Mercury stepped back again, restoring a buffer between them. "Think carefully before you tell anyone, Mitch. You witnessed an attempted abduction and interrupted someone's plans."

Mercury dug through a pocket, procured a card.

"Call me if you need help." He extended a hand, holding the card by a corner.

Mitch took the card, grabbing the corner opposite Mercury's fingers, and glanced at it. He could do better with his laptop and home printer. The card had the word "*Mercury*," a phone number, and the title, "*Investigator.*"

"You don't have a first name?"

"Does it matter?"

Mitch watched Mercury turn to leave. He was unaware of the tension in his shoulders until it dropped away. The man reached his car, a boring Ford. Mitch tensed again as Mercury stopped, car door partway open, and turned back. Even from fifteen yards away, those orbs danced with energy.

"Just a thought, Mitch," the cop said, raising a finger and inscribing an intricate pattern in the air. "It takes guts to run *to* the sound of guns."

The words settled on him like a gossamer net, but instead of entrapping him, they wrapped him in a fold of comfort. A nugget of emotion, pride, moved through him.

With that, the cop settled into the car, and Mitch turned to go inside.

The blare of the television, some dumb reality show, hit him as soon as he cracked open the door, closely followed by the smells from the kitchen.

"What he want? You going the same damn road your dad went?" demanded his uncle, tossing out twin accusations without ever shifting his full attention from the smack-talking from the set.

"I'm not crazy." *Or lazy and stupid,* he thought.

"What dija you do, then?"

"Nothing."

"Cops don't come 'round for nothin'."

"He came to pin a medal on my chest."

His uncle glared at him. "Smartass, just like your dad."

Your brother, Mitch thought, but didn't say it, expecting to be hit for thinking it, but his uncle had already shifted back to the show.

Mitch strode down the hall to his room, shutting the door firmly. The light was too bright, so he switched it off. Lying on his bed in the dark, he let his thoughts roam. He rolled onto a hip and checked his back pocket for the permit, pulling it out and rotating it between his fingers and thumb. Finally, he got up and put it under the foot of his mattress with the stun gun.

As he dropped off to a fitful sleep, he saw her again, dressed in gold, the hair with a hint of waviness to it, held back by the ponytail, a cute nose. Then the touch, and his heart ached.

Who the hell are you, McKenzie Graham?

CHAPTER SIX

The next day, Jackson, Kenzie's new bodyguard, picked her up for school, waited for her after school, drove her to martial arts, watched her there, drove her home, and only let her out of his sight when she fled to the bathroom or her bedroom.

Jules noticed.

"What's going on, Kenzie?" she asked, pulling her aside and earning a reproving frown from Jackson. The rest of the class filed out past them.

Kenzie fibbed, because it was easier than telling Jules that she was under house arrest.

"Somebody threatened my mom, so Dad's being extra cautious." She held Jules's gaze while she lied. Some lies she had practiced so long they seemed true. This one she had to work to sell.

Jules wasn't buying the manure that Kenzie was offering, but, thankfully, didn't press her.

Her mother had reacted to the attack in an entirely predictable fashion—by overreacting. In a flurry of activity, Sasha Graham ordered her husband to find a bodyguard for McKenzie and both of them launched investigations. Her dad launched a quiet operation with his trusted underlings at the police department. Her mother researched angles from the tech company she ran, pulling in its resources behind the scenes.

In the meantime, Kenzie was stuck with Jackson.

He carried himself well, and as befit his job, his eyes never stopped moving. He stepped outside first and then held the door for her with one long arm while the other hand rested at his hip. He kept his body angled so that he could scan in both directions. She noticed as she passed close to him that he had a clean scent, as masculine as the ropy muscles that flexed under the wine-colored sports shirt he wore with khakis.

Kenzie followed him out into the afternoon. The cheerful chatter from the busy sidewalk greeted them as it blended with the street noise from Rainier Avenue as cars accelerated away from the stoplight.

Jackson led her to a silver Audi, parked in the first space directly in line with the studio. He hit the button to unlock it while they were still ten feet from the vehicle. He secured her into the passenger seat, walked around the vehicle, and slid behind the wheel.

Seconds later, he pulled out of the parking space and headed for the exit from the parking lot, dodging pedestrians headed for the Safeway that anchored the other end of the strip mall.

"Home next?"

"Yeah."

He made the turn onto the avenue, and the silver car joined the herd, blending into the mix of upscale autos on the road.

Kenzie absorbed the view out the window. The sun was shining again, the fourth day in a row, which seemed like a new record for Seattle in April. Perfect running weather. An ache in her chest reminded her that she hadn't run today. One day, but she missed the endorphin rush already.

"Stop the car," she said. She tried to make her voice carry the authority of her mother's, but it lacked weight, emerging with a shrill note instead.

Jackson's concentration did not break. His focus swept from the dash to his mirrors to the road ahead. The car didn't betray a flicker of change.

"Did you hear me?" Mentally she kicked herself for the dumb question.

"You have good technique," he said, keeping his eyes on the road.

Kenzie turned from the window and faced Jackson. "I'm going to run home."

Jackson kept the car in the right lane, slowing to leave space for cars turning in front of him. He shook his head.

"Kenzie, no can do. That's the one spot that you're most vulnerable—showed up like a neon light during the threat assessment session we did with your folks. Until your father gives me the all clear, we drive, even if it's across the street."

Kenzie's lips curled down. She'd be stuck with Jackson until her mother relented, whatever her father thought. She lifted her right hand up from the armrest to the door release, fingers resting on the lever.

Sighing, she dropped her hand back and shifted to her left to fiddle with the sound system with her other hand.

"Thank you."

Kenzie glanced up, saw Jackson give her a brief smile.

"I didn't want to have to stick you in the back and set the child-proof locks."

Kenzie ignored him and chose a song, and then hit Play, ratcheting up the volume. Turning back to the window, she pressed her temple to the cool tinted glass as "Be Your Everything" resonated inside the vehicle. The lyrics wrapped around her, and the heaviness in her chest grew. She told herself she needed to run, she'd forget if she ran, let the movement take her away.

What kind of idiot runs out into the street like that?

No answer came to her, just slow-motion pictures, earnest and yet somehow tragic, as he said hi through the veil of pain. Then the sensation when she touched his chest, felt the deeper pain that didn't show.

Hands clasped unconsciously against her stomach below her belly button, she stared at the world gliding past her, normal people doing normal things, and wished she could be a part of it.

The church windows spied on her, knowing her. They were tall and rounded at the top, with smaller circular windows set above them, each with wooden muntins separating the panes of glass. They watched without blinking, all the people in their crosshairs. Above them rose the cross, set on the top of the bell tower. The tower, rising from a bald, barreled roof, was capped in wood, freshly painted and bloodred. The cross strained her vision, outlined in black against the intense blue of the April sky.

The large brass bell in the tower had been removed from the old church a generation ago after the congregation had fractured.

No sign announced the church, no mention of denomination or times for services. Instead of open doors, a keypad stood anachronistically against the grim gray-blue basalt block of the foundation walls, allowing entry to the chosen. Kenzie's skin cooled as the rock stole her body heat. She waited for her parents to make their way up the steps. She shivered. Until midsummer, the walls held the chill of winter; it would be cooler still inside.

The earliest lie she remembered being taught surrounded this old building: the imperative to tell others, Meat, that it was a church—an exclusive one for the wealthy, but no different than a thousand similar houses of worship in Seattle. Only the adults held the codes to get in.

Once, a couple of years ago, Kenzie had surreptitiously watched her father entering the digits that would unlock the door. Memorizing them, she had tried them later, feeling pleased with the snick of the lock opening. She had pulled open the door barely wide enough to weasel through, then shut it behind her, hearing it latch. In the musty and dim interior of the entry alcove, Kenzie had seen that the heavy wooden doors, darkly stained and inset with etched stars, were shut. Beyond those doors lay her target, *The Incantaraus,* the book that held all the spells, charm-making, and potions known to the congregation.

She had taken precisely one step into the alcove before a *Linius* ward had captured her, weaving her into a cocoon that left her barely able to breathe and blink. Instant panic had made her squirm and thrash to remove the enmeshing spell, to escape. All the movement had accomplished was to leave a sheen of sweat on her skin. Kenzie had forced herself to take several deep breaths to quell her initial panic. Thinking rapidly, she began to form canceling spells, an unraveling spell, and, getting desperate, the only banishing spell she knew. Her attacks on her bindings squandered a profligate amount of energy, but without the proper focus, the magic dissipated into ethereal wisps lacking the power to accomplish the simplest task.

An hour later—it seemed so much longer!—the lock had buzzed and clicked, and her father entered. Kenzie sagged against the wall, too exhausted to stand.

He stood and assessed her. His eyes displayed no humor. "Well, I'm glad it's not Meat, at least."

Humiliating.

After he had released her from the *Linius* ward, he had driven her home. She held her tongue, but the voice in the back of her head wondered what would have happened to an ordinary stranger who'd stumbled into the church.

Kenzie shoved the memory away as her mother and father met her at the pad. She felt a twinge when she followed them across the threshold to the alcove, alert to the protective spells hung by the Council of Protectors. After her foray, the wards had been changed and strengthened. Her parents hung their coats while she waited.

The inlaid stars on the massive doors glowed as the three of them approached, Kenzie in the lead, and soundlessly the doors hinged open as though waiting for them.

Kenzie stepped into the nave, seeing row upon row of empty pews flanking the long aisle to the open altar at the front of the church, which sat devoid of decoration. The polish on the hard benches gleamed in the light from the clerestory.

She kept walking, and the view in front of her rippled and ran like watercolors bleeding off the bottom of a canvas. A lightness touched her skin, sending quivers of excitement along her nerve endings as she entered the transition. Three more steps and the colors ran back up the canvas, the hues lifting up until they touched the glittering stars above her and spread to the far reaches of the woodland.

The tightness of her jeans and blouse, her dressy shoes, even her undergarments, disappeared, replaced by the delicate touch of silken fabric as her clothes transformed into a flowing robe. Glistening white, it signaled her status as an enchantress, a woman of power, but not a wizard—yet.

Kenzie paused, feeling the comfort of mossy earth below naked feet, and offered gratitude to the magic.

Spread before her, lit with the light of a perpetual moon, lay the Glade of Silver Night, home to the Gathering, home to the Family.

CHAPTER SEVEN

Hunter Rubiera scowled at him in disbelief.

"You need better dreams, bro," he said with a sad shake of his head. "Any dream that involves a pretty girl and you on your back should not end with you bleeding."

Mitch hid his face while Hunter offered his advice, but watched him from the corners of his eyes. He was working on their joint project in the school robotics lab, the heat from his face obscured. Spying the problem with the bounce that had almost tipped the machine on the last trial run, he added tension to the suspension of the robotic arm. He turned the robot ninety degrees, placing it back on its base on the lab bench.

He hadn't told Hunter everything, leaving out the stun gun, which was sitting under his mattress at home, and the learner's permit, burning a hole in his mind and pocket. He was an idiot for carrying it, he knew, but the impulse to keep it close overrode common sense. He stopped short of mentioning anything as random as instantaneous healing.

"You done messing with that yet?" Hunter asked.

Mitch traced the linkages. "That should work."

Mitch and Hunter had paired up the first day of the semester and quickly discovered that their skills complemented each other's: Hunter a genius with electronics and controls, Mitch nimble and clever with motors and mechanical systems. Now Hunter switched on the remote control, also hand-built, and tapped the joystick. The mechanical arm jerked. The motion attracted the attention of the other nerds at nearby tables. They muttered then returned their attention to the robots they were building.

"Easy."

Hunter shot Mitch an amused grin. "No worries."

He manipulated the arm, increasing the range of motion with deft adjustments on the remote. The mechanism responded precisely to each command.

"Pretty sweet job, Stumble. You might not be able to walk without running someone over, but you can build the hell out of stuff." He worked the pincers, opening and closing the four-fingered claw, slowly at first, speeding up as he got the feel of the modifications that Mitch had made.

"You know, if I were under a pretty dream girl . . . ," Hunter started.

The articulated metal turned sideways, the artificial fingers closing in a mechanical pinch in the direction of an intensely concentrating girl bent over her own contraption a few feet away.

Mitch saw Paulson, the instructor who ran the loosely organized robotics lab, give them a frown and a head shake. Paulson allowed almost infinite experimentation with the mechanical equipment and electronics but drew bright lines at uncontrolled explosions and "socially inappropriate behavior."

Mitch squirmed and muttered, "Paulson's watching."

"Yeah, so." But Hunter retracted the mechanism, rotated it around the pivot of the motorized base, and sent the arm to full extension. "Go get the blocks. We'll try stacking."

Like he'd know what to do, Mitch thought, still stuck on Hunter's comment about McKenzie as he ambled to the front of the room.

Hunter, with his dark good looks and compact frame, seemed to draw girls to him. He relished the attention—*Who wouldn't?* a little voice whispered inside Mitch's head—and chatted easily, using his hands in graceful gestures that mesmerized his audience. When the girls weren't around, Hunter would comb through his wavy hair or stretch his shirt a little tighter across the muscles of his shoulders and chest.

Mitch wondered what it would be like to have girls want to touch his arm, get his attention, to smile at him like *that.*

In the middle of his reverie, Mitch's hip hit the edge of the front-row lab bench, jostling it and earning a grunt of contempt. He ignored the noise with practiced inattention.

Better to cultivate a reputation as "most likely to be an ax murderer" for the yearbook than as a wimp, always saying sorry. He'd learned early, long before he got to Seattle and high school: Constantly apologizing only got your ass kicked.

For all his big talk, Mitch never saw Hunter with any girls, and he felt a moment of curiosity about it.

He passed Paulson on the way to the ubiquitous gray storage racks that sat under the high windows. A chill gray-filtered light, typical for the Sound, fell into the room from the windows. Hitchings Charter

School for Advanced Technology didn't rely on natural light, treating it as a decoration. The lab facilities utilized new-generation LED lighting, lending a starkness to the space.

Paulson, the lab leader, glasses tucked into the front of his button-down shirt, looked up from the laptop on his desk.

"You two are making good progress."

Mitch shrugged and went to the shelf with the blocks, the green numbers visible through the translucent plastic of the bucket. The project that the class had was to design an articulating robotic arm capable of three different compound tasks. The easiest was a simple stacking exercise, picking up numbered blocks and stacking them with their bright green numbers right-side up.

He turned with the bucket in hand just in time to see Hunter making odd gestures, but not at him. His partner was staring at another team and seemed agitated. Mitch followed the direction of his eyes and saw that the other team was close to having the arm mechanism capable of grasping. Big deal. They still hadn't mastered the pivot points; the controls to handle the pivots were wicked hard to get right.

He looked away and then quickly back to them when a burst of frantic activity drew his interest.

The other team's arm, which a second ago had appeared stable, lurched, extended all the way out, then collapsed like a dying brontosaurus, complete with the counterbalancing weights on the back lifting as the arm fell, missed the bench top, and hurtled to the floor, while the two students flung themselves forward to catch it.

Heads all over the lab lifted, surveying the wreckage, and the closest offered encouragement to the guys who stood gazing dejectedly at a week of rebuilding.

The only head that didn't turn belonged to Hunter. Mitch had watched his hands stop moving and his partner duck down just before the mishap.

A queasy feeling blossomed in his stomach as he walked to Hunter. He rolled his shoulders and dismissed it.

Getting neurotic, he thought.

Mitch dropped the bucket of blocks onto the surface of the workbench and studied Hunter. He did not see any guile there, and the worry in his stomach unknotted.

"What?" Hunter asked, raising his eyebrows as the stare went on too long.

"Nothing," said Mitch. "Except . . ."

Hunter waited.

"Have you ever played with a stun gun?"

CHAPTER EIGHT

The air tasted of honeysuckle, and the silver light of a double-sized moon hung over the class. The students sat with their backs straight and their expressions eager, apostles in the world of magic. They sat on rounded stones, metamorphic rock marbled with reds and browns, their surfaces polished by a millennium of wear. All of the students were older than Kenzie, many of them by decades. The hard seats on the far side of the circle were unoccupied. As though caught in a still-frame picture, the mottled rocks took on the appearance of turtles dipping into a sea of grass and swimming away. In the distance, a waterfall added a muted roar as it splashed into a narrow lake at the far end of the Glade, beyond the woodland.

The focus of her attention, though, stood within the center of the circle: a venerable old man. The wizened wizard, lit with an inner humor, demonstrated the sign again, his gnarled hands carving a simple pattern in front of himself, then sweeping the hand to the side. As he completed the gesture, he spoke the command, *"Anemosa."*

A stiff breeze swept that side of the circle, the air ruffling the robes of the enchanters and enchantresses to Kenzie's left. The bottom of her alabaster robe ruffled and caressed her ankles. A busty blond woman, probably about thirtyish, tittered annoyingly, and held the bottom of her robe tight to her legs.

"Try," Harold said to the group, voice croaky with his years, but energetic. Harold had long ago refused a wizard's name, and used his own, setting a tradition for the rest of the Family. He lacked raw power, but was a gifted and precise technician who dazzled with his array of spells and potions. The gnomelike man made an outstanding instructor in the craft.

Kenzie lifted her hand in the argent glow of the moon and scribed the same motions, but without reaching for the magic inside her yet. Around her, hands moved. Gusts swirled and collided, collapsing into each other.

Now, she thought. She calmed her mind and let the potency of the magic well forth, then cast the spell, whispering *"Anemosa"* as she released control of the energy, pointing to an aspen tree outside the circle. A vacuuming sensation grew at her fingertips. The tree quivered and shook, and a leaf floated down out of season.

"Gently, McKenzie," Harold said. "A baby's breath, not a tornado. Anyone can release magic in volume, but all magic has a cost. Try again, this time with more control and less power. Be subtle."

Kenzie nodded, face hot. She caught a glare from the tittery twit. Not all the neophytes were born into the Family. Wilders emerged, usually in vivid and unexplainable events as their uncontrolled magic exploded on them. The Family wooed them with the promise of still more mastery as well as recognition from similarly evolved beings.

The flattery usually succeeded.

Kenzie frowned.

The newest members sneered at ordinary people the most. The term "Meat" started with them and infected the rest of the Family. Still, without the new acolytes, the Family would have disappeared.

A blast of solid air interrupted Kenzie's reverie, almost knocking her from her perch. Her arms flailed as her feet left the ground. Instantly she shifted her balance to her right hip and slid with the force of the blast, letting it flow up and over her. Getting her right foot back on firm ground, she stood, swinging the other leg down, facing the direction of the spell.

She shook the tendrils of hair that lay across her face, hands already building a reply to the bullying move. She locked stares with the woman, saw the momentary pleasure change to concern as the other enchantress saw Kenzie's hands moving, followed by relief as Harold stepped in.

"McKenzie, please sit down."

He turned. His voice turned waspish. "Belinda, what did I tell McKenzie? Baby's breath. And aim away from people, for goodness' sake."

Stone-faced, Kenzie returned to her place in the circle. Anger churned below the surface. As Harold worked with a man two rocks away, she sought her center, breathing deep to cool her emotion.

Useless; worse than useless, total crap.

Her attention shattered, she couldn't tap the reservoir of energy inside her. Frustration built on the anger as she cast one ineffective spell after another. She tried closing her eyes to envision in her mind the effect of the spell, to watch herself casting it, but the magic stayed quiescent, blocked by her emotions.

Lips compressed into a line and nearly squinting with the effort to hold her mind quiet, she finally managed to create a movement in the air, a gentle touch that moved gradually across the circle. It dissipated by the time it reached the far edge.

Old Harold noticed and misconstrued. "Excellent, McKenzie! Control, very good, very nice."

Kenzie snorted and looked away from him, cloaking her reaction. If she had cast the spell properly, it would have released enough force to uproot the trees.

The lesson ended a few minutes later with Harold offering his usual cautionary suggestions: Don't use magic outside the Gathering unless absolutely necessary, visualize the newest spell for practice, all magic comes with a cost. He beamed at them benevolently.

Harold was a fuddy-duddy. Nice, even if he did repeat himself a lot.

Dismissed, Kenzie stood and turned to leave the circle. In the distance, she saw the leaders of the Family in deep discussion, a veiling spell over the group. The conversation appeared heated, her mother pointing to underscore the importance of whatever she was telling them. With her mom, it was always telling, and Kenzie recognized the finger-point. She would have felt sorry for the other women, but they were all hard-edged themselves.

Kenzie headed in the opposite direction, toward the waterfall. A hundred yards from the teaching circle, she reached the brook and turned to the right to follow it. The burble of the water over the mossy stones was pleasant in her ears, and a peaty smell blended with the honeysuckle scent.

The horizon moved with her as she meandered. No one ever reached the edge of the Glade. Like a soap bubble, it deformed and elongated to adapt to the interlopers. All sorts of theories had been advanced to explain the Glade, but Kenzie, born to the magic, contented herself with the knowledge that it existed without troubling herself with the unknowable *why*.

A peaceful sense of well-being overtook her on her walk along the waterway. Unselfconsciously, she rolled her shoulders and lifted her arms above her head, fingers intertwined, stretching as though reaching out to touch the silver moon that loaned its luminous glow to the land around her. The tension released from Kenzie's muscles like a burden set down.

She reached the bank of the lake, and sat with a satisfied sigh, watching the billowing spray at the base of the falls. Her skin cooled, not uncomfortably, as the warm mist, delicate as gossamer, left a sheen of warm water on her skin, and a fresh, clean scent in the air.

She missed the animals that should have enlivened the Glade, but the land, air, and water stood barren of fauna. The lack reinforced the oddness of the Family as she made her solitary way to the falls. Nearly all of the new members came as Wilders, enticed into the Family and taught to harness their abilities. There were only three children, two of them younger than Kenzie, one a boy, the other a girl.

The magic can't die, she thought, repeating a mantra laid on her since she first stood in her crib. The words sat heavy on her heart, and the solitude of the falls darkened, tarnished by her drifting melancholy. To distract herself, she sought a spot in the water and touched it with magic, raising a delicate shape that reminded her of pictures she'd seen of undines, elemental spirits that inhabited pools and waterfalls. She lifted the shape free of the water and let it pirouette.

A song reached her ears, sad and audible over the sound of the falling water. The melody carried a pang of regret, of what could not be. Kenzie knew that she had imbued her creation with her pain, the magic holding it forth.

The magic cannot die. It was the law of the Family that magic married magic. The women who led the Family expected her to choose from the eligible wizards from within their own ranks, preferably a Wilder, to improve the genetic diversity. There was no other choice. The genes that allowed magic must be reinforced. The Family must flourish.

In a year, two at most, the eligible bachelors would court her.

A shudder ran through her body, and the watery undine swept back into the pool without a ripple, taking the song with it.

She glanced to the moon setting at the edge of the Glade, glittering stars accompanying it, and knew that it was time to leave. She stood, brushing her robe straight, and, as she did, a spark leapt from the fabric to her hand. She jerked her hand away, eyes widening.

At the edge of her vision, she caught movement on the lake. A single wave rolled in toward shore, low and fast, and washed onto the white sand of the small beach. As fast as it arrived, it withdrew, and the lake returned to placidity.

Coldness touched her spine, and the hairs on her arms rose.

On the beach, an object gleamed, brought in on the wave.

She crept close, drawing together a defensive spell. Better to be careful than cooked.

A necklace, Kenzie saw. She knelt next to it, careful not to touch the chain or the rounded charm attached to it. The silver charm bore four filigreed petals that resembled hearts, with an empty setting in the center. From the bottom of the fitting, a translucent green gem hung, square cut with beveled edges. The chain was choker length, with a simple clasp.

It's beautiful, she thought, but basic caution kept her from touching the piece. Magic existed, neither good nor evil, as neutral as gravity. Things *created* by magic, though, were imbued with their maker's purpose.

So who made this? ran through her mind, then, *Why?*

She didn't have much time to decide what to do. Should she take it with her? Could she? The rules here were perplexing. The size of the Glade was shrinking as the rest of the wizards began leaving in ones and twos. Her parents would be waiting, unless their councils ran long.

She extended her arm and touched the gem with a hesitant forefinger, half-expecting to trigger a spell, but nothing happened. Kenzie bit the inside of her lip and pondered. Then, making a decision, she scooped the jewelry into her hand and stood.

As she hurried away from the waterfall, she thought she could hear the song again, and wondered if she was making a huge mistake.

CHAPTER NINE

Mitch left the door of the garage down.

"This thing run?" asked Hunter. He sounded dubious as he wandered around the Camaro, inspecting the dings, dents, and rust. The crunching sound of plastic breaking made Mitch wince.

"You got a busted taillight, too."

"Runs great," Mitch said as he slipped behind the wheel and cranked the engine over. It grumbled to life, the bass reverberations vibrating the walls of the garage. For fun, he punched the gas. The engine roared, then tailed off to a steady vibrating purr.

He got out and left the door open.

"Wanna sit inside?" Mitch indicated the open door with a sideways jerk of his head.

Distaste flashed on Hunter's face, making the answer clear.

Figures, thought Mitch. *No getting the chinos dirty.*

"You could buy something better and not have to work on it constantly, you know."

Mitch didn't answer him. He didn't know how to explain the pleasure he derived from rebuilding the classic car. His uncle controlled his small inheritance, but let him buy the parts that got the small-block V8 engine running again. The project had started with a lump of inert steel hauled in on a trailer, and he felt a sense of gratification in the rumbling proof that he had been successful in transforming it into a functioning vehicle. The body work would come next. The big thing was that she ran.

The fumes from the exhaust sat in the air, slightly acrid.

"Can't work on a new car, with all the electronics crap," he said, walking to the back of the long, narrow garage to pop open a window.

"You don't *have* to work on a new car. That, dude, is the point of new."

Mitch shrugged his shoulders, stepping on an ancient couch that might originally have been green. "I like it." He forced the window open and took a lungful of fresh air.

The springs creaked as he hopped off the couch. He pointed to the beat-up olive green dresser across from the couch. The stun gun rested next to the television and game console.

"Ready?"

"You first," said Hunter, sounding less confident than when he had agreed to the "experiment."

Mitch picked up the weapon from the cluttered surface. "Chicken."

"You gonna turn off the car first, before we choke on the exhaust?"

Mitch turned and reached in through the open car door and turned the ignition off. A memory of the throbbing sound lingered in his ears for a few heartbeats. Outside, he heard the sound of his uncle's car rolling up, his shift at the plant complete. He faced Hunter and lobbed the stun gun over to him.

Hunter caught it sure-handedly, using both hands. The two of them had become friends during tryouts for the basketball team in their freshman year. Hunter had displayed a solid handle dribbling and an excellent three-point shot. He'd started on the JV, and swiftly been elevated to the varsity team on the strength of his outside shot.

The coach had been almost apologetic when he cut Mitch. A big believer in statistics, the full-time calculus teacher and part-time coach had the team managers chart everything. The coach summed it up on Mitch's last day of tryouts.

"You got a great motor that never quits, and you seem to play good position defense, but whoever you guard always hits eighty percent of their shots. At first, we thought it was a statistical fluke." The coach, a genuinely good guy to Mitch, had been perplexed. "Never seen or heard of anything like it."

Mitch had expected the cut, and nearly laughed in the coach's face when the older man stuck out his hand and said, "Good luck."

Mitch worked on the car as he reminisced. Rousing himself, he offered instructions to Hunter with a head bob to the stun gun.

"The slider turns it on; the trigger is the red toggle."

Hunter located the switches and turned it on. He stared like he expected the stun gun to do something, but it sat in his hand, quiescent.

"You want to be standing or sitting?"

Mitch thought about it. "Standing, I guess. How much can it hurt?"

He said the last with an ironic grin on his face. A knot in his stomach was asking Mitch the same thing, but he was committed. He walked back to the couch. If he fell, the couch was softer than the concrete. He took a deep breath.

Hunter's face scrunched into an anticipatory grimace, and his hand slowly brought the device near Mitch's bare right arm.

The cone-shaped probes dominated Mitch's vision as Hunter snapped the slider on. He tried to relax his muscles, but his whole body felt ready to launch into runaway mode any instant. Mitch took another deep breath. Nope, didn't help. The skin on his arm was hypersensitively waiting.

The silver tips wavered as Hunter seemed to get distracted rethinking the whole "You shock me, I'll shock you" deal.

"Scared?" Mitch asked him, and smiled, daring him.

Hunter jabbed the stun gun forward.

There was a crackle and Mitch flinched away from the burst of pain. "You okay?"

Not as bad as I expected, he thought, rubbing his arm.

"Yeah."

They both looked at his arm, but there was no indication on the skin to show the shock.

Hunter gaped at him. His face was pale, and his eyes were wide. He licked his lips.

"Wonder how it works through clothes?" Mitch thought out loud. "Shoot me in the leg this time."

"You want to do it again?"

"Honest, it wasn't so tough." Mitch paused. "It's like a hard sting, like maybe from a wasp. Enough to make you pay attention, that's all."

"Right," said Hunter, unconvinced.

Hunter put the gun against Mitch's thigh, pressing it into the meaty part of the quadriceps. He didn't need to be urged on this time. Mitch heard him hit the button, but instead of an instantaneous *zap!* there was a perceptible pause.

*Uh-*Mitch had time for the physics of electrical resistance to whiz through his head before the snap of the charge sounded-*oh.*

Pain, like a burn, accompanied the shock this time. Mitch didn't twitch, but he did blink rapidly and draw a deep breath.

A hint of an ironic smile crossed Hunter's face. "The clothing increases the resistance, so it takes a greater voltage differential to cross the spark gap," he said. "Plus it was tighter against you, improving contact."

"That thought occurred to me about the time you hit the trigger."

Mitch started to chuckle, twisting his shoulders back and forth in countermotion to his shaking head.

". . . increases the resistance . . . ," Mitch said between breaths. "Why didn't you just call me a dumbass?"

Hunter laughed with him. "Why say it when you can prove it?"

"Gimme the thing. Your turn." His leg still hurt at the point where the electricity had been released, but he didn't want to act like a baby and check it until Hunter was gone.

"No way, man," said Hunter, raising his hands and backing up a step. He flashed the smile he used on the ladies—lots of white teeth and charm.

"Yeah, right. Gimme." Mitch closed the gap by taking a step forward. At the same time, he held his hand out for the stun gun.

Hunter backed up another step and bumped into the dresser.

"Here," he said as he sailed the weapon to Mitch, "but I'm not getting shocked."

Mitch caught it with one hand. He held a steady gaze on Hunter. "You screwing with me?"

Hunter gave his head a single shake. "Learn from others, that's my motto."

"Boring," said Mitch, and thought, *Kind of gutless.* "You sure?" he asked, offering Hunter a chance to redeem himself.

"Not happening."

They both stood there, uncertain. Mitch operated on unspoken rules, and Hunter had broken two of the biggest. Finally, he sighed.

"Let's go get something to eat then," he said to Hunter. He wasn't too sure how well he covered his disappointment.

Relief showed in the relaxation of Hunter's shoulders, and he stepped toward Mitch. "Sounds good."

Mitch waited another beat, and as Hunter came within range, he thrust the stun gun, turned off and dormant, at his friend's midsection.

Shock and surprise, along with a sense of betrayal, appeared on Hunter's face, and Mitch almost laughed.

Then, he felt a buildup of tension flowing along his arm, forcing the limb out. He tried to withdraw the hand, but the resistance was too great. Mitch tried to let go of the stun gun, and his hand opened, the weight of the plastic case falling away. A roar of sound disappeared with a soundless flash between his hand and Hunter, hitting his friend in the chest.

Hunter howled and wrapped his arms around himself. He fell forward, eyes rolled back in his head.

Mitch reached to catch him, missed him.

Hunter melted down to the floor, and his dark complexion turned waxen.

Mitch hesitated, stunned at his friend's collapse. Help Hunter himself or get help? He turned to go for his phone in the car when a heavy weight crashed into him. The weight smashed him into the garage floor next to Hunter, and a fist pummeled his kidney.

Gasping, Mitch twisted his head and recognized his uncle.

Face-to-face, his uncle spoke, low and vicious. "Just like your goddanged father."

CHAPTER TEN

Kenzie had nowhere to hide the necklace.

The transition from the Glade had reverted her clothing from the voluminous robe back to her jeans and blouse, with a pair of low heels, the stylish casual she wore for "church."

She fumbled the choker into a small ball and followed her parents into the dusty rose light of the sunset. The shift from the Glade to the real world—*which was real?*—came abruptly each time. The outside world was noisy, with traffic and a streetcar, green with orange stripes, like an old-fashioned bus, crawling down the boulevard. Dusty too—Kenzie suppressed a sneeze on the walk to the car.

Seizing on a moment of inspiration, she fake-sneezed, bending in half to sell it. Kenzie took advantage of her doubled-up position to shove the necklace between the folds of cloth that opened at the lower buttons of her blouse. When she stood, she sucked in her abdomen to keep the bulge from showing.

She need have not worried. Her parents were oblivious, engrossed in their own conversation.

Her dad was talking as he unlocked the car, but she could see her mother already preparing a reply.

"The Protectors are in agreement that the threat to McKenzie is almost certainly an outside, non-magical operator. No indications that magic was used in the attack. An interview with the Meat that interfered with the attack and helped McKenzie suggests a few unusual elements, primarily the use of a high-end electric car. Certainly not very nondescript, and I have the staff pursuing it as a lead."

Her mother was talking almost before he finished. "I don't really care if it was a threat to the Family," she said.

She paused to buckle into her seatbelt. Kenzie did the same without thinking, and relaxed her stomach muscles.

"The attack was on McKenzie, presumably either because she is a young female and thus vulnerable, or as leverage against you and I."

"If it weren't for your project, it would have all the makings of a stranger abduction. Though," her father added, "the use of two assailants indicates a nonsexual intent."

"What project?" Kenzie asked. The car started in motion.

"Don't blame the project. It could as easily be someone trying to get even with you for sending them to jail."

"Creeps that get sent to the slammer do not conduct high-profile kidnappings in broad daylight using cars that cost a hundred grand." Her father sounded exasperated. Kenzie knew that he often sounded like that when talking, arguing, with her mother. "A device that threatens to upend the balance between the Families, on the other hand, and make Meat obsolete, attracts exactly this type of criminal."

"What device?" Kenzie piped up again. Curiosity piqued, she momentarily forgot that they were talking about her.

"MAGE does nothing of the sort. It's the natural merging of technology and our own . . . special abilities, like a gear that amplifies the output of a motor," Sasha Graham said, in an obviously practiced tone. Even the hesitation sounded practiced.

Kenzie struggled with the idea, contemplating a distant mountain as she tried to understand a . . . *an amplifier?* . . . for magic. She cocked her head to the left as she thought.

"The idea of such a device threatens the other Families. We've already seen a reaction. One of the Families is recruiting heavily. Every time we get a report of a possible Wilder, we discover that someone else has already gotten to them first, and they're gone. Worse, I can't find out which Family is involved, or their intentions."

He let that sink in.

Kenzie filled the silence with a tentative question.

"Why would the other Families be threatened?"

She understood that ordinary people would be threatened by them. History was replete with examples of mortals discovering wizards and denouncing them as evil. Horrific stories from the medieval period of the early Families being hunted and drowned—or worse, set afire— were retold as examples of why magic should work from the shadows and never in direct sight.

Her mother answered her question. "There isn't a reason for them to worry."

Her father snorted at this but kept his eyes on the road as they traveled next to Lake Washington.

"Tell her of the fracture," he dared his wife.

Kenzie's attention sharpened. The Splintering happened before she was born. The whole subject was taboo, but rumors slithered from mouth to ear.

A tingle of a thrill went up her. She waited.

Her mother shook her head in disagreement, slow and sad, and the thrill was replaced with disappointment.

"No need to revisit troubled times, and certainly not for someone as young as you."

Her father's phone, the one he kept for work, buzzed. Her mother turned to him as the car pulled into the driveway.

"Find whoever tried to kidnap McKenzie. If the attack is of magical origin, we," she said, meaning the women who were the leaders of the Family, "will deal with it." Her posture showed how unlikely she thought that was.

Her father parked the car, and they exited. Kenzie started to stretch, sensed the fabric of her blouse pulling tight on the necklace, and resumed her slightly slouched stance to hide its presence.

Her dad checked his phone and said, "I have to go."

He gave Kenzie a puzzled glance, and she could see his brain working on some problem, turning it over, seeking the keys that would unlock it.

And that expression meant that whatever problem the text message signaled, it somehow involved her.

CHAPTER ELEVEN

Hunter whimpered and leaned against the yellowed drywall in a semi-curled ball.

Mitch elbowed his uncle and twisted out from under the overweight man to help Hunter.

Panicked, he scanned the visible parts of Hunter, but other than fresh dirt stains on the pressed chinos, he couldn't find any damage to explain Hunter's reaction. He triple-checked the stun gun, and each time, it was off. There was no way that he had hurt him by shocking him.

"Dude, where's your phone? I'll call your folks."

Hunter shook his head. His voice was weak, and Mitch strained to hear him. "You're . . . meat." Hunter made it sound more like a question than a statement.

"Yeah, right, I'm dead meat, but later. Where's your phone?"

Uncle Henry had shouted incoherently at them, probably because Mitch's elbow had caught him in the throat, and fled. He was nowhere around to help. Big fat surprise.

Mitch reached to search Hunter's pockets, but his friend skittered away on the seat of his pants, craning his neck back and staring.

"Dude, I'm sorry, man," Mitch said. "I thought it was turned off."

He had his hands out in front of him, demonstrating they were empty, and willed Hunter to listen.

Behind him, the door to the house swung open. Anger welled up. He kept his gaze on Hunter. Without looking, Mitch spoke over his shoulder to his uncle. "Go away, you worthless turd."

The air movement told him he was being rushed, and he started to stand up straight and turn to face Uncle Henry.

A hard, muscular arm grabbed him, and Mitch found himself airborne, slamming into the trunk of the Camaro, bent backward and staring at a very pissed-off Seattle cop.

"Hey, whoa—"

The cop flipped him onto his belly, and an elbow pinned his neck to the scratchy, peeling paint.

Shit.

"I thought you were Uncle Henry!"

"Shut up."

The pressure let up for a fraction of a second, and Mitch tried to turn to face the cop, to explain. His right arm twisted up behind him, and he lifted onto his toes to relieve the sudden pain in his shoulder. The cold, cutting plastic of a cuff restraint bit into his wrist as the officer ratcheted the strap tight.

"But—"

"Shut up."

The voice carried no inflection, just the expectation of instant and complete obedience.

Two seconds later, Mitch's other hand was cuffed.

"Leave him alone."

Mitch turned his head to see Hunter standing, dusting himself off.

"Sit down."

Hunter stepped closer, talking with his hands again, but slowly and agreeably. "Mitch didn't do anything," he lied. "Took me by surprise, that's all."

Then what was the flash?

The pressure on Mitch lightened.

"Please sit down, sir," the cop responded. "The report came in that someone had been shot. I want everybody nice and calm while we get this straightened out."

Hunter moved to the couch, keeping his palms open to the officer, about waist high.

"Okay." He disappeared from Mitch's limited view.

"Can you get off my friend's neck in the meantime?"

The pressure went away, and Mitch lifted his shoulder and head. He twisted his head side to side and saw his uncle in the doorway, watching expectantly. Mitch shot a contemptuous glare at him.

Frickin' idiot.

Anger and resentment blackened his uncle's face, as though he could read Mitch's mind.

That's right, get all pissed off, Uncle Henry, Mitch thought. *That's the last time you swing at me.*

"I'm going to leave those cuffs on you," the cop said, trying to sound reasonable, "but you can turn around. I'd like you to stay here by the car, 'kay?"

Mitch nodded his acceptance. He stood, turned, and stretched. With his hands hidden, he started probing for a way to get the nylon straps off his wrists. The cop saw the movement from the corner of his eye and stared hard at Mitch. Mitch met his glare, face tight from trying to keep the swirling mix of resentment and anger, confusion and fear, off his face. He stopped testing the bonds.

The cop was young, blond, and trim. The name patch on his right chest pocket had "D. Blaine" in gold letters on the royal blue short-sleeved shirt. On the opposite side were his badge and radio. He stood where he could see both of them.

"You," said the cop, pointing to Hunter, and removing a small pad of paper and ballpoint pen. "Name?"

"Hunter Rubiera."

"Where do you live?"

Hunter told him. The officer wrote it down. After each entry on the pad, Blaine glanced at Mitch before refocusing on Hunter.

"Occupation."

"Uh, student?" replied Hunter, voice rising at the end.

The cop appeared startled and gave Hunter a wry grin.

"Gotta ask, right?"

"No worries."

Hunter had a way with people, for sure. Blaine was darn near smiling.

"What are you doing here?"

"We were checking out the work Mitch has done to his car, and then we played around with a stun gun that he had."

Blaine's gaze flicked to the rectangular plastic case on the floor. "That's pretty dumb."

Hunter grinned and shrugged, but didn't answer.

"Where did you get the stun gun?"

"It's Mitch's."

Blaine faced Mitch. "True?" His voice lost any warmth.

"Yeah," Mitch replied. He didn't add any more, but he started sifting excuses and reasons for having a stun gun, where he got it. He sure didn't want to admit to withholding evidence of a crime.

Blaine sighed. "Describe for me what happened," he said to Hunter.

Hunter shifted on the couch. A hint of the calculations going on in his friend's agile brain showed briefly, and after the barest hesitation, he spoke.

"We got done firing up the car, and it was running great. That's when we opened the window," Hunter said, tipping his head toward the open pane. "I already knew that Mitch had the stun gun from school—"

Blaine jumped in. "He had it at school?"

"I'm not stupid," Mitch said, cutting off Hunter's reply. "I researched up the law. It's legal, no registration required, but not allowed on school grounds."

Blaine considered this, then replied with incredulity. "So you're smart enough to look up the relevant law but dumb enough to nearly kill your friend?"

This is why I should let Hunter do all the talking, thought Mitch.

Thankfully, Hunter slipped himself back into the conversation, diverting attention back to himself.

"I shocked Mitch first," he said.

"Keep going," said Blaine.

"We tried it on his arm first—"

Blaine was shaking his head. "You did it more than once?"

Hunter blinked, then grinned. "Yeah. First time on his arm, and Mitch here says, 'Oh, it's like a bee sting, wonder what it's like through clothing,' not thinking it through. He's like that, jump in and figure it out as he goes." The grin got wider, and Blaine visibly relaxed.

Hunter continued, using his hands again to make his points.

"Anyway, I shock him in the leg and he yelps like a big baby. Then he wants to shock me." Hunter shook his head. "I didn't want to, but he lunged at me and caught me by surprise in the stomach."

"That's battery," said Blaine, writing a note on his pad.

Thanks, Hunter, that's a big help.

"It was a prank, and if it was battery on his part, then I guess I'm guilty, too."

Blaine clearly did not want to ascribe the same crime to Hunter. While he sorted out his response, Mitch watched another man walk in.

Cop.

Confident, not in a uniform, dressed neatly but casually. Medium height and build, but in an indefinable way, he arrived with a larger presence.

He did a swift assessment, taking in Mitch, the cuffs, Blaine, the stun gun, Hunter, all in one fast, perceptive sweep of the room.

"Blaine, why is the second suspect not in restraints?"

Blaine stiffened. The tips of his ears reddened, and he stammered as he replied. "He's the, I mean, it looked like he was, uh, the victim, Lieutenant."

The man stood there staring at Blaine.

The flush spread across the rest of Blaine's face. He pulled another pair of restraints out.

"Right away, sir!"

The man waved his hand and Blaine halted.

"Too late, but you endangered your own safety."

Blaine swallowed and waited for direction.

"Take that one," the lieutenant said, pointing to Hunter, "and get his statement. Take him outside while you're at it. Who taught you to get statements with both suspects together?"

Blaine bundled Hunter out of the garage, tension plain in his shoulders as he left. Mitch tried to feel sorry for him, but it was too funny watching Blaine act like one of the girls busted by a teacher for fawning over a football player. His amusement ended when Blaine was safely out of earshot.

"Tell me, Mitch," the man said, "why is it that my officers have been out here twice in less than a week?"

Déjà vu hit as the lieutenant used his name. He transferred his gaze to the stun gun on the floor, avoiding the new cop's face.

"I'm just lucky?"

"It doesn't seem terribly lucky to me."

Mitch didn't have an answer for that, so he kept his mouth shut.

"I want you to start at the beginning, and you're going to tell me everything that happened, no matter how small, okay?"

His words were friendly enough, but Mitch could feel . . . *distaste* emanating from the cop. A surge of resentment, bitter-tasting, made his face twist. The expression wasn't lost on the lieutenant.

"You don't like me now, contemplate what happens to you if you lie to me. Now, talk." As he spoke, his hands moved in a graceful arc. It reminded Mitch of the way Hunter spoke, hands gesticulating, pointing or swooping like a conductor directing an orchestra.

Mitch dragged the words out reluctantly, and more honestly than he intended.

"Hunter and I hang out together sometimes. Today, he came over 'cuz I told him that I had a stun gun—"

"Where did you get the stun gun?"

"From the kidnappers," Mitch said. He winced as the words emerged.

Stupid! So much for not admitting to felonies.

The cop absorbed the information as though he expected it.

"So go back to the start of the story, back to the attempted kidnapping."

Mitch felt a sense of relief at the word "attempted."

She's okay.

Mitch dutifully began to tell the story again, while ignoring the voice in the back of his head that tried to warn him that he was talking too much, being too truthful. The words rattled out in a rush, heedless of his inner censor. Shocked, he listened to himself describe the attack, his efforts to help the girl, his injuries, everything. Even the effect of her touch.

The cop interrupted the gushing confession, anger plain on his face.

"So you believe that because she touched your chest"—the distaste in his voice was like vinegar, biting and acidic—"your injuries were healed."

Mitch felt his stubborn gene kick in. His face flushed and radiated heat. Frickin' cop thought he was lying.

"I told all this to the old cop that interviewed me that night," Mitch said.

The cop froze. Mitch saw gears turning in the man's head.

"Officer Pho is about thirty-five," he said, enunciating the words carefully.

It was Mitch's turn to freeze, and the cop saw it.

"Describe the man who interviewed you before."

The hackles on Mitch's neck rose at the tone of the cop's voice, cold like the worst day in February.

"Older, like maybe sixty, gray hair, really green eyes."

"Name?"

"He called himself Mercury, said he was an investigator."

For the next ten minutes, Mitch felt his brain picked to pieces as the cop probed for ever-increasing detail. Once Blaine wandered in to ask what to do with Hunter, but the boss cop sent him away with the wave of a hand. Mitch tried to hold back details, but they spilled out. *Shut up already,* he thought, watching anger building on the face of his inquisitor, but the tumble of words continued.

The cop never took a note, but Mitch knew he was mentally recording every detail about Mercury, even some that Mitch didn't consciously remember, every word that the old man had said. Then they moved on to Mitch's life, his routine, what school he went to, his relationship with Hunter.

Finally, the cop relented.

"Go get that business card he gave you," directed the cop, "and tell Blaine to bring your friend in here."

Mitch held his arms out, demonstrating the impossibility of getting anything while cuffed.

The boss cop tilted his head over as though Mitch might be mocking him.

"Fine," he said. Using a folding knife from his belt, he carefully cut the bonds.

Mitch scurried for the door to the house, rubbing circulation back into his hands. He opened it to the smell of pizza—dinner—and strode across the kitchen. His uncle was in his chair, beer open, while Blaine and Hunter sat at the dining room table.

"The other cop wants you guys in there," Mitch said as he passed.

The card was sitting on top of his dresser, right where he left it. He grabbed it and turned, then stopped. Snatching a pen, he jotted the number from the card onto a scrap of paper.

He walked/jogged back to the garage. Hunter seemed bemused at the angst that Mitch was feeling. Mitch gave him a *screw you* eye roll as he delivered the card, which only made Hunter smile more.

"Blaine, get the stun gun, put it in an evidence bag."

The young cop hustled to follow his superior's order.

"You two."

They both turned to face him.

"Teenage boys should be locked in closets until the testosterone wears off." He paused. "You were stupid, both of you, especially you," he said, indicating Mitch. "Withholding evidence is a criminal offense. However, it seems that the person who interviewed you impersonated an officer of the law, making this a gray area. Next time, call us first instead of making us come to you."

Hunter bobbed his head in assent. Mitch shuffled his feet without answering.

"Also, this is part of an ongoing investigation. Don't discuss it with anybody else, period."

"What about our parents?" asked Hunter.

The cop stared at him, then replied. "Okay, but nobody else. I find out you're compromising my investigation . . ." He left the threat hanging in the air, gave them a frankly hostile glare, and left.

Blaine returned with a clear plastic bag with illegible words written on the side in black magic marker. He slid the stun gun into the bag, sealed it, and took it with him to his cruiser.

Only when the cops were gone did Hunter speak.

"Dude, what kind of trouble did you stir up this time?"

Mitch wondered the same thing.

One thing he knew, though—he had to get rid of the permit in his back pocket, pronto. . . . *Tomorrow,* he thought. The idea of going to McKenzie's scared the crud out of him. Right now, the slim rectangle felt like an anvil, and the deep water was already closing over his head.

CHAPTER TWELVE

Kenzie locked the door of the stall and leaned her head against the painted steel. She heard the scraping sound as someone else entered the girls' bathroom, retreated to the commode, and sat down, her backpack stuffed with books on her lap.

Two, maybe three girls entered.

"My god, how can she not realize how big it makes her ass look?" one of them snarked.

Kenzie recognized the voice. Alicia Rowbury, heiress to an internet fortune. Two girls laughed, high and mean, to agree with the lead bitch.

Kenzie breathed as softly as possible. She willed the pack to go away, prayed they wouldn't notice the door that stayed closed too long.

Instead, they lingered, probably touching up the makeup they wore. She caught a whiff of flowery perfume overriding the clean pine scent that lingered from the cleaners, and wrinkled her nose.

Set on verdant grounds with elegant white-painted buildings, All Friends Private Academy boasted of the number of students who went on to the Ivies, or Duke, or Stanford. The institution was very private, relentlessly educated the sons and daughters of the new wealthy, and lied in its name.

With overly loud laughs, the other girls left, and the ensuing silence settled on Kenzie. She wanted to run away from the school, or just run, run until she was as far from her life as she could get. She kept her eyes closed, trying to ignore the voice of her father nearly yelling at her, except he would never lose control enough to actually yell. Against the black background, the scene rewound, and replayed, a rumination that left her exhausted in the morning, and hiding in the bathroom during lunch.

"You used magic on Meat!"

He had found out about the boy, that she'd healed him. She couldn't tell if he was more disgusted at the waste or worried at the risk of exposure.

"You do it all the time," Kenzie had said, arms crossed and fists balled, leaning against the marble of the kitchen island. Long and flat, it was like the deck of an aircraft carrier parked in the house. Her dad had stood on the opposite side and lectured, palms flat on the black stone.

"My use of magic is condoned by the Family and is used in furtherance of the goals for the Family. What you did was unsanctioned. Did you even calculate the cost?" He punctuated the speech by leaning in as he pointed a finger. "The boy's a waste, even for Meat."

"He tried to help."

"You know nothing about him. Saving him from the natural results of his own actions and exposing yourself was foolish."

"It's not like I flashed him!"

She had managed to shock him silent. The muscles at the side of his jaw popped out, and she thought she could hear him grinding his teeth.

When he responded, the words contained so little warmth as to sound brittle. He began to recite the details.

"Mitchell Merriwether lives with his uncle, Henry Merriwether, because his father is in the Orofino prison in Idaho for the shooting death of one LeighAnn Merriwether, his mother. That was six years ago. He was present, watched it happen, and by his own admission at the time, did nothing to stop it. Interviews with the people at his school indicate that he is an antisocial influence, though apparently competent at mechanical tasks. He's Meat, and damaged Meat, at that. The call that I went on was to his house—he injured his supposed best friend by shocking him with a stun gun. That stun gun, by the way, was previously used in a crime, namely the attempt at kidnapping you. He didn't tell anyone about it, putting him on the same path as his father."

Kenzie had stopped listening. Now, in daylight, she still felt a surge of sympathy for this gangly boy.

That's why you run out into the street, she realized.

"That's the kind of Meat that you wasted magic on," her dad said, mistaking her silence as acceptance, if not agreement.

The depth of his callousness to Mitchell, his contempt for ordinary people, made her lash out with words. "You stand there and preach about how great we are compared to someone like Mitchell. When we're at the Glade, all everyone talks about is being one—not a person, but one part of Nature. That, and how to use your magic," she waved her hands in a meaningless gesture, "to help the Family. And they always make it sound like the Family includes everybody, don't they, but what you really mean is 'use it for us.' Well, too bad, *Daddy,* but I used it to help someone who tried to help me. Too bad he's ordinary, but he at least cared enough to help me. You couldn't even look me in the eye when you took my 'report,' didn't ask if I was okay?"

"I have my job—"

"I don't care—"

"Do not speak to your father that way."

Her mother, returning from an evening meeting for work, entered from the laundry room that stood between the kitchen and garage. She wore a sour expression and had her gaze fixed on Kenzie.

That ended the argument, with Kenzie stuck in the middle, the words she still wanted to say choking in her throat as she stormed up to her room.

But she left her door open a crack, just enough that she could hear the heated discussion. Even from upstairs, she could sense the urgency in the briefing. Momentary sadness swept through her and she wondered how many other families had briefings instead of conversations.

The news that someone had interfered with her father's investigation, impersonating one of the officers, alarmed her, and the chill of the aftereffects of the attack returned. She quelled it by clenching her teeth tightly together until she heard the hiss of blood in her ears from the pressure.

"It has to be related to the project." Her dad's voice was adamant as he continued, "A straight kidnap for money is rare as hell, and nobody would have gone back to the primary witness to interrogate him. Not only that, but an ordinary criminal can't make one of my officers believe that he went to Merriwether's house and conducted an interview. That single fact points to someone using magic, and at a very high level."

"Only a handful of people are aware of the full ramifications of what we're doing in the lab, all of them members of the Family." A pause. "It would be a . . . a betrayal."

Kenzie perked up at the emotion in her mother's words, a hint that her mother was not only concerned with elegant, unfeeling efficiency but could feel emotions. Her hopes crashed a second later when her mother spoke again, cold steel injected into the air, replacing the scandalized tone.

"Never mind, we'll run a security review. I've initiated the process at the company. You follow up on the wizard that interfered. He can't be with the kidnappers, or he'd have known all the details."

"Exactly—"

Her mother became contemplative, and Kenzie had to strain to hear her. "We need to address McKenzie. She's clearly besotted with the boy. That must end."

Kenzie blinked and swallowed.

"She knows her duty," responded her father.

"Knowing it and accepting it are completely different things. Trust me, I could see it in her when I came in—if we leave it to her right now, she would choose the path away from magic, to try and reform the Meat that got himself tangled up in something that's none of his business. History will repeat itself."

Kenzie had her mouth open to shout a protest down the steps when caution stole her voice, and she caught the final word from her mother.

"It's time to tell the menfolk of the Glade that McKenzie is open to courtship. She will be made to choose one of them, as is her duty. If she refuses, we will choose for her."

The bell rang, a gentle tone suitable for the emerging leaders that the school produced. The rushing noises of students heading for class drifted into the stall. Kenzie waited until the restroom was empty, wiped away tears, and stood to go. It took all her willpower to unlock the door and step back into public.

It's my life, she thought, and hated it.

CHAPTER THIRTEEN

There was no place to park.

Mitch rumbled past the Graham address three times, but both sides of Lake Washington Boulevard were posted with No Parking signs. He turned around again at the entrance to Seward Park and doubled back. He slowed as he came to the huge house, a Tudor set back from the road with white gates set in brick columns guarding the driveway. The gates were open, the same way a trap is open, and he slowed more, then sped up.

Finally, he pulled into the deserted lot for the Lake Washington Rowing Club. He looked around, didn't see anyone watching, and got out of the Camaro.

He flipped his hoodie up and tucked his chin down during the mile-long jaunt back to the house. The misty rain soaked into his jeans and the mossy-smelling damp April chill insinuated its way past the layers of clothing he wore. A boat floated by, and gentle waves lapped up onto the shore.

He huddled his shoulders and kept walking.

When he reached the address on McKenzie's permit, he stopped on the sidewalk to gaze at the gates, the foliage rising behind the walls, and the graceful home with an upper balcony giving an uninterrupted view of the lake. He stepped forward, heard the hissing sound of car tires on wet pavement coming toward him, and stepped back to avoid the slime thrown up from the wheels. That much, at least, was the same as home.

Mitch took a deep breath and crossed the street.

This is stupid, he thought as his hands began to shake, but he went through the gates and up the driveway. Mitch stuck to the side of the driveway, keeping himself partially hidden by the shrubs. He absorbed details from the veranda, the high windows, the feeling of emptiness.

She won't even be here.

The thought rambled through his mind as his heart thumped. His stride faltered, and he almost turned to leave again. He wavered there until an image of Hunter laughing at him tipped him past the moment of paralysis.

He climbed the steps to the front door, trying to be quiet. Another set of deep breaths, but Mitch's heart collided with ribs, spine, and seemed to end up lodged in his throat. He stopped in front of the first window, peeked in from the edge.

A table lamp burned in the corner of the formal living room, and he saw a shadow on the wall entering from the far doorway. He slipped past the window and was reaching for the doorbell when he caught movement from the corner of his eye.

His jitters disappeared instantly, and all the nerve fibers in his body shifted to high alert.

Not again, he thought. Reversing his strategy of the last two times he'd faced imminent threats, he tried ducking and moving away.

He gained a momentary advantage as the man's arm fell on open air.

Mitch stepped forward again, swinging his right elbow in a hard arc. It caught the man behind the ear, but his assailant was already moving away from the attack. He slipped his arm under Mitch's left armpit, seized him, and, continuing the turn, rammed Mitch into the support column on the veranda.

Mitch felt the hard grip of hands around his throat as he met the man's eerily calm eyes. Mitch, face pinched with anger, lifted his right forearm to knock away the hand. The man shoved his shoulder into Mitch's, blocking the motion.

In the confusion, he heard her voice.

"Jackson, he's a friend."

Mitch saw a hint of surprise, tempered with doubt, but the shoulder came up, and the hand fell from his throat.

She stood at the doorway, taller than he remembered.

McKenzie Graham.

Mitch tried to breathe.

She wore her hair down, and it fell across her shoulders in a bouncy wave, framing her fine-featured face. Her permit showed her with her hair pinned back, the same as when she ran. He hadn't pictured her in anything but the running clothes, but now she was wearing a brown leather jacket over a T-shirt and jeans.

She fit the fancy house like she belonged.

He realized he didn't, but it was too late to leave. Mitch ducked his head and tried to talk.

"I, uh . . ." He swallowed. The pressure of her gaze on him made him lift his eyes, and he glanced at her. She just looked at him, waiting.

God, those eyes, honey-brown, were gorgeous.

"You want to come in?"

The man next to him stepped in front of Mitch, blocking him with a broad shoulder.

"I doubt that's a good idea."

"You're supposed to protect me from strangers. My father hasn't forbidden me from having friends over, right?" the girl said. She spoke past Jackson. "Please come in, Mit—cheal. . . ."

Mitch caught the hesitation, and the sudden swerve from his name. With a practiced reflex, he smoothed his face.

Why lie about my name?

She stepped back into the house and held the heavy oak door open. Jackson walked in ahead of him, shielding her. "I still don't think—"

"It will be fine. I asked Michael over to help with some homework. He's a brainiac."

Mitch followed the Jackson dude in. Before the man could turn, Mitch lifted his shoulders up and sent a questioning nod at McKenzie. She turned her head a quarter of an inch to the side and back.

Okay, later, he thought. He stepped past her into the living room. She closed the front door with a click of the latch.

He surveyed the room, the abundance of real wood, something dark like mahogany. All the colors were deep and natural, the walls cream colored. It smelled lemony, like someone had polished recently. An arched doorway on the far wall showed a slice of a formal dining room with a mahogany table and cushioned straight-back chairs. A matching arch on the next wall created the surreal illusion of never-ending openings. To his left, French doors enclosed a den.

He thought of his cluttered bedroom and his uncle's crappy small house.

The damp on his clothes chafed.

"We'll be in the kitchen," said McKenzie.

She walked away, toward the back of the house. Mitch shuffled after her. Jackson *humph*ed but stayed put in the front room.

Boots, that's why she seemed taller. Leather, like the jacket, probably real leather. There were sparkles on the pockets of her jeans.

A jittery feeling grew in his chest. Mitch fumbled in his back pocket to pull her permit out.

The kitchen gleamed. The granite island, flecked with gold, dominated the space. Tile floors, expensive cabinets, a frickin' refrigerator for wine.

McKenzie shrugged the jacket off as she walked in. Mitch watched the play of her shoulders, petite, as she shed the extra layer.

She smelled nice.

She plopped the jacket next to a backpack and turned to face him.

Unable to speak, he held out the stiff plastic ID.

It took her a second to recognize what he held, then her hand reached to his, and took it. Her fingers brushed his.

"Thanks," McKenzie said, slipping it into a pocket with a wriggle.

She indicated the doorway they had passed through with a worried jerk of her hand and kept her voice low.

"Do you know anything about math?" she asked. Her voice was noncommittal; not mean-cold, just not friendly. "Jackson is cool, but he's going to tell my father you were here."

"I just wanted to, you know, get your license back to you."

He diverted his attention to avoid her questions. The refrigerator was big enough to swallow a steer and then some. A whirring sound came from it, and then a grinding sound. *Ice maker,* the mechanical part of his brain categorized. Or the fridge was digesting that steer. Mitch pulled at the neck of his sweatshirt. He should have mailed the thing.

She was busy digging out books from the pack. "Mitchell."

"Mitch," he corrected automatically. He gazed at her. She stood, arms folded across her chest, holding a textbook. Upside down.

He spoke. "Why did you lie about me, out there?"

"I told you. Jackson's going to report everything, that's part of his job." Bitterness tinged the words.

"It's not my name."

"He's my bodyguard, ever since . . ."

She's not listening, thought Mitch. Heat filled his face as reality collided with his imagination. What the hell had he thought was going to happen, she'd be so happy to see him that she'd fall all over him . . . and *what?*

He locked his face into don't-give-a-damn mode, but his heart hurt as it banged in his chest. His eyes wandered back to the fridge, took in the reflective sheen of the high-end appliance that cast them in funhouse caricatures.

"I gotta go."

His shoes cemented themselves to the tile floor, though, making a liar out of him. He could see them right there, disobeying orders. Finally, the left foot squelched and pivoted, and he could move again. He waited for McKenzie to say something, make him stop.

He struggled to focus on something other than the thin grout lines between tiles and risked a glance at her.

McKenzie held the book tight to her chest, hair in a cascade. The bruise on her arm had faded, but a faint smoky ring remained as testimony to the welts he had seen on her. As he watched, her chest rose softly and fell with a hint of a shudder, but she held her chin up, proud.

He lost control of his face and words fell out of his mouth, quiet like his mother taught him: *Quiet, quiet, Mitchell, it'll be okay.*

"Are you okay?"

CHAPTER FOURTEEN

Three words, and he hit her in the heart.

Mitch slipped past the layers of Kenzie's carefully constructed protection that made it possible, barely, to function as a caricature of who she was, by always pretending to be someone else: daughter to a fortune for the girls at school, normal to Jules and Jackson, a dutiful member of the Family, submissive daughter. Always something others thought she should be, should be, should be . . .

Mitch didn't ask who she should be.

Three words.

Are you okay?

Kenzie had locked herself behind doors, each with different locks, marked with red warning letters: *Lies! Control! Indifference! Anger!* Rather than stopping at each door, he bypassed the fortifications and found the back door, which had a rusty sign loosely attached.

Honesty.

She had forgotten to lock that door, and Mitch had found it.

He stood in her kitchen, sodden but straight and tall, waiting for her answer.

"Yeah," she said, shaking her head. The waver in her voice betrayed her, but she met his gaze. She did not blink. Teardrops would prove her lie.

She saw a softening of his expression and a tilt to his head.

"You don't look it."

He kept his voice down, glancing at the doorway to make sure that they were alone enough. She heard sadness in the undercurrents, like unanswered echoes from a lonely place.

She clutched the book tighter to her chest. That's why it was so hard to breathe. She opened the door to *Control.*

"I said I'm fine," Kenzie said. "I made a mistake. You can leave."

He gave her an appraising squint, the kind she associated with old people when they seemed to know too much.

She turned away from his scrutiny and walked to the counter, heels clicking on the tile floor. She put the book down with a thump. She heard him step closer, but not too close.

"Did they catch the guys that attacked you?"

Her breath caught, and she gave a sharp shake of her head.

Don't blink, it'll pass.

The fluttery feeling in her chest moved to her stomach.

For a fleeting instant, she could feel his arms around her, feel her head leaning into the muscle of his chest, then she shoved the image away.

He isn't Family, he's—she caught the thought and despised the word even as she changed it—*normal.*

But the feeling persisted, so right that she could see pictures of the future slipping one at a time into her mind, first kiss, first date, first . . .

"Go away."

"No."

Startled, she peered at him. His unguarded expression said he was as surprised as she felt.

She tried locking the door marked *Anger.*

"What do you mean no?"

Her voice sounded loud to her ears, too loud, *crap!*

A rustling sound from the other room, Jackson getting up, checking on her.

"Everything okay?" he asked before he reached the door.

"Fine," Kenzie said, lying. She flipped open her book.

Mitch took the hint and stepped closer to read the pages. With a flick of his wrist, he spun the book so that it was facing the right way.

"Why don't you get your notes," he said, louder than he needed to.

Jackson reached the doorway. His expression showed skepticism as his gaze shifted from Mitch to Kenzie. She gave him a hurried half smile and bent over her backpack to pull out a tattered notebook. Mitch had his head down, studying the book with a quizzical eye. As she walked back, he turned a page, then let it fall back.

Jackson turned wordlessly and left them.

"It's calculus," she explained, speaking softly, spreading her papers out. "Sorry."

Mitch bobbed his head. She could see his eyes flitting first to the book, then to her work. In a burst of intense concentration, he squinted at the arcane equations.

She grimaced, imagining what it would be like to get tossed an advanced—

Mitch's finger stabbed out, touched the page where she had erased the same problem repeatedly.

"You dropped a sign when you did your substitution into the integral."

She gawked at him, and heat filled her face. She checked the page, and her brows climbed her forehead. The heat ratcheted up two more notches. She saw it now.

He glanced at her, face impassive.

"Math is one of the things I kinda get." He paused. "And putting things together. I'm good at that, too."

She continued to stare, and Mitch shuffled from one foot to the other. He took a half step backward.

"You didn't really need any help, the rest of the problems are right. . . ."

"You figured that out in what, thirty seconds?"

He lifted his hands up and shrugged as a blush tinted his cheeks. He took another backward step and stared at her boots. His hands moved aimlessly, as if to ward off his nerdliness.

"Yeah."

Kenzie stood staring at him and tried to solve the puzzle of Mitch. It was hard to imagine the boy in front of her as the guy who'd run into a street to rescue someone he didn't know. Five minutes ago, he'd refused to be driven away. Now he was ready to bolt for the door, all because he could do some math?

The sound of their breathing was the loudest thing in the house.

Which meant Jackson was listening, too.

"Thank you."

Mitch shrugged. A frown crossed his forehead, and she watched as a stubborn streak showed itself in the way he held his chin, turned his shoulders like he was wrestling with a choice. His gaze darted up to her face, seeking.

"Who are you?" Mitch asked.

Blindsided again, she felt answers blossom in her mind.

She was Kenzie Graham. . .

. . . *ordinary teenage girl . . .*

. . . *but ordinary girls didn't have uber-rich parents . . .*

. . . *an ordinary teenage girl . . .*

. . . *who hid in the bathrooms at school . . .*

. . . *an ordinary teenage girl . . .*

. . . *who led a secret life as an enchantress, bound to the Family . . .*

. . . anything-but-ordinary teenage girl . . . who wished sometimes she was ordinary, or at least, invisible . . .

She discarded all the answers as too truthful under his stare and, in the void left by her hesitation, shrugged.

"I'm just me."

Mitch didn't say anything, and the weight of the question grew.

"My friends call me Kenzie . . ." *What friends?* ". . . and I do martial arts and run." That was true, she thought.

"Normal stuff. School. You know." She added another shrug and evaded his eyes by checking the time. An hour until her father came home.

"I think," Mitch said, an odd inflection to his voice, "that you're anything but normal. I know you have secrets, just like the rest of us. You don't want to tell me, or can't, doesn't matter which, but if you're normal, nothing fits."

Kenzie stifled a gasp. Mitch saw it and ignored it.

"It doesn't matter. I don't care about"—his voice wavered—"I mean, if I can, like, help . . ."

The ruddy color had spread from his cheeks to the tips of his ears and Kenzie could feel a matching heat on her face. The heat grew and warmed her insides, which went rubbery. Almost as though they belonged to someone else, her hands began a slow, intricate movement. The heat ignited and spread into her abdomen. Her fingers turned and made a brushing, come-hither gesture. Her breath moved faster. . . .

Mitch watched her hands, and his breathing matched hers. His enraptured gaze returned to her face.

Startled, Kenzie clenched her hands into tight fists, then splayed her fingers wide. Her whole body quaked as the gathered magic dissipated.

A worried thought followed the shakes: How had she done *that?* Even in the Glade, where magic flowed to them like sunshine onto flowers, she had never drawn that much power. A quivering *aliveness* permeated her core and left her tingly all over.

Mitch watched her, head pulled back, cautious. "What was that?"

His voice came out hoarse, and he shook his head in a side-to-side motion as though he was recovering from anesthesia and found his senses addled by the experience.

"I don't know." She forced the lie out as a taint of her shame spread on her face. She bit down on her lower lip as the *aliveness* panted and answered, *I do.* She looked away and drew in a great gulping breath.

As she exhaled, she sought her core like Jules had taught. She centered herself before she tried speaking.

Words would not come.

Kenzie could read the suspicion in Mitch. Mouth dry, she turned away and took the two steps to the dishwasher.

"Want something to drink?"

Lame, lame, lame, Kenzie thought, but removed two sparkling glasses from the washer. They sang with a clear song when she set them on the marble. She hazarded a fast glance at Mitch. He stared back with relief overriding his doubts.

"Yeah, thanks."

She filled the glasses with water from the fridge. The edge of the glass rattled against the dispenser as she carefully filled each one. The routineness of the act let her rein in her thoughts. Glasses filled, she turned and extended the one in her right hand toward Mitch. She held herself steady and placed a smile on her lips as she did.

"Here."

Mitch stepped forward to retrieve the water. He grasped the bottom of the glass, paused until she let go, and then backed off a couple of steps. Together, they sipped their water, eyes making contact before veering away. Kenzie tried to find something to say that didn't sound idiotic. Instead, she took another sip.

A rustling sound came from the other room. Jackson appeared in the doorway. He glanced at them, measuring the distance between them with suspicion.

"Hunh, I could use some water, too," he said, staring at Mitch. "I don't recall seeing you at All Friends, *Michael.*" Jackson's skepticism was clear.

Kenzie saw the defensive shields slide into Mitch's demeanor as he assessed the bodyguard. He stopped slouching and lifted his shoulders. Kenzie noted that Mitch stood several inches taller than Jackson.

"Because I don't go there, sir." His tone was polite on the surface, but with a sharpened edge below that discouraged more questions. "I go to Hitchings. It's a tech charter school."

Mitch put his glass on the countertop. He faced Kenzie.

"Thanks for the water," he said, turning to the doorway, "but I should get going."

Kenzie set her glass next to his. "I'll walk you to the door."

This earned a reproving frown from Jackson. Kenzie glared at him and silently followed Mitch through the dining room, living room, and out the door.

Outside, she apologized. "It's his job, ever since, the . . ." She hesitated, uncertain how to phrase it. "The, uh, attack."

"Sucks living under a microscope."

Something in the way he said it made her search his face, and he was the one to avert his gaze. Her breath caught in her chest.

"I have a private lesson tomorrow at the studio," Kenzie said, rushing the words together. "You could, maybe, swing by after?"

Mitch's mouth gaped open, and surprise lit up his face.

"Me? Um . . . sure." His fingers fidgeted with the pull cord of his hoodie. "When?"

"After school?"

He nodded.

Kenzie gave him directions, casting a nervous glance over her shoulder to make sure that Jackson wasn't in earshot.

"I can find it," said Mitch. He scanned the yard and shoved his hands into the front pouch of the sweatshirt. He stood, out of place and unsure how to proceed.

Kenzie indicated the door and relieved him of making a decision. "I got to head inside, or Jackson'll be out here in a minute."

"Yeah, sure, I get it."

"See you tomorrow?"

Mitch bobbed his head and ducked as he walked out into the misty rain. Kenzie watched him go.

Mitch glanced back as he reached the sidewalk, and Kenzie gave a half wave, fingers curling over.

She turned to the door and found Jackson watching her.

"That's kind of creepy," she said as she opened the door and reentered the house.

"Tell your dad," was his reply.

Kenzie thought that was a pretty crappy idea.

As she walked back to the kitchen, she started figuring out how to get around Jackson so Mitch could visit her.

CHAPTER FIFTEEN

Mitch stood next to the Camaro and stared out across Lake Washington Boulevard to the stately houses made gloomy by the mist. Behind him, a Mercedes hissed by on the wet asphalt, the black paint of the body work in glistening contrast to the manicured lawns that fell down the hillside to the asphalt.

He put both hands on the roof, the cold paint slick under his palms. A deep breath and a long exhalation didn't help. Everything still seemed topsy-turvy.

His imagination re-created the scene in Kenzie's kitchen, and he watched the weaving of her hands. Her sudden mortification surprised him and, at the same time, electrified him. An aching need inside threatened to take over. He stifled the feeling, buried it with the other emotions that would hurt if he brought them into the light.

It wouldn't be ignored, a heavy lump in his chest, squeezing his heart.

He curled his fingers and scraped his nails over the faded paint. His pinkie fingernail caught on a chipped spot in the paint job. This much felt real.

The smell of the grass and the rain, they were real.

The rain was real, and in Seattle a constant, he thought, then remembered the blue skies that had framed Kenzie's face the day he raced out into the street. *Almost constant,* he thought, *with occasional bouts of stunning clarity,* and deep inside, the observation surprised him.

The lump grew, and he inhaled until his ribs stretched his skin. He held the air inside for the count of three. It came out in a rush when he let go.

It helped some, not much.

Kenzie wanted him to meet her tomorrow.

The lump in his chest froze into a solid block.

Does this qualify as a date?

His brain stopped, grinding to a halt like a computer instructed to process cheese. Data went in, hit the processing center, got blasted by the concept of a date with a real girl. No, not a real girl. Well, okay, Kenzie was a real girl, and pretty, too, but not like the other girls. Those he watched from across a room or ignored because he was not going to humiliate himself by asking them out.

Kenzie was different.

Mitch made an effort to force his thoughts into logical patterns, but he could not hold on to them. Violently, he shook his head until droplets of water sprayed off his hood. Other than making his neck hurt, nothing happened. His mind continued to dart in scattered directions.

He'd meet her—

What time?

She said after school.

Her school? His school?

Why didn't he ask?

There were lots of things he hadn't asked her.

Chicken, he thought, and agreed with himself. He didn't want to know, especially now.

He had a date. Why mess with a good thing?

Hopeless, his internal watchdog said, walking away from the mushiness of his thoughts.

A sharp pokey spike shattered the lump in his chest. Not hopeless. Hopeful.

It scared the crap out of him.

CHAPTER SIXTEEN

The rattle from the garage door opening vibrated up through Kenzie's bedroom floor to announce the arrival of one of her parents. Kenzie ignored it, gazing out her window. High above the hillside behind her house, a spark of sapphire blue sky burst through the late-afternoon gray. Through the opening, light played down to the ground, the rain at the edges shimmering, caught by the rays.

Kenzie exhaled in a long, depressed breath.

He won't show, she thought to herself. Heat rose on her cheeks again as she glanced at her hands. She repeated the gesture, without the focus needed to summon the magic, a swirl of her hands leading up to the crook of a finger, bent to summon, urging Mitch to come closer. She sensed a wrongness at the end of the movement, and repeated it, flattening her right hand as the left began the dance to the call forth, and then, relaxing and letting intuition guide her, folded her hands between her breasts and over her heart.

Rumors abounded in the Family of portents and hidden spells, and especially of wizards who refused to honor the magic. The rogues would turn the magic on the ordinary, taking what they wanted from them. That was how the Wilders got discovered, pushing the magic too far, inviting discovery. There were rules, set up to protect the other wizards.

The Family relied on stealth to hide their assets, both in terms of wealth and influence, never letting any of the wizards gain so much of either that it sparked interest. When you could manipulate others in subtle sorcery, acquiring a bankroll took very little effort. It did not take much to influence people into deals that were consistently profitable. Money left more time for magic. Everyone agreed with that rule and policed everyone else to make sure nobody got too greedy.

The strictest rules applied to using magic on others, bewitching them into doing your bidding. Wasting magic for personal gratification. Kenzie heard the whispers of the scandalous stories, of women luring men into bed, of men doing the same. They targeted ordinary people so they wouldn't get caught. Belinda, the blond Wilder who had blasted her with the spell at the most recent Gathering, featured prominently in the gossip.

She had made her living with her magic, they said. No one ever said how, but they would nod, and the way their accusing eyes would dart in her direction made it clear.

Belinda, they said, had made a very good living.

Kenzie turned with her face to the distance.

It would be so *easy*. . . .

A shudder ran down her back, and she squashed the repugnant thought.

No, not that way. An ache filled her. In her mind, she pictured Mitch, standing close, near enough for her to lay her head on his chest, hear his heartbeat, and feel his arms around her. Because he wanted to, and she wanted to, not because either of them *had to*.

Footsteps clicked in the hallway, and Kenzie opened her eyes and unwrapped her arms, which had unconsciously folded around her. She turned as the door to the room opened. Her elegantly dressed mother leaned into the room, one foot still in the hallway.

"I called a Gathering for this evening," said Sasha. "Please be ready by seven, okay?"

Kenzie raised an eyebrow and then shrugged.

"Sure."

She turned back to look for the blue patch, but the gray mass of clouds had swallowed it.

CHAPTER SEVENTEEN

The garage door closed on the gray gloom outside as Mitch stared through the dusty windshield of the Camaro. The door of the car creaked as he popped it open and again when he closed it. The garage door, heavy wood, did not creak anymore, not since he oiled the hinges. It opened smoothly and silently.

He waited, listening. The house around him felt tired in the drizzly weather. Nobody else was home. He moved into and through the kitchen, mentally comparing the dingy Formica with the marble, the battered cabinetry with the polished wood at Kenzie's. An odor wafted from the dirty dishes stacked haphazardly in the sink, and for a change, it bothered him.

The color of the day filtered in on the filmy glass of the windows, leaving the inside of the house depressed. The light petered out at the hallway, and Mitch traversed the near-dark to the door of his room, opened it, and entered a deeper shade of melancholy.

He fished his wallet out of his back pocket and tossed it onto the top of the dresser. It hit, slid, and fell to the floor. Something white from the dresser's surface fluttered down next to it.

Mitch bent to pick up the worn brown wallet and saw his handwriting on the torn slip of paper. He pinned it with a thumb against the flat of the faux leather as he retrieved both items from the floor. He placed them on the top of the dresser, careful not to pitch them since they'd slide off again.

The paper didn't let go and clung to his thumb.

I hate the gray, he thought ritually, without wasting extra emotion on it, and peeled the paper loose.

He stared at the phone number.

Mitch knew exactly who the number should reach, and he was equally sure that calling it would be a mistake. He didn't know who the hell Mercury was, but he still remembered the grilling he'd gotten yesterday from the unnamed supervisor about every aspect of his meeting with the fake cop the day of the attack. Based on the reactions of the real cops, Mercury had to be some kind of fake.

Still, Mercury had treated him better than the SPD dude had.

Mitch had given up the business card, of course, and more. He shook his head about how much he'd blabbered to the cop, the words tripping out as he tried to answer the questions. Meanwhile, Hunter had lodged himself in a corner, staring at all of them, whites showing around his irises. Hunter had been okay—Mitch thought he was okay, at least—when he left, almost running over the cops in the process of vacating.

Curiosity finally overcame his good sense, and he pulled out his phone, dialing with his thumb. It hovered over the button to initiate the call. Reflexively, he jabbed down and lifted the phone to his ear, hoping that no one would answer.

One ring, two, three . . .

"Museum for Magical Arts," Mercury's voice announced, "a repository for learning about the craft. We cater to the gifted amongst us, as well as those too curious for their own good. Each talisman comes with a money-back guarantee, but spells are not returnable. Books are available for loan, but we're in no way responsible for any misuse of the materials, anticipated or unanticipated side effects, or liability for your personal safety."

"Fracking joke number," muttered Mitch, though bile rose with disappointment at the recording. He hit the button to terminate the call. The screen faded to black in the dim light of his room, but the voice continued like the phone was set on speaker, warmth replacing the practiced ease of the sales greeting.

"Since this is the private line, though, you don't care about any of that, do you? Hello, Mitch."

"Um, hello." The sudden transition confused him, plus, now that he was talking to Mercury—how was he talking to Mercury?—he didn't know what he really wanted. He turned the phone over and considered removing the battery. Would it make a difference?

"I presume that it is safe for me to guess that you're not a wizard?"

Mitch deflected. "I gave your number to the real cops."

"No, Mitch, you gave them a number, not the number. Only you could reach me this way."

"I don't understand."

"Don't worry about it. It's important for you and me to meet again. You've been very busy."

Mitch popped the case off the phone, removed the back cover, and checked the battery.

"Mitch?"

"Yeah?" The skin on his face felt tight and numb.

"Relax, kid." The phone fell silent for a moment. "Trust your instincts. You just need to have a little faith in yourself."

"I don't need a pep talk!"

A sigh emerged from the phone and dissipated. "Fine. You said you were never lucky, right?"

"I'm not."

"How do you tell good luck from bad luck?"

The son of a . . .

"By the bad shit that happens." Mitch's words came from between clenched teeth. "That's how you can tell, when everything goes wrong, and there's nothing you can do to stop it—"

"This time there's something you can do to stop it," Mercury said, his voice rising hard over Mitch's.

Mitch fell silent, and Mercury continued. "We need to meet. I would not ask if it weren't important, Mitch. And sooner would be better than later."

"None of this fits together."

Frustration ripped the words from Mitch, and he winced. It sounded too close to a whine.

"It does, trust me, but you don't have everything you need to recognize that. You only have part of the pattern."

"And you can give me the whole thing?"

The silence lasted several seconds. Mitch willed Mercury to respond. A strange excitement built, mixed with fear. He needed answers.

Mercury's words were a letdown.

"No," said the older man, regret filtering through. "I probably would, if I knew the whole thing myself, but I don't either. I just know a lot more than you do."

"Probably?"

"Mitch, this is a limited-time offer. Will you come meet?"

He could almost feel the pressure of Mercury's green eyes on him, boring in, as if he were asking a different question entirely. He remembered the old man's comment about running to the sound of the guns and decided. In the instant of deciding, he felt something irrevocable change, deep inside.

"Where?"

Mercury gave him an address. Mitch recognized the general area. Close to the studio he was meeting Kenzie at. The coincidence made him suspicious. "When?"

"Yesterday would have been better, tomorrow is not too late."

Mitch grimaced. He wasn't going to get any straight answers from Mercury. "I've got school tomorrow and a . . . another person to meet first. I can be there at five?" The inflection rose at the end, making the statement a question.

"I'm not going anywhere." There was a click and Mercury was gone.

Mitch held the phone tight. With his right hand, he pulled the battery, but he suspected that it didn't make a difference.

The pieces might not fit, but he was starting to at least see the shapes of them.

CHAPTER EIGHTEEN

The Glade was as small as Kenzie had ever seen it and the moon dominated the horizon. The scent of lilacs floated on the air this time. The Glade presented itself in beguilingly different ways every time she came. The size she understood, a function of the occupancy and position of the wizards, but the blooms seemed random. She meandered toward the training circle, stopping along the brook to scoop a handful of sweet-tasting water. She let the excess dribble through her fingers, the droplets catching the bright light of the moon as they fell like a shower of tinkling diamonds back to the softly flowing stream.

To her surprise, old Harold was at the circle, hands folded under his long robe. He had his back to her, and his head tilted down. In this pose like a statue of a wise man, he greeted her with a serene, "Hello, Miss McKenzie."

"Where is everyone?" The rest of the teaching circle lay slumbering.

Harold spoke with his back still turned. "Special session, I think. Only the council members were invited."

Kenzie studied him. "If you weren't invited, why are you here?"

"I like it here."

Made sense, thought Kenzie. She liked it here, too, but the short notice for the meeting so close on the heels of the conversation between her parents made her nervous.

"What are they meeting about?" She tried to keep it casual, but her words came out forced and needy.

Harold turned to face her. "You don't know?"

He studied her face. Kenzie held her features still, knowing that the answer wrote itself in her lack of surprise at the meeting. Sympathy lines etched into the creases along Harold's forehead. "I see," he said.

Involuntarily, Kenzie's lips formed a hard line. It took a deep breath to force them to relax. She changed the subject.

"So what do you do here? I mean, all by yourself?"

"Practice. Play." He waved a hand, and a golden glow appeared a foot in front of her. He flicked his wrist, and the glow danced around Kenzie. Distracted by the motion, she missed the next gesture. The globe of light expanded, engulfed her, and bathed her in the warmth of a summer evening. Across from her, Harold smiled.

The spell faded from the outside edges into her, leaving a peacefulness behind where the anxiety had been.

"How did you do that?"

Harold laughed. "It's a parlor trick, that's all."

He lifted his hand again.

"First, it's a version of a healing spell."

"Æsculapium?"

"Yes, very good." He hesitated. "I don't remember teaching you that spell."

Dummy! Kenzie thought to herself.

"I watched you teaching some of the others when I was little," she confessed.

He arched his left eyebrow. "You and I will need to talk," he said, "about what you know and what you're supposed to know. Some of the lessons are much too advanced for you yet, and the magic dangerous." He half-turned away from her.

She tracked him and watched as a creature took shape. The murky outlines solidified into a mangy black animal with scary pretercanine eyes that burned sulfurously. The animal stood as tall as a lion and presented itself with a vulpine loll of its massive head. Kenzie stepped back as the snout swung toward her and the jaws gaped open.

"A gytrash," explained Harold. "You can summon one to you, being magical, but the gytrash seeks to lead humans to their doom." He beamed at her like a showman hitting the high point of his act, balancing between the trick and the audience. He waited until he had her full attention. "It can also guide the lost to the correct path."

The gytrash's gaping mouth curled in a canine grin. Then, it faded back to wherever Harold had summoned it from.

"That's magic."

Kenzie let out a lungful of air, the image still clear in her head.

"You conjured that . . . that gytrash," she said, struggling with the pronunciation, "without a spell." She winced, hearing an accusation where she meant amazement.

Harold cocked his head to the side. "True."

"How?" The question tore out of her. Harold was a dear, but frustrating, and she loved the way he taught the classes. Now, with him for what seemed like a private lesson, she couldn't curb her impatience.

"When we practice spells, we move our hands and say the words, but until we cast them, nothing happens." He let her digest the information. "Potions are the same way. We mix all the ingredients, but the concoction stays inert until what?"

"We add magic," Kenzie said. "I know all tha—"

"But you don't question what it is that a wizard must add. Like following a recipe to bake a cake, all of you think"—and the diminutive man indicated the distant council with a turn of his head to remove the sting—"everyone forgets that the wizard adds a bit of himself to the process."

He stopped and raised a finger.

"Do this," said Harold.

She lifted her right hand and pointed up with the forefinger. It trembled like her body had before her first sparring competition at the studio. She sought her core as Jules had taught her, and the hand steadied.

Harold waited, and scrutinized her effort. "Good."

Behind him, the globe reappeared, wobbled in a circle, and flashed out of existence.

"Do it."

"But I didn't see you do anything."

Harold bent his finger down and touched the tip of hers. A jolt flowed down her finger, traced up her arm, and lit her mind. She staggered back, blinking to clear her vision.

"Feel the magic, use it to re-create the light," Harold instructed her. "Don't worry about spells. You saw it, felt it. Now, use that and the energy inside you."

"What's with the finger, then?"

"A distraction. You watched me to see a spell cast."

Chagrined, Kenzie dipped her chin. Harold was right. Sneaky, too. She chanced a glance at his face. He had a hint of a smile. Her lip curled down, and she tried to remember the essence of the honeyed glow. Her limbs grew warm as she crafted a mental representation of Harold's parlor trick. He said to use the energy. *How do you add magic . . . ?* Kenzie sought the moment of calm in casting a spell, summoned it without moving or speaking. Her hair floated away from her neck.

A pleased sigh came from the man, and Kenzie's head jerked up. In front of her floated an orb, more daylily orange than spun gold. It popped as she lost concentration, and disappeared.

Kenzie felt a bubbling excitement grow until it overflowed her. "I did it."

"I saw."

She threw her arms around Harold's neck and hugged tight. She felt Harold stiffen, and then relax.

"Thank you," she whispered, and then wondered why she whispered. Harold cleared his throat and Kenzie released him. A tinge of red graced Harold's cheeks.

A murmur of voices reached her. She glanced over her shoulder. The meeting must be over, but she still had questions for Harold. It wasn't fair that she had to leave now when she was finally learning something useful, not how to blow air around.

When she glanced back, Harold held an orange sunburst of a bloom in his hand. "A reminder," he said, and handed it to her.

She heard the footsteps and read it in his face, before he covered up his sympathy.

Her parents.

He spoke quickly but softly. "Practice, but carefully and privately. Very few wizards are ever able to trust and touch their own magic like you did. It's a gift. Some of the others will be jealous if they learn about it and you aren't strong enough to defend yourself."

Kenzie's jaw dropped at the implication in Harold's words. She wanted to question him, but he moved his right hand in a flat cutting-off motion to shush her.

He shifted his gaze from behind her to her face. Worry disguised itself in a smile. "Time for you to leave."

He nodded affably in the direction of her parents and turned away. She turned around to face them, flower still in hand. Both parents glanced at it.

"You'll have to leave the chrysanthemum here," said her mother. She shot a hard, searching glance at the retreating Harold. "It won't survive the transition."

The statement startled Kenzie. She almost contradicted her mother and then squashed the thought.

It would, she knew. The necklace had.

"Yes, ma'am."

As her parents escorted her from the Glade, she searched for a way to preserve the flower. Passing a pool of water, she stopped, forcing both of the adults to do the same.

"Just a sec," she said, without explaining.

She carefully set the mum into the water, gently swishing the petals in the liquid to free any remaining air bubbles. Satisfied, she decorated a green-covered rock with the flower. As she stood, she touched it lightly, willing it to stay preserved until she returned.

"Really, McKenzie," said her father. He sounded exasperated. "It'll be gone the next time. Very little is permanent here. You know that."

Kenzie didn't answer, not trusting herself to lie successfully to him.

The soft grass and moss absorbed all the sound of their footsteps on the walk to the grotto to leave.

She felt a twinge of regret at abandoning the flower and hoped the gentle caress of her magic was enough.

CHAPTER NINETEEN

Mitch's nose wrinkled from the acrid smell of burnt electronics.

"What the heck is the matter with you?"

"Shut up," said Hunter. He was staring in disbelief at the control board he had painstakingly put together. The scorch marks on a half-dozen resistors obliterated the paint markings that identified them. One capacitor had exploded, leaving an uneven sooty star across the fine filaments of circuitry. A thin tendril of smoke showed a hot spot in the plastic.

Across the lab, Paulson tried to troubleshoot another team's equipment failure. Like random lightning bolts, groans or curses came from all the teams as their circuitry cooked off. By the time the fourth one had fried, the students actively searched for signs of sabotage.

Mitch simultaneously shrugged and shook his head. "No worries, let's figure out what happened." He inclined his head toward the other teams. "It's not like we don't have company. Check the juice first."

Hunter grabbed a tester and inserted it into the guts of their robot.

"Naw, man," said Mitch. "Test the bench supply. If it was just us, it'd be our setup, but it's hitting everyone."

His voice must have carried, because Paulson turned to them. "Good thinking, Mitch." He raised his voice. "The rest of you, unplug your equipment. Let's not cook anything else."

The teams with still-functioning bots snatched at the cords supplying power. The other teams moved more slowly, dejected at the weeks' worth of work gone.

Hunter put the probes of the multimeter into the receptacle side mounted on the lab bench. He shifted the selector, checked the voltage, shifted again, tested amperage, and let loose a disgruntled sigh. "Normal."

"It can't be frickin' normal, dude. Something cooked off our board. Maybe it was a surge." Mitch frowned as he fumbled for an explanation.

The expression Hunter wore placed him in the category of village idiot. "The supplies are protected against spikes and surges."

A telltale pop came from across the room, and both boys turned to face it.

"What the hell—" yelled a redheaded youth, fist clenched to strike at something as frustration twisted his face. He turned, faced Paulson, and extended his hands palm up, asking for answers. "It wasn't even plugged in."

Paulson glanced up at the clock, and Mitch followed his gaze. Ten minutes left in class.

"Pack it in, everyone. Unplug all your gear. Make sure you pull the batteries, too. We have a few minutes. The teams that had failures, I want full documentation of what cooked. If you know the sequence, get it written down. Teams that didn't fry, help the others, *after* you get your robots de-powered."

The frustrated kid spoke up. "Why are we pulling batteries?"

"Because we have a major anomaly and energy can transmit in forms other than through the wires."

They all knew this—it was basic physics—but Mitch's forehead wrinkled as he realized that he had fallen into the trap of believing his eyes instead of considering the full range of options. The equipment had fried from some freak spike, either natural or manmade. Direct connections such as those to an inconsistent voltage supply were the most likely culprit for the malfunctions, but most of their electronics were unshielded. A solid pulse of energy could conceivably damage the circuits.

Mitch looked into the distance. "So why'd only some of the gear cook, if it was a pulse?"

"Good question. Once we know the answer to that, we might be able to reverse engineer the process. Finish out your thought, Mitch. How?"

Mitch squirmed under the inquisitiveness of the other students in the lab. They paused in their cleanup activities to listen. Uncomfortable as the center of attention, he gazed past them as the options swirled and sorted themselves into some kind of order.

"Each one of us built a slightly different set of circuits. Finding out which ones cooked and how will give us the information to determine the source of the energy." He shrugged and glanced at Paulson.

"If it's the same capacitor"—he inclined his head toward the blackened interior of his robot—"for all of us, then we'll have an idea of the magnitude of the surge. We'll also be able to find out about where the circuits picked up the current by tracing forward from there to potential entry points." He stopped, his mind racing ahead.

"You don't think it was a spike on the bench power." He checked Paulson's reaction. He was close, no cigar. He considered it a second more. "Pulling the batteries might not help. You're thinking it's some type of electromagnetic pulse that hit the lab. The pulse might be transmitting right into the unshielded wiring. So nothing is safe until we figure out where did it come from."

His voice rose slightly on the last, sounding loud as the other lab rats alternated disbelieving glances at him with worried touches to their precious robots.

"That's the other question, Mitch. Once we get the first one answered, we'll have a better idea of how to finesse the second." Paulson shot an approving smile at the student before addressing the group again.

"A lot of you have some major catching up to do on your projects now," he said, and a faint chorus of angry muttering agreed. "I'm going to keep the lab open this afternoon. Those of you who want to get started rebuilding today can come on in." He surveyed the wreckage. "And I'll open up next week during spring break."

Around Mitch, kids with the broken machines were nodding, and talking to their partners in quiet voices, making arrangements to meet. The ones who had weathered the event sat taller, relieved. One, the Asian girl at the bench next to theirs, spoke with downcast features and a diffident voice.

"Our robot is working. I can come in and show you what we did. Maybe that will help."

A couple of "thanks" came from various corners of the room. Mitch turned to find Hunter glaring at him, a dark scowl cast across his face. Hunter turned his head away.

"I got places to go," said Hunter. "You're going to have to fix the damn thing."

He's still pissed, thought Mitch. He still hadn't figured out how the stun gun had misfired. It was another mystery, like the blown circuits. Like Kenzie.

"Can't," said Mitch, without elaboration.

Hunter did not disguise his scowl. "Whatever, then," he said, and tossed the tester on the table as he turned on a heel and pivoted away. He strode over to Paulson and spoke to him. His words were spoken too quietly to hear but were delivered with an emphatic hand gesture, a sweep of his pointer finger in a half-moon arc with his wrist rotating over that, finished by indicating the door.

Paulson nodded, and to Mitch's surprise, Hunter walked out of class five minutes early. He sighed and began to catalogue the full extent of the damage. It was going to take a while.

CHAPTER TWENTY

Kenzie stood in the center of the training floor, wearing a blindfold. She strained to hear Jules moving, but other than muted sounds from the street and Jackson occasionally shifting position, the studio was silent. She flinched when she felt a gentle tap on the muscle below the base of her neck.

"Let go, Kenzie," said Jules's voice. "Stop trying so hard to use your senses. Be aware instead."

Kenzie's eyelashes brushed against the silky material tied around her head, but Jules had made sure that no light made it through, though it did not feel overly confining.

"Relax."

She turned her head toward the voice.

"Try to feel where I'm at, try to feel where I'm moving to," said Jules, her voice soothing and rhythmic. "Don't think about it, don't try to follow me with your usual senses. Breathe and relax. Do it. Take a deep breath—"

Kenzie did.

"—and hold it—"

Again, she complied.

"Now, relax and let it flow out, and with it, feel the edges of your perception grow as it follows your breath. Feel it and then do it again. Keep doing it."

Jules fell quiet.

The traffic sounds slid off into space, but Kenzie gradually could feel the presence of Jackson on the bench. Each time he shifted, the picture in her head reordered itself. A sensation like floating pervaded her body as she measured the breaths, in, gentle hold, out. A pressure grew on her right side, near her cheek, and she turned her head imperceptibly in that direction.

"Very good," said Jules. Kenzie could hear the smile, and her subconscious built an image of the dusky face.

A rasping sound of the door to the studio opening, accompanied by the tinkling of keys, dragged her attention sideways, and a ball of tension deep in her abdomen released the serenity like a flock of mourning doves scattering to the heavens. Her eyes fluttered open. The pulsing beat of a car stereo thumped into the studio as someone held the door open.

Not a student, she thought, and then, *Mitch?*

Her breathing changed, coming from high in her chest, and faster.

She heard Jules speak, her words measured.

"This is a private lesson," she said. "If you would like to wait in my office, I will be with you in a few minutes."

"Um, 'kay."

It sounded like him. The feeling inside her split, settling lower in her abdomen and higher in her chest. The closing door cut off the pulsing beat. A pair of seconds later she heard the seat in the office creak.

The feeling down low was like a wire galvanizing her nerve endings, radiating from below her belly button. She drew a deep breath.

It caught at the back of her throat.

Jules apologized. "Sorry, Kenzie, I thought I locked the door."

You did, thought Kenzie. She had unlocked it when no one was paying attention.

"Relax, find that place that you were at, and breathe, focus on the breathing, nice and easy, in and out." The black belt modulated her voice downward, to reestablish the atmosphere that fled with the interruption.

Kenzie forced her body to relax, but even the slightest noise distracted her. The office chair squeaked, and the muscles between her shoulder blades involuntarily twitched. Twice, she completely lost track of where Jules was. She jerked her arm at the delicate pressure of Jules's touch on her left forearm.

Jules sighed. "He's not here to see me, is he?"

Kenzie gave Jules a microscopic shake of her head.

"Your companion"—Jules never called Jackson a bodyguard—"is looking daggers at him."

"It's his job."

"Understood."

Kenzie waited, unsure whether the conversation meant that the lesson was over or not. She wanted to get the blindfold off but knew not to touch it until Jules gave her permission.

"You might as well go change. We're not going to get anything done with you wound up like this."

Kenzie sensed amusement rather than disparagement underlying the words. She reached to the blindfold and removed it. She blinked rapidly at the light streaming around her. The afternoon sun cast her slim body in a long silhouette stretching to the wall. The interior lights were off, but even the limited natural light overwhelmed her. With each blink, she could feel her pupils adapting until the illumination felt bright but not painful.

She glided across the mat to the small barrier that defined the training floor as separate from the spectator section, paused to turn back and bow her respects, and backed off the training floor.

Kenzie jogged lightly on the balls of her bare feet toward the changing rooms. As she passed Jackson, she slowed and spoke.

"I asked my father, and he said it was okay. Next door, in the yogurt shop. I told him you'd be keeping an eye on us."

Jackson nodded, his face impassive, but Kenzie could feel his uneasiness with the arrangement as if he sensed the parts that she had left out. She had asked, laying out her case that it was a study date with "Michael," not anything else. When he balked, she'd pointed out that Jackson would be there, and promised to only go to the highly visible eatery.

She hustled into the narrow changing room, quickly swapping the *dobok* for jeans and a cotton shirt with ruffles along the sweetheart neckline, the front plunge curling in from the shoulders to a point. Kenzie shrugged the garment on and adjusted it to make sure her bra didn't show. The sleeves flared at the middle of her biceps with a matching ruffle. She slipped on her socks and running shoes. Kenzie dropped her workout clothes into her gear bag. Her hand wavered, then reached into the small zip pocket on the end.

Kenzie pulled out the necklace she had secreted from the Glade and considered it. The open setting in the middle of the heart-shaped leaves intrigued her, like a work of art that was nearly, but not quite, perfect. The past several evenings, when she knew that her parents would not interrupt, she would take it out and stare at it as though, if she tried hard enough, she could divine its purpose. It defied her inspection.

Today, she had smuggled it from the house, uncertain of whether she had the guts to wear it. Now it sat lightly on her hand, untarnished, and she still couldn't make up her mind. An impatience grew inside her, and she pictured Mitch shuffling his feet and fussing at his watch.

Annoyed with herself for dithering, she quickly reached behind her neck, holding back her ponytailed hair with the backs of her hands, and closed the clasp. There was a very quiet click when the hasp snapped shut, and Kenzie waited, muscles tensed to react if there was embedded magic in the necklace.

The murmur of Jules's and Mitch's voices, too indistinct to make out individual words, brought her back to the moment.

Kenzie gathered her stuff and exited the confining space.

Jackson was standing guard, arms held loosely at his sides, scanning the pictures above the wall of spectator seats. The instant she appeared, he pivoted, first to face her, and then continuing until he had ascertained the position of everything in sight. His gaze lingered on Mitch, and a cloud of discontent emanated from him.

She followed his gaze. Mitch was the opposite of the shuffling goof she thought she'd see. He exercised a quiet animation as he spoke, rolling his head and shoulders side to side in short arcs. He finished his point with a lift of his hand. To Kenzie's surprise, a slender smile appeared on Jules's face. The black belt nodded to Mitch and then inclined her head in Kenzie's direction.

Mitch jerked around. Kenzie could see him stiffen as she walked to him. He glanced down, and then his gaze darted up, tracing the lines of her body. A hint of heat touched her cheeks as she noted that his eyes slowed their movement at the top of her blouse.

Kenzie knew she should be offended, but instead her hurried walk took on a hint of a sashay. Still, as she got closer, she wondered if her bra showed through anyway, or whether . . . or whether . . . or whether . . .

His eyes sought hers, realized she had been watching him watching her, and his face matched hers, a hint of a flush coloring his skin.

Kenzie smiled, and Mitch visibly relaxed.

Jackson fake-coughed. "Study session, right?"

Kenzie did not even deign to recognize him as she met Mitch by the door. "Ready?" she asked, drawing close.

He's taller than I thought.

"Sure," said Mitch.

He reached for the door, but Jackson pushed past him and pulled it open first. The security man sidled into the doorway and gave the parking lot a hard-eyed sweep. Only then did Jackson finish opening the door.

Jules glanced at Kenzie but spoke to Mitch first. "A pleasure to meet you, Mitch."

He nodded as she turned her attention to Kenzie.

"Next week, Kenzie, same time." Something in the tone forced Kenzie to focus on Jules. "Please remind Mitch that your private lesson ends at four. I'll make sure next time that the door is actually locked." A smile softened the mild rebuke.

"Yes, ma'am."

Amusement curled Jules's lips, transforming the woman's face. "Go, I've got to get ready for the next class."

Mitch hustled out the door first. Kenzie followed him into the heat of the sun, with Jackson behind her. She let the rays warm her skin for a second before heading right to the shop two doors down that offered coffee, sweet treats, and frozen yogurt.

A shadow fell in beside her. "You look nice," Mitch said, repeating what his lingering ogling had already told her. He reached for the handle of the coffee shop door and pulled. The smell of roasted coffee permeated the air.

"Thanks," Kenzie said.

The place was modestly busy. Jackson staked out a table in the corner and pointed to one next to his.

Kenzie nodded.

"What do you want?" she asked Mitch. She swung her pack down and unzipped the front pouch where she kept her money and ID.

Mitch raced her getting money out to pay for the yogurts and won. "My treat?"

A barista with blond hair tinged red at the tips took their order. Kenzie ordered a coffee, black, for Jackson. Mitch paid and dropped a spare dollar into the tip jar.

"Be back in a second."

Kenzie dashed over and dropped her bag at the table that Jackson was saving for them. "Watch this?"

She didn't wait for an answer. She rejoined Mitch. The barista placed the coffee on the wood counter with a bored sigh while a second employee scooped out yogurt: spearmint for Kenzie, vanilla in a cone for Mitch.

"I wasn't sure you'd come."

A furrow creased his forehead. "Why?"

The question flustered her. Thoughts dashed through her head as she remembered the pain she'd felt when she touched him, the hassle that must have come with his reckless charge to help her, and deep inside by her heart, a recognition that her cloistered existence left her with no idea how to interact with Mitch right now.

Cloistered.

She had seen the word in a short story for English class and felt the pain of the protective life, of lost opportunities.

"I thought maybe my father had scared you."

"Your dad?" Confusion crossed Mitch's face.

The bored girl serving them passed over the desserts. They had put chocolate sprinkles on hers, and multicolored sugary specks on Mitch's.

"What about your dad?"

She picked up Jackson's coffee and turned away from the counter, headed for their table. "I thought that maybe he might have, I guess, scared you off or something."

Her voice faltered toward the end. In a flash of intuition, she saw Mitch had no idea of what she was talking about. The furrow deepened, and she could see Mitch sorting everything he knew. . . .

Oh, hell.

She had to tell him first. She didn't know why, except that she didn't want to keep secrets from Mitch.

A voice in the back of her head whispered, *Really?* and the image of the Glade of Silver Night rose in her mind.

She shook her head hard once to rid herself of her internal hall monitor and spoke quickly. "He's a lieutenant with Seattle PD."

Mitch had turned with Kenzie. Now he stopped dead, face losing color. He stood slack-jawed.

"Oh shit," he said, barely above a whisper.

"He's not that bad," she lied. She searched across the restaurant, found Jackson staring at them with hard suspicion.

"Keep walking."

Kenzie took the lead, and Mitch followed her. She could feel his reluctance. Reaching the tables, she forced herself to smile, her lips twisting to sell it.

Jackson's face was grim. He wasn't buying it.

"Here's your coffee," she said, bending a knee almost like a curtsy, setting the paper cup in front of him.

"What's goi—"

Her hand now free, she inscribed a spell in the air, her thumb and pointer finger coming together in a movement that resembled the closing of a zipper or the pulling of a thread.

Jackson's voice faded away, and he grew disinterested. His hand reached for the coffee.

She wheeled to face Mitch. "We have to talk."

"No kiddin'."

He was pale, switching focus from Jackson, to Kenzie's hands, to her face. He flopped into the padded booth. The cone wobbled, and Kenzie worried that the frozen mess was about to land in his lap.

"Scoot." Kenzie sat next to him.

A squadron of hummingbirds were flitting inside her, and her hands shook. She put the yogurt down and clasped them together and squeezed.

Mitch shifted away from her, creating some space. "I told him everything," he said.

Distress carried plainly with the simple declaration.

"I know," said Kenzie. Even clasped, her hands showed a visible quiver. "I know."

They both took a deep breath at the same time. Kenzie let the air out first, and spoke to Mitch, careful to keep her voice down so Jackson wouldn't hear. The spell she had laid on him made him lose focus and drift, but he would remember anything he heard.

"He told me, actually, yelled at me. He said he went out to answer a call at your house. It's all because you rushed out into the street to save me—"

"That's not exactly my fault!"

"I didn't say it was. Would you listen?"

Mitch's jaw was set, but he dipped his head once, agreeing.

"You didn't have any choice about telling him, you really didn't." Her mouth dried out, and she tried to swallow, something to get the rest of the words out.

Mitch gave her time.

"You said nothing made sense yesterday. It's going to make less sense today."

She stopped again.

Telling an ordinary person about magic carried defined consequences, none of them pleasant. If she were lucky, they'd only banish her. A shudder shook her shoulders as she considered the ultimate penalty for being an apostate.

Mitch saw the movement and lifted his hand as if to comfort her. Before it could touch, he dropped it back to his lap.

Kenzie blinked, and blinked again, and then talked in a low voice, rushing to get all the words out before she lost courage. She focused on the melting mint yogurt in front of her.

"The day those thugs tried to kidnap me, you hurt yourself trying to help me, hurt yourself, and I couldn't leave you there like that, so I cheated. I used . . ."

Her voice broke.

Keep talking, don't stop, tell him. . . .

"I used," she said, and nearly lost her nerve. *Quick is best,* she thought, and carried on, "Magic, a spell that I had heard of, but never used. And it worked, but I used so much energy, too much energy, I thought I'd hurt you instead of healing you, and then you were okay. I had to get away, so I put you to rest, and ran like a coward and hid in my room."

Mitch's long fingers closed around her clenched fists, gently and protectively covering them. His touch galvanized her skin, a different kind of magic.

"You are pretty frickin' amazing."

She twisted to face him, to see if he was mocking her. He met her with a steadiness, a little wide-eyed maybe, but she couldn't blame him.

Looking at him, she lost her train of thought for a moment. Her eyelashes fluttered, and she recovered. "You can't tell anyone about this."

Mitch laughed with a hint of bitterness in response, and said, "Seems like everyone but me already knows."

Kenzie winced. "Just me and my dad."

"And Hunter," said Mitch.

"Who is he?"

Mitch gave her a worried glance. "You don't know?"

Kenzie felt control of the conversation's momentum shifting to Mitch. Obviously, she was missing something, and internal warning bells were sounding. Beneath Mitch's calloused hand, hers began to shake.

"No."

Mitch quickly explained the flash of light with Hunter. The warning bells shifted into a full-fledged clamor when Mitch told her of Hunter's reaction.

He concluded with, "And that's when I met the lieutenant. He knew all about me, which seemed weird, and I couldn't stop talking."

He paused.

"He used a spell or whatever you call it on me, didn't he?"

Kenzie dipped her chin. "Probably."

She drew a deep breath to center herself, as Jules had taught. In a moment of insight, she realized Harold had taught the same thing, just differently.

"What do you know about Hunter?"

Mitch hesitated. "Know or guess? His family has bucks, he's smarter than crap, and the girls hang all over him. He's about my only friend. That's what I know."

Kenzie waited.

"What I guess?" Mitch waved his free hand, fingers together in a small circle. "He's like you. He does stuff with his hands, kind of like you but not quite the same, and everybody starts agreeing with him. He did it with the cop that showed up after I shocked him, before your dad showed up."

Kenzie watched Mitch drill down in concentration. The hummingbirds had left her stomach, replaced by circling vultures. The Family would never let Mitch know that they existed. Their survival relied on staying at the outer fringes of light.

Her next words hurt, but she had to warn him.

"They'll kill you if they think you know about them. The Family will."

Mitch's mouth twisted into a wry grin. He was ahead of her. "Yours or Hunter's?"

"Probably . . . both?"

"And what happens to you?"

"I can protect myself."

"Un-huh."

Kenzie snatched her hands out from under his and balled them in her lap.

How come he never did what she expected? she wondered.

While Kenzie sorted her thoughts, Mitch cleared his throat. He shifted to Jackson.

The spell was wearing off.

Wary amusement lit in Mitch's face. "None of this makes any sort of rational sense, you know that?

Kenzie shrugged. Nothing ever made sense except when she was at the Glade and could be herself, all of her, without having to hide anything.

"Can you sneak out Friday night? Tomorrow?"

The recklessness of the question totally gobsmacked her.

Numbly, she nodded and said faintly, "Sure."

In her head, klaxons replaced the bells as her good sense shouted, *What are you thinking?*

CHAPTER TWENTY-ONE

It smelled old.

Mitch let go of the door, and it swung shut, a dark scythe cutting into the sunlight, until the click of the latch left him in the gloom. In the middle of the room was a long oaken counter, easily six feet wide and thirty feet long. Curved drawer pulls gave an approximation of the size and depth of each container, some so small as to be designed to hold stamps, others large enough to fit a cadaver. Shelves made from plank oak lined the wall, glass jars and jugs arrayed in haphazard order to the left, a wall of ancient-looking leather-bound books to the right.

It took another few seconds to adjust.

The glass jars bore yellowed paper tags with faded handwriting. He took a hesitant stride to the left, almost against his will, impelled by curiosity. The first jar on the shelf at eye level held some kind of plant leaf. The writing, slender and looping, had three lines. The first looked like the Elvish runes from *Lord of the Rings*. The second line, written in English, read "Elf Leaf." The last line had "Rosemary" in parentheses.

"The stuff you buy in the supermarket will never do."

Mitch recoiled from the jars, spinning to face Mercury.

The older man beamed, and shuffled around the end of the countertop, extending his hand as he did so. He wasn't in a suit; instead, he wore a formless gray shirt that bagged heavily over the shoulders and past the waist. His pants were black, thick cotton that made swishing sounds as he moved. Mitch would have sworn he saw slippers on the man's feet.

"I'm glad you decided to come."

Mitch squinted at the man in the low light, met the steady gaze of the green eyes, and made no effort to shake hands.

"It looks more like a weird-ass store than a museum."

Mercury emitted a sad sigh as his right hand returned to his side. "The proper response upon being greeted by a friend is to say hello."

"Who says we're friends?"

Mercury raised a bushy eyebrow. "Fair enough, I suppose." He shrugged, and an impish smile broke up the lines on his face and rearranged them into an expression of warmth. "Let's go over to the back room, and we'll chat there."

Mercury led the way, opening a door that Mitch hadn't seen on his first inspection of the interior. Mitch stopped at the doorway. The room, running longwise to his left, was bright. The wall directly in front of him had a row of windows that received abundant light tinged golden with morning sun instead of the hot yellow of the afternoon.

A trick of the window glazing, Mitch decided. He noted the wildness outside the window with a frown before being distracted by the oddities of the room.

The space looked more like a garden parlor than an office. Plants grew from odd pots; some vines wound up to the high, arched ceiling before traversing across. Mitch recognized some of the flowers, periwinkle and rose. A pair of large orchids occupied places of honor on either side of an old-fashioned wood desk. Between the blooms sat a thick ledger book, the kind used a couple of hundred years ago. He half-expected to see a quill and inkwell. They would have fit with the ledger. Instead a simple pencil sat on the desk next to the ledger and a pair of straight-backed chairs shared the near corner of the desk.

Unlike the front of the building, this strange room exuded the sweetness of the flowers and a powerful underlying mint.

"Tea?"

Mercury stood at the far end of the room, his left hand out, gesturing to a battered metal pot and a pair of mugs.

"Uh, no," said Mitch, taking another step into the room. The carpet was the color of grass, and spongy. He stepped back, then forward again, testing the floor. Same thing, the gentle give like a well-manicured lawn. He swiveled his head to take it all in.

"I like to work in natural spaces," said Mercury, by way of explanation.

"You said you were a cop," said Mitch. The mint smells were soothing, and he kept filling his lungs with the scent. Today was going from weird to crazy. Hunter acting squirrelly, the electronics blowing up for no reason, Kenzie, Mercury.

"Mitch, are you okay?"

Mitch shook his head. "No."

"Come sit down, son."

Mitch did as he was told. The seat of the chair was hard, but not uncomfortable. Mercury sat in front of the ledger. He procured a glass of water from somewhere on the far side of the desk.

"Here," he said. "It will help."

Mitch sipped. The water tasted delicious, like liquid fresh from a deep mountain lake. It woke a memory of camping, when he was tiny, and his parents still loved each other. The lake was cold, and the craggy mountain still had snow on it, reaching down like a white velvet cape to the far edge of the shore. Memories whispered: splashing with his father, the droplets brilliant in the air, the sparkling laughter of his mother.

He put the glass down, chest heaving, and shoved the images far away.

"You said you could give me answers."

Mercury's face bore an expression of sympathy, and Mitch felt a reflexive anger build to shield against it.

"Some of the answers, yes. Let's start with what you already know, and build."

Mitch nodded.

"Good," said Mercury, leaning an elbow on the tabletop and squaring up to face Mitch. "Your first introduction to this mess was the attack on one McKenzie Graham. You rushed out to save the fair damsel—" An upraised finger forestalled commentary from Mitch. "—taking out the knees of one of the men. The fair damsel had already dispatched the other with what you've described as a rather vicious kick to a perilous region.

"Since then you have discovered, probably the hard way, that Miss Graham has a father who works for the Seattle Police Department. Mr. Raymond Graham can be rather unpleasant to confront. He also is a master at interrogation. Hence he found out about the card that I left you. He has since tried to trace the number, with, I'm afraid, very little success.

"Mr. Graham is married to a Sasha Graham, who is CEO of a very specialized technology company that is proceeding with an investigation into certain esoteric subjects that have attracted the attention of some rather predatory actors in the technology field.

"With me so far?"

Mitch held his face blank. "Yeah," he said, processing the information and seeing the enormous chasms of missing data. He bet himself that Mercury was going to dodge the important stuff.

"Your role has been protector for young Miss Graham. The attack was a direct response to the research efforts, to try and use the leverage of the kidnapped child against the mother. They want that technology, want it quite a lot, actually."

Mercury distractedly scratched the stubble on his chin.

"The technology is world-changing."

"What is it?" Mitch said, slipping his words in quickly and stopping Mercury's monologue.

Mercury glanced away to the scene outside the windows, then turned his gaze back to Mitch.

"The nature of the device is open to some conjecture."

"You don't know?" Mitch tried to keep from sounding incredulous, without success. "Some geek in a lab builds a machine that you think is *world-changing* and you don't even have a clue what it does?"

A fire lit in Mercury's eyes, and to Mitch, the room darkened. The older man straightened in his seat and leaned forward. "We have suspicions, but none fit to share with a fledgling such as you."

As he spoke, his hand reached out to thump Mitch on the meaty part of his leg above the knee with a closed fist. Mitch recalled the strength of those hands from their previous encounter but refused to be cowed by Mercury.

"Well, you're going to have to share something, because so far you haven't told me anything that I hadn't already figured out myself. Tech is changing constantly without thugs resorting to kidnapping, so it's not tech, it's the application."

Pieces shifted, coalesced in Mitch's mind, and, with a snap, things sharpened into focus.

"It's a weapon of some kind, or can be used as a weapon?"

He was pretty sure of his guess but phrased it as a question. More pieces shifted, but he held his tongue and waited for Mercury's response.

"That is our presumption, that it could be used as a weapon. It appears that someone else has made the same connection and wishes to possess it." Mercury frowned. "Obviously, such a person should not be permitted control of the . . . power."

The slight stumble in Mercury's speech caused a spasm in Mitch's gut. Mentally, he substituted the word "magic" for "power," and Kenzie's role, and even Mercury's, became much clearer. The puzzle piece labeled "Hunter" still didn't fit, but somewhere there was a connection tying Hunter Rubiera to the rest of this mess.

Mercury sat back, head tilted like he was looking through the bottom of bifocals, and gave Mitch time to think. Mitch ran a hand through his hair and stood. He paced. At the far end of the room, he turned back and spoke.

"Kenzie's still in danger."

Mercury nodded but did not speak.

Mitch trod across the accommodating softness of the floor. He was nearly even with Mercury when it clicked.

"Why me?"

"Why you what?"

"You want me to look out for Kenzie, so why me? She's got Jackson." Mitch shot a glance to Mercury to see if he knew of Jackson, found the old man nodding. A deadly chill filled his stomach, and the hair on his arms started to lift. "You don't think Jackson is enough. Why?"

"The threats almost certainly will overwhelm Mr. Jackson, fine man that he is."

His vision narrowed onto Mercury, the edges fading to black, until there was just the man's face, each line stark and sharp. Mercury's lips pursed, and words reluctantly fell forth into the air between them.

"Mr. Jackson is very competent against ordinary threats, but the competitor—or, shall we say, enemy—has the resources to defeat him. More importantly, Mr. Jackson is only cognizant of a single thread of attack. We are aware of at least two."

"Magic," whispered Mitch. His voice strengthened. "It's not two threads, it's two modes."

Mercury's normally gray face drew grim and ashen.

Mitch continued, gesturing with his right hand in a herky-jerky flutter. "You want me to what, back up Jackson? You said he's competent."

Even as he uttered the words, the implication of Mercury's request released more memories, not the happy ones like the water, but the last minutes of his first life. The coldness took over, tied up his muscles, making his limbs clumsy, while the memory played itself out, the nightmare that haunted him because it wasn't a nightmare to awaken from.

They were at the cabin, high in the mountains. Unexpected June snow had trapped them overnight, and his mother fretted, sending nervous glances toward his father. He watched the mood change overtake his dad as the meds, psychotropic drugs to take the sting off the lows and the edge off the highs, wore off. The rest of his supply resided in the cabinet above the master bath sink at home, unreachable as the darkness filled him.

His dad drank. Mitch later understood the effort to self-medicate, but in the moment the alcohol simply reinforced the death spiral in the warped areas of his dad's brain. The fight started when his mother tried to take the booze away. The first blow came when she reached for the bottle. Not the first time ever he'd hit her, just the opening act for that evening.

His father raged and hit his wife again, and Mitch, ten years old, flew to intervene. A hard backhand launched him across the room to land in an ungainly heap next to a bunk. His mother had run to him, and he had looked to her face, the tracks of the tears. A freshening bruise under the red weal on her porcelain skin.

"No, Mitchell, don't fight him."

The rest blurred, stumbling into the snow outside where the falling sun tinted the clouds ruddy. A single shot, and then . . . nothing except a soul-stealing cold.

"Mitch," said Mercury. The tone was controlled and insistent, as if he had repeated the name more than once.

Mitch clenched his teeth to keep them from chattering as the sight of Mercury's room replaced the memory.

"I . . . ," he said, blinking rapidly, unable to finish.

The thought was stark, unassailable truth.

I failed. I couldn't stop him, save her.

Mercury gave his head a sorrowful shake. "Yet you helped save McKenzie. As to your mother, you were too young to find your measure in such an act. There is always the possibility of redemption, if that provides motivation for you. McKenzie is not safe. Will you help?"

"I'm not, you know . . . magical."

God, that sounded stupid! But he'd rather talk about anything than start reliving and re-dying in his memories.

Mercury eyed him, and then seemed to make a decision. "That is the second time you've mentioned magic. Why?"

"Because I don't have a better word. Kenzie did it when she healed me, that's why you were asking those questions at my house."

Mitch stopped talking as a question drifted through his mind. "Why did you care if she used words?"

Another thought, another question, asked before Mercury could reply to the first.

"What's with the hands? All of you . . . well, not you, but everyone else does this stuff with their hands." Mitch demonstrated a looping circle with his right hand, emulating Kenzie and Hunter.

I need to talk to Hunter, he thought, in the gap between his questions and Mercury's response. The back of his neck crawled at the thought. Mitch stopped his pacing to face the old man.

"Are you a magician or wizard or what?"

Mercury laughed, deep and rumbling. "Probably 'or what.' Some people who can do what we do call themselves witches, some warlocks, some think of themselves as wizards. All are convinced that they are superior. I started as a wizard, became a fool, and now hope to grow old and wise. The first happens quite easily, the latter will tell in time."

Mitch scrutinized Mercury's face. "I didn't expect you to admit it."

"It's safer. To answer your other questions, the use of words implies training versus natural ability simply manifesting. Both the hands and the words are ways to concentrate properly to use the energy, or magic. Understand?"

"Yeah, but I don't know how I can help." Mitch's left shoulder lifted in a half shrug while his lips twisted into a grimace. "It's not like I can do any of that. I'm lucky when I don't get hit by a car."

"You do, however, have a habit of being in the right place at the right time. I do not believe that the world operates randomly. You were there to help Miss Graham for a reason, even if I am not able to divine why."

"'God doesn't play dice with the universe,'" Mitch murmured.

"Exactly, Einstein was quite correct," agreed Mercury.

Mitch kept the surprise off his face. He hadn't expected Mercury to recognize the quote.

The wizard continued. "Since the universe has seen fit to include you in this squabble, my interest is to see that you participate on the side favoring freedom. Not every problem can be resolved with force, whether of the brutish sort employed already or by magic, as you called it. The use of intelligence can often defeat either, when properly applied. You possess both intelligence and a resilient mind."

Keeping his attention on Mercury's hands, Mitch gave another half shrug. "You're leaving parts out."

"I told you I didn't know everything."

The answer was less than satisfactory. Mitch approached the proposition the same way a hungry dog approached tainted meat. He couldn't see the trap or poison, but his brain worried at the voids. What was the device? Why would wizards give a damn about a new glitzy piece of electronics? Why would magic be opposed to magic? This last question followed logically from Mercury's statements. At that thought, Mitch snorted. Magic kind of negated logical thinking.

Mitch searched Mercury's face. He judged the sincerity of the man and made his decision. "I'll help Kenzie."

Mitch went out the door he'd come in and turned left into the street, crossing at the first intersection. He opted to walk the mile back to his house rather than hop the trolley. He needed time to think. He glanced back at the building he'd left. Behind it sat more commercial property and rows of houses hanging on to the flanks of the hill that formed the geographical separation from his neighborhood and Kenzie's, on the other side of the spine, down to the edge of the lake.

He stopped next to a sign advertising Kenyan food, the smell of roasting meat from the restaurant triggering his hunger. He got his bearings relative to the inside of Mercury's fancy little museum.

Nope, he thought. *Should be a park there.* The sunlight was wrong, too, a different color.

He looked back to the building, looking under the stately maples shading the other side of the street.

The door he had entered was gone. Now there was a bookshop there, spanning the storefront.

Somehow, he wasn't surprised.

CHAPTER TWENTY-TWO

Mercury sat in the chair, staring out the door where Mitch had left. Behind him, he heard soft footfalls.

With a sad sigh, he spun around on the wooden seat of his chair. From there he could see his brother, and the doorway into a darker realm that contrasted with the view out the windows.

"He's keeping secrets from me already, Harold," said Mercury. "Did you see what he did with his hand? Looked pretty close to a compulsion spell from the old days."

"One of the Families that broke away in the Splintering? The *hechiceros?*"

Mercury felt a shudder ripple down his spine. The Spanish Family traced its lineage back to the wizards of Arthurian legend and the era of knights. Some of their thoughts, at least a half century ago when they were last heard from, had not evolved beyond the master and serf feudalism of the Middle Ages. He doubted that they had changed much at all. The Spaniards were not for change. They had even attempted to turn other, lesser wizards into chattel.

"This would be much easier if I could ensorcell him with a spell," grumbled Mercury.

His brother, a year older, didn't smile. "We need his willing cooperation. The energy required to force him to sacrifice himself against his will is beyond either of our abilities." Harold paused. "Tremendous power is gathered; I can feel it, as you can. The thunder is coming, just as with the Splintering. This time we must gain control of the magic and direct it to safety."

"If the *hechiceros* still live, they will try to beat us to it," replied Mercury. He stood abruptly and faced his brother. "He also didn't promise to help me. The boy is deep in puppy love. Still, he fulfilled part of the prophecy. 'A hero will come to save her—and us.'"

"'Trust his heart,'" finished Harold.

Mercury pointed a finger at his brother's chest. "How sure are you of McKenzie?"

"Sure enough to call you back. She's the most naturally gifted enchantress I've encountered and, despite her parents' best efforts to adopt the contempt of the Family for the rest of humanity, she resists. If anyone has the ability to mend the rift in the Families and heal them, it is she."

They stood, eye to eye, each taking the measure of the other.

Mercury nodded as if reassured. "Then we gather the storm and ride the wind."

"Agreed," said Harold. "And we protect McKenzie, so she can repair what we broke so many years ago."

Harold turned to leave, striding to the door that led back to the Glade. At the threshold, he stopped and turned.

"Do you think you can keep the youngster alive, brother?"

Mercury had the same question, and didn't answer. They held a long look that shared the same understanding. McKenzie must be protected. Anyone else, including Mitch and themselves, was expendable.

CHAPTER TWENTY-THREE

Kenzie opened the door to find her mother had beat her home. Not good. Her mother was forever working late and was always the last one home. Jackson trailed in behind her, looking hungover from the spell. Kenzie diverted her mother's attention with a forced but cheerful greeting.

"Hi, you're home early."

The response was slightly warmer than icicles. "Yes, I wanted to talk to you."

Kenzie managed to keep guilt off her face. She had a harder time with anger. "About what?"

Her mother raised an eyebrow at the tone. She glanced in Jackson's direction. "Mr. Jackson, thank you very much. Please excuse my daughter and I. We'll see you in the morning."

"Yes, ma'am." He looked at Kenzie. "See you at seven thirty?"

"Sure," came the surly reply.

After Jackson had left, Sasha turned to Kenzie. "That was quite rude of you with Mr. Jackson."

"I'm tired of being babysat. Jackson doesn't bother me much, but you haven't let me have a single minute to myself since the—"

"Since armed men tried to abduct you," interrupted her mother. "I think our precautions are perfectly reasonable, even if your manners are not."

"You could always have Father lock me in a cell someplace."

Red appeared high on Sasha's cheekbones. "The sarcasm is unwarranted. And you could try calling him 'Dad' like most other girls do with their fathers."

Inwardly, Kenzie was delighted that the small insurrection bugged her mother.

"We're not like most others, are we, Mother?"

Her mother ignored the provocation and redirected the conversation. "I am planning a dinner party, and I will need you in attendance."

"Why? It's not like you need me for one of your business thingies. Anyway, they're boring."

Sasha Graham sighed. "My business 'thingies,' as you call them, provide opportunities for the Family. However, that is immaterial. This is not a business dinner. Your father and I have decided that it is time for you to be presented to the eligible young suitors of the Family. I have invited a young engineer from the company to meet you at this dinner, and I expect that you will show him every courtesy as a young lady. Do you understand?"

"But—"

"There will be no buts. There are quite a few bachelors that meet the criteria set forth by the Family. Ideally, you will find one that you can find happiness with. Regardless, you will marry one. The magic must survive."

With a sick feeling, Kenzie saw that her fate was being determined not by a mother but a high priestess.

"I will instruct Jackson to take you shopping for a suitable dress." Her mother handed her a credit card. "Use this," she instructed. "Dinner will be at six thirty tomorrow evening. See that you're ready on time."

CHAPTER TWENTY-FOUR

Mitch jacked up Hunter twelve minutes before the first bell, pinning him to a masonry wall in a side hallway that was momentarily deserted.

"What the hell!" yelled Hunter.

Got to be quick, Mitch thought, casting glances down both ends of the short hallway.

"Need to talk to you," said Mitch from a distance of six inches away from Hunter's face.

Hunter struggled against the armbar, but Mitch leaned in and saw surprise register on Hunter's face, swiftly replaced with an icy fury.

"Get your dirty hands off me."

"Sure," agreed Mitch, forcing his face into hard planes to belie the easygoing tenor of the words. "You start moving your hands, though, and I'm going to knock your teeth into your throat. Deal?"

Color fled Hunter's face as shock and the first signs of fear overrode the other emotions.

"Deal?"

"Yeah."

Mitch eased back as a tall brunette turned down the hallway. Both boys pivoted their heads to watch her. Mitch kept tabs on Hunter from the corner of his eye.

Her steps faltered as she approached, and a self-conscious blush lit on her cheekbones. She looked away and scurried into the independent studies room at her end of the hall.

Hunter lifted a hand.

Mitch instinctively clenched a fist, shoulder pulling back.

"I heard you," said Hunter, his hand seeking his chest, moving carefully as he maintained contact with Mitch's hard expression. "Chill." He used the heel of his hand to massage the spot where Mitch's elbow had dug in.

Mitch could see the thoughts racing through his friend's mind. He started talking before Hunter could bury him under a load of horse crap.

"What I want to know, dude, is what you know about—" Mitch paused to force Hunter to pay attention. "—magic. Not like pulling rabbits out of hats. The kind that you do with that fancy hand-waving stuff that makes all the girls fall over for you. The kind that shuts up a cop in my garage."

"You're nuts," said Hunter. He straightened himself, and his face slid to neutral, only the glint in his eyes betraying him.

"Yep, totally. Except I keep running into people more nuts than me."

Hunter wagged his head side to side. His hands stayed stationary.

"I didn't put it all together until yesterday, but it all makes sense, everything since the goons tried snatching—"

Recognition popped as Hunter added up things up. "You said it was a dream."

"I wish," said Mitch, kicking himself for the admission and lying in the same breath. He was very, very glad that Kenzie was not a dream.

"Look," Mitch said, "I know stuff, not enough, though, and what I don't know is about to bite me in the ass."

The contrary part of him that lurked in the back of his mind to cause him trouble murmured, *True, that.* Mitch blinked three times to clear the voice.

Hunter stared at him. "What kind of stuff?" He spoke like he was addressing a dolt.

Mitch glared at Hunter and then lifted his hands in mock surrender. "Weird crap, like making me talk when I don't want to. Like you did with Paulson yesterday. You short-circuited him with a wave of your hand and freakin' walked out of class."

Hunter blanched. "You got any evidence or data? I mean, you sound seriously crazy, or would if anybody would listen to you." Hunter shook his head, a sneer twisting his features. His voice raised to a mincing falsetto as he mocked Mitch. "Hey everybody, I believe in magic, and unicorns, and *faeries.*"

Blood thundered in Mitch's ears, and his fist closed again. He drew a long breath and forced the muscles in his arm to relax, ignoring the impulse to clobber Hunter.

Mitch's voice was thick. "Knock it off."

"Why? You're the one assaulting me, right? Shouldn't I be saying that?"

"Because Ken— the girl needs my help and I need yours."

The urgency that made him feel desperate served to strengthen his resolve. He paused, gazing steadily into Hunter's eyes. Below the surface, below the anger was a fear, but not directed at Mitch, because a bare trace of sympathy showed too.

Hunter responded to the open plea in Mitch's voice. "You want my help, then run away from all this as fast as you can."

"Not going to happen."

Hunter gave Mitch a hard stare. "Then you're screwed. Too many people know about you."

A tingle ran the length of Mitch's spine, and he resisted the urge to shudder. He could count three people other than Hunter who knew for certain. Two he trusted, and Kenzie's dad had only interrogated and warned him. That left Hunter.

"Who did you tell?

Hunter's words came out low. "I had to. He could tell."

"Who? About what?"

Hunter shrugged and didn't answer, looking away down the hallway.

Mitch considered the data. "The flash. It's the only thing you knew about."

"I told Father," said Hunter. His scowl deepened. "I had to. There's no way to disguise that much power. He's gone nuts, raging about some other Family. I had to go over the whole thing, explaining you're about as magical as a toothbrush. He couldn't believe that a piece of Meat—"

"Meat?" Mitch glared at his best friend.

"Ordinary people, okay, we call them Meat. None of you have any ability worth talking about. No one has ever heard of Meat acting like you did, like some kind of capacitor. That's the way I explained it and the only reason . . ." Hunter's voice faltered. ". . . the only reason they don't kill you immediately."

Mitch's mouth dropped open, and it took him a second to find words. "You can't be fricking serious."

"I told you, run away, go back to Idaho or wherever, just get away from here."

"I can't."

Above them, the fluorescent lights began to dim and flicker. Mitch formed an image of Hunter at the bottom of a whirlpool with an ocean of energy sucking down toward him. Mitch latched onto the idea that the odd flash, the way Hunter used the term "capacitor," the magic, were all related. He pieced together the implications and spoke, the words tumbling out to keep pace with his thoughts.

"Energy. That flash of energy, then the lab goes into the toilet. All the other magic stuff, it's all some wild application of energy."

Hunter's head was turning back and forth, dismissing the words as fast as Mitch uttered them. "You can't know this."

Like sparks leaping from a bonfire, ideas and connections leapt in Mitch's mind.

"If it's energy, then it's subject to the laws of physics—energy can be neither created nor destroyed, but transformed into a different form."

In his excitement, he saw the change in Hunter's face without comprehending the reasons.

"And for every action, there is an opposite and equal reaction. It's not magic, it's crazy weird physics." Mitch stopped the torrent of words long enough to understand what he had said.

"That spark, from Kenzie," he said, forgetting that Hunter didn't know her, "through me to you, it's all part of the chain of reactions. And you're like, what, an overloaded battery?"

Hunter's façade crumbled, and he let the fear write itself onto his face, dark and shadowy. "It's like a fire hose," he said, "on full blast, and I'm the only one on the end of the nozzle."

"Well, figure out how to chill, dude, before you blow up the lights."

Hunter glanced up, saw the flickering. The effort to control himself wrote itself in his strained look and the flat compression of his lips. The illumination steadied.

"So what happens now?" asked Hunter. "You can't tell anyone. Most people will think you're crazy, and my Family will destroy you as soon as they understand how you did whatever it was you did to store energy like that."

The bell sounded, and Mitch jumped.

"I guess we come up with a plan that saves everybody's ass," he said.

"How do we do that?"

"I got no idea, dude, not even a clue."

CHAPTER TWENTY-FIVE

Kenzie stormed into the martial arts studio. Behind her, she heard the door open and close. Little Bo Peep only had sheep following her. She had Jackson. In the car, she had a "suitable dress" for her mother's "party."

She changed into her uniform in a couple of fast shrugs and a tug, tied the red belt around her waist and knotted it, and stepped back into the open. Jules met her eyes through the glass window of the office and twitched her head to one side.

Come here.

Kenzie, chin out, blew a breath of air up, a mixture of a sigh and a snort. She stomped past Jackson, or tried to, but the carpeted floor and her slight build defeated the effort. To make up for it, she dumped her bag at his feet.

"Yes, ma'am?" she said, from the office door. The skin on her face was tight from chin to hairline, and she kept her gaze down to the floor.

"I think," said Jules, in measured tones, "that you need some practice on the heavy bags. Set up two speed bags across from the hanging heavy bags. Begin with a straight progression, ten kicks each leg, front, side, round, and use the speed bag for hook kicks. Then hit the basic hand and elbow attacks. Once you're warmed up, begin to set up combinations, and keep moving from bag to bag."

Jules glanced at the clock. "You have thirty minutes, then class starts."

After the barest of pauses, Kenzie nodded. "Yes, ma'am."

Kenzie retraced her steps, stopped at the entrance to the training floor, and bowed deeply. She crossed the floor to where the portable heavy bags lined the wall, red pads on sand-filled black bases standing sentry next to the black-on-black speed bags. With a grunt because even the smaller training targets weighed more than she did, she dragged a pair of free-standing reflex bags into position.

Kenzie faced the hanging heavy bag. Teeth clenched, she settled into a back stance, weight on her right leg, hands coming up into defensive position. Her left foot lashed out, lifting and snapping toward the bag. With her toes pulled back, Kenzie struck the bag at waist height, the rough canvas making a rasping sound as the force of the impact sent the bag away.

In her mind, she pictured the kick striking the solar plexus of ferret-faced Ashley Rowbury.

Hana, she thought, counting in Korean as Jules had taught her.

The bag creaked back toward her, a heavy pendulum tied to a support beam by stout white rope. Kenzie launched another front kick.

Dul . . .

The bag started to pivot.

. . . *set* . . .

The kicks and words worked together to build a rhythm that settled her mind.

She finished the left leg with a loud mental yell. *Yoel!*

She switched legs and repeated the sequence. As her body warmed to the work, her mind drifted to the hallway of All Friends, and Alicia Rowbury, with a pair of minions, because nothing says *I'm popular* like mindless followers.

She shifted again, sending a powerful side kick into the meat of the bag with a thunk that lifted it on the rope and popped the canvas-covered weight backward.

Alicia, looking down her nose, mocking her as she spoke. "I thought you'd be interested, *McKenzie*"—always a heavy accent on her name, like there was something wrong with it—"that my father was asking about you."

While Kenzie searched for a reason for Miss Bitch's dad to even know who she was, Alicia opened her lips in a fake smile and handed Kenzie the information.

"I suppose mostly he wanted to know what you said about your family's little company," the tall ash-blonde said. Her voice changed from mocking to sugary-sweet venom. "My father takes over crappy little companies and rebuilds them into successes. Of course, he has to fire all the old people and bring in his own management team to fix them."

The other girls had laughed. Kenzie's face burned, but there was no way to respond, short of hurling insults, and she'd seen too much of

Alicia destroying other girls with wickedly fast and mean statements to dare it.

Kenzie, done with the heavy bag, stepped to the speed bag. The pad was set at head height. Alicia's head height.

The hook kick, a deceptively fast and effective attack, set the target oscillating.

Hana.

I got answers, thought Kenzie, with a glare.

Dul.

Except I can't use them.

Set.

Kenzie nearly missed the next kick, her heel scraping along the side of the canvas as she misjudged the movement.

A firm voice called from the office doorway. "Kenzie, you're thinking. Stop."

Kenzie broke out of her stance to acknowledge Jules with a nod. The black belt walked onto the floor and toward the heavy bags and Kenzie.

Kenzie refocused her efforts, aware that her instructor analyzed each movement. She finished the warm-up sets with a sheen of fine sweat on her skin, nervous because the tall woman beside her was quiet.

"Better." With the single word of encouragement, Jules retreated back to the office.

Kenzie ripped through the hands-and-elbows sequence. In the middle of a hard step-in strike, she recalled the elbow Mitch had delivered to Jackson the day he returned her permit. The question slipped away with the sounds of her fists hitting the bag.

Then it was time for the combinations. Kenzie mixed hands and legs into attacks on the bags. Without a real threat, she delivered them like she was guessing at right answers. Finally, she decided to pretend that each target was an enemy and to visualize a scene in her mind. The heavy bag became the men that tried to abduct her, and the speed bags represented Alicia and the minions. Her movements smoothed out. She flowed into one attack on the heavy bag, broke away to deal with a "threat" from the first speed bag, and kept moving. As she did, a new image formed.

The image lasted one sequence and changed. The walls grew indistinct, absorbed into a damp fog of gray. The heavy bag represented an ogre, the smaller bags knaves; a trio, intent on her. The lights above dimmed, and now she breathed faster, moved faster, as her imagination supplied sounds to match her movements. She spun to her right, engaged a knave, but in her mind's eye, drab brown cloth, coarse and thick over a muscled forearm, blocked her spinning backfist.

She kept moving.

She sunk a side kick into the distended stomach of the ogre. Hard contact that generated a foul expulsion of fetid breath, but he didn't fall.

Turn, an elbow to one knave, and a lightning-fast spinning hook kick snapping like a whip to the head of the second.

The second knave dropped, but the ogre came into striking range.

Instinctively, she stepped under the arms—*Can't let him grab me!*—and launched a fast combination of punches into the kidney area, then ducked under again, before the ogre could turn.

Her momentum sent her toward the last knave. He bobbed his head as the distance closed.

Kenzie gathered herself and leapt. Her right foot slashed up and out, slipped between his arms, and caught the knave under the chin.

He's finished.

She landed, balanced on the balls of her feet. She stared at the ogre, feinted right, and crossed over to deliver a spinning sidekick. The ogre lurched, folded, and charged with a roar as she landed and recovered her footing.

The space between them closed in a blink. In that instant, Kenzie pivoted and, uttering an explosive *"Kai!"* that shocked her ears, unloaded a mule kick straight behind her with all the force she could gather.

With a bang, the rope holding the heavy bag parted. The sound was enough to break Kenzie out of her fantasy.

She looked at the bag crumpled to the floor in dismay. The first speed bag was on the ground. The second was "headless," the pad lying twenty feet away.

A group of young students gaped at her, Jules towering over them, a peculiar cast to her face.

A yellow-belted girl named Sophie, no more than ten, with corn-colored pigtails and an oval-shaped face, looked wide-eyed at Kenzie and then to the bag.

"Daaaammnnn," she said, voice filled with awe, and embarrassingly, hero worship.

Jules ran the class through forms, the choreographed movements that simulated an attack and response. Starting with the first form, the class stepped forward, punched, and blocked in unison.

The black belt glided among them. She corrected the smallest flaws in each student's action, sometimes by gently lifting a fist targeted too low, occasionally demonstrating the form to highlight a flaw in stance or technique. When the forms became more complicated, Jules broke the less-advanced groups out to practice their forms off to the side of the main floor with the guidance of a more-advanced student.

Kenzie welcomed the form drills. The shake in her hands lessened with the ritualistic activity. She concentrated on perfecting each action, her heavy pants popping on each kick. Her sick-to-the-stomach reaction to her destruction of the heavy bag faded.

She had one *what the hell happened* thought, and skittered away from it, afraid of the answer. It came back and demanded attention.

Magic had to be summoned, it didn't just show up and infect inanimate equipment, but her experience had seemed wholly real. Her arm hurt where the knave blocked her backfist. Surreptitiously, she looked. No bruise.

Jules worked with Kenzie, who was the only red belt in the class, and picked on her smallest flaws. Kenzie sought to meet the exacting instructions down to the nearest millimeter in targeting, and a fraction of a second in timing.

Jules, finally showing a hint of satisfaction, nodded.

"Good," she said, though her voice held a guarded quality that was unfamiliar to Kenzie. "Take over the yellows and run them through the first form. We'll break in about ten minutes for the end of class."

"Yes, ma'am," replied Kenzie.

The class finished on schedule, and Kenzie bowed off the floor after the mad rush of the youngsters. Jackson handed her the gear bag, and with a quick thanks, she slipped the strap over her shoulder.

"Kenzie," Jules said.

Kenzie stopped at the door, stepped aside to let Sophie hurtle past, and glanced at Jules.

That expression was back.

Kenzie's stomach fluttered. "I was doing what you told me to do."

With a wag of her head, Jules said, "I know. It's equipment, and you were not abusing it."

Kenzie stood without speaking, dreading whatever Jules would say next. She gripped the strap on the gear bag until her knuckles went white.

The soundless moment grew, and Kenzie's vision narrowed to Jules's face. Finally, the older woman spoke, keeping her voice low, but touched with bewilderment.

"Did you know you were fighting with your eyes closed?"

CHAPTER TWENTY-SIX

Mitch stared at the screen of his phone, and specifically at the time, which still showed thirteen minutes to eight. Finally, the digit changed, and the next eternity of a minute began.

Kenzie had texted him after the yogurt date. It had been short, and sharp, like she was mad at him. After that, twenty-four hours of nothing.

He had clocked the drive to the meet-up spot after school. Eighteen minutes, and they were supposed to meet at nine. Per the text, she'd meet him at the road that overlooked her home. He'd walked to the meeting spot, dropping down the winding roads from the top of the ridge. The houses got fancier and more expensive with every hairpin, and they aligned themselves with the lake, large windows or decks facing Lake Washington. He found the spot right where Kenzie said it would be, a small gray-graveled turnout. He didn't stay long, and remained hidden by flowering rhododendrons, careful to make sure the Jackson dude didn't spot him. Then, reconnoiter completed and the route memorized, he had headed home.

Now Mitch shook his shoulders, loosening them, releasing the memory to worry about the moment.

He sent a text message, letting Kenzie know that he'd be there, nine sharp. He almost asked what was wrong, thinking there was a reason her message had been abrupt. Thought about it, but didn't.

Hated, hated, hated feeling needy, but no word, nothing, all day.

Did she change her mind?

What would her father do if she told him about Mitch?

He worried over that for five more minutes, before reaching the unsettling conclusion that no one had tried to wipe his memory—or run him over in a fake hit-and-run.

Needing another thing to fret over, or distract him from his impending date with Kenzie, he let his thoughts shift to Hunter. Now that he'd confided in his friend, the dude was on his ass with a thousand questions. Bonus points for the ones Mitch hadn't already thought of.

He still kept a close watch on Hunter's hands.

What the hell had he been thinking, asking her out?

Cute girl, kissable lips, the honest but inconvenient voice in his head said in answer.

Leave early, he decided, *and leave the voices, second guesses, behind.*

He hoisted himself off his bed, eased open the door, and peered down the hallway.

The house smelled of burned dinner, and sounded like the gunfight at O.K. Corral. Nobody'd even know he was gone. Maybe. Until he fired up the Camaro. It was parked up on the street and down one house. His uncle's total lack of curiosity, or hell, basic intelligence, was not his problem.

He meandered past the entrance to the living room like he was headed to the fridge, then kept going into the garage. Four seconds later, and cursing vehemently with a skinned shin because he forgot about the forty-ton car jack in the middle of the concrete floor, he exited out the pedestrian door to the side yard.

The Camaro was conveniently close to this side of the house, and he sprinted for it, leaping over the crappy-looking shrubs that the neighbors planted a couple of years ago, and crossing their yard in a flash.

On the other side of his house, Muffles sounded the alert that all was not well.

Stupid dog can't even see me.

A stray thought crossed his mind on who was smarter, his uncle or Muffles. He smirked in the almost-twilight. His uncle, but only by a whisker.

Mitch went around the rear of the car and opened the driver's door, dropping into the seat in a rush. A metallic smell permeated the air, with fresh Bondo dominating. He gave the interior a fast once-over. The seats were freshly cleaned, and the floor was swept out. It would do.

He pumped the throttle twice and squinted as he turned the key. The engine came to life with an agreeable, if too loud, rumble. With a twist in his gut, he shifted into first, eased out the clutch, and glided away from the curb and onward, toward Kenzie.

From the rear, Mitch looked down on the two-story Tudor, weathered brown timber beams crisscrossing with stucco that looked like buckskin stretched on the wood. Moss grew on the weathered cedar shakes on the roof, with the mottled sea-green surface of Lake Washington for a backdrop. A flat black asphalt driveway to the left snaked past the iron gate that he'd entered by when he'd returned

Kenzie's permit. It followed the running ivy on the red brick of the perimeter wall and wrapped around to the back. Past the unruliness of the ivy, the landscaping gave way to precisely trimmed lawn, the kind he assumed all rich folks had because they never had to mow and rake it. The flagstone path pulled extra color from the setting sun. It disappeared at a gazebo dripping in purplish wisteria blossoms.

An attached garage extended to the rear of the compound. It bore an anachronistically modern look and felt like an afterthought to the rest of the home. Probably was, thought Mitch, guessing that the house might have predated the advent of automobiles.

A trio of towering old red cedars stood sentry at the back wall beside the garage and obscured his view to the remainder of the yard, so Mitch turned his attention to the upper story of Kenzie's mini-mansion.

On the rear gable, a pair of large windows, the frame and purlins stark white against the rustic wood trim, straddled the peak of the garage, situated like eyes over a downturned mouth.

He wondered how Kenzie planned on leaving the property undetected; the brick wall securing the perimeter of the compound stood tall and uninterrupted along the back.

Mitch hunkered down to wait. Burnt reds of the fading sun reflected in the glazing, lending the profile a steady and demonic glower. He shivered under that gaze but told himself it was excitement.

CHAPTER TWENTY-SEVEN

If he didn't stop checking out her chest, she was going to stab him with her fork, Kenzie decided. Across from her sat Aric, a twenty-something engineer. She slid sideways to hide behind the centerpiece, red and pink dahlias in a clear vase set in the middle of the white tablecloth. Aric ate in jerky twitches and, with his dark eyes and narrow face, reminded her of a ferret.

"No, I think we have the worst of the problems resolved," he said, talking shop with her mother, who sat to Kenzie's right at the head of the table. His voice grated, unctuous and arrogant at the same time.

She could see him smile like he was humble. It came across as condescending. "The mathematics is pretty intense stuff, even for me."

He's bragging that he's good at math? thought Kenzie. She stopped her eyes from rolling with a determined effort.

It wasn't that hard to fill in between the lines. Knowing that Aric was a wizard, even if a lame one, and an engineer, she figured that they were talking about the amplifier for magic. She turned her wrist just enough to check the time. Thirty minutes until she was supposed to meet Mitch.

Move it along, people.

The idea of increasing her power with an amplifier left her scary-excited, though, and she had to know more.

Her heart thumped against her chest, and she ducked her head for a moment, unsure whether Mitch, the idea of sneaking out, or the invention was responsible. All three, maybe.

The mock battle at the studio weighed on her. She'd had no idea what to tell Jules at the studio and had mumbled something about using her imagination, but the tightness in her gut questioned that. She had never heard of magic bleeding over unbidden, but two weeks ago, mechanical magic would have been incomprehensible. Consequently, she paid close attention to Aric, which had the unfortunate side effect of making him think she was interested.

Kenzie fake-smiled to keep him talking and sliced off a bite-size piece of the T-bone lamb chop. The smell of the garlic rub added to the taste as she put the piece into her mouth and chewed. Her Brussels sprouts sat untouched and unloved on the side of her plate closest to Aric.

The smile worked at getting him talking again, mostly to the other adults. That didn't stop the man from sliming her with his eyes as he periodically glanced at her.

"I don't want to make this too technical, but the essential bottleneck entailed designing the nanoelectronics, mostly quantum dots, to handle the random inputs and simultaneously store energy. The theoretical underpinnings have been known for quite some time. French physicist Olivier Costa de Beauregard suggested the possibilities back in the seventies, but trying to translate the base theory into an operable piece of equipment has been difficult, to say the least. Since our abilities derive from innate qualities permitting us to directly manage quanta, what the less educated call magic—"

Kenzie saw the fast wrinkle form and disappear on her father's forehead at the implication that using the term "magic" was for rubes. Her father had been quiet during dinner, setting a steady and uncompromising gaze on the engineer.

Aric plowed on, oblivious.

"—what we had to do was create an electronics device that could not only detect energy at that level, but act on it. Events at the level of quanta are subject to probabilistic outcomes, and the more closely we tried to control one aspect of the quanta, say spin, the more the others would diverge. The randomness made designing anything tricky."

"But you have a working model now?" asked her father, interjecting himself into the conversation for the first time.

"A prototype, yes. We've been able to increase the input by over fifty-two percent, but we've encountered some scattering issues. Until the lab gets better shields, we don't dare try to move forward."

"The repairs should be complete this week," said Sasha.

Aric nodded and shoveled a forkful of potatoes into his mouth. His eyes wandered again while he chewed. Always in the same direction. Gross. Kenzie gripped her fork tighter and slouched behind the flower arrangement.

Her father put his fork down in a deliberate fashion and placed both palms on the tablecloth. The expression on his face put Kenzie on alert.

"Why don't you dare to move forward, as you put it?" asked Raymond Graham. His tone was detached, and though the question was directed at Aric, the cop coldly evaluated his wife.

"Stray energy," said Aric, with a breezy wave of his right hand. "There is a certain amount of background energy, 'noise' if you will. Think of MAGE, that's what we called the amplification hardware, think of it like a laser, highly concentrated energy. You get normal background interference, and it creates a speckle pattern, degradation of the beam. Same thing happens with mag— with our manipulation of energy, except our speckle pattern causes unpredictable changes."

"It's really quite under control, dear," said Sasha, exasperation written on her face. "The extra shielding will mitigate the problem. There's nothing to worry about."

Her father drummed the table with his fingers like he was preoccupied with another thought. He seemed to make an internal decision, and fixed his gaze on Aric.

"How did you discover the problem with the background radiation?"

"It's not really radiation—"

Raymond interrupted, with words that had zero warmth. "The problem."

Kenzie recognized the tone: cop voice, master inquisitor. *Uh-oh.*

Aric sat taller in his straight-backed chair.

Kenzie sneaked another look at her watch. Eighteen minutes.

She needed to get out of here.

Aric spoke, trying to match her father's gravity and failing miserably.

"We had an accident at the lab, no big deal. All the equipment is replaceable, and one person got hit with some glass, but nobody was seriously hurt."

"Raymond, the company and the manner in which it is run are my purview. I think interrogating one of my employees, at a dinner that we invited him to no less, is plainly interfering, and beyond rude."

Kenzie glanced from one parent to the other, seeking an opportunity to vanish from the table. Her mother sat stiff with anger, lips pursed. Her father bent his head fractionally to acknowledge her words and then turned to Aric.

"Flying glass implies an explosion of some sort."

"An 'explosion' is not accurate." Aric sounded testy. "It was an energy overload with diffused effects throughout the lab."

"The lab was unshielded."

"I told you that we're fixing it."

"You have a means of detecting such an overload."

"Raymond," said Sasha, but he froze her with a look and a pointing finger.

"You should have told me," he said. She blanched and looked away, putting her hands on her lap.

Aric shifted in his seat. Kenzie read the confusion in his fidgeting. He turned to Sasha, seeking help, saw her face, and with reluctance turned back to Raymond.

Her father continued his line of attack.

Kenzie observed, fascinated even as the time slipped away.

"Yes or no, you have a means of detecting a release of magic."

"Yes."

"The means of detection is based on science, not magic."

Aric appeared ready to argue the use of the terms, thought better of it, and answered. "That is correct."

"Your device is replicable."

"Well, only if someone knew what they were looking for. It's not like—"

"Yes or no."

The harshness in her father's voice cowed Aric.

"Yes," he said, shoulders slumping.

Her father turned to her mother. "You really should have told me. It would have saved chasing after the ghosts of missing Families."

"The incident in the lab had nothing to do with . . ." Her mother didn't complete the statement.

Kenzie's face tightened. She looked back and forth between her parents. With a sudden clarity, she knew that the explosion and the attack on her were somehow related, and that her mother had withheld the information from her father.

The rattling of her fork against the rim of her plate attracted the attention of the adults. Kenzie stood. Her chair grated against the wood floor as it slid back.

"I can't believe you lied," she said, staring hard at her mother. She snorted. "No, wait, I can. I mean, what's a daughter compared with magic and the chance to increase the fortunes of the Family, right, *Mother*? The assholes that attacked me were trying to get to you, weren't they? It was never about me, but I'm the one that gets to get babysat by Jackson forever, and can't run, or go hang out or anything."

A rushing wind filled her ears, and her hands itched to move, but a scrap of memory from the studio intruded.

Control, gotta get control.

Kenzie ground her teeth together and gave a hard shake of her head. She spun, banged her knee against her chair, and managed not to curse out loud even as the chair stuttered over the hardwood.

"McKenzie, your behavior is inexcusable. You will come back to this table and apologize to Aric," said her mother to her back.

Kenzie held her course, headed for the stairs. She couldn't trust her anger not to engulf her.

Another chair scraped. A moment later tendrils of unseen gossamer touched her skin, almost tickling with their lightness.

She stopped on the first step and pivoted against the increasing pressure. Before her stood her mother, face like a high priestess betrayed by a novitiate's apostasy. Her hands wove the *Cordaesus* spell without the usual grace, the interlocking motion taut with rage. Meanwhile, she muttered the incantation, binding the magic tighter and tighter to Kenzie's skin until it began to pinch. Surprise overrode anger, and she stood stock-still.

A detached part of Kenzie's mind analyzed the spell, and she drew upon the swirling energies around her. It was as though she could visualize the knots; she also saw how to undo them. The glow of the energy shone for her only, faint but definite.

Kenzie's mouth pulled down at one corner, and her shoulders lifted. *Innexustrum,* she thought, and sent the spell into the world.

The bonds fell free, parted like string meeting the sharpest of skinning knives.

Three sets of startled eyes weighed on her, each carrying its own meaning. Sasha stood, hands frozen in the midst of conjuring, shock radiating out. Aric's face faded to a sickly gray, and his mouth hung open. He closed it with a gulp. Her father had his head tilted at an angle, peering at her as though reassessing what he knew.

Kenzie gathered herself and said, "I'm going to my room." She swung around to ascend the stairs, and paused, looking over her shoulder at her mother. "And I'm locking the door."

Silence met her announcement and her exit.

Kenzie checked her watch at the top of the stairs and ran as softly as she could to her room. She slipped in and closed the door with enough violence to ensure that it would be heard and felt below.

Safe.

Kenzie leaned her back against the flat panel of the door. The last red glow of the sunset painted the wall to her left.

"Thank you, Harold," she said into the dim space.

She looked at her watch again. She was going to be late. No choice, she had to change. Kenzie prayed that Mitch would wait.

CHAPTER TWENTY-EIGHT

A ladybug crept over the blossom of the rhododendron that concealed him, and insect noises rose in the dusk. Crouched behind the vegetation, Mitch's knees ached, almost as much as his chest. What if she didn't show? The last rays of the sun touched a cloud, making it bleed as the night closed in. To the right of the house, a halcyon moon grew over the trees, full to bursting.

She's late, he thought. *That's all.* He checked his watch again. Five after. How long should he wait?

A man stalked out from the front of the house. Not Kenzie's dad or Jackson. Mitch evaluated the slacks, button-up shirt, attitude, and placed the guy into the "dork" category. Whoever he was, he left, and Mitch turned his attention back to the house.

A light blossomed in the right-hand window. Then it died, came back on for another two seconds, and disappeared.

His inner voice cautioned him that it wasn't a sign, but Mitch's heart leapt.

He caught sight of movement on the other side of the glazing, but couldn't make anything out in the gloom. The window slid open and then he watched the screen shake and pop loose. It vanished into the dark room.

A slender jean-clad leg appeared and hooked over the windowsill. A slender bronze arm reached out the window, and he saw her fingers clasp the top of the window trim. The slender profile of Kenzie emerged, one limb at a time. Her ponytail touched the top of the transom as she ducked to get her head out and then had to hop to get enough clearance from the windowsill to draw the second leg out. She stood upright.

Mitch rose to his full height, mesmerized. He had asked her to sneak out with him; he hadn't meant it literally.

Kenzie closed the window behind her and made some kind of gesture with her hand. She tugged at the bottom of her ivory gypsy blouse to straighten it as though she had stepped out the front door.

With her hands spread for balance, she ascended the slope of the roof to the peak. As lightly as a sparrow, she walked along the ridge until she reached the end of the shingles, her shirt pressed against her by a slight breeze. Kenzie descended the opposite slope, the one closest to him. She kept her knees bent and her weight back.

The wall, he guessed, as he figured out her plan. It was a couple of feet from the edge of the roof to the top of the wall.

Kenzie reached the lower eave and stopped.

The angles were funky, coming from a pitched surface to the flat top of the wall. He might be able to step over the gap, but it looked too wide for Kenzie. Mitch took one step from hiding, to go help, but Kenzie lifted her knee and jumped sideways. With a ninety-degree pivot in midair, she landed on her left foot, arms opened wide, with only a hint of a wobble. She folded down, tucked her trailing leg under her, and then she was standing on the wall. She walked the length of the wall and disappeared behind one of the trees at the edge of the property.

Kenzie swayed to avoid the branch that hung over the eight inches of brick at the top of the perimeter wall. The tips of the needles pricked the palms of her hand when she clutched at the bristly limb and used it for balance. She released it too soon, and it snagged on the loose bottom hem of her blouse. For a scant moment, she thought that it would sweep her from the wall before the natural tension pulled it past her and the branch returned, vibrating, to its original position. The quiver that had started when she opened the window and divined the ward set there grew to a full case of the shakes.

Kenzie crouched down and let her butt settle onto her heels.

This is silly, she thought. *Heck, the wall is twice as wide as the balance beam in the studio.* Except the beam was on the ground, and the wall dropped away about ten feet here. She looked ahead to the point where the hillside ran into the masonry work. The clearance there looked to be about four feet.

Doable.

The scent of the pine stayed with her. She rubbed her thumb across her palm and fingertips, touched the sap. She grimaced, but repressed the urge to shrug.

What if he's not there?

Kenzie quieted her nerves, mostly by ignoring them and her doubts, and stood tall.

Only one way to find out, she thought, and resumed her traverse.

She had clicked the light switch a couple of times to let him know that she was on her way. That was before she had found the ward across her window. Just like her father to be paranoid. It had taken a few seconds to analyze the ward. It wasn't a binding spell, but a tripwire to notify him that someone had breached the window.

She'd sought out the essence of the magic—stupid Aric, calling it anything else!—and found this to be slipperier than the binding spell her mother used. *Does the person casting a spell change the nature of the energy?* she had thought, and filed the idea away to discuss with Harold.

Kenzie glanced downward.

Close enough.

She faced the hillside, looked again, and changed position, worried that she'd fall backward into the wall because of the slope. The shakes threatened to take over again, so she jumped before she chickened out. Kenzie kept her uphill leg bent, hoping to get both feet down at the same time. She had enough time to realize the wall here was taller than she thought, and then she fell through the low greenery and landed.

Mitch fidgeted with his feet until Kenzie reappeared, side-hilling instead of forcing her way through the overgrown brush. Bushes blocked her from view as she traversed the hill. Mitch moved on an intersecting course with her, his long legs moving faster as he strode down the shoulder of the road as it wound down toward Lake Washington.

Mitch found the terminus of the trail, a faint trampling in the ground with the damp soil showing partial footprints laid over each other in a mosaic of personal journeys. A gentle swish of a branch alerted him to Kenzie's presence before she stepped into the open.

Kenzie had a leaf stuck in her hair. She brushed her hand back to put her hair over her shoulder and looked up at him with luminous eyes filled with stifled anger.

"Hi," Mitch said to cover his confusion. Was she mad at him? For what? If she was, why'd she meet him?

The light of her anger faded, and the corner of her mouth twitched. Mitch's mounting confusion gave way to sudden panic, sure that he had confirmed he was an idiot.

"What?" he asked. Crap, he sounded frickin' eager.

'Cuz you are . . .

"Nothing," Kenzie said.

It wasn't nothing, it was definitely something, but Kenzie's voice had been light, so it wasn't something tragic.

He was making himself crazy. Short drive.

"So what's the plan?" asked Kenzie.

"Uh . . ."

That was intelligent sounding.

He started over.

"Uh . . . I don't really have one," he admitted.

The ultimate in smooth, yessir.

"We could drive someplace and get something to eat." He poured the words out too quickly, almost tripping over them, but he needed her to want to stay, not decide this was the worst idea in her life.

Kenzie smiled, and Mitch found himself fascinated by the curve of her lips. His gaze slipped down, and his innards tingled as he saw the necklace. His gaze lingered on the chain, followed the hanging stone down. . . .

His face got hot in the silence between them.

"Can we walk instead?" Kenzie asked.

Relief coursed through his body. "Anything you want," he said.

Kenzie smiled again, wider this time, and Mitch could see the gleam of white teeth in the moonlight.

"Come on," she said. She glided away into the falling darkness as she made her way down the street.

Mitch chased after her and worried that they'd come too close to her house, but Kenzie ducked onto another backyard path that led diagonally away. He ducked under the same branch she did, dipping low, and stood still long enough to see where she went.

He stepped forward.

"Son of a—" he swore as his face tore through a spider web.

Kenzie *shush*ed at him. Mitch clamped his lips shut.

He flailed at the air around his head to knock down the rest of the web. Strands clung to his skin and, for a split second, he thought he could feel the legs of the spider tickling his cheek. He rubbed his face to get the silk off.

"We're in somebody's backyard," said Kenzie.

"Freaking spider web," came the aggrieved response from Mitch.

Shadows from the trees hid her face, but by the angles of her silhouette, he could tell she was facing him. The shape shifted and moved away without saying another word. Mitch hurried to follow, crouching down as he went.

The path dropped them out on Lake Washington Boulevard, Kenzie's house behind them and obscured by the trees lining the broad street. The briny smell of the water twitched at his nose, shifting away on the breeze. A green light slid across the surface of the lake, and the heavy rumble of a diesel engine drifted onto shore. Mitch judged the boat's size from the height of the illuminated wheelhouse and raised an eyebrow, figuring it to be about a fifty-foot cruiser. Farther away, a red dot moved in the opposite direction while specks of steady yellows sat on Mercer Island, set in the middle of the lake.

Kenzie broke into a slow jog.

Mitch ran to catch up and settled in next to her.

She crossed the street and opened her arms wide.

"This feels amazing," she said, turning onto the dark ribbon of asphalt that wound along the shore.

"What does?"

"Running."

Mitch panted as he adjusted to her pace. Thankfully, she wasn't running fast, or he'd be sucking major wind.

Kenzie started to talk. The bitterness on display earlier faded.

It's not me, he thought with relief.

"Martial arts and that stuff was all my father's idea. One day, Jules took us out to a park for an outdoor workout, and we did laps to get warmed up. Running on the grass barefoot put me in a happy place. We did it again a couple more times, and I told my parents I wanted to start running for real."

She rolled her shoulders as she shrugged in stride. One shoulder fell bare as her blouse shifted.

Mitch admired the delicate architecture of her shoulder, the muscles moving smoothly under tanned skin.

She pulled up the wayward fabric.

"I got some shoes and stuff, and went out."

Say something, he thought, but nothing came to mind.

"You don't talk much, do you?"

"Trying to keep up," Mitch fibbed.

Kenzie slowed a touch. She reached up with a practiced motion and tightened her ponytail. Her blouse tightened across the front as she did. She slipped to a walk.

Mitch, caught by surprise, overran her by two steps.

"So where now," he asked, surrendering control of the adventure to her. Kenzie pointed to a dark mass a half mile away. "There."

According to the sign, "there" turned out to be Seward Park, and it was open until ten. Mitch checked his watch automatically and recorded the time.

They wove their way around the sculpted grounds at the entrance and rounded the trees in the middle of the deserted parking lot. The Audubon Center sat dark in front of them, nested down for the night. The tall conifers behind it provided a curtain against the white beams of the rising moon. The stucco-and-brick façade reminded Mitch of Kenzie's house.

"Aren't your folks going to miss you?"

"I don't care."

Hearing the anger, Mitch kicked himself. *Dumbass.*

Kenzie strode ahead, and he played catch-up again. She turned toward the water and halted so quickly that Mitch had to sidestep to avoid plowing into her.

"Holy heck," breathed Kenzie.

Mitch diverted his attention from the girl.

Before them, the full moon climbed the snow-covered flanks of Mount Rainier. Mitch stood awed, even as the numbers crunched in the back of his head, calculating the height of Rainier (fourteen thousand feet plus a bit) and distance (better than fifty miles away.) Confronted by the majesty of Rainier, the statistics washed out, and a naked portion of him reacted with awe. From Seattle, especially his side of the ridges, Mount Rainier sightings were rare. Tonight, some trick of the air brought the silvery snowcapped peak closer and made the moon seem huge. Mitch imagined he could see each pockmark on the surface of the moon, each crevasse on the glaciated side of the dormant volcano.

A sigh escaped from Kenzie. She lifted her right hand like she wanted to touch them.

"Everything should be this beautiful," she murmured.

"The second prettiest thing I've seen tonight." The words, spoken without thinking, tumbled forth. Mitch froze up at his honesty, stupidity, air trapped in his lungs.

Oh, crap. . . .

A fleeting flash of a smile graced Kenzie's face at the timbre of Mitch's words before their full import reached her brain. All the air left her lungs. Tongue-tied, she tried to form a response. All she could do was swallow.

Guys at school ran their mouths and said all kinds of stuff, either to pump themselves up or to wrangle their way into a girl's pants. She could hear it in the voices of the players, with their "hey, girl" and roaming hands. At All Friends, they were all players, trained from toddlers to be the next generation of alpha males, full of themselves. Well, not all of them, but the rest of the boys hid, sneaking wistful glances when they thought nobody was looking.

And now Mitch said she was pretty, and meant it. It put her brain into a tizzy. A pleasant and scary tingle didn't help her think, either.

The moon and Mitch waited for her answer as the words slipped across the water. The disoriented feeling fell away, replaced by clarity.

I like *being called pretty,* she thought.

The tingle responded and added a flutter.

Face hot, Mitch waited for the explosion.

Kenzie stepped back and turned to face him. Her eyes glowed with the luminosity of the moon, and the gem at her throat sparkled in the captured rays of moonlight. Color touched on her cheekbones.

"Thank you," she said, and she sounded flustered.

Mitch let the air rattle out. His brain hunted for an escape route that would move them onto safer ground . . .

She's not mad, dude.

. . . when out of the corner of his eye, he registered motion closer to the water. Something floated in midair, and the skin at the back of his neck prickled.

Indistinct shapes sat darkly between them and the horizon. It took a second for the lines and curves to resolve themselves into familiar configurations of playground equipment. Nearby, picnic tables lined the sawdust-filled play zone. The floater turned into a swing.

"Wanna sit?" asked Mitch. That seemed a safe enough offer.

Kenzie nodded.

They walked side by side. Mitch kept sneaking glances at Kenzie, hoping to see another smile. They reached the bench, and Kenzie sat down facing out to the water at the reflection of Rainier. She stretched out her legs, pointing them toward the light spilled across the surface of the lake. A tall, angular bird, maybe a heron, stood on a silent vigil on a piling.

Mitch endured a second of indecision. Sit on the other side of the table? Sit next to her? Sit facing her?

Mitch deposited himself on the bench, too, but left a clear two feet between them. From the trees, he heard a rustle of branches as a bird or squirrel moved, and the water continued a gentle lapping at the sand of the beach. Around them were the lights of moving cars and houses, even a plane headed for Sea-Tac, but the sounds of the bustle were muted.

He leaned an elbow on the concrete surface of the table. Kenzie continued to gaze out onto the water, and Mitch gathered a feeling of sadness below the anger she'd displayed earlier. He put his chin in his cupped hand and unabashedly ogled, soaking in each detail of her face. She lacked the glow of their first meeting, but it was still the face that he dreamed about at night.

Her eyes flicked in his direction. He could see the muscles at the edge of her jaw clench tight. A minuscule shake of her head warned him that she was getting her courage together, so he sat upright and spoke first.

"So what do we do now?"

"If you had any sense, you'd run away."

He hurried to reassure her. "Yeah, except I seem to run to, not run away. I told you I wanted to help. That everything got weirder than snot doesn't change that. And besides, you've told me this much, you might as well tell me everything. Like, who tried to kidnap you? That part doesn't make any sense with all the magic stuff. I mean, if you can wave your hands around and make crap happen, why resort to a felony?"

The muscles clenched even tighter as Mitch spoke, and the anger resurfaced on her face.

Dude, you're a dumbass. Do not piss off the girl. It's not a hard rule, amigo.

Pictures of Kenzie stomping off because he gave her the third degree shuffled through his head. In about half of them, she slapped him first.

"You don't have to—" he began, but Kenzie shook her head. He watched the cute bounce of her ponytail and zipped his mouth.

"It's okay. My mother invited a jerk to dinner—the engineer who is building the invention I told you about. It's an amplifier for magic. They were trying to kidnap me to get to my mother. Whoever wants the stupid thing must know about Aric's—he's the lead engineer, I think—his work in the lab, though I don't know what good it would do them if they can't do magic in the first place."

Suspicion nibbled around the edges of Mitch's mind. He thought about telling Kenzie about his meeting with Mercury and decided against it. Mercury's instructions or requests or whatever the hell they were didn't square with the older wizard being involved in the attempt. Just the opposite—he'd asked Mitch to protect Kenzie.

"Maybe they can do magic?" He was thinking aloud. "What if they found out about it and wanted it? It would make a great weapon, wouldn't it?"

He fumbled with ideas, seeing which would match up.

"Are there, like, organizations for wizards? Ones that would fight for something like this amplifier?"

Kenzie tucked her legs back underneath her and made a quarter turn to face him.

"We call them Families. Supposedly there are more than just mine, but I've never met anyone from another Family. Mostly, I thought my Family was pretty much the only one, and that my parents used stories of other Families, the Spanish Family, to scare us. I don't think it would surprise my father if there were others, though. He's in charge of keeping us all safe, so he'd already know if they were around and messing with us."

A warning sounded when Kenzie mentioned the *Spanish* Family. Mitch drew a deep breath, making the connection to Hunter *Rubiera*. Kenzie stood up while he dithered over how much to tell her.

"Come on, I don't want to talk about it anymore."

Kenzie rolled her shoulders as she walked away from the picnic table. The moon that resembled the orb in the Glade had settled back to a normal bright fullness, but Mount Rainier still glimmered across the rippled water to her.

She didn't want to talk about the Family or the amplifier or anything else. More than anything, she wanted to disappear into a crowd so she could be herself, have a boyfriend who . . .

Her thoughts ran up against a hard upswell of emotion. When she thought of *Mitch-boyfriend* that new tingle-tension set her on a delicious edge.

More than anything, she had a reckless urge to run away to Mitch.

Mitch saw her wrestling with her thoughts as she crossed the woodchips. She was headed for the swing. A pang of sympathy for her predicament softened his features. He followed, giving her a little space. As Mitch got closer, he saw that it wasn't a regular swing. Rather than being attached to poles, the seat hung by chains leading to a roller on a zip line. The cable bolts were attached to tube steel framing that resembled elongated upside-down Us.

Kenzie settled onto the swing. The action made the whole thing spin slowly.

"Push me?" Kenzie asked. "Please?"

Mitch hesitated, trying to figure out where to push from. With little kids, he knew to push down by the butt.

Kenzie was definitely not a little kid.

He thought about pushing higher on her back, but a fast vector analysis in his head gave him a fifty-fifty shot of knocking her off the swing. He compromised by placing his hands at her waist the next time the spin put her in the right position.

Through the thin cotton of Kenzie's blouse, the heat from her skin warmed his palms, and the scent of her hair twisted him up inside. He pulled her in a couple of inches before giving her a gentle shove. The pulley at the zip line hissed as she bounced away. Kenzie laughed and lifted one leg, putting herself into a fast spin. As she came around, she switched legs to slow herself. She ended up with her back to him.

Bobbing on the wire, she leaned back and looked at him upside down. She balanced there, with her feet up, Mount Rainier lined up between them. She kept her focus on him. Mitch's gaze traversed from the petite-looking shoes to the snap on her jeans. Kenzie's blouse parted at the ruffles on the bottom and pulled up, leaving her tummy exposed. Tight lines of her taut ab muscles kept her from overbalancing on the swing, and she had an innie belly button. His eyes stopped moving when they reached her breasts. The twisted feeling at his gut straightened itself out.

He was glad it was dark.

Kenzie looked at him from an upside-down position as the blood rushed to her head and her cheeks warmed. He stood there gaping at her. He looked silly with his mouth open like that, she thought.

A zephyr of wind lifted the bottom ruffle of her blouse and billowed out the top. The slight wind threatened to unbalance her, so she dropped her feet a couple of inches to maintain equilibrium.

"You ever think of running away?"

"Not really," Mitch said. His voice sounded weird, husky.

The magic is right there, she thought, *I can feel it, so easy to hold. . . .*

"Why not?" Her question flowed out on her breath, a murmur, not a hard interrogative.

"You can only run so far, and then the bullies find you anyway, and you still have to fight. Might as well start it first."

Kenzie nibbled at her lower lip, and her eyes drifted sideways. Breathing stretched out like this seemed hard. The heat of her face expanded to her torso and moved lower. She gave Mitch an intent stare.

"Did you have to fight?"

Mitch's face went hard and his unblinking gaze touched hers with bleakness.

"I . . ." Mitch set his jaw. "Never mind."

Kenzie's brows gathered in as she read the answer to her question in the scars that she had picked at. She met his look.

He's too far away.

She wanted him closer, near her. Holding her, while she put her head against his chest . . .

As if reading her mind, he took a step toward her.

Kenzie sat up, looking over her shoulder at him. With her hair falling to the side and the stone at her throat and the big, big eyes, she looked like a fairy-tale princess. The seat rotated, and Kenzie spun until she faced him. Mitch extended a hand and grasped the cable. The coldness of the wire strands gave him an anchor to cling to.

A hard crack, a broken branch, made it through the rushing roar of blood in his ears, but he disregarded it. Even the persistent sounds of the lake got submerged.

Kenzie tilted her head up to him. Her lips were parted, and he saw her chest rise and fall. She shimmered with an internal glow that melted any restraint he had.

He bent forward, lowering his mouth toward hers. Vaguely he recalled all the warnings from school. He disregarded them.

His lips touched hers, lightly, felt hesitation—her hesitation, his hesitation. He let his lips linger and then drew away, trembling, vibrating with pent-up energy, more than he thought he could stand. He waited for some reaction, dreading what it might be, unable to move or speak. Just vibrating, while the voice in his head laughed and said, *I told you they were kissable.*

His hand shook on the cable, so he squeezed his fist tight until the knuckles were ready to burst from the skin.

He watched Kenzie's face, desperate for a sign, and his heart fell out when she dropped her chin.

"Why did you do that?" Kenzie whispered.

"You looked like you wanted to be kissed."

She lifted her face. He caught the stars in her gaze.

"Do it again?"

Mitch leaned toward her, and Kenzie reached up. As his face approached hers, she closed her eyes and parted her lips.

Another crack came from the trees and, as Mitch was about to kiss Kenzie again, a flash of red crossed her face.

Mitch went onto high alert, as tense as an impala scenting a pride of lions. He froze, inches from Kenzie. The dot flashed again and disappeared.

Mitch slowly stood up, swinging Kenzie around behind him.

His hand shook on the cable again, but not from excitement. No self-respecting gamer could fail to recognize a laser sight when he saw one.

"Hey," Kenzie said, sounding hurt.

Mitch looked into the trees, mind racing with calculations and angles. Laser light traveled in straight lines. *If it had been on Kenzie's face, it had to come from about there,* he thought.

He faced the darkness, keeping himself from looking down to see the dot on his chest.

"Who's there?" he shouted into the dark, defiance loud in his words while dread slithered into his heart.

CHAPTER TWENTY-NINE

Kenzie's lips burned from the kiss with Mitch, then she was spinning away from him, pushed hard enough that the pulley above sang.

Mitch stood with his face away from her and hands clenched at his sides.

Her father.

He found them!

She jumped from the swing's seat, hands already initiating a defensive weave as she tried to anticipate the spells that her father would use. Her attention scattered, the opposite of earlier in the evening with her mother.

"Miss Graham, may I ask you to stop conjuring, please, or I will be forced to have my man execute Mr. Merriwether."

Kenzie's hands froze. Frantically, she tracked the smooth baritone voice. She focused on an older man, silver at the temples, less than ten yards from them. She recognized the look, though not the man. He stood at ease, like a master overseeing the boardroom, impeccably turned out in a suit that fit so well that it had to be custom made. A silver tie clasp gleamed in the moonlight, and he held his hands folded in front of him.

"Thank you," he said.

"Who the hell are you?" demanded Mitch. He started toward the stranger.

Kenzie left her hands in the air. She found the magic, but it slithered away like an eel escaping into a reef. She panted as she sought the calm to reacquire control.

The man raised a hand in the universal sign to halt.

"Mr. Merriwether, I will have you shot if you continue." There was a pause as he touched something in his ear. "Miss Graham, very impressive, but you will cease your magic now and not try to call it forth, or whatever it is that you do, again, agreed?"

Kenzie went numb with shock and dropped her hands. Mitch lurched to a halt. Kenzie saw that he had placed himself directly between the man and her.

He knows when I'm using magic, she thought.

Mitch spoke, rank suspicion coloring the words. "What do you want with Kenzie?"

"How do you know it's about me?" said Kenzie, directing her question to Mitch.

"He hasn't offered to shoot you twice in the last thirty seconds."

The man laughed with a practiced ease that belied any humor. Unease settled on Kenzie. She stepped sideways to get a clear view of the man, head tilted at an angle like a peasant totally engrossed by a cobra.

Cobras are safer, she thought.

"Very perceptive, Mr. Merriwether. My business *is* with Miss Graham, though I must thank you for getting her out of her house and away from Mr. Jackson. I can assure you that Mr. Jackson's family will thank you as well. He is quite good at his profession, and I was beginning to believe that I would need to remove him in order to approach Miss Graham."

Mitch's shoulders hunched forward, but Kenzie was relieved to see him hold his ground. The semi-paralysis that had seized her muscles at the first appearance of the man, when she feared her father had located her, transformed into a smoldering anger. The threat to Jackson added fuel.

She took a deliberate step forward.

"I'm going to stand next to Mitch," she said through tight lips.

As opening gambits for negotiation went, it sucked, but not as much as doing nothing.

"Certainly, Miss Graham, please do." The man met her with dry calculation. Lifting one hand, he stretched out an index finger toward Mitch. "If you wish, inspect the evidence that your very alert young man noted."

She needed information and time.

"What's your name?" asked Kenzie.

"That is quite unimportant."

"Then we don't have anything to negotiate," said Kenzie, projecting strength though her legs wobbled under her. She reached Mitch's side and glanced up. Two red dots sat on his forehead, one over each eye.

"I am not here to negotiate."

Mitch *hah*ed under his breath and spoke up. "Yeah, you are, at least some, otherwise you'd just shoot me and be done. You haven't, meaning you want Kenzie's cooperation for something. You tried to force it before, but the kidnapping didn't work, so you're back again, talking. So answer the lady instead of being a prick."

Kenzie drew a deep breath. Mitch was provoking a corporate tiger, the kind that crushed people who refused to "yes, sir" the boss, namely him. The kind that destroyed lives if it added two percentage points of profit to the bottom line. She put a hand on Mitch's forearm to shut him up. His trembling anger roiling under her fingertips reinforced her will.

"Your name?" she asked. "Please."

"You may call me Mr. Lassiter." Mitch's words had shredded Lassiter's debonair façade, and Kenzie saw the feral intent in his eyes. The man's glare never left Mitch as he answered. "Mitchell, I had high hopes that you might prove a useful addition with more seasoning and training. I see now that such a thought is untenable."

"Don't call me Mitchell." Mitch shrugged one shoulder while his head bobbed to the same side. "Doubt I wanted to work with you anyway."

The idiot is trying to get shot, she thought.

"What may we do for you, Mr. Lassiter?" A tremor accompanied the words, and she prayed that Mitch would keep his big mouth shut.

Lassiter looked away from the boy. He spoke, and Kenzie's skin goosebumped like the temperature had dropped to near-freezing levels.

"It is quite simple, Miss Graham. You will locate a storage device that your mother keeps in her possession. You will ensure that the device is not damaged in any way in the process of acquisition. You will deliver it to me, in intact condition, within seven days. You will ensure that no magic is attached to the device. Failure to accomplish these things within a seven-day period will result in a breach of our agreement, and I will begin imposing penalties. Do you understand?"

Kenzie spoke over Mitch's snort. At least he wasn't talking. She imagined her mother standing in her place, corporate CEO, and channeled that alien persona.

I can do this. But her knees quaked.

"First, what does the storage device look like." She took a deep breath and asked her second question, the one that she already knew the answer to, but she wanted in the open air. "Second, what are the penalties? Next, where is the device to be delivered? And finally, what is the inducement for me for successful completion of the project?"

Lassiter examined her. Kenzie held her chin up and refused to break eye contact. He moved his hand again, that same type of gesture he'd used earlier.

"Look at your right leg, Miss Graham."

She looked down as instructed. The hand on Mitch's arm clenched while the other one drifted up to her stomach. Mitch leaned forward to see.

One of the red dots held steady an inch above her knee.

"It will be very hard to perform martial arts or run without your leg. The correct type of ammunition delivered to that precise location on your leg will have the effect of amputating it. That is your inducement."

Kenzie's insides heaved, and she tasted bile in the back of her throat.

"As for the penalties, in five days—"

"You said seven," said Mitch.

"The young lady wanted to negotiate. It was, and is, a poor decision for a person with no leverage to attempt to change the terms."

Lassiter consulted his watch. "It is nine minutes after ten. In five days' time, Mr. Jackson will be removed as an impediment."

Kenzie gasped. "Jackson hasn't done anything," she protested.

"Nevertheless, he is a pawn on the board. It will be your decision whether you sacrifice him or not. In seven days, you will have a similar decision regarding Mr. Merriwether." He paused. "This presumes that Mr. Merriwether does not flee, so his inducement to help you is your right leg."

Mitch stiffened, head dropping at the same time that his hands rose. The white across his knuckles showed in the pale light.

"I'm not the gutless asshole hiding behind scopes in the middle of the night."

Kenzie cringed.

"*Shut up*," she said in an angry whisper. To Lassiter, she said, "Is it a hard drive, a thumb drive, or what? And once I have it, where do I deliver it?" She hoped her voice sounded more professional than she felt. She fought to keep her teeth from chattering and one fist in a tight ball while the other had to be cutting off circulation to Mitch's fingers from the death grip on his forearm.

"You will have to discover the media yourself, as my information does not extend to that. Do not take that to mean that you can substitute a forgery for the item, though. I will have an expert to inspect the delivery to ensure that it conforms to my expectations. As for the point of delivery, I will have instructions sent to you when I receive confirmation from you."

"How?"

"In the parking lot, you will find a container holding two disposable cell phones secured within a Faraday bag."

Kenzie felt Mitch stiffen. The silver-haired bandit in front of them saw it, too.

"Precisely, Mr. Merriwether. While in this specialized bag, the phones are 'invisible' to routine surveillance. There is a second Faraday bag in the box for the device, which you are to use to deliver the item on the assumption that your mother would not be so foolish as to not have a GPS tracker attached.

"When you have the media for me, you, Miss Graham, will remove and turn on one phone from the first bag. It does not matter which. A text will arrive within three minutes to give you the time of the exchange. Dispose of the phone in the trash receptacle immediately across the street from your home, by the lake.

"Two hours prior to the assigned time, you will turn on the second phone for a text with instructions on where the exchange will be."

Kenzie felt a surge of hope. Her father could investigate the cell phones—

"Do not involve your father in this transaction. Any attempt by the Seattle Police Department to identify me through the purchase of the phones, or similar investigative efforts to locate me, will result in the immediate forfeiture of Mr. Jackson's life." Lassiter paused for emphasis. "Trust me, I will know, and I will have Mr. Jackson removed. Are we clear?"

Kenzie scrambled to find a gap that she could exploit.

"Miss Graham, are we clear?"

"How am I going to get out with only a couple of hours of notice?"

"I expect that you will need to be creative. Perhaps Mr. Merriwether can help, as he's demonstrated a certain proclivity for such things."

"Can I join her at the meeting?" Mitch said, rushing to add, "Not that I don't trust you or anything."

Lassiter considered it. He gave Mitch an infinitesimal nod. "You may. In fact, I insist. I'm afraid that left on your own, you might convince yourself to be a hero, and that would be quite a shame for Miss Graham."

He returned his gaze to Kenzie. "Now, I believe that concludes our business, does it not, Miss Graham?"

Kenzie, chest tight, thought of Jackson and his innocent family, and whispered, "Yes."

"Excellent." Lassiter half-turned, paused. "In ten minutes, the laser lights will be turned off. That will be your signal that it is safe to leave. Take a step before then, and I will regretfully need to find new business partners."

Two statues watched as he left the park.

CHAPTER THIRTY

Crimson trickled down to Mitch's wrist from the nasty gash on the middle knuckle of his right fist; he could think now.

It would have been nice to have destroyed Lassiter instead of leaving a gaping hole in the garage wall. The dust he'd knocked loose in the violent attack to the helpless drywall threatened to make him sneeze, so he put his left forefinger under his nose and pressed to discourage it.

The rage had built over ten excruciating minutes. The minutes crept by as tears, one at a time, dropped down Kenzie's cheeks. She kept saying "I'm sorry" and Mitch kept telling her it wasn't her fault.

She knew that, he knew that; not that it mattered. They believed Lassiter that the clock had started on Jackson, and him.

A plan, some way out, seemed impossible.

He had escorted Kenzie home, head on a swivel looking for any new threats. Silent, both of them walked and thought. He didn't kiss her good-bye. Instead, he gave her a leg up onto the brick wall. His breath caught in his throat when she wobbled, jumping back onto the roof, and he exhaled only when she reached her window safely. Once she was inside, Mitch had sprinted for the Camaro and roared into the night, his vision tinged red at the edges.

The urge to pummel something, someone, Lassiter, overwhelmed him. Mitch held it together until he sneaked into the garage. Then he exploded, punching the wall with every ounce of force he could muster.

That release of adrenaline jump-started his brain.

Lassiter had all the advantages, including the biggest one: a willingness to destroy lives to get what he wanted.

Wrong.

The analytical part of Mitch flagged his assumption, manipulated it, and recognized the falsity. Lassiter had advantages, huge ones, but one, no, two weaknesses. First, he didn't have the device, whatever the stupid thing was. Two, he was playing chess.

Mitch smiled, a grim-faced thing that would have scared the crap out of Kenzie if she had seen it.

Yes, Lassiter was playing chess, and he stood ready to capture a pawn named Jackson and remove him from the board. What, thought Mitch, would happen if he pulled him from the board first?

An innocuous brown paper bag sat on the workbench, covered with particles of white gypsum board. They'd found it right where the asshole said it would be, smack dab in the middle of the parking lot. Kenzie insisted that she needed to take it with her.

All Mitch did was ask one question: *What happens when your dad finds it?*

She'd deflated, and the mean streak he faked to keep everybody else away faltered, and he almost gave in. That he'd guessed right, that she knew her dad would spy on her, tore at his heart. It wasn't like he had a whole a lot more privacy, but he carved out space for himself. Score one for being a pain in the ass.

You ever think about running away?

Until tonight, never.

Now he'd reconsider, if she'd run away with him.

But first, they needed to defuse Lassiter, and do it without getting Jackson dead. The SOB shouldn't be allowed to screw with people like that.

In the dark of the garage, with the smell of old oil in the air, the rudiments of a plan coalesced, pieces dropping one by one into place. He didn't know where everything would fit, didn't need to yet, but at least he could see a way forward. Same as basketball, attack, attack, always attack, get inside the other guy's head, stay unpredictable, never give him a second to catch up.

Lassiter wanted to play chess, and he had them in check, three moves from mate.

Fine, thought Mitch. *Hate chess anyway, so screw it.*

Let's see how well he plays a different game.

Calvin-ball.

Mitch fished his phone from his pocket. He turned to the sooty window at the end of the garage. Punching numbers into the glowing screen, he faced his reflection. A chill crept down his spine as he recognized his father in the reflection, the same fracking crazed look in the eyes, the blood dripping darkly from the torn skin on his hand.

Not the same, he swore. This time things would be different.

A sleepy voice answered on the third ring with an unintelligible mumble.

He met his reflection's accusatory stare, rock-steady and determined. The reflection looked like a wild man.

When he spoke, the man in the glass provided the words.

"How good are you at kidnapping people?"

CHAPTER THIRTY-ONE

Sweat broke out on Kenzie's temples as the warding spell slipped away from her control. Breathing suspended, she fought to keep the recalcitrant magic from alerting her father. Trembling, she steadied the wayward flow by canceling stray vibrations in the pattern. She exhaled softly.

She prised the screen out of the channel and, placing her fingertips onto the white vinyl of the window frame at the middle, slid it sideways an inch, enough to open a gap at the side jamb. She wrapped her fingers around the open edge and pulled in one strong motion to finish opening it. She climbed through, catching a heel in her haste. She freed the foot and got both feet on the floor.

Once inside, she worked efficiently to reset the screen, let the ward slip back, and then close the window. Only then, willpower spent, did she let the accumulated reaction overwhelm her.

She dropped to the floor like a piece of origami falling and unfolding simultaneously. As her knees hit the carpeted floor, she refolded into a compact shape with her arms crossed and hands, still shaking, clasping the tight muscle at the back of her arms. She rocked herself side to side even while her mind sought an opening, some way to protect Mitch—and Jackson, she reminded herself—without giving in to Lassiter.

Kenzie's chest rose and fell, picking up frequency. She recognized the symptoms, less intense than after the kidnapping attempt, and forced herself to her feet. The action wetted her cheeks again, the luminous moonbeams refracting in the threatening tears.

No crying like a little girl, she ordered herself. *Think.*

She wiped her face with a hand. The tears stayed in her ducts, and her hand erased the gritty salt tracks left behind on her cheeks.

Poor Mitch.

Mitch had kept grunting "It's not your fault" every time she apologized. The more he said it, the worse she felt. All he had tried to do was help her. Each iteration also brought greater concern as she listened to his voice, and heard the rage emerging from the depths where he kept it buried, bound tightly by the pain she had felt the first time she'd touched him.

The casual violence promised for Mitch and Jackson, using her like a pawn, to the point of even coldly stating that they were all pieces on a board in a game Lassiter controlled, infuriated her. Kenzie felt the touch of that fire, now that she was safe. It grew hotter, until there was an acrid taste in the back of her throat and brimstone in her nose.

She sensed the potential in the emotion, the intensity that she could access, now that she didn't need it. For a moment, she was tempted to seize it, to prove that she could. Kenzie gave in to the feeling. She drew it to her, to touch, not to hold. The potency filled her senses, the color of the anger a deep, ruby claret, while the burning brimstone took on the sweetness of wine. The touch built, lapped over the wall of her resistance, and Kenzie absorbed it like a parched woman who drank deeply on a life-saving draught. On the tip of her tongue a word sprang, full of malevolence, strange syllables readying themselves to terrorize Lassiter, if only she could find him.

If she could harness it when the time came and not freeze.

It was the mirror that saved her before she surrendered into the bleakness of the poisonous fire. The image of herself, lit from within, with ruddy flames upon her hands, and hair lifted like a banshee in an ancient picture, glowed from the reflective surface.

She choked, and the shock dropped her to the floor.

Desperately, she released the bloodred rage, let it spill away. From the vision that came from her mind, it seemed to slither, slink away, as though it were a spurned lover leaving, reluctant and truculent at the same time.

Kenzie fell back against her bed, shaken. Inside, she was sapped, without the energy to lift herself from the floor. Arm leaden, she pulled her quilt from the bed. Her pillow rode with it and fell against her.

Wearily, she wrapped the comforting material around her, the astrological patterns a familiar touchstone. Kenzie arranged her pillow and lay against it, gazing up at the mirror, half-fearing the menace would return. A shudder wracked her, and she clenched the soft fabric tight to her body. The vertebrae in her back pressed on the metal rail of the bed frame, so she shifted deeper into the comforter and pillow.

Her thoughts turned slower, shifting as each priority strove for supremacy. She ached to save Mitch, save Jackson. This was replaced with a repugnant need to find the abominable device that Lassiter demanded. Briefly, she thought to save herself, but that gave way to a longing to protect her magic, her Family. Despite herself, she drifted into a half sleep.

Just before she lost consciousness, it occurred to her that she should talk to Harold. The last thought she had as the darkness completely closed in was that she'd dispatch Lassiter to hell before she'd let him hurt Mitch. She knew the way now.

CHAPTER THIRTY-TWO

"Answer the damn phone already," said Mitch, as the ringing dragged on. When the recognizable click of the voice mail answering system resonated in his ear, Mitch hung up. Again.

Disgusted at the limitations of technology when he needed it *right this second*, he shifted his attention to a storefront that contained a museum. As best he could figure based on drive-bys, it appeared and disappeared on alternating Saturdays, the third Thursday of every month, and the twelfth of fricking never. Today, the door sat dark, with a "Closed" sign visible, resting cockeyed behind the grimy safety glass that reminded him of juvie.

Mitch had rolled out of the sack at dawn and had smacked his hand on the dresser, resulting in a slew of bad words and a hand that throbbed and hurt like hell. Exhausted by a brain that refused to shut down, he had thrashed in his bed, the sheets tangled and his pillow on the floor. Fading nightmares of Kenzie bleeding out from a hideous wound mixed with ruminations of plans, counterplans, schemes, and an overpowering desire to inflict pain on Lassiter, disturbed his rest.

I hope Kenzie did better, he thought, but doubted it.

He had dressed in the dim light, ears attuned to the sounds of wheezy breathing that came from the room next door. Much better than the nights when he could hear the bedsprings complaining and the headboard hitting the wall.

Why, why, why do old people do stuff like that?

He had sniffed a shirt, decided it would do, and donned it. Grabbed at socks, shoes, wallet, and gotten out of the house before anyone woke to stop him.

Now he stood on the deserted street, staring at the museum. Odors from the dumpsters next to the restaurants added a sour wrinkle to the damp morning air. A scratching sound caught his attention. Behind him, a mottled gray-brown rat quivered, beady eyes staring unblinkingly at him. It was joined by a larger rat. They watched him like they were waiting for him to turn his back again before rushing him.

A shiver of revulsion coursed through his body and he stepped out onto the street. A prickly feeling at the base of his neck made him cast a glance over his shoulder at the vermin.

Once across the street, Mitch banged on the door with his left hand, rattling the glass.

He wiped at the pane, cleaning off the particulate left by the city air. He peered in. The space inside stayed dark. He scanned up and down the street.

"Mercury, open up, man," he yelled at the building. He hammered the door again with the bottom of his fist. Inside, the sign jumped and fell with a clatter audible through the thin glass.

"Mercury!"

A light blossomed at the far end of the interior space. Mitch breathed out a sigh of relief. A figure approached, dressed in gray sweats, a large purple W on the chest. A clack from the door handle and the door swung open.

"You could have just walked in, you know," said Mercury. His hair stood in clumps, and his bushy brows crawled together.

"No, I didn't know," said Mitch. "Why would I?"

Mitch's mind boggled at the purple W and tried to reconcile the Mercury he knew with a U-Dub fan. He expected the old wizard to be, well, wizard-like. Magical people should be different, he thought, then tried to reconcile that idea with Kenzie. And Hunter. He'd thought both were pretty normal until this week.

Mercury shook the door. "Come in or get out," he said, and shambled away, leaving the door standing ajar.

Mitch followed him in and swung the door shut, plunging the room into gloomy darkness. For an old man, the wizard moved fast. He was already out of sight. Mitch walked around the display cases toward the sole source of light coming from Mercury's weird garden room.

He halted at the door.

Mercury stood in front of him, a pair of speckled brown stoneware mugs in hand. Around him, the room had changed from a brightly lit garden room to a library. The windows still opened to a wild profusion of vegetation but the interior now resembled a bibliophile's dream, old books—they all seemed to carry a weight of years on their leather spines—lining shelves on two walls. Two high-backed armchairs of worn brown leather and dark wood lined the third wall. Between them sat a matching table with a Tiffany lamp burning.

"Want some tea?" asked Mercury.

Mitch shook his head. "Got coffee?"

"Heathen pup," muttered the wizard without a trace of animosity. He held out one of the mugs.

Mitch wrapped his hands around the mug, and the warmth permeated through to the damaged skin on his knuckles.

"Come, sit down," instructed Mercury, "and tell me why in the world you want to kidnap someone."

Mitch took a sip of coffee and grimaced. Bitter as wood chips mixed with month-old grounds that had soaked for a week.

"Crap, this stuff is terrible," Mitch said, wiping his tongue on his upper teeth.

"No refunds." Mercury pointed to the left-hand chair. "Sit. Talk." As an afterthought, he added, "Please."

Mitch sat, and recounted the threats Lassiter had made, leaving out the reason they were made. He failed to keep the anger out of his voice when he described the businessman's promise to destroy Kenzie's femur but glossed over the threat to himself. When he got to the point where he needed Mercury's help, he stood and paced, coffee mug forgotten on the table.

"So the jerk thinks he has the initiative. Until we break that, he's got all the control. You asked me to help Kenzie, you didn't say to sacrifice somebody else, so we need to get Jackson out of the way."

Mercury sat brooding over his tea. He pursed his lips and spoke. "So the kidnapping is solely to remove Mr. Jackson from harm. You understand that this Mr. Lassiter will simply accelerate the time schedule for your demise."

"I think he wants to kill me anyway. I can't see any reason he needs me alive after he gets what he wants."

Energetic eyes peered from under the bushy eyebrows, and Mitch had the impression that the wizard was weighing his next words, sorting through the options until he settled on one.

"So what does Mr. Lassiter want?"

Mitch had rehearsed lies, but under the penetrating stare of Mercury, he resorted to the truth.

"A memory-storage device, as near as I can tell. I don't think he really knows what it is or where it is, so he's using people around Kenzie as targets to get her to do what he wants." Mitch paused, phrasing the next part as a question. "Do you know why he would use me and Jackson as blackmail instead of her parents?"

A filter dropped behind the wizard's eyes, and Mitch prepared himself to be lied to.

Mercury surprised him by speaking the truth. "Because I think she cares more for you."

Mercury spread his hands. "It's not relevant now. I can help you with Mr. Jackson and with his family. We can't very well remove him without also protecting his wife and children."

Mitch mentally kicked himself. "Yeah, okay," he acknowledged. "When does the exchange take place?"

"When Kenzie finds the thing, she's supposed to contact him. Lassiter, I mean."

Mercury shifted his attention up to the right and a thoughtful expression settled on his features.

"Yes, we'll have to work on the time, but I can help you." He gave Mitch a hard stare. "Do you have a plan for keeping yourself safe?"

"I'm working on it," said Mitch. He bore Mercury's scrutiny by avoiding the wizard and gazing at the tropical scene out the window. He saw an unfamiliar bird land on a branch of a large-leafed tree. The branch sagged under the weight of the bird, which looked about a foot tall. Resplendent with a rosy chest, blue-purple feathers on the nape, and emerald green wings, it stared back at him over a beak that curved downward as if in disapproval.

"It's a red-and-blue lory," said Mercury. "Quite endangered."

"Do you collect them?"

A sad silence filled the room. Finally, Mercury answered him.

"No," he said in soft tones, "I give them some space and time to find their destiny. There are fewer than five thousand left now. Saving them is more than I can do, any more than I can reanimate a dead person."

The bird cocked its head to the side and Mitch imitated it. "No zombies to worry about, then?"

"We have enough to concern ourselves with as it is."

Mitch's phone vibrated against his thigh He slipped it from his pocket in an automatic response. He checked the screen, saw an incoming message from the house, and killed the call. He glanced up to see the wizard considering his next words.

"If I am to help you, I need the details, Mitch. All of them, anything that may affect McKenzie."

"Yeah, I've pretty much covered it."

Mitch watched a fleeting expression of weariness come and vanish from the wizard's craggy visage.

"What I don't know can get you killed."

Mitch laughed without even a trace of humor. "Take a number. Lassiter seems pretty intent on wiping out anybody around Kenzie."

"True, and we will find ways to handle Mr. Lassiter. He is not the first mortal to try to harness us. Most should count themselves lucky to live to regret it. The Families," he said, his green eyes turning to sea ice, "have suffered persecution, seen their members burned and drowned. Some think the time has come to remove the threat the mass of humanity, blind as it is, represents. As cold as you may consider me or Raymond Graham, we are the least dangerous to you. There are those that would extinguish your life in a moment if they were aware that you suspected that they existed."

The words hung in the air like ice crystals, glittering and dangerous.

The chill reached into Mitch's stomach. The old codger knew something.

Hunter?

Should he tell him?

No, he decided. *Not yet.*

"So is that a threat?" he asked, brows pinched.

"A warning, to the wise."

Mitch's phone went off again, but he ignored it this time. He needed to meet up with Kenzie somehow, and then bust his butt to get over to the school.

"I got to go. You can handle Jackson? When we're ready?"

Mercury looked suddenly ancient. "I can," he assured Mitch. A sigh slipped out after the words, though.

Mitch managed an embarrassed shrug. "Thanks."

He headed for the door, aware of the pressure of the wizard's gaze pushing between his shoulder blades.

"Mitch," the man called out.

Mitch turned at the doorway.

Mercury was standing. He lifted a forefinger, pointing at Mitch.

"Look at your hand."

Mitch glanced down. The knuckles had fine white scars, and the swelling was gone. He met Mercury's glare.

"I can't heal dead. Be careful."

Mitch nodded and left. He flexed his fingers and closed them into a tight fist.

Knowing wizards had some advantages, he thought. Except for the part where he might end up "unhealable."

CHAPTER THIRTY-THREE

Kenzie woke clutching at the top of the pillow while her legs entwined themselves around the bottom. She looked past the open curtains to the rays of the sun walking up the trunks of the trees behind the house, a pure, rich light that lied about the birth of a beautiful day.

Dismaying thoughts reemerged with her from the abyss of sleep, a fitful rest that had finally come when she hit mental exhaustion. She left her head on the pillow for a minute longer, considering and discarding a slew of ideas in rapid succession.

Find the device, Lassiter had said, and deliver it. All will be well.

Big fat liar.

It didn't take a genius to figure it out, especially for a girl whose father worked as a detective during the business day and led the security council for the Family the rest of the time. Jackson might be safe since he didn't know anything, but Lassiter had stamped an expiration date onto Mitch as surely as if he'd tattooed it into his skin.

The dummy would ignore it—he was too bright not to realize the smooth criminal's intent, too—to help her.

Guilt finally motivated her to get off the floor.

Kenzie's right shoulder and hip ached from sleeping on the floor, and her back felt bruised from the bed rail. She staggered over to the door, put a hand on it, and paused.

She still wore her clothes from last night.

Working fast, she stripped down, slipped on a pair of pajamas. Though the room was comfortably warm, she put on her bathrobe to hide the lack of wrinkles on the pjs. She pulled the hairband off her ponytail and gave her head a gentle shake. She faced the mirror over her dresser. The unconstrained mass of hair lent a wild look that matched the hunted stare that reflected back.

She tried to smile, but her visage in the glass grimaced like a woman who had eaten one prune too many.

She practiced, making sure to relax the rest of her face. The face in the mirror fell short of sincere.

Got to avoid Father, she thought. *Mother's pretty oblivious, but not him.*

The lower half of the house was silent as Kenzie padded down barefoot to the bottom landing. A stray beam of morning sun blazed a path across the floor and made the rest seem darker.

Crud. She was the first one up. Now what?

She dithered for a second at the foot of the stairs, torn between the urge to retreat to her room and the pressure to *do* something useful.

With a sigh, she went to the kitchen.

In the early morning, with the recessed lights off, the wood and marble took on a sterile aspect, highlighted by the stainless steel appliances. The floor radiated cold through the soles of her feet. She should have put on her slippers. Kenzie curled her toes under as she made a pot of coffee.

While it brewed, she pulled her mug from the artsy stand next to the coffeemaker. She fetched cream from the fridge and organic cane sugar from the cabinet. She spooned one overflowing heap of the golden granules into her mug and added a large dollop of the thick liquid. The aroma of brewing coffee surrounded her, and she inhaled, savoring the sensation.

Impending doom took a step backward, and she realized that simple actions, like making coffee, created space for her mind to process. The drip of the coffee ended with a gurgle, the loudest sound in the house. She poured, making sure not to spill.

She pulled a spoon from the drawer to stir and left it in the mug when she turned to go to the breakfast nook. She put her coffee on the table so she could open the blinds. The sunlight would have been better in the front of the home, almost blinding at this time of the morning. Instead, she saw the backyard, the same trees she could see from her bedroom window. The whole hillside glowed as the day came alive. She slid the window open to smell the fresh air, perfumed by the shrubs and flowers of the neighborhood.

Without looking, Kenzie picked up the mug and held it tight with both hands. She sipped, the sweetness of the sugar spreading from the tip of her tongue to fill her mouth. The flavor of the coffee emerged at the back of her mouth.

A depressing thought emerged from the mélange of ideas that presented themselves for inspection. Without Jackson or her parents, she couldn't leave the house. Jackson didn't work weekends, and she wanted him as far from her, and Lassiter, as possible, anyway.

The house seemed much smaller than normal.

Circling high above the trees, a red-tailed hawk screeched. It scrolled through the heavens, already searching for prey. A turn on the currents brought it closer.

She brought her eyelids down and pictured herself in the place of the hawk, imagined the freedom to fly away on the wind. She took a tremulous breath and let the feeling go.

A spark of red and blue dancing across the rhodies in the yard caught her eye. A bird, much too large and tropical to be native, fluttered and settled on a shrub bespeckled with pink blossoms, seeking nourishment. It flashed into full sun, the colors popping, the red vivid, the blue taking on an iridescent sheen, the green wings.

A raspy scream from the raptor above made Kenzie look up. She sensed the predatory change in the hawk as it shifted a wing to alter its trajectory toward her. The glide took on an eager purpose, the intensity of the hunt.

A wave of sadness gripped Kenzie, and she put the coffee mug on the sill. Lifting her hand, she repeated the motions that Harold taught the class, and said, *"Anemosa."*

She imbued the air spell with sufficient power to build an upswell of air that captured the hawk and lifted it away. Kenzie held it until the bird of prey had risen hundreds of feet vertically and drifted away to vanish behind the trees.

She released the spell and looked for the bright plumage, but the tropical beauty had left. Kenzie hoped it had sense enough to avoid the hawk. In the meantime, Kenzie knew what she had to do.

Kenzie was still standing at the window when her mother came downstairs. She could tell it was her mother by the weight of the footfalls and the air of frostiness that entered the kitchen with her.

"Mother," she lied without turning, "I owe you an apology. And Aric, too. I should not have lost control like that."

"Indeed."

Kenzie pressed her lips together but kept her annoyance hidden. Her mother never compromised, not in the office, not at the Glade, not at home.

"Aric is not the one."

She heard the sound of coffee being poured. A stalling tactic.

"All right, then we will find you another suitor."

Like hell you will!

She maintained her composure despite her shock at the blatant disrespect from her mother and the immediacy of the defiance it triggered.

Stick to the plan.

"I would like to get in some time at the studio this morning, please. It's Jackson's day off, so either you or Father would need to drive me. Jules can act as bodyguard while I'm there, and I won't leave until one of you arrive to take me home."

She heard her mother sip at the coffee. "Hmm, good," her mother said.

Kenzie stood stoically watching bees flitting through the irises. She could feel the burn of her mother's gaze on the back of her head.

Her mother sighed. "What time is the class and how long do you think you'll be?"

"It starts at nine and lasts a couple of hours."

"We'll make the arrangements." Another sip. "To be clear, there will never be a repeat of your behavior last night, McKenzie."

"Yes, ma'am," said Kenzie. The lie rolled off her tongue easily. "Last night will not happen again."

I'll make sure of it.

CHAPTER THIRTY-FOUR

Mitch's stomach turned queasy, and he could taste acid at the back of his throat. Mitch didn't believe it was possible, but the Rubiera clan had no internet footprint at all. He tried to think of another series of searches and came up blank.

Mitch had left Mercury's place and driven around, finally settling in at the coffee and yogurt shop next to Kenzie's studio, more because it was familiar than for anything else. He got a cup of strong dark-roast coffee to wash out the taste of Mercury's swill. Hunter still hadn't called back, so Mitch decided he would force the issue by pounding on the Rubieras' door until the jerk answered. Which would work, except he had no clue where Hunter lived.

Now, staring at the screen on his phone, he wondered how he managed to know nothing real about Hunter. The Rubiera name didn't come up in any searches. No phone numbers, no addresses, no social media. Mitch resorted to the results from the basketball season to prove that Hunter existed.

Hunter's name was missing from the box scores.

Online was forever, except for Hunter. He found a Rubiera commune in Italy on Wikipedia, records of a Spanish family that emigrated at a genealogy site, and a former Tour de France cyclist, but nothing in Seattle.

It took some mad webfu skills to disappear someone digitally.

Mitch took a sip from his cup while his stomach grumbled, and tried to fit the new information into the pattern. Something niggled, but he knew enough not to force it.

Out in the parking lot, a stream of cars dropped off youngsters dressed in white karate outfits. Maybe ten or eleven years old, a mix of girls and boys, most walking like they'd rather be any place but practice on a Saturday morning. A gleaming black Mercedes pulled up.

Crud!

Cursing his ever-present rotten luck, he slipped down low in the bench seat. The features of the man speaking through the open passenger door to Kenzie were indistinct, but he had no trouble making out the dour face of Lieutenant Graham of the SPD. Kenzie nodded once and swung the door shut. She crossed behind the automobile. Only when she was inside did the sedan pull away and Mitch start breathing again.

Mitch stood, coffee forgotten.

Across the parking lot, an Audi pulled in and parked. Jackson, dressed in the red polo and khakis that he wore almost like a uniform, got out. The bodyguard talked animatedly on a phone, checked both ways before crossing the main drag in front of the shops, but resembled the kids, as though he'd rather be someplace else this morning.

Mitch flopped back onto the plastic seat. The worry buffeting the inner recesses of his mind grabbed hold of the image of the phone in Jackson's hand. His mind strayed to his phone, the implications of Faraday bags stashed at his house, and the synapses closed. His shoulders slumped at his stupidity.

He knew how Lassiter had found them.

Their phones, more likely Kenzie's phone. Lassiter and his organization traced the phones and knew when she strayed from the house. They'd been waiting for the opportunity, and he had led Kenzie right to them by encouraging her to leave the safety of her house. It was a wonder that her father hadn't done the same thing.

Their cell phones were a humongous liability.

How much info can they hack from them? he wondered. A wave of light-headedness engulfed him.

Do they know about Mercury? Hunter?

Mercury was a cagey old guy and had already proven smart enough to avoid Graham. No way to check on Hunter now. He picked up his phone, pried the cover off, and was about to remove the battery when another idea hit him. Fingertips on the edge of the battery and his head down, he delved deep in his own thoughts.

No, leave it. If he pulled the battery, killed the phone, they might figure out they had lost an advantage. Take it away later, when it would matter. Carefully, he snapped the components back into place.

He pressed his fingertips to his forehead and rubbed. What now?

He needed to be able to talk to Kenzie, and the phones weren't safe. If they weren't, neither was the internet, or landlines, probably. He might be able to hide in the dark web, the hidden places where hackers, drug dealers, and investigative reporters lived. In the hidden bowels of the internet, people worked at nefarious and noble endeavors, protected from exposure.

No bueno. Kenzie probably didn't know how to get there.

Frustration grew as he recognized that every avenue of communications could be corrupted.

He snorted in disgust.

Might as well try radio messages in code, or smoke signals, that's what they did in ancient times.

Only one other possibility seemed likely to be safe.

Talking face-to-face.

Which was fine with him. He liked Kenzie's face, and it lived behind his eyeballs all the time.

Mitch was pretty near certain it wouldn't be fine with Jackson. Or Kenzie's dad.

He huffed on the coffee to cool it, which it didn't need, while he thought. He slugged down a couple of gulps, tried to find another answer, and gave up.

He stood, leaving the half-finished coffee on the table, and left.

Kenzie had her back turned when he walked in. She stood hunched over, explaining how to tie the belt properly to a pair of nervous young white belts.

Jackson spotted him immediately, as did Jules. The bodyguard gave him a fast once-over, checking hands, pockets, waistband in a practiced examination to determine threat level. Jules gave him a noncommittal smile, though she flicked a look in Kenzie's direction. He sensed more than saw her shift her alert level.

Mitch strode with more confidence than he felt to the seating area. Butterflies multiplied in his stomach as he approached Jackson. He kept his hands open but avoided eye contact. He selected a seat one row in front of Jackson and to the man's left so that the bodyguard could maintain an uninterrupted view of Kenzie. The pressure of the man's gaze on his back made him itch between the shoulder blades. He shifted his attention to the padded floor in front and the mirror that lined the front wall. He glanced in the mirror, saw Jackson squinting at him in overt suspicion. Mitch switched his focus to the kids on the floor, most not even coming up to his waist.

At Jules's direction, the class came to order. Kenzie spotted him. He gave her a minuscule shake of his head at the questions expressed in her raised brows. She broke eye contact, lining up in the senior position in the rows of students. As Jules led the class into their warm-ups and the high-pitched shouts of the children counted the reps, Mitch shifted in his seat to speak past his right shoulder to Jackson.

"You know, sometimes you get caught up in crap bigger than you know," he said, keeping the volume down, "just by trying to do the right thing, like running out in the street to stop a pair of ugly goons with stun guns from abducting a pretty runner girl that you don't know from Adam. Natch, you get hammered for your trouble. Nobody, not the cops or your family or anyone else, believes a damn thing you say, but that's okay, too, because that girl turns out to be probably the best thing that's ever happened to you. And since that's only the start of her trouble, you stick around to help even when it rains hell on your head."

Mitch shut up and held his breath, waiting for Jackson's response. He watched Kenzie set herself, pivot, and kick high over her head. The snapping sound of the stiff cotton pants carried over the grunts of the other kids. Kenzie refolded the leg and dropped back into her stance, hands held ready.

"Any regrets?"

The question caught Mitch by surprise. He resisted the urge to look over his shoulder at Jackson.

"Not really."

A sigh greeted his observation. Mitch glanced at the mirror. Jackson kept up his roaming search. Briefly, their eyes met. Mitch clenched his fists in a reflexive gesture and then spread his fingers wide.

"You need my help," said Mitch. It sounded lame, even to him.

"Really?" replied the bodyguard. "Funny, I was trying to figure out the best way to get rid of you."

"Join the club. The last guy promised to shoot me."

Jackson's professional veneer cracked as his lips twisted into a wry grin, gone in a flash.

"Messy. There are better ways to handle teenage boys."

The undercurrents in Jackson's tone triggered a spark of recognition. The bodyguard looked at him as a threat as *Kenzie's boyfriend!*

"You didn't know McKenzie before the attack?" Jackson asked, redirecting the conversation.

Mitch shook his head. "Just saw what was going down and didn't think."

"Well, I need you to think now. My job is to keep that *pretty runner girl,* as you called her, safe. I don't need some kid at my elbow getting in the way, and if you cared about her—and I think you do—you'd figure that out and clear out until this whole adventure is resolved."

Mitch didn't answer. Jackson was right, except he didn't know the whole story and Mitch couldn't fill him in. As a boyfriend, he was in the way of the man's mission. As Kenzie's partner in crime, which stealing the device would make him, he needed to hang tight.

Neat box, he thought. *Now, how the heck do I get out of it?*

Play the boyfriend angle, he thought. He sat up and turned to face Jackson.

"I think they're tracking her cell phone," he said.

Jackson arrested his room scan, and his whole attention zeroed in on Mitch.

Mitch read the cold competence in the man's posture as he evaluated the information. This close to the man, he had no doubt as to how formidable the bodyguard was. He had a sudden vision of Jackson wearing battle paint, protecting the tribe and, before there were tribes, the family clan, in multiple iterations receding into history. Not a man to fool with.

Mitch hurried to explain his reasoning.

"Everybody carries phones now. The news is filled with stories on how the government tracks everybody, knows who you call, everything. If the government can do it, criminals can too. The technology is there if you know how to make use of it, and nobody ever thinks about it. We all carry phones with us everywhere. Heck, the phone companies advertise tracking apps for parents so they can keep tabs on their kids. If you wanted to find someone, you'd just need to find their phone."

"She was running when they attempted the kidnapping. No phone." Analytical and precise, Jackson looked for the holes in Mitch's argument.

"Part of a pattern," said Mitch. "She followed the same route she always did"—Did she? He didn't know, but it sounded right—"so they could predict when she'd hit the cul-de-sac. With a spotter at the top end . . ."

His voice tailed off. It made more sense that way, using a full team. Lassiter wouldn't have taken any chances. Mitch shrugged and picked up the thread of his thoughts, dancing as close to the truth as he dared.

"It wasn't a couple of guys, but a well-organized team with tech resources backing them up."

"Which is exactly why you need to walk away and let me do my job," said Jackson. His hard demeanor softened. "Look, I get it. You did a nice piece of analysis, but we have pros that have been managing these types of situations for years. We'll keep her safe, and her father will track down the perps, and the two of you can live happily ever after."

Mitch sagged in his seat as his effort to recruit Jackson foundered on the rocks of the man's professionalism. He looked for some wiggle room, a gap that would let him meet with Kenzie without arousing the ire of her bodyguard.

"May I meet Kenzie at the yogurt shop like we did this week? Or does Kenzie need to be isolated from everything while the cops try to catch the bad guys?"

He winced a little at the edge on the second question, unsure how the man would react. Still, he met Jackson's gaze.

"Don't test me, kid."

Jackson went into scan mode while Mitch waited. He swept the studio and then focused on Mitch.

"Okay, here's the deal. Only here, the shop next door, and her house. Schedule it, so I know what's going on. You follow all my instructions without any of your charming mouth. One surprise and I shut you down. Got it?"

"Yeah, that's fair."

"It's more than fair. One last thing. If hell breaks loose again, you forget your Sir-Galahad-to-the-rescue routine. You get in my way, and you're likely to get us all hurt."

"Deal," said Mitch, relieved.

He turned to watch Kenzie acting as an instructor, leading a group through their forms. She corrected one of the girls, a waif in white. The little girl must have said something, because Kenzie smiled.

Like clouds falling away from the sun to brighten the world, the smile radiated joy and transformed her face, and his heart ached.

Mitch wished he believed in happily ever after.

CHAPTER THIRTY-FIVE

The last session ended, and Kenzie tarried to put away the target pads while the other students filed out. The last exercise of the day had been simulated sparring on a four-inch-wide balance beam that stretched a dozen feet across the floor. The goal was to force opponents into upsetting their equilibrium with attacks aimed at misdirection rather than to knock them from the narrow platform by brute force.

Unobtrusively, Kenzie glanced at Mitch and Jackson. Both of them were watching her, Jackson as part of his usual I-spy-everything routine.

Her heart had sunk when Jackson walked in.

Of course they called him in, she thought. They were too occupied with their careers to give a flip about her.

When Mitch ambled into the studio and nonchalantly sat near Jackson, she'd frowned. Figuring out what went on in his head made her dizzy. Watching him sneak in a conversation with Jackson made her nervous.

Now Kenzie located Jules and sauntered in her direction, putting them both out of her mind for the moment.

Jules saw her coming. "Kenzie, give me a hand with the beam, please."

Kenzie altered course and went to the nearest end of the unwieldy piece of apparatus. Together, they lifted it and, with Kenzie walking backward, moved it to the storeroom. Kenzie maneuvered the beam into position and stood up.

Before she could take a step to leave, Jules caught her eye and spoke. "So, why are you here on a Saturday, as are both Mr. Jackson and Mitch?"

The woman towered over her, but not in a way that intimidated. Instead, Kenzie pictured the protective embrace of a mama bear standing between her cub and a hunter.

"I'm sorry about Jackson and Mitch," she said.

Jules interrupted her. "You're evading the question."

Kenzie dropped her chin. "I'm in trouble and—"

"What do you mean by trouble? You and Mitch together kind of trouble?"

Kenzie's head came up at the startled, faintly sad quality to Jules's words. They took a moment to process. When they did, Kenzie's face lit with a fire so hot that she thought the walls should be glowing cherry red.

"Boy . . . trouble . . . um, no-o-o," she stammered, "Mitch and I . . . haven't, I mean, aren't . . ."

She didn't finish, the necessity of denial tying her tongue even as the memory of the heat of his kiss sent a quiver through her. She shook her head as her fingers fidgeted with the thick hem at the bottom of her *dobok* jacket. Kenzie drew a deep breath. It failed to calm the flush on her face, or the twitchiness inside, but gave her air to talk with.

"Someone . . ." Kenzie's voice broke. She started over. "I thought hitting something would help."

"Well, it's probably better than hitting some*one*," said Jules, "not that I'm the one to offer premarital counseling."

Kenzie opened her mouth to protest again, but Jules pinned her with a shrewd glance, stopping the objections before they were uttered.

"It's not a Mitch problem, but he's out there looking like he hasn't slept in days, your Mr. Jackson seems perturbed, and you can't focus worth a darn. You say you're in trouble. Okay, what kind of trouble? Because the only reason I can see that you stuck around was to talk to me, and I can't give you any advice if I don't understand the question."

Kenzie shook her head at Jules's perceptiveness, and in the same elongated instant, understood that she could endanger the black belt by telling her the full truth.

She met the black woman's eyes with an unflinching gaze of her own.

"The trouble isn't with Mitch." The words fell from her mouth the same way they had last night, as though she had become an imitation of her mother. "Someone has asked me to do something that violates . . ." She fought for the right phrasing. ". . . my principles, and placed me into a position where I have to choose who gets hurt."

Jules rocked back a bit. Her voice felt soft as velvet on Kenzie's ears. "Well, look at who got all growed-up all of a sudden."

The drop into vernacular unsettled her. The gentle praise— *Was it praise?*

She searched Jules for mockery, saw sympathy. Shaking her head, Kenzie answered, "I wish I was. What do you do when you're forced to choose between two things, both bad?"

"Search for the third one," came the swift reply. "When we study ground fighting, what do we do? Especially you, tiny as you are?"

"Redirect your opponent's energy," replied Kenzie. "But I know how that works on the mats."

"The art isn't a way to fight, you know. Most of the arts end in –*do*, which means 'the way.' The discipline that you learn on the training floor translates to the manner in which you live your life. The physical component, which, unfortunately, is what most people see at the movies, is the smallest part. As your instructor, my goal has been to first teach you to use your body as a tool so that you can learn to use your mind and *chi*—your spirit, if you will—in harmony."

"I don't see how that helps," Kenzie said.

"Right now, it won't. Maybe it won't ever," said Jules, "but I think that you have a chance to reach real enlightenment and, if you do, the understanding will follow. It's up to you to reach for that future."

Chills marched along Kenzie's spine as a vision of a competing alternative to her mother's plans manifested itself. A yearning for freedom, from the Family and the unwritten sacraments her mother enforced, pushed its way forward.

She shivered and responded, "It's not that easy."

"I never, *ever*, promised easy, did I?"

"People can get . . . hurt." Kenzie internally recoiled from the obfuscation. *Dead is way past hurt.*

"Then look for the places where you have control. You have some, or you wouldn't be facing a dilemma. Exert that control."

"Redirect."

Jules nodded. "As much as you can. Somewhere in there is your answer, if there truly is one, because that's another lesson: understanding we have no control over others, only ourselves."

Kenzie let out a long sigh.

"One more thing, Kenzie," said Jules.

Kenzie glanced to Jules's face. The serious expression remained, but it was leavened by an amused twinkle.

"Boys lie." Jules's smile softened the accusation.

"Not this one."

She decided against changing into regular clothes. She untied the red belt from her waist and stripped off the jacket. She stuffed them into her gear bag and walked barefoot toward the waiting men.

"Is it okay if we go next door?" Kenzie asked Jackson as she approached, forestalling Mitch. She sat to slip on sandals.

Jackson took his time replying. "Are you two going to tell me what's going on?"

Kenzie shot a glance filled with questions at Mitch, but he maintained a sphinxlike impassivity.

"I thought you had today off," she said, to deflect his question.

"When duty calls, you answer," said Jackson.

Kenzie stood up with her bag slung over her right shoulder. "I'm sorry. If I had known that my parents were going to make you babysit me, I'd have stayed home."

Jackson smiled ruefully. "Too late, and it's not your fault."

Mitch stood. "Coffee?"

"Food," said Kenzie. "I'm starving."

Ten minutes later, Mitch had a cup of coffee in front of him while Kenzie worried at a large white chocolate yogurt, toying with the cashews and blueberries she had added as the toppings. Mitch had selected their table. Their backs were to a wall. He looked like heck, she thought as she watched his head swivel, taking in every detail.

Jackson sat at a table a discreet distance away. Kenzie noted that he was positioned between her and the door, with his back to a wall, too.

"Crud," Kenzie said, and spooned another bite into her mouth. She contemplated using a spell on Jackson, but a sense of revulsion at using the magic with the same casualness that Lassiter used fear changed her mind. Instead, she lowered her voice. "I didn't sleep."

"Yeah," said Mitch, "me neither, but I think I've got the beginnings of a plan."

"We don't need a plan. I've got to find that memory storage, and Lassiter didn't give me anything to work with. Until I do, I've got to put everything into figuring out where my precious mother would hide something that people would kill for. It could be hidden anywhere, the office, our house, the—" Kenzie stopped herself before she revealed the existence of the Glade. "If it's at the office, we're in big trouble, because I can't get in there."

Mitch leaned toward her to say something, and then stopped cold, his gaze disassociating and drifting into the distance. It snapped back to her face. "How did he know that it isn't at your mother's office?" he asked, staring at her intently.

"He can't—"

"He's got to, otherwise it makes no sense to go after you. He'd nail someone with access."

She watched the intensity of his gaze ramp up and the corner of his left eye pinch down into wrinkles as another idea hit. His ability to seize data points and race ahead made her feel incompetent. A budding anger toward him glowed.

"How did he even know about the chip or disk or whatever?" And, then another question, ripping fast behind the last one. "And what's on it that's so damned important?"

Kenzie blinked. She should have thought of those questions, but the immediacy of the threats against them all had kept her locked in on protecting them. She watched as Mitch's fingers on the right hand tapped on the tabletop like he was playing a snare drum. She noticed that he only used the first three fingers on his right hand, and recognized the irrelevance of the observation.

"Is it related to, well, you know?"

"Would you stop for a second and let me think?" Kenzie said. The volume of her voice got Jackson's attention—from the corner of her eye, she saw his head swivel their way.

Mitch went back to work the tabletop with his fingers. He used the other hand to lift the coffee. The surface rippled and betrayed a tremor. The *tap, tap, tap, pause* sounded like a three-legged horse.

"Stop that."

"Sorry," Mitch said. "Thinking." He folded the offending hand into a fist and then relaxed it.

Kenzie scowled, analyzing the situation. *Mitch is right,* she decided, *it must not be at the office.* The implications of the leaked information getting to Lassiter scared her. Someone at the company had to have sold them out. The only project of any note that she knew of was Aric's. Words from dinner last night played back. "*. . . create electronics that could not only detect energy . . .*"

An ominous dread overcame her as she recalled how casually the well-dressed snake had directed her to stop using magic. Twice, he knew when she tried to use magic, even the second time when she hadn't made any physical moves to give herself away. *They already have a detector, and now they want the rest.* Her mind recoiled at the idea of Lassiter grasping after the invention, and what he might do with it. The memory device must contain the full details of the amplifier. She knew her mother was cautious enough to have backups for everything, and maintaining her own private copy should anything go amiss would fit with her untrusting nature.

She wondered how much of this she should tell Mitch. Breaching the secrecy of the Family, even indirectly, would lead to swift and terrible punishments.

"We have to give him something else." It came out in a whisper, like doing otherwise would be a blasphemy.

"He's not going to be fooled. He'll have experts check out the schematics. . . ."

"How do you know they're schematics?" asked Kenzie, staring at him. She expected to find some type of drive with plans for the amplifier. How much did Mitch know or guess? She racked her brain. She was certain she'd never mentioned the device, or anything like it, to him.

He avoided her eyes when he answered. "Your mom works at an electronics outfit. What else would be on there?"

Mollified, Kenzie nodded. "We can't give him what he wants. We have to find a way to delay things until we can get help."

"No way. We do that and Lassiter will do exactly what he said. He's a bully in a suit who's never been knocked on his ass. We gotta find the data he wants, give it to him, and then kick his teeth in. He's not going to come out of hiding without the real deal sitting within his reach," Mitch said. He was staring at her now, and the intensity of his gaze made her blink.

He wants to take him head on, she thought. Anger at Mitch's suicidal surety in his ability to defeat the businessman roared to life, fed by a combination of loathing for Lassiter and the conflict between selling out the Family and the dread of losing Mitch. Just like last night, he wouldn't—couldn't—back down.

Mitch mistook her silence for agreement. "We need to move quickly and force him into mistakes. There's a couple of ways that we can do it. I think the best is to—"

"Would you shut up and listen!"

His head snapped back. Kenzie saw high spots of red on his cheeks, but her own emotions overrode her caution and flowed out as she spoke. "You keep talking about plans, but you have no idea what kind of person you're dealing with. He's the same kind of ruthless creep that teaches his kids how to take advantage of every situation and has them practice at school. Some of the kids that can't hack it end up dopers, baked half the time. Some jump. Whatever plan you put together, he's going to be two steps ahead of you, because that's the way all of them do things: plan, test, prepare for every contingency. You don't think he has it figured out that you're going to try to cheat him—"

Mitch interrupted, his voice harsh and the words abrasive. "Me, cheat him? The bastard pointed guns at us, threatened to blow your leg off. He can go to hell. No way we can play his game, unless you want Jackson dead, and me along with him, 'cuz that's what's coming."

Kenzie shook her head hard twice. From the corner of her eye, she saw interest perk up in Jackson's face, an eyebrow rising as his chin set itself like stone.

"We can find other options," she said. The leaden feeling of being trapped sapped her words of conviction. "Once he knows that we have what he wants, we have a bargaining chip."

"Lassiter knows that, too," Mitch said, punctuating his words by nailing the Formica table top with his forefinger. "It's part of his game planning. Like you said, he's got plans, but he's only going to figure on the reactions of normal people and, if there's one thing you aren't, it's normal."

Kenzie glanced to Mitch. He wore an inner fire born of rage. She drew back from him, from the intensity of his stare. *He's losing it,* she thought. *And wrong.* Compared to him, she was the normal one.

"Look, all we have to do," she said, hoping to persuade him, "is give him what he wants. Once he has that, we have more time, and we can get help—"

Mitch laughed, a hard sound without humor, and Kenzie's face grew hot. "Fat chance!"

Kenzie's face grew warm, and it took effort to unclench her jaws.

Jackson spoke over the hubbub of noise in the restaurant. "You two okay there?" He locked on Mitch.

Mitch lifted a hand in a dismissive gesture without looking at him. Kenzie saw a flicker of annoyance cross Jackson's face.

"It's okay," she said. She accompanied the reassurance with a forced smile.

"Right." Loads of skepticism encased in a laconic response.

She reached for the spell to hold the bodyguard at bay. Stunned, she realized she couldn't feel magic. Could the stress Mitch and Lassiter exerted on her overwhelm her connection to the energy? A Harold question. She sucked in a panicky breath, seeking her center.

Kenzie turned back to Mitch and spoke. "It's better to let the game run its course and find a strategic point to make our break." It sounded reasonable to her ears.

"That works great if you're trying to escape, but this clown isn't going to go away. We need to take him down, and for that, we need some help."

"Your friend? Hunter? We can't get anyone else involved." Guilt made her glance away from Mitch. She still had not told her parents about the odd friends Mitch had. Part of her liked keeping secrets from them, part of her was scared for Mitch. Instinctively, Kenzie knew that coincidences like this—her meeting Mitch, the Hunter guy being his friend, the whole Lassiter problem—weren't accidental. Somehow, they all tied together even if she couldn't see how. A queasiness in her belly agreed.

Mitch, looking out the window, ignored the injunction. "Yeah, he's smart, I already told you that, and really good with electronics. He can design a couple of things for me."

He broke off as she grabbed his wrist. Her knuckles stood out white against Mitch's tanned skin.

"You can't tell him."

They swapped looks.

"Lassiter needs to be put down."

The arrogance in Mitch's words stunned her. Not the promise of violence implied in putting him down like a rabid dog, but the complete dismissal of her suggestions was breathtaking. And infuriating. She wasn't some little helpless girl who needed a big *strong* boy to save her. Her breath came faster, and her heart thudded against her ribs as indignation built. She sensed the magic pulling closer, and at the back of her mind she wondered why it came and went with certain emotions. She lost that train of thought when Mitch spoke again.

"You can't call me."

Her reaction was instantaneous. She backhanded him across the upper shoulder. The hard smacking sound brought silence to the clatter of the restaurant. Her eyes swept the room with embarrassment heating her face. The other patrons watched voyeuristically for a potential spectacle. Jackson lunged out of his seat and strode toward them. He brought a welcome distraction from those prying looks.

"Jackson," she said, but he wasn't looking at her. His grim gaze was fixed on Mitch.

She glanced to her side.

Mitch sat, every muscle in his arms and up across his chest set hard in rigid knots. His face was frozen into hard, implacable planes that sent a shiver along her nerves. He didn't raise his voice. When he spoke, the words came as stinging as a dead arctic wind that bore slashing ice particles. "You don't hit me," he said. *"Ever."*

His reaction shocked her and chills danced at the base of her neck. *You idiot,* she thought, *you expect any different from someone who got the crap beat out of him. . . .*

"We're done here," said Jackson as he arrived at the table.

"No, we're not," Kenzie responded. Her hands shook, but she tilted her head up so she could show him her face. "Please, Jackson, go sit down. This is my fault, okay?"

"I was leaving anyhow," said Mitch. He slid sideways on the bench.

Kenzie laid her hand on his arm but didn't close it. She couldn't force him to stay, but she pressed his firm flesh with a gentle pressure. "Wait?"

Mitch stopped but didn't turn to face her.

Kenzie shifted her gaze back to Jackson, eyes pleading. The bodyguard expelled his pent-up tension with an annoyed sigh.

"No more of that crap, either of you," he said. He went back to his seat. Kenzie heard him mutter but couldn't make out all the words, only "teenagers," as though it were a derogatory term.

Kenzie's fingers were cool against the warmth of Mitch's arm. She twitched them to get his attention.

"I'm sorry." The roller coaster of emotions that had started last night swept her along, off-balance and waiting for another plummet.

"The phones aren't safe," said Mitch, avoiding her eyes.

"Wha—" Comprehension filled her, and her fingers closed. His skin was hot against the cool of her palm. He hadn't meant "don't call me, I'm dumping you," but rather "don't call me, they're monitoring our phones." Naturally Lassiter would spy on them. She had absorbed enough of the tech business from her mother to understand that none of them had an altruistic bone in their greedy corporate bodies.

"I'll figure out something," said Mitch. His jaw stayed hard set, and his eyes, locked with hers now, simmered, but he sat next to her instead of getting up. She let relief and thanks show on her face.

With a solvable problem, her mind raced ahead. In rapid order, she dismissed landlines and computers. The first required her to explain to her parents why someone was calling—*and who!*—while computers were even less secure than her phone.

"That's why you met me here," Kenzie guessed.

Mitch's clipped answer disappointed her. "It was an accident. I needed someplace to hang out. I wasn't expecting to see you here. Doubly surprised to see your dad dropping you off, until Jackson pulled up." He gave a tug of his arm against her fingers. "I got to go," he said.

"Why?" She blinked. *Guys don't like needy chicks,* she remonstrated herself. *Cut it out.*

Mitch, sounding calmer, as though he had forgotten her slap already, though his expression revealed otherwise, said, "Can you get out of your house to the backyard, or are you, like, in solitary confinement there, too?"

"What?" The lack of sleep and the excess of stress made her stupid, she thought, and Mitch's fast changes of direction created a whirl in her head.

"There's a blind spot behind the garage next to the wall. I can slide down the hill later, and we can meet there. Until we figure something else out," Mitch amended. He shifted restlessly.

"I guess," she said.

It seemed like a dumb idea, but Kenzie couldn't think of anything better. It was a big chance to take. She avoided the obvious question about what would happen if anyone caught them.

Mitch stood up. His back was to Jackson. "'Kay, I'll text you, something boring, then give me thirty minutes." A ghost of a strained smile flashed, faded into a sigh.

He stepped back in a half pivot. He nodded to Jackson, who was staring at them both. "Thanks, man," Mitch said to the bodyguard, and headed for the doors.

Kenzie watched his sure stride and wished for Mitch's confidence. She saw nothing but disasters on every horizon, for him and for her, even if they got past Lassiter somehow. She still had to deal with her mother and the Family. An urge to visit the Glade came upon her. She pictured the peacefulness there. In her mind's eye, she saw the chrysanthemum set in the pool, smelled honey, heard the tinkling of the brook. She wanted to be there so much it hurt, to be someplace where she felt safe.

Like an awakening, another feeling overcame her.

She wanted Mitch's arms around her.

CHAPTER THIRTY-SIX

Hunter and Uncle Henry both moved to face Mitch as he plowed through the doorway. His uncle wore a cheerful smile that brought him to a full stop. The fragrance of fresh-brewed coffee permeated the air, and Mitch's stomach reacted with an acidic lurch.

"Hi, there," said Uncle Henry, beaming. "You were sure out early this morning. Tried calling . . ." His eyes went momentarily blank as a fat crease formed above them. ". . . can't remember why now." Uncle Henry's voice wavered, then drifted off into the distance. He picked up a half-full cup of coffee and sipped from it as though he had forgotten Mitch was there.

Unnerved, Mitch looked from him to Hunter and raised his eyebrows to silently ask, *Whaaat?*

Hunter greeted the unspoken query with a broad smile. "Your uncle said you'd be back pretty quick. We were having a little chat." He lifted two fingers on his right hand, and Uncle Henry grinned. Hunter dropped them again, and his uncle's expression faded to bland indifference. Freaky.

Mitch jerked his head in the direction of his bedroom. "Dude."

He stalked down the hall, hearing Hunter behind him. He twisted the knob to his door and swung it wide. He glanced at the disaster zone, and his lips curled. He'd worry about that later. He dumped his tattletale phone on the bed.

He launched into an interrogation as he turned. "What the hell—" He stopped when he saw Hunter leaning against the wall in the hallway, arms held loosely at his sides.

"Just making sure I don't get slammed into a wall again," said Hunter. "You going to be reasonable and listen?"

"What the hell did you do to him?" asked Mitch. "And get in here. You look stupid out there."

Hunter joined Mitch in the room.

"Close the door," said Mitch.

"No need."

Mitch frowned at his friend's cockiness. "Okay, spill it."

"I figured that you needed some, um, *help—*"

"Why?"

Hunter laughed, showing perfect white teeth. "You called like eleven times before nine o'clock this morning. Needy, man, totally needy."

"Shut up," said Mitch. He almost flipped his friend off and wondered what would happen if Hunter or Kenzie flipped someone the bird. The idea had potential—he roused himself. Not now.

Mitch peered at Hunter. The other boy wore his usual chinos with a button-down shirt and looked as though someone had told him to be ready for a photo shoot. The difference between the Hunter who'd twitched and trembled in the school hallway forty-eight hours ago with this version of the guy, standing there with complete self-assurance, struck Mitch like a blow.

"What kind of *help?*" asked Mitch.

"Your uncle is a major pain in the ass, so I manipulated his reality subtly so that he's both easier-going and pretty much disinterested in anything you do." Hunter shrugged. "It won't last. It's more like anesthesia."

"You manipulated reality?" Shaken by the thought, Mitch let his eyes dart around the room. It looked the same as it did this morning. *How much of what's going on is real?*

"His reality." Hunter's face took on a speculative cast. "I think."

"That's encouraging," said Mitch. "Not."

"Doesn't matter right now," said Hunter. "I've dialed him down so you can motor and do your thing without him riding you about it. Never mind about that, what happened?"

"How come you, or anyone in your family, don't show up in an internet search?"

"We like our privacy. Surprised it took you this long to put that together. Now, give."

Mitch's gaze dropped to the pile of bedsheets. He didn't hide the small grimace that accompanied the gesture. "I need to get into the school. Can you fix it?"

"Yeah, easy enough," Hunter said. "Why?"

A silence accumulated and weighed heavy in the atmosphere of the room. Mitch felt the pressure to say more, to explain. He checked Hunter's hands. The other youth stood motionless. A bird trilled outside, accentuating the tension. Mitch recognized the tactic. Hunter wasn't going to talk. Mitch didn't have time to wait him out. He dodged the question. "I also need a piece of gear, a trigger circuit, and it'll need to be hand-designed, I think."

This last piece of information caused Hunter's gaze to focus on Mitch, sharp as a spear tip. Mitch knew it would. More importantly, it distracted his friend from the school. Only for now, though.

"What kind?"

"A transmitter, but it's got to run on a delay, be nearly invisible in the dark, and have enough power to reach about a quarter mile to a booster."

"So you need a booster for the signal, too?"

Mitch dipped his chin. "Yeah."

"Sounds fun. Why?"

"I can't tell you."

Hunter shook his head. "Anybody going to call the cops?"

Mitch gave Hunter a stony stare. "No one will call the cops on us," he said. It wasn't a total lie. More like a misdirection. He held his eyes steady, almost daring Hunter to challenge him.

"You ought to clean this place up."

"I can't wave a hand and make all the crud put itself away."

"Doesn't work that way in the real world, dude." Hunter turned serious. "And you need to not say stuff like that. It took forever to convince my dad that you're an asset, and he's still not convinced that you aren't more trouble than it's worth to him."

"Thanks." Mitch dragged the word out sarcastically. He glimpsed a hint of anger in Hunter.

"Yeah, be a jerk, man. You don't know how close my dad was to . . ." The anger petered out, replaced by a hard look. "You owe me, even if you don't know how much yet."

A hard knot formed in Mitch's gut. He had thought that Kenzie's comment about someone killing him if he knew about her—which paled in comparison to Lassiter's very real promise—was hyperbole, like so much of what other teenagers said. He saw his mistake, thinking that Kenzie and Hunter were in that same group. Mitch grimaced, and the knot tightened. They weren't.

"How am I an asset?" Mitch asked. That part confused him, but he wasn't certain he wanted the answer.

"I told him you have a knack for putting things together. Someone that can read patterns like you do can be very useful to him. Also convinced him that you had no idea what you did the other day."

"I don't."

Hunter waved a hand in dismissal. Mitch kept track of it with a cautious glance.

"What exactly does your dad do?" Mitch asked.

"What do you need to get into the school for?" Hunter countered.

Mitch hesitated before answering. "Powdered aluminum and ferrous oxide," he admitted.

Hunter's face went blank for a moment as he processed the chemical equations, then sharpened. "Thermite? You're going to need an initiator for it."

Mitch hid his smile, and the bunched feeling in his gut relaxed at Hunter's response. Thermite wasn't an explosive, but it burned with incredible intensity. In Mitch's plan, the metal, aluminum, would steal the oxygen atoms from the ferrous oxide, a fancy name for plain old rust. The reaction was exothermic and released enormous quantities of energy as heat and light. Railroads used it to weld broken axles on boxcars without pulling the whole unit off the track and to fix cracks in the tracks themselves.

The military, of course, had a whole series of less benign uses for thermite.

"Yeah, I was hoping you could handle that, too. Electronic, though, not chemical. Plus I need to borrow the bot and make a few modifications."

His eyes strayed to the paper bag containing the Faradays. *How to get control of the communications?*

Hunter did not answer. Mitch glanced up to find Hunter regarding him with curiosity.

"Sounds like you're planning for a war, bro, and if you're going to drag me into it, I want to know what's going on."

"Remember when you said I was screwed?" Mitch asked. "That too many people knew? I thought you meant you and Kenzie—"

"That's her name? Kenzie?" asked Hunter.

Mitch mentally cursed his verbal slip. The near-exhaustion was making him stupid. He had no choice now but to answer truthfully or he'd lose the help he needed.

"Yeah," he said, nodding.

"Do I get to meet her?"

The subtle anxiousness in Hunter's voice caused a suspicion to form in Mitch.

"Why?" he asked. Immediately, he regretted the question.

"You got major trust issues," said Hunter. He snorted in amusement. "You think I'm going to steal your girl?"

Didn't until a second ago, thought Mitch.

"Another guy showed up last night," he said, deflecting away from the subject. Quickly, he recounted the events of the previous evening, highlighting the threat to him, but keeping Jackson out of it. He also skipped over Mercury's presence in the whole affair. He finished by explaining his suspicions about his and Kenzie's tainted cell phones.

"Hell, you need a couple of burner phones. No problem."

"Two problems. First, the cost, and second, more importantly, the second I buy phones this Lassiter dude's going to know. He'd be stupid to not keep me under some sort of electronic surveillance. He might even have somebody watching the house, for all I know."

Hunter flashed a broad smile. "But he's not going to be watching me, is he? I can buy the phones for you through a shell account and drop one off for you and another at this Kenzie chick's house."

The worrisome feeling about Hunter and Kenzie strengthened.

"No," Mitch said. "If they're watching her house, they'll see you. Right now, you're in the shadows."

"I can take care of myself," said Hunter, with a meaningful motion of his hand.

"Yeah, no," said Mitch. "Forgot to tell you that they can detect whatever the energy is that you use, and I doubt that you can stop a thirty ought six slug mid-flight."

Hunter blanched at the mention of Lassiter's ability to know when magic was in use.

"*Meat* can tell when magic is applied? No way—"

"I watched it happen, dude." Mitch said it in a flat voice, with no emotion. Let Hunter believe what he wanted, but Mitch was there. "And stop with the 'Meat' comments already."

"I want to know how he can tell when one of us summons. You don't know what he really wants?"

"Just that it's some kind of data storage. I'd guess that it'll be encrypted, but I don't know what the physical form is, or what the heck is on it. It's almost certainly related to tech," he said, not offering the information about Kenzie's mother.

Hunter fell silent. He paced away two steps, turned, and paced back. "I'll pass this on to my father, but I think you have an ally."

CHAPTER THIRTY-SEVEN

Kenzie dismissed Jackson—she'd catch hell for that when her mother discovered it—and searched the house while her parents were out.

She started in her mother's study. Before entering, she scanned for alarm or capture spells. Eyes half closed, and without quite knowing how she did it, she let her sense of magic wander along the frame of the French doors. The desk, set under the window, dominated the room with its broad and Spartan work area and trio of drawers on each side, forming a stout box. A touch of vertigo swirled around her as she "saw" both the dust particles coating the top of the white trim and, through the door, a computer passively occupying the center of the handcrafted mahogany desk. The sensation passed as she closed her eyes entirely and finished her exploration.

Nothing.

If her mother had constructed a protection system, like the supernatural wards her father built around the house, her abilities proved incapable of discovering it. She reached for the knob—and halted before touching it. A tech CEO would feel comfortable with a more mundane security system. She peered through the rectangular panes of glass. No wires or minuscule sensors were visible. A twinge of guilt hit her as she grasped the handle with a shaky hand. Kenzie took a deep breath, twisted her wrist, and invaded her mother's private sanctum.

She stood inside the threshold and let her gaze travel left to right over the bookshelves and credenza, with their lustrously dark wood to match the desk, past the leather executive chair to the well-polished gleam of the desktop, and over to a bank of custom-made filing cabinets. In the middle of the floor, an intricately wrought carpet displayed white and red ornamental flowers arranged in the rough shape of a pentagram. The woven black background absorbed the light from the window and lent it to the petals so that they seemed to radiate the patina of life.

Where first? Kenzie thought with a frown. She contemplated the filing cabinets. That would be the logical spot, which made it likely the wrong location, but it gave her a place to start. She angled to her right, leaving the door open behind her. Her path took her to the edge of the rug. With one foot already lifted into the air, it dawned on her that her mother might well have concealed her spells inside, not outside, the office.

In the rug, for example.

Kenzie leaned and recovered her balance.

Quit being paranoid, she thought, but she tried to see if the rug carried an imbued power. Again, she did not find any, but she sidled along the edge anyway to reach the drawers. She tugged on the top drawer of the first cabinet she reached and raised an eyebrow when it silently glided open. She had expected locks. Only by standing to one side could she fully open the drawer and avoid stepping on the flowers.

Hands shaking, Kenzie rifled through the folders, paper and more paper, but there was nothing that looked like the kind of electronics that a snake like Lassiter would be interested in. She closed the drawer. Methodically, Kenzie inspected each of the others in turn. She shut the twelfth and last with a hard push, punctuated by a frustrated puff of breath. She glanced at the other side of the room, at the credenza.

Thirty minutes later, Kenzie had swept through the bookcases, the cabinets in the credenza, and the nearest desk drawers. A mental timer ticked away the minutes that her parents would be absent as she calculated the effort needed to get to the far set of drawers. Short of climbing onto the furniture, she could not get into position to open them, and it would be impossible to explain why she lay sprawled over the desk. Besides, the study so far held the most innocuous of possessions and boring business briefs. She gave up.

She retraced her steps to the glass-paned doors and pulled them closed behind her as she vacated the room. She chewed on the inside of her lower lip. The next logical location was her parents' bedroom. Or her father's office. Both ratcheted up her heart rate. She picked the bedroom and headed upstairs.

The hallway lay in perpetual darkness, with closed doors lining the walls. Feet silent on the thick ivory-colored carpet, Kenzie padded to the farthest door, where she repeated her inspection for traps and tricks. As she expected, the door held no secrets.

With less trepidation at getting caught, but more embarrassment at voyeuristically peeking into her parents' most private room, Kenzie slipped into the master bedroom. The curtains were open, and the view to the lake made the large room even more expansive. She left the door open behind her.

Hiding places were limited. Kenzie went to the bedside table on her mother's side. Two hardback novels sat neatly stacked next to the reading lamp. It had a small drawer and single cabinet below. Heart thudding, she pulled the drawer open, hoping against surprises. Tissues, a collection of letters, a couple of pens, a small scratchpad with a pair of dates written in blue ink, and a pile of envelopes that appeared to hold photographs. Curiosity drew her to the pictures, and she picked up one of the packets and lifted the flap.

The edges of the photos were curled and yellow. She slid the top image out. She recognized the faces that smiled back, her parents and Harold, others from the Family. Some faces seemed familiar, but she couldn't place them. She shuffled through three more pictures. The last showed a graying man with captivating emerald eyes standing with his arm over Harold's shoulders. The two could have passed for brothers, down to the sad lines of their smiles. Maybe she could ask Harold who he was, if she could figure out how to bring it up without admitting she was sneaking around. She stuffed the pictures in the envelope and returned them to the drawer. She tested the cabinet doors and found them unlocked. With a sigh, Kenzie opened the lower cabinet. She discovered a stash of chocolates and another couple of books.

Her father's table bore teetering stacks of historical and technical books. She skipped his end table.

The master closet, the size of a small bedroom, had a window to let in natural light and a small padded bench to sit on when dressing. To the left were her mother's smartly tailored suits, dresses hung next to them, and then her casual clothes. Her father's suits occupied three linear feet of space, the rest given over to slacks and sports shirts.

Shoe boxes and plastic storage containers filled the floor space under the hanging rack. The shelf above was filled to overflowing with more boxes and a spare pillow that brushed against the textured ceiling near the scuttle for the attic. The sheer number of boxes argued against searching them. She'd be here all day.

She eyed the scuttle. It was the least obvious place she could think of for hiding anything, but it made more sense than the end tables, and she was running out of time. Kenzie clambered onto the bench seat and, hanging onto the clothing rod, leaned out and simultaneously reached for the inset cover. With her fingertips, she pushed the lid and felt it skitter up. As it cleared the lip, she saw wood forming a box around the opening. She went to her tippy-toes at the edge of the bench. Even at full extension, she couldn't quite nudge the cover over the framing.

The vibration of her phone in her back pocket startled her. She twitched, and her toes slipped off the edge of the bench. The bottom dropped out of her stomach as Kenzie plummeted to the floor. She stumbled on impact and fell against the wall with a loud crash, the shoes at the floor scattering as she kicked them. She came to a rest, panting heavily, half-crouched with her shoulder jammed into the wall and hangers swinging above her.

The phone vibrated again, and she yanked it from her pocket. She glanced at the screen, ready to yell at Mitch for scaring the hell out of her, when she read a number that she didn't recognize. Her thumb hovered over the screen. The phone vibrated three more times while she suffered through indecision. Before she made up her mind, the phone sent whoever it was to voice mail. She stuffed it back into her pocket and surveyed the damage.

Her father's slacks lay in disarray. Working with urgency, Kenzie put them back into proper alignment, careful to match the spacing. She stepped back to check her work, and her calf hit something. She teetered but avoided falling again. Glancing down, she saw the bench seat out of kilter. She must have broken it on the way down, though she had no idea how.

An odd angle at the edge of her vision momentarily distracted her. Glancing up, she saw the lid to the attic space jammed into the opening, with one corner hanging.

Great, she thought. A quick glance at her watch showed the time closing on noon, about the time she could expect her parents home. Not time to panic, not yet.

She made the expedient decision to fix the bench first. Without it, she couldn't reach the hatch.

Kenzie grasped the cushioned seat. To her surprise, the whole thing moved smoothly. Kenzie stooped over the wooden frame of the bench, resting the cushion against the edge. As the space below the seat was exposed, she gasped.

A safe, built into the floor, was visible through the opening. The door sat round like a face with a single eye at the dial and a handle as an offset line of a mouth. Her eyes darted from the minutely numbered dial, to the silver handle, to the wood frame that protected it from accidental discovery.

Satisfaction welled up in Kenzie's chest as she knew she had found the hiding place, even if the presence of the safe introduced another problem, namely that the combination could be anything. She balanced the lid with her knees and checked the time again. She was cutting it close.

Rotating the bench seat exposed a plywood bottom, with the outside edge thinner so that the whole thing would sit into the box frame like a cork. Carefully, she maneuvered it into position and nudged it until it dropped down with a solid *thunk*.

Hurrying, she remounted the bench. This time she didn't go right to the edge. Extending a lithe arm, she pushed at the rectangle of drywall wedged into the attic opening.

Drat. It was stuck.

Kenzie analyzed the angles. She'd need to lift the hatch cover up and straighten it before it would drop properly. Doing so required two hands. She needed a ladder. Which was in the garage, of course. With her mother due home any minute, the last question she wanted to answer was why she had the ladder out. Her mother wouldn't buy the suggestion that it was time to hang Christmas lights.

Double drat.

She stood, staring up, looking for a way to apply steady pressure.

Anemosa.

The air spell that Harold had taught her came back to her. If she could apply the force of the wind against the panel evenly, she could lift it, and then taper the flow to let it drop into place. If that didn't work, she'd fetch the ladder.

Kenzie closed her eyes to help her focus. She inscribed the spell in the air in front of her. As she completed the motion, she slowed the wind and directed it upward with a gradual lifting of her palm. As she did, she imagined the air spreading to cover the entire surface area of the hatch. She tilted her hand to match the angles and apply more pressure to the lower corner.

She opened her eyes, seeking the ceiling.

The hatch cover vibrated, a dry rattle. A hint of white powder fell from the edges, only to get caught in the updraft. Kenzie gave a push with her hand, and the drywall responded with a scraping sound as it slid up. The corner wrenched free. Kenzie dampened the air flow at once to balance it above the opening.

Through her feet, she felt the vibration of the garage door going up.

No time, she thought, never breaking eye contact with the levitating lid. A nervous excitement made her teeth chatter. She clamped her teeth together to quell the reaction.

The lid wafted on the air but oriented at fifteen degrees off the maw of the opening. She tried adjusting the pressures. The white rectangle darted like a kite in an awkward wind.

Can you do two spells at once?

Her gaze rock-steady above her, she sought another thread of magic with her other hand detailing the spell. Kenzie crafted a delicate air spell, whispered, *"Anemosa."* A baby's breath of air struck the edge, turned it. Estimating the point at which the rotating panel would line up, she released the second spell.

Hah!

Her lips pulled back into a grim smile at the pleasure of discovery, though the clatter of her teeth had become a vibration throughout her torso. Her hand lowered the panel and closed to cut the wind pressure. A corner hung up, and she tapped it with the air. The hatch dropped soundlessly into the ceiling.

Kenzie scrambled off the bench. On tiptoes, she ran from the closet back through the master bedroom, checking to make sure she'd put everything back, and down the hall to her room, closing the door behind her.

Breathless, she stayed by her door, the earlier tremors transforming into a knot of anxiety. She'd know soon enough if she'd gotten away clean or not.

CHAPTER THIRTY-EIGHT

Breaking into the school turned out to be anticlimactic. The doors were unlocked. The nerds and geeks operated on their own schedules, even on the weekend that started spring break.

Hunter strode next to Mitch through the dim hallways as they headed for the lab.

"It's not something we talk about," said Hunter.

"I mean, you all are like wizards or witches or whatever you call yourselves, but you don't know each other. There can't be that many of you," said Mitch, reframing his original question.

Hunter glanced around the vacant building. The antiseptic smell of floor cleaner masked the spring weather outside.

"Wizards," said Hunter, distaste crossing his features. "The so-called witches are a neopagan religion, bound up with dogma like any other sect. Wizards can actually manipulate the energy around them in a physical manifestation that can be readily discerned."

Their shoes squeaked in time when they hit the vinyl floor at the lunch room. They turned left at the first hall, and the carpet swallowed the sound of their footfalls.

"Sounds like a dogma to me on your end, too."

"Observable fact is not dogma. You're thinking like a mush-head. We have generations of experience analyzing our Family. Magic is simply evidence that the human race is evolving into new abilities to interpret and interact with the universe. A feature of that is that each wizard is typically much healthier and more intelligent than Meat. We tend to succeed to high levels, and all the members of my Family are solidly in positions of power or leaders in their field. It is nature at work, like Homo sapiens meeting Neanderthal. Only one branch of the species will survive, completely supplanting the others." Hunter shrugged. "Of course, that won't happen until we either achieve sufficient numbers or our power becomes unstoppable."

Mitch glanced at Hunter to see if he was serious. The other youth's eyes held a queer glow that triggered a revulsion deep inside Mitch. He glanced ahead, saw a light on in the lab, and buttoned his lips rather than make a joke about master races. He didn't think Hunter would find it funny, anyway.

Paulson was hidden by a stack of boxes marked with the Amazon smile. He craned his neck around to peer at them as they wandered into the room.

"Hey, guys. Getting some extra work done over the break?"

Mitch answered ahead of Hunter. No need to do the whole hand-waving routine when the teacher would probably simply give them what they wanted.

"Hi, Mr. Paulson, we figured we might borrow Alice for a couple of days and work on tuning her up at home, if that's cool with you."

"You got her rebuilt?"

"Mostly," said Hunter, taking the lead. Most of the damage had been in his domain of electronics. "We might want to check out some components, just in case. If we don't use them, I'll check them back in."

Five minutes later, Mitch tucked Alice under his arm, making sure all the cords were bundled up so he wouldn't step on them. Hunter held a small box that contained an assortment of capacitors, resistors, transistors, and a small roll of soldering metal.

"See you, Mr. Paulson," said Mitch as the two of them left.

"Have fun. Don't blow anything up," said Paulson with a laugh.

"That's no fun," said Hunter, matching Paulson's tone. Mitch saw his free hand lift, but the teacher already had his head back down, working on his laptop.

"Let's go," said Mitch.

They went left from the doorway, in the opposite direction from where they'd come.

"Hit the chemistry lab and out the side door?" asked Hunter.

"Yep."

Apprehension tightened his shoulders. Once they hit the chem lab, they'd find the powdered aluminum and ferrous oxide, though the second item wasn't critical. Mitch could find plenty of rusty things in the garage, although the rendering of that rust wouldn't have the same purity. Until then, the two of them were students working through spring break. Stealing materials for thermite put them into teenage terrorist territory, worthy of SWAT team responses.

Which is why, Mitch thought, he'd brought Hunter and his hand jive along. If he was supposed to be keeping Kenzie safe and out of trouble, staying out of jail, even over a "misunderstanding," was essential. He counted on Hunter taking control of anyone who interrupted their excursion. A chill traversed his spine at an image of his uncle, jolly and laughing one second and blank-faced the next.

He glanced at Hunter. Did he ever think that denying a person their own identity was wrong? Another thought hit. Was he any better, using Hunter to do it for him?

He shook the thought away with a short but violent arcing shake of his head.

Hunter saw the motion. "What? Losing your nerve?"

Mitch responded by increasing the pace of his casual walk into a brisk stride that forced Hunter to half-jog to catch up. They turned one more corner. The room they wanted was closed up. Mitch slowed and grabbed the knob.

Locked.

Mitch signaled to Hunter with a come-on crooking of two fingers, then pointed to the door. "You're up."

"You didn't tell me that we'd have to break in."

"What did you think? They'd leave everything in the hallway with a note to be super damn careful not to blow ourselves up?"

Hunter fidgeted, glancing up and down the darkened halls as if he expected the janitor to show up any second. "I don't know how to open locks," he admitted.

Mitch leaned his head to one side, mind swirling. "Just use your . . . ," he said with a suggestive motion of his hand.

"It doesn't work like that," said Hunter. He shuffled his feet. "I mean, there are spells for all sorts of stuff, but it takes years to learn how to do all that, what all the rules are."

"Well, I don't have time for rules, and I don't want to smash in the door, so you need to figure something out. Can you use your magic to recess the tongue of the lock long enough for us to slip in?"

Fear trembled in Hunter's eyes. "Maybe, but you really don't understand. If I get caught by my Family acting like a deviant, they'll . . ."

"They'll what?" Mitch didn't mean to mock his friend, but the tone in his voice carried his exasperation. Hunter and Kenzie could do amazing things, the crazy stuff that you read in fantasy books, but both of them seemed totally locked in against using their powers, to the point where something that seemed simple and straightforward brought them to a trembling stop.

"Deviancy is not permissible," said Hunter, sounding like a student repeating a formal lesson. He took a step back from the door.

Alarmed, Mitch spoke quickly. "Deviancy would be operating against the interests of your dad, right? And you said that we probably were allies now, so you're in effect helping your dad when you help me."

Hunter gave him a sharp look, and Mitch saw a wavering in the fear. Maybe he was getting through.

Mitch pressed his advantage. "All we have to do is acquire the materials by getting through the locks. There's no one here except you and me, so the chance of discovery doesn't exist." Mitch took a breath. "Plus, I double dog dare you to try."

Hunter laughed, and the tension in his face disappeared. "Oh yeah, because you can never turn down a dare." He shook his head, but he kept smiling. "Okay, I can try. The worst that happens is that my father kills you." He turned to face Mitch. "Just kidding, man."

Hunter focused on the door. Mitch scrutinized his friend's face for some clue as to what he was doing. Other than a narrowing of concentration, Hunter did not display any indications of the efforts he was making.

"Push," said Hunter.

Mitch interpreted that to mean the door. He placed the back of his hand against the door and applied a steady pressure. Nothing happened for a moment. Then, it opened. The snap of the tongue returning to the locking position echoed from the concrete and metal that lined the hall. Both boys checked to see if anyone came to check what disrupted the silence.

Mitch leading, they passed through the opening.

"Toss me a book," said Mitch, propping the door open with his foot.

Hunter removed the first one that came to hand from a nearby shelf and handed it to him. Mitch leaned it against the jamb and let the door fall back.

The inside of the lab would have been familiar to anyone who had ever taken a chemistry course. The black bench tops were made from a nonreactive epoxy resin designed to be durable. Gas fittings for Bunsen burners were built into the counters. The peculiar odor of the lab awoke a sense of pleasant familiarity. Mitch got the same sensation from the electronics labs with their pervasive ozone taint. Above the benches were the ventilation and exhaust hoods, and there was an eye wash station at each end of the laboratory.

The various chemicals, mixtures, and solutions were secured in a second room, past the instructor's desk. The door on this one was constructed from solid metal, and the lock was a stiff deadbolt, not a relatively easy doorknob.

"Don't know if I can do that one, Mitch," said Hunter, doubt clear on his face as well as in his voice.

"Nothing ventured, nothing gained," said Mitch. "I don't suppose you can teleport, too?"

"Don't think so," replied Hunter. "Never really thought about trying. Plus, making a mistake could be really messy. Any suggestions on how to break this bad boy are welcome."

Mitch thought. He knew Hunter would wait for an answer. A detached part of his brain, not currently occupied on breaking and entering, realized that this was all part of the pattern between the two of them. For all of his genius with electronics, the guy lacked the spark to initiate projects.

"We can't use simple pressure with that lock," said Mitch, surfacing from his calculations. "The best bet is to emulate a key using force and lift the pins in the lock until we find the right combination. If I remember correctly, most locks have five pins inside, with ten possible positions, I think. So, if you lifted the pins until they reached the shear point in the cylinder, it should open."

Hunter's eyes flitted around the lock and door. "'Kay. So, how do I know when the pins are in the right spot?"

"Can you see inside?"

"No," said Hunter. "It's more like a feeling, like you can touch something with a hand you don't have."

"Phantom limb syndrome, like an amputee," said Mitch.

"Close enough," said Hunter. "Let me give it a try." His eyes closed. On his right hand, the fingers twitched like those of a sax player riffing to a jazz routine. Mitch surmised that the movements corresponded to Hunter's efforts at moving the pins. He could hear ticks from the mechanism. Sweat broke out on Hunter's forehead.

"It's no use," said Hunter. "I can't feel when I get it right. As soon as I try to shift the pressure from the pins to the cylinder to rotate it, everything goes to hell."

"What if I applied the sideways pressure?" asked Mitch. "I mean, if I don't get in the way."

"Unless you can climb into that lock, you won't be in the way," said Hunter. "It's not like physical objects interfere with magic."

"It's not like I know," said Mitch, with a wry smile. "Hold on, I'll get something to work the cylinder."

Mitch rummaged around the teacher's desk. A slender metal letter opener—a tool for the teacher, a weapon if a student got caught with it—looked perfect. He took it to the door.

"Let me know when you're ready," said Mitch, dropping to a knee at the door.

Hunter nodded, and his eyelids dropped.

"Now," came Hunter's strained voice.

Mitch inserted the tip of the letter opener into the key slot and very gently twisted it sideways. The pins' movement made the metal in his hand vibrate nearly imperceptibly. He held the pressure and felt a sharper click.

One down.

In quick succession, the trembles of pins releasing tingled through Mitch's fingertips, and with a smooth motion at the fifth, the lock turned, and the door opened.

"Good job, man," said Mitch, straightening out the kinks in his back and lifting his right hand to fist-bump. The other boy met the gesture with a tap of knuckles.

"Grab the stuff and let's get, buddy," said Hunter. "We still have to lock it again."

Mitch hurried into the room. The supplies were laid out on the battleship-gray shelves while an exhaust fan whispered overhead. Mitch looked at the markings at the front of a bank of cabinets holding the corrosives, flammables, and acids, special items segregated due to their potential for booms and burns. Each cabinet bore a warning symbol indicating the contents. What he needed would be on the shelves. Separately, the metals were reasonably inert.

A quick glance showed the remaining containers were grouped according to their properties instead of alphabetically. Made sense, Mitch thought.

He found the ferrous oxide. He pulled a pair of sandwich-sized Ziploc bags from his back pocket. He opened one, squared the bottom to get it to stand partially open, and then loosed the catches of the container with the iron rust. Using the scoop inside, he quickly took as much of the black powder as he needed, plus an extra scoop just in case. He squeezed the excess air from the bag and pinched it shut.

Using the bottom of his shirt, he wiped the surfaces he had touched.

Mitch walked to the section with the metals, though in his head he classified the aluminum as a post-transition metal, which is how it appeared on the periodic table. He had considered using copper for the metal component of the chemical reaction, but it was too reactive, giving more of an explosion than a fast-burning sizzle. Kenzie would be near the thermite when he set it off, and he didn't want to take any chances of splatter reaching her. His stomach clenched at the thought of molten copper cauterizing her skin.

There were two types of aluminum, granulated and powdered. He stole the granulated—aluminum powder could become unstable in certain conditions, and he had no desire to have a premature eruption.

Mitch shoved the baggies into different pants pockets and repeated the cleanup process. He strode to the doorway. Hunter turned his head as Mitch swung the door shut with a shove of his shoulder.

"Ready," said Hunter as Mitch put the letter opener back into the cylinder lock and applied pressure in the opposite direction. The snapping of the pins back into the locked position happened so quickly that Mitch was taken by surprise.

Hunter shrugged. "Practice," he said.

"Fine with me," said Mitch. "Let's wipe down everything we've touched and get the heck out of here."

Two minutes later, the lab door snicked shut behind them, and a minute after that they were sucking in deep breaths in bright sunshine.

Hunter started to laugh. "Dude," he said, "you know how to break up a boring day." He put up a hand for high five.

Mitch smacked the proffered palm with a loud whack and smiled himself, though not from humor or relief. He had the first part of his arsenal against Lassiter. His mind was racing on to the next point of attack.

"Let's go get some phones."

CHAPTER THIRTY-NINE

Kenzie was suitably impressed.

"As you can see, the *Estatosa* spell is possible," said Harold, "but the strain is quite significant."

His feet were several inches off the ground. He allowed himself to descend to the grassy interior of the teaching circle. He wheezed a bit as though he had run hard, and he ran a hand across his brow. He had begun the lesson with a discussion of moving physical objects and the raw power that was necessary to use magic to overcome the effect of gravity.

The demonstration of the incantation for flying had left them all spellbound.

"Mind you, not everyone can perform the necessary magic at that level, either due to a lack of natural talent or physical vigor, or not applying the careful attention such a spell requires."

"When do we get our brooms," said Belinda, staring big-eyed at Harold. The Wilder perched on her seat with a definite curvature to her spine that must have hurt, but managed to pull her virgin-white robes against her chest.

You don't need one, Kenzie thought. She chalked the uncharitable judgment up to fatigue but didn't retract it.

"That actually brings up an interesting theoretical point," responded Harold, "about the stories from the Dark Ages of witches flying. In the literature of the period, and especially the art, witches would always be depicted as riding brooms, chairs, or animals. The spell I performed," he lifted his hands to imitate the levitation, "was unheard of. Theories within the Family abound, but the most prevalent is that the early wizards and enchantresses, our ancestors, would imbue a physical object with magic, much as we do with amulets. The mundane world"—Kenzie felt oddly reassured at the way Harold avoided the term "Meat"—"resorted to slanders that the witches would put herbs with psychoactive properties on the broomstick to administer the effect of the drug more directly."

He paused, and Kenzie tried to picture applying a drug from the broomstick through clothes. It didn't fit, until she realized that the robes would have gotten in the way and been abandoned. Then the picture came too clearly, and she blushed. She saw burning cheeks on the brother-sister pair who were the only others in the Family close to her age. Wilders filled out the rest of the group. Ten feet away, Belinda laughed throatily.

Harold saw the discomfort in their faces.

"Maybe that was too much information," he murmured, not quite to himself. He gathered himself. "Right, watch closely."

His hands, graceful as a pair of mourning doves courting, weaved themselves into a rolling motion, with the right hand sliding intimately over the left three times, always in contact. At the end of the third roll, the fingers on the right overlaid the finger of the left to form an inverted V with the thumbs pointed out. The Vs sank toward the ground, fell apart from each other, and then rose cupped as though describing the bottom of a large urn.

Kenzie noted that Harold inhaled as his hands lifted.

In front of Harold, a fist-sized stone, smooth as a river rock, flecks of red in the grayness catching the moonlight, elevated to the height of the wizard's hands and hovered. He left it suspended for a few seconds before turning his palms down and releasing the stone. It landed with a muffled thud.

"I've placed smaller pebbles in front of each of you. See it clearly first; I don't want you tearing the living," he said, referring to the grass laid across the circle like a carpet. "Take your time and concentrate. Do not get discouraged if you can't make this spell work the first time out. Very few people can. Most of you will not even realize how ingrained to your subconscious the idea of gravity is. Contrary beliefs will inhibit performance, so try to open yourselves to the infinite and allow for the possibilities that imbue the universe." Harold swept his eyes around the students.

"Begin," he said.

The two embarrassed siblings immediately launched into a hurried version of the spell, hands darting like herky-jerky finches. Their pebbles stayed safely snuggled between the blades of grass.

Kenzie stood while the kids wasted time, and took two casual steps to look at her pebble. She lowered herself with a curtsy-like motion to touch it with a tip of her finger. It bounced slightly at the contact. A frown creased her face. Other than shape, none of the other characteristics of the pea-gravel manifested. Unsure of the reason, she picked the stone up between her thumb and forefinger.

Inspecting it more closely, she saw that the stripes of color, taupe, umber, and faded yellow, testified to the origins of the rock. She put it into the palm of her other hand. The skin of her palm picked up the chill of the pebble. She focused on the small object. Kenzie's peripheral vision darkened as the tightening focus on the pebble left her mesmerized. Specks of individual grains appeared under her close examination, and a definite weight became apparent.

Kenzie breathed deeply and replaced the stone. The two kids continued in their race of futility, and mutterings reached Kenzie's ears, along with a pleased-sounding *yes* from Belinda, but all the sounds washed over and around her without leaving a mark. The scent of the Glade when she had arrived, like tangerines, drifted to an older, earthier odor.

Eyes half-closed, Kenzie held the idea of the pebble in her mind, and let her hands inscribe the sign, emulating Harold as closely as possible, conscious of the fluid grace of his gestures in the forefront of her mind. Just as she released her hands and began to lift, she inhaled. She swayed, light-headed. Through the slits of her eyes, she watched the pebble grow larger, felt it grow light.

Now, she thought. She closed her eyes and exhaled.

An audible gasp filled the circle and startled her. Kenzie's eyes flew open. Unlike Harold's stone, her pebble glowed like an earth-bound star eight feet above the ground. Shock relaxed her arms, and they fell to her sides. At the edge of her vision, Harold turned a palm down as though he were swatting a fly. The pebble glowed a fraction of a second longer, then fell back to the circle.

"There is no extra credit, Kenzie," said Harold. The modulation of his voice carried a worried subtext below the gentle humor of his words.

A dozen faces gaped at her with something akin to awe. One face, though, twisted into a malevolent snarl. Belinda's.

Kenzie shook her head and turned her back on the circle, wrapping her arms around her torso.

Behind her, she heard Harold instruct the rest of the class, "Focus on your own process. Belinda, you did very well. You others, slow down and remember to focus. Go ahead and begin again. I will be right over there."

Kenzie had no doubt where "there" was. Her suspicion was confirmed a moment later when Harold materialized at her side. Feeling the weight of the sleepless night and her tiff with Mitch, she waited for him to speak first, to chastise her for her screw-up.

He harrumphed under his breath, and then asked, "Who else has been teaching you, Kenzie?"

The question took her by surprise. "No one, why?"

"You don't know what you did?"

"I did what you showed me," Kenzie said. She didn't like the defensiveness in her voice. "I don't break the rules on training in the arts."

Guilt seized her at the mention of rules. One of the reasons for bringing Wilders into the fold of the Family was to train them properly. The laws that governed all the societal interactions, from marriage to conduct outside the Glade, also dictated the steps that every acolyte had to complete on their journey. Her relationship with Mitch, her telling him of this existence, shattered those rules. Her knees quaked.

Harold put a hand on her shoulder and let it rest there lightly.

"You picked up your pebble, held it. Why?"

Kenzie's mind raced. "I wanted to understand the pebble." Since that sounded stupid, she added, "In my Tang Soo Do class, the martial arts I take, the black belt, Jules, has been teaching me how to use what she calls the third eye. It's kind of like seeing without looking."

Harold dipped his chin, and his eyes narrowed. "I think I should meet this Jules. Your sensei—"

"*Sabomnim.* Sensei is Japanese. Tang Soo Do is Korean." She thought of Harold joining Jackson and Mitch on the benches at the studio. *I have an entourage.* The idea almost made her smile.

"I stand corrected," said Harold. "What you're learning is how to reach a higher plane of consciousness, to tap into your intuitive capabilities. These are skills that we attempt to teach young enchantresses as they approach full wizard status." He raised a bony finger. "Every living thing moves within its own energy potential, and it is possible to jump those levels in leaps without passing through each lower level. Sadly, very few can reach inside themselves to attune their greater selves to the universe."

"Why did the pebble glow?"

Harold graced her with a shadow of a smile while warmth lit his eyes. "You made an amulet."

"Hunh?" Kenzie glanced over her shoulder. The pebble remained hidden in the grass. The rest of the class was staring at the pair of them despite Harold's instructions to continue practicing.

Harold explained. "Whether or not you know it, you sought the underlying nature of the pebble. When you applied magic to lift it, you also added a . . . *charge* to it." His eyes drifted to the horizon. In a voice that bore an abiding sadness hidden in its depths, he continued, "Very few others could do such a thing."

"But how?" Kenzie asked.

Harold rolled his shoulders and turned a sheepish gaze to her. "I don't know. Can you explain how you did it?"

"But I don't know what I did," said Kenzie. She clenched her hands, the frustration showing in the tendons popping out on the backs of her hands.

This was met by an understanding nod from the old wizard. "I thought not. *The Incantaraus* lacks a mention on it. As with many other things, we know that it is possible, but not how. Much of what we teach you is based on tradition. We know it works, even if we don't fully understand why."

Kenzie pondered Harold's admission. She realized she took magic for granted, a part of her everyday reality. Why were there any rules about training in the Arts if no one really knew how magic worked? She closed her eyes, touched the swirl of magic around her, and opened them again.

Before she could ask her next question—*so many questions!*—Harold spoke. "Rejoin the others, Kenzie. Focus only on the exercise of lifting your pebble," he said, voice crisp.

Kenzie hesitated, contemplated forcing answers from the wizard. "Yes, sir," she said, reluctance clear to her ears. "One last question?"

Harold was good at sighing. "One," he said.

"That doesn't explain why it glowed, just how. Why did my pebble, my amulet, glow?"

A fleeting expression of concern showed on his face, and he was slow to answer. When he did, he kept his voice down. His gaze was direct, and his words shook her. "Amulets are almost always created by a wizard in great need. They take many forms, but the magic they are imbued with is there to guide, defend, or empower the wizard."

He paused.

"I think, and only you will know for sure, that you are in a dark and frightening place and seek a light to the way out."

The rest of the lesson was a disaster. Kenzie found herself unable to perform the simplest of spells. Harold watched her, and she sensed his sympathy. Thankfully, he left her alone. When the class was over, she paid her respects to him with a minuscule bob of her head, then fled. In her hand was her pebble, inert and unassuming.

She crossed the brook and followed it to the solitude of the lagoon. The small beach extended to the water's edge with its white sand undisturbed. She wavered and walked to the water, her feet leaving pockmarks in the sand. A shudder started in her chest and moved to her shoulders, and she sniffled. She clutched her robe and held it tight against her body.

How deep is the water?

She dipped a foot into the lagoon. The liquid surface broke, and water warm as tears accepted her entry. She took another step, the bottom hem of her robe brushing across the surface.

A drop from her eyes splashed the surface and rippled forth. The pattern of rings intersected with waves from the waterfall, and the sad song of the undine rose with a delicate apparition that formed into the shape of a woman. From across the pool, Kenzie stared and, for a dizzy second, felt as though she were looking into an aqueous mirror. The sprite tilted her head and words formed in Kenzie's mind, feminine and comforting.

Believe, daughter.

Kenzie, alone with no one to witness her weakness, sobbed.

She heard her name being called from far away. Startled, she looked to the silver light above. She was late, really late.

The tears had stopped much earlier, but she had stayed with the embrace of the water. A semblance of calm had come with the cleansing of the tears. She hurried to shore. The wet cloth of her robe stuck to her skin. She'd have some explaining to do, although to the best of her knowledge, there was no prohibition against getting in the water.

She hustled along the brook, the dashing music of the water heading in the same direction she was. She skipped across to get to the side closest to the exit grotto and found the trail leading away. She broke into a soundless run, bare feet caressing the soft footing of the trail.

She turned a bend and skidded to a stop, her mortification spreading in a hot stain across her face. Belinda and Aric, only partially robed, were engaged in the kind of carnal acts that Kenzie had assumed were absent from the purity of the Glade.

Belinda saw her first, and if the look during Harold's class had been malevolent, the expression Belinda wore now contained black hatred. The Wilder lifted an arm from under Aric, causing him to tip over.

Kenzie had no idea what spell the woman planned to cast, but she didn't intend to stand there while Belinda conjured. With a voice that cracked, she whispered, "I'm terribly sorry," and sprinted away from the pair of lovers.

"Damn it," she heard Aric say, while Belinda spat invectives at her. She ran and didn't look back. *Definitely don't look back.*

Out of breath, she found her parents waiting.

"Where were you?" asked her father, glancing at his wrist and remembering too late that that watches did not exist here.

"Why are you wet?" Her mother's tone came across as an accusation.

"I soaked my legs in the lagoon." She had planned to come up with a better excuse than the truth, but the encounter in the woods had flummoxed her.

Her parents shared glances. Her father asked the question. "What lagoon?"

CHAPTER FORTY

Mitch leaned against the railing with the sun over his left shoulder and faced toward the large flat circle of a fountain with the Museum of History and Industry in the background. At his feet was his backpack. In his hand was one of the two cell phones that Lassiter had given Kenzie. The secure bag for it was folded and in the backpack. He might need it later.

It had taken an hour and three streetcar transfers to get downtown. The swaying motion of the electric cars had relaxed him as the bustling neighborhoods sped past the window. He had jumped off at the museum at South Lake Union and Terry Streets and walked across the park on the concrete paths that wound across the greenscape of meticulously tended lawns. The grass was freshly cut and the smells mingled with the saltiness of Puget Sound drifting past. On the far side of the fountain was an observation deck jutting into the lake. Gulls wheeled overhead, their calls shrill. One tucked its wings and dive-bombed the water, searching for food.

Instead of looking out to the lake, Mitch kept his eyes trained on the foot traffic to and from the park. Three minutes after he'd exposed the phone and turned it on, the promised text message had arrived. He had glanced at the message, which bore the single word "acknowledged," along with the day—*Tuesday*—and time—*10 PM*—for the rendezvous. He closed the lid.

Thirty minutes later, they started to gather. It confirmed his suspicion that Lassiter would have monitored the locations of the phone used to signal when they had what he wanted, as well as his and Kenzie's personal phones. Lassiter had been explicit that Kenzie should signal him. Mitch deliberately violated those instructions. His phone was in his backpack, acting as confirmation that it was him, not Kenzie, that had used the first of the throwaway phones. Lassiter would be pissed, but he'd have to investigate.

First, a man and a woman, dressed in business suits too warm for the day, meandered into the park and settled on a bench across from the water feature. The next to arrive went to the pier to the left of his mini-peninsula and took up residence, nonchalantly scanning the waves made by the passing boats, with his opaque glasses hiding his eyes. The dude held himself balanced like he was a professional fighter. Mitch could see knots in the man's arms and decided he did not want to tussle with the guy.

The last to arrive was a woman. She was petite and in yoga pants, hair up in a ponytail, a dark blue lightweight jacket with baby blue piping. She had stopped to stretch, but the right pocket of her jacket hung heavily. Might be a cell phone, Mitch thought. He wasn't positive she was one of them until he saw her exchange glances with the others.

He straightened up, and they reacted as a team, the man to his left cutting off that avenue of escape, the couple splitting to follow the perimeter of the fountain. The cutie closed off the right.

Mitch allowed himself a small, self-satisfied smile that earned a frown from the woman in the activewear. He held up the phone, turned, and with a fully cocked arm, hurled Lassiter's phone out into the lake. All four of the watchers stopped. The runner put her hand up to her right ear. Mitch watched her lips moving. They must all have been connected via earpieces and mikes like the FBI used.

She nodded and walked toward him.

She was even prettier up close and barely came to his shoulder. When she spoke, her voice carried warm overtones. "Mr. Lassiter is questioning why you have elected to violate his instructions. What should I tell him?" Her smile encouraged him to answer. Mitch bet that not too many guys turned down that smile, in that face.

"Tell Lassiter that I have the other phone as well. I've stashed it away, and Kenzie doesn't know where it's at. When we find what he's looking for, we'll get hold of him on that one. He gets to set the time, I get to set the location."

Mitch held his breath, waiting for her to relay the information. Her hands stayed put. She regarded him with amusement, as though she were privy to a private joke.

"Are you going to tell him?" Mitch asked. He forced his eyes to keep moving. He glanced to the other three. They stood sentry, facing out.

As if to answer, a phone at her waist emitted a tinkling tone. She unclipped it, checked the number, and answered, all in the space of two rings.

"Yes, sir, he is right here." She listened. "Yes, sir, understood."

She held the phone out to Mitch.

"Our microphones are quite sensitive. Mr. Lassiter heard your message and would like to converse with you for a moment, if you have the time."

Another incredible smile. Mitch's fingers took the phone, brushing the lady's as he did. He glanced at the screen, but the number was blocked. No luck backtracking that trail, then.

Phone to his ear, Mitch said, "Hello."

Lassiter spoke, voice as precise as a laser. "Mr. Merriwether, every action has attendant consequences."

Mitch interrupted. "You can't hurt Kenzie, because she is the one that needs to dig up the flash drive for you. Me you need, because I have the last phone."

"Mr. Merriwether, I believe you have miscalculated your importance. If need be, I could remove you and arrange for another means of communication."

"Maybe," Mitch said, a tremor in his hand, "but her dad's a cop, a detective. How many coincidences do you think it will take before he switches from protecting Kenzie to nailing your ass to the wall? Me showing up dead might be one event too many."

"Playing percentages, Mr. Merriwether, is called gambling. I choose not to gamble."

"Then do it my way. You'll get what you want, and I can protect Kenzie."

Mitch quashed the urge to wipe his free hand on his jeans while Lassiter made him wait. His fingers rubbed against each other, gliding on a thin layer of sweat, matched by the dampness he felt at his brow. He saw movement from the corner of his eye. The big dude had abandoned his position and was walking toward him.

Come on, he thought, making eye contact with the fighter.

"Mr. Merriwether, this will be the final change to our agreement, do I make myself clear?"

With an explosive release of pent-up pressure, Mitch said, "Yeah, you do."

"Please hand the phone back to my representative."

Mitch handed it back to the woman. He kept his eyes locked on the man. Lassiter wouldn't let him off that easy. Mitch glanced to the water. He could always swim for it.

A scuffing sound brought Mitch's head around in time to see the cutie pulling something from her jacket pocket. He had time to recognize his mistake, the heaviness of her pocket earlier, the phone at the waist.

The electrodes struck him in the chest. Unlike the bee sting of the stun gun, the Taser hit him, and hit him, and hit him, and wouldn't let go. Red pain filled his sight as he fought to grab the leads embedded into his muscles, but wave after wave of high-voltage electricity short-circuited the commands from his brain.

He tried screaming, *"Enough, enough"* but the words never made it past the immobile muscles of his mouth. His whole body joined with the screaming, and he heard the runner speaking, he could hear everything, while he stood rigid, the voltage destroying any ability to move.

Her voice still carried the deceptive overtones of compassion while she electrocuted him at nineteen shocks per second. Her words broke up the eternity of pain into discrete blocks of agony. "Mr. Lassiter wished me to reinforce his point that there will be no more alterations to the plan. Also, that if he truly wanted to know where the second phone is, he has the wherewithal to get that information. He asks that you do not further abuse his patience or kindness."

Mitch didn't know how much longer it went on, just that it stopped. When it did, he faded to blackness, but not before feeling gratitude that his gamble had paid off. He was still alive. . . .

CHAPTER FORTY-ONE

For them, there was no lagoon. Kenzie tried to wrap her mind around the fact that her parents had walked the path along the brook and never discovered the waterfall and the pool of water below it. In a hurry, they refused her offer to lead them to it, to prove its existence.

With a numb feeling from the tip of her head to her toes, she followed them out through the portal back to the mundane world. Her robes transformed back to jeans that bound her hips, a blouse, and her running shoes. The pebble, still clenched in her hand, came through as she expected, so she slipped it into a pocket.

Staring out the car window as they drove home, Kenzie looked at the oncoming sunset and wondered if it were any more real than the lagoon.

Her father drove, threading through the traffic along the most efficient lines. In the rearview mirror, Kenzie saw his eyes flick from the dash to the road ahead. Her mother, sitting in front of her, maintained a rigid posture, face straight ahead, mouth downturned. Silence piled on itself and turned the atmosphere palpably anxious.

"How do the wards work?" Kenzie asked, making her father jump. He sent her a searching glance before getting his eyes back on the road and the vehicles around them.

"Why do you want to know?" asked her mother.

"Hush, it's a fair question," Raymond said in response to his wife, who visibly tensed. To Kenzie, he said, "In principle, the ward is a barrier of magic. It acts as a physical barrier, though a lighter web can be used as an alarm. The important part is that the ward must be connected to an object."

"So it's like an amulet," said Kenzie, thinking of the round stone she'd purloined from the Glade.

"Not quite. A ward doesn't alter the object of attachment, while an amulet is created by changing the item, whatever it is, at a fundamental level and imbuing it with magic of its own." As he lectured, Raymond relaxed. "Wards are simple enough that almost any wizard of reasonable capacity can fashion one."

"Can you teach me?" asked Kenzie.

He tipped his head to see her in the rearview. "I can," he said in a pleased voice.

"I think you should be considering how the council is overreacting to MAGE," said her mother.

Kenzie's ears perked up at the mention of the amplifier. News?

Her father's lip curled at the edge of his mouth. "I don't consider an electronics device that can locate the Family nearly as benignly as you and the other technocrats seem to. Aric made it clear that MAGE is a dangerous progression into the realms of magic."

Kenzie felt her eyes widen. Her father rarely spoke against her mother in such a direct manner.

"We'll discuss this later," said Sasha.

Kenzie caught the implication. It was an adult conversation and not for her ears, which was stupid after Aric had shot off his mouth at dinner . . . *yesterday?*

It seemed *so* much longer.

Like a bolt, a thought hit her and made her jerk. Trying to keep the apprehension she felt from her voice, she asked, "Are there any other companies that are doing this kind of research?"

Because sure as heck, Lassiter had a detector, which meant that the secret her mother thought was safe had already been discovered by someone.

Her father sent her a probing glance, but her mother answered first.

"No, it's a relative backwater for research, since there's no money in it. If we were involved in a politically popular field, like climate research, there would be significant competition for the federal funding. There is nothing there for you to worry about." The last bit was directed at her father, in a frosty voice.

They don't know.

Panic clutched at her. Down at the emotional level, she felt abandoned, as though her parents, by not divining the threat Lassiter posed, had let her down, even as her brain, at the intellectual level, argued in their defense. Not just Lassiter, evil as he was, but their failure to find the lagoon. And, as she admitted to herself, the way she kept slipping from magic to the mundane world frightened her.

She didn't know what was real anymore.

"McKenzie, did you still want to learn to set a ward?" Her father stood at the doorway of her room, a reprise of their positions after the kidnapping, him there, her on the floor in the corner. The thought appeared to occur to him, too. "Are you feeling okay?"

"Yes," Kenzie said, the weariness she felt oozing into the word. She struggled to her feet and forced a smile. Even the muscles in her face felt tired. "That would be cool."

He gave her a searching look and turned, the momentary crack in his professional demeanor forgotten. She followed.

Once they were downstairs, he faced her. "The process is not complicated, but you do need to be precise. More magic is not better in this case, as the ward will act as a steady drain on your energy." He hesitated. "You've used up considerable reserves in the last day or so, first with the . . . incident last night and then the lessons Harold taught today."

"Did he tell you?"

"About the amulet? Of course." He shrugged. "Harold should keep better control of the neophytes."

So much for expecting praise.

"Now, as I was saying, it doesn't take much power." His pointer finger first etched a pattern of the *Linius* spell and then described an arc like an igloo, and then traced along the bottom. As he closed the circumference of the circle and clenched his fist, she felt the ward come up.

"If it doesn't use much energy, how come I can feel it when you put it up?"

Her father's forehead furrowed. "Can you 'see' it, too? Not with your eyes, but with your magic?"

She tipped her head. She'd never really tried, but recalling the way she'd broken the binding spell last night, she let loose the lease of her senses. Dimly set, as though the lines of force were a double-exposure picture laid over the rest of the room, the gridwork of the ward materialized. She stuck out a hand. A tracer leapt from her fingertips and attached to the existing spell by the living room windows. She tugged at her end, and the whole ethereal firmament retreated in size toward her.

A squeal from the kitchen and the sound of breaking glassware shattered her composure. Kenzie let the web expand back to its original dimensions.

"Raymond!" came the shout from Kenzie's mother in the kitchen. An aggrieved Sasha appeared at the doorway. "What in the name of—"

She stopped both walking and speaking when she saw Kenzie. A heated flush reached her mother's cheeks.

"Teach her control." Sasha spun on her heel. Two seconds later, they heard the tinkle of glass being swept with vigorous strokes of a broom.

"Now," said her father, "you don't have to use a capture spell. The ward is a combination of two or more spells, with the first defining the nature of it"—he reiterated the *Linius*, but without calling magic— "with the second, which places it into a stasis." He completed the motion.

"As you grow, you'll learn to include warnings to go with the spell. In the event of absolute need, you can take a tingle spell that delivers a mild shock and dial it all the way up to a charge that will knock a rhinoceros on its butt."

Tingle spells were taught to the little kids and the Wilders when they first joined the Family. Harold used them occasionally as an attention-getter when the students lacked the appropriate focus on lessons. Like sticking your tongue on a nine-volt battery, it emitted more of a shock than any actual damage. It was an aimed spell, the same as the air spells, and unlike the frame of the ward.

"*Astrapius*," Kenzie said, giving the spell its proper name, and demonstrating it with a flick of her fingers without any energy attached, "is a kid's trick. All of us tried to boost the shock, but it always stays the same no matter how much magic you put into it." She waited for an explanation.

"Not exactly," he said. "You were taught a scaled version of the spell. Having Wilders electrocute each other seemed like a bad idea."

Kenzie sent a sidelong glance at her father at the atypical hint of humor. His demeanor remained studiously serious.

"Some of them could use it," she ventured, a picture of one person firmly in mind.

"True," he said. "Watch. This is the way to conjure the full power of *Astrapius*." The motion was substantially more complicated than the flick she knew. "You try, but don't use any energy. Go through the process."

He spent the next ten minutes correcting small flaws in her casting, reminiscent of the way Jules would adjust her arm for a block or strike. Finally, he seemed satisfied.

"Why are you teaching all this to me?" asked Kenzie. "I mean, not that I don't want to learn, it's . . . "

Her father stared directly into her eyes. The glint of determination in his eyes, so familiar, almost caused her to miss an underlying uncertainty. Seeing her father not fully in command of a situation was unsettling.

"You said you wanted to learn." He shifted his gaze to the kitchen doorway. With a lowered voice, he said, "Trouble is brewing. I can feel it—"

Not brewing, it's here, she thought. Still, it was spooky how he could read the vibes that way.

"—you can, too, or you wouldn't have asked to learn how to ward. It's not the attempt at abducting you, though I still haven't found the man that ordered your kidnapping. There are other powers at play." He transferred his gaze to a point over her shoulder and broke off.

"Dinner is ready," said her mother in a peevish announcement from the doorway.

"Be right there," said her father.

Kenzie turned. "Yes, ma'am."

Kenzie felt a hand on her shoulder. She faced her father.

"I know Jackson is looking after you, but some of our enemies have no respect for the sanctity of the living. They're worse than the lifelong criminals I catch, because they're not only totally amoral but intelligent and *gifted.*"

A trembling shook the hand on her shoulder.

He's scared, too, she thought, *and he doesn't know the half of it.* The implications of "gifted" settled on her. Lassiter was not of the Families.

Her father was warning her of someone who could do magic, that would use the Arts as a weapon. That's why he was teaching her the full power of *Astrapius.* To defend herself.

"You need to be ready," he said, the intensity of his eyes piercing as he delivered his instructions. "Keep yourself safe, even if it means you sacrifice Jackson."

Kenzie readied for bed. Her phone sat on her dresser, inert as a lump of clay. Mitch still had not sent her word about when they would meet. The silence made her anxious. Plus she wanted to see if he had any ideas on how to break into the safe.

Her mind dwelled on the hidden compartment in the floor of the master closet. It was big enough to hold some electronics. She clenched her jaws at the thought that Lassiter couldn't give her some idea of what the heck she was looking for. Until she was alone in the house again, she couldn't play with the safe and figure out the combination. And then, even if she did stumble onto the right turns of the intricately marked dial, there was no guarantee that it held the treasure she sought.

Feeling overwhelmed, she switched off the bedside lamp and tucked herself deep into the white comforter. As emotional exhaustion claimed her, an image of the gytrash stalked her sleep. Her last recollection was the supernatural canine stepping between her and Mitch, as though on guard.

CHAPTER FORTY-TWO

Mitch waited until after dark to slip in through the door at Mercury's place. Shutting the unlocked door behind him, he called out.

"Yo, Mercury?"

The inside of the shop wore the darkness like a cloak and muffled his voice. Mitch fumbled for the light switch to his right and came up empty. Patting the wall on the other side of the door proved equally fruitless.

Well, okay.

Mitch closed his eyes and pictured the room as he'd seen it that morning. Two steps to get past the cases to his right. He let his knuckles trail along the wood until they left the edge.

One step more forward and his other hand found the center cases. Turn right, again letting his hand track the picture in his head. He felt the corner at the end where the junction of the side passage was.

Time to turn left. He stuck his right arm out, making contact with jars on the shelves. He retracted his hand, touched the front edge of the shelf, noticed the cool and smooth texture under his fingertips.

It should be about eight steps to the door that led to Mercury's lair. He took a breath and counted as he walked. At "four," his shin collided with something solid. The impact sent red waves of sudden pain to his eyes. The clatter suggested a small stepstool. Wincing in the dark, he reached down to rub his abused lower leg while he waited for Mercury to come investigate. Nothing doing, so he dropped to a knee. Finding the object, a low chair based on the wood spindles he touched, he carefully put it to the side.

It took five more steps to get to the next door. This knob turned freely in his hand, too. Mitch wondered if Mercury ever worried about people breaking in.

The library stood as he remembered it, right down to the lit lamps on the table. Outside, though, had transformed from a jungle to a surreal glade with a waning moon glittering down onto the dark grasses and trees. Mitch squinted at the moon. Yesterday's moon was normal sized, as big as a quarter, and full, not a silver half-dollar and halved. This moon, strung from the heavens, seemed odd. *An optical illusion?*

Shaking his head, Mitch reminded himself not to trust anything he saw. The whole magic thing was screwy, even if, against all logic, it was real. He went to the nearest bookcase and perused the titles. A pair of shelves were devoted to the classics, from Plato to Melville. The next shelf down held tattered copies of books with titles like *The Sworn Book of Honorius* and *Magical Treatise of Solomon*. Next to these was a three-volume set with the tantalizing title *Three Books of Occult Philosophy*. He pulled the Solomon book from the shelf and creaked it open. The pages exuded the odor of time, and the curled letters of print were unreadable, Old English or High Latin or something. He snugged it back into the hole he had pulled it from.

He selected a ragged copy of *For Whom the Bell Tolls* on the second bookcase to read while he waited for Mercury. With a half-audible groan, he eased down onto the polished leather seat. His body ached like a cranky ogre with a meat-hammer had tenderized every square millimeter of muscle. Getting Tased was on his never-do-again list. He shoved the self-pity out of his head and opened the book to the first page.

The click of a door latch woke him. Bleary-eyed, he saw a door swing wide where a blank wall had been, and Mercury enter. The door swung the other way and disappeared once more into the featureless wall.

"Ah, good, you're here," said the wizard, as though he had been expecting Mitch to show up. "Everything is nearly set for the removal of Mr. Jackson. The Jacksons will find out on Monday that they have received an all-expenses-paid trip to Aruba. I'll give them a little prod to move them along, but by Tuesday morning, you can stop worrying for them."

Mitch labored to get up, still feeling groggy. The muscles on his face tightened as the period of immobility in the chair turned the aches into spikes stabbing into his arms and legs. He wobbled and held on to the top of the seatback.

"That's good," he managed to say as he wobbled. He succumbed to an overpowering pressure to yawn. "Sorry," he said from behind the hand he used to cover his mouth.

"You look like hell," observed Mercury. The wizard's eyes swept up and down Mitch's body.

"Lassiter doesn't like disobedience," said Mitch.

Mercury gave him a long, considering stare. "I imagine not."

They both fell silent. Fuzzy thoughts trickled across synapses in Mitch's head as the old man watched. Finally, the question that kept bugging Mitch forced its way to the front.

"Can you tell me more about magic? Not how it's done, but the history of the people."

"Most teenage boys would want to know how to do it."

"Can anybody learn?"

"Magic is very selective," Mercury said after a brief hesitation.

Natch, thought Mitch. "So what about the people, the wizards? How does Lassiter fit in the framework, because I'm not seeing it."

The hesitation this time was palpable. "I can't answer the last. Mr. Lassiter is an anomaly, a man who does not appear to belong to a Family and does not, to the best of my ability to determine, work for one."

Mercury peered at Mitch. As at their first meeting, Mitch was struck by the *aliveness* within those green orbs.

The wizard continued. "Those circles are very small. The Families are not large. For whatever reason, those that practice the Arts do not often have offspring. The larger part of each Family is made up of what some call Wilders, those who spontaneously demonstrate or manifest magical ability. To complicate matters, the Families are not unified. If you thought of them as tribes with different cultures, you would have a decent idea of the structures. Some cultures are modestly permissive, as is McKenzie's, others are much more rigid in the way that they view the mundane world.

"At one point, the tribes numbered about two dozen, before they consolidated. Now there are two dominant ones, at least in this area. For rather obvious reasons, they don't advertise."

"You keep saying 'them,' Mercury. What Family do you belong to?" asked Mitch.

The wizard weighed his words. He wore a pensive expression as he answered. "I have no Family. Some of us are solitary wizards, bound by oaths to perform a duty that supersedes the life of Family and friend."

Mitch sensed a chasm of loneliness in Mercury's words. The wizard picked up the thread of the lesson.

"The people chosen to work for the Families are an even smaller group, and number in the handfuls. These are almost always selected for specific skills that they possess. In the earliest days of our awareness, we sought out the protection of the lords. As our ranks grew, and especially after the nobles sacrificed us to the mobs, we retreated into enclaves. Behind the myths of the druids and covens lay kernels of truth. The Families take advantage of people that can advance the species—"

Mitch raised an eyebrow at the term. He doubted Kenzie was a totally different species from a biological perspective.

"—while holding the vast majority of the population in a general sense of contempt."

"Meat," said Mitch, his voice flat and emotionless.

"A somewhat despicable term that has gained currency among the Families." This was delivered with a piercing look. "It originated with the Spaniards and is spreading."

Mitch shifted his feet and avoided Mercury's eyes by assessing the waning moon. The features weren't quite right. The Sea of Tranquility was missing.

"It's a wonder you all put up with us," Mitch said, joking.

"Some think we ought not."

Mitch caught movement from the corner of his eye. He swapped gazing at the moon for checking the foliage.

"That's why Lassiter doesn't fit. He's not magical or anything like that. He's a dude with hired guns who is looking to steal something. I'm guessing he can't go directly at Kenzie's mom without getting chopped into hamburger, so he's trying to backdoor the situation. And while he's an arrogant jerk, he doesn't think he's an evolutionary upgrade on the rest of us."

An extended sigh met his words. "Mitch, I could help you more if you were a bit more honest with me."

Mitch's head snapped around. The old man didn't flinch away from the confrontational cast of Mitch's face. Mitch searched for words to deflect Mercury. The wizard beat him to it.

"You've had some contact with at least one other person of power, someone not affiliated with the Graham family."

The accusation lay in the air. A buzzing grew in Mitch's ears as he locked stares with Mercury. He froze his face but stayed alert to the other man's hands.

How much does he know? competed with *How much do I tell him?*

"It's not like there are that many of you guys out there," he said, and let derision drip from his voice.

"No, but you do seem to have a knack for encountering them. First McKenzie, then her father, and, somewhere, one of the Spanish Family."

Crap, crap, crap . . .

Mercury stepped back, and Mitch relaxed a fraction.

"When you first came in here," said Mercury, "you used a hand gesture for a compulsion spell that Kenzie's Family hasn't used in a generation. The Spaniards, as befitting their history, were among the first to use that spell with that motion." Mercury opened his palms. "Like this, but no magic."

Mitch tensed. Mercury's hands flashed through the sequence that Hunter used at school.

"There was no way for you to know that specific cast if you hadn't been introduced to it somewhere else. You would also need to know that the person using it is one of us, or the significance would have been lost on you. The last piece, though, was implication of a master race."

Mercury's eyes gleamed and his voice deepened. "The two remaining Families have a difference of opinion about whether or not wizards are a new species, destined to walk the world as its rulers, or simply human beings with a new skill that someday everyone will possess."

"So where does Lassiter fit?" Mitch retorted. "He's not wizard material."

"But you said that he does have a means to know when we use our magic. That implies the means, at some point, to control it. Mr. Lassiter may not be a wizard, but my instinct suggests that he would like to be. And a man that ruthless will not be thwarted. He will need to be destroyed, root and branch. Your Spanish friends will be more than willing to assist," said Mercury.

The echo of Hunter's words, *"you have an ally,"* rang in Mitch's head.

"Why?" Mitch asked, despite knowing the answer.

"The Spaniards consider themselves the rightful lords of the planet, and the rest of humanity a plague to be cleansed. The only reason there has been a reprieve is that people, in all their stupidity, still outnumber the Families a million to one."

Mitch did the math on instinct. Six or seven thousand people total in the Families.

"Is that here, or worldwide?"

"Just the ones known. Wilders appear all the time, but no one knows why," said Mercury, glittering shards of icy green replacing the normal warmth of his eyes. "Now, enlighten me on how you found them when I couldn't in a search that took me to four continents and spanned most of two decades."

CHAPTER FORTY-THREE

Mercury watched as his brother warmed his hands over the fire that crackled in the corner, well away from the books. After draining Mitch of all the information the boy possessed, he had sent the exhausted youth home with a strong injunction to rest. He'd set the fire in an invisible hearth and turned out the lights, preferring the flickering along the walls, to encourage some deep thinking. That the Rubiera clan had never left Seattle stunned him to his core, and he could only imagine what else he might be missing.

"I find it somewhat amazing that Mitch managed to discover both Families in an act of cosmic accident," said Harold, "and more surprising that the children of both Families are so careless as to tell him what they really are. As a bonus, he's still alive afterward." He stood straight and turned to face Mercury. "Would you like my news, or are you depressed enough already?"

"Lassiter?" said Mercury.

"Related, I think," said Harold, appearing to glide to the other chair, his legs hidden below his robes. "According to Raymond, Sasha has engineers building an amplifier for magic, and they already have an electronic device that will detect us. Sasha, in her very assertive way, has assured anyone who would listen that her research project presents no threat to the Family. Raymond has a suspicious mind, so doubts her statement." He sat and crossed his ankles. "Based on young Mitch's testimony, we know that he is correct to question her security."

Mercury rolled his neck, generating a crack. "Has Kenzie approached you?"

"Nary a word, though she looks as though she's tussled with an anaconda. Her power is growing faster than we expected. She created an amulet today."

Mercury peered at Harold. "Was it wise to teach her how to do that before she gains full control?"

Harold's lips twisted into a wry smile. "No, that would not be wise, so I did not teach her. She transformed an ordinary pebble into a perpetual lantern. Quite impressive, and slightly terrifying. She has both range and power."

"Well . . . ," said Mercury, considering the ramifications. "I'm beginning to suspect that we've lost control of the situation."

"Indeed," said Harold, unruffled. He changed the subject. "Lassiter poses a threat to all the Families. We are too few to survive a purge. Raymond is of the opinion that we should join with the Rubieras to expunge him."

"He should know better," murmured Mercury. "The Families need to stay hidden as much as possible, not from the designs of Lassiter, but from the *hechiceros*. They have a long memory, and the last thing we need is another wizard's war."

Harold gave his head a slow shake. "So you still propose to sacrifice the boy?"

"It's not a sacrifice. He is in the matrix of forces for a reason, even if I am too much of a dullard to understand it. You talk of the power of magic gathering like a storm front roiling on the horizon. It's not happenstance that he is both friends with Hunter Rubiera and is in exactly the correct spot to thwart Lassiter. Those speak to a grander plan for Mitch. He is cast in the role of hero. I suggest we let him fulfill the part." Light from the flames flickered in Mercury's eyes. "Of course, that doesn't mean that we don't help him along the way."

Harold cast a disparaging glare at Mercury. "He has no training."

"So I'll arrange some training."

"Assuming the Rubieras, Raymond, or Lassiter don't murder him first."

"There is that," agreed Mercury. He turned serious. "We need to trust the arts, I think. We've looked at this as a new occurrence, but what if it's the culmination of the break between the Families? It's in the best interests of all wizards to have a united nation in order to grow to our fullest potential."

"What of Lassiter? He's not one of us," said Harold.

Mercury smiled, feeling the lack of mirth as he did. "He is."

Harold protested. "He's mundane."

"So are we," said Mercury, and waited.

Harold rocked back at the blasphemy. His lips parted to speak, closed again to a thin white line. Anger glowered from his features. He swallowed, then said in a strained voice, "Is it your intention to be deliberately offensive? The average person not only cannot manage magic, but they act as cattle, dull in their senses, and resist the effort to think as though the attempt would shatter their skulls."

"You spend too much time within the safe confines of the Glade and not enough among the people," said Mercury. He purposefully maintained an even tone. "The mass of humanity is a mob, but meeting them as individuals reveals kindnesses and courage that we might do well to emulate. However," he continued with an unconscious twitch of his pointer finger, as if consigning the previous statement to the settled past, "the point that I am offering is that the wizards, while clearly evolving from the current rendition of humans, are only one step along the journey. Many other people are taking those steps beside us, some of them spontaneously like the Wilders. Some, like Kenzie, seem a step and a half ahead on the path."

"Lassiter isn't interested in your path, or even in magic. He's a grasping conniver, the same kind that sought to enslave our ancestors."

"*Au contraire.* I think his sole purpose is to be able to gain access to magic. There is no power on earth that one person possesses that another does not covet. We have been under the impression, mistaken I think, that our abilities are founded within biological imperatives, that we are evolution's favored children. We conflated the imperative with the magic. We should have recognized that the imperative affects everyone. We sought the biologic and philosophical. Lassiter seeks the same thing in the mechanic and technological."

"Machines have no soul," said Harold. His glare radiated his offended dignity.

"Still, the machine world grows, its slithering tentacles intruding into every aspect of life, while we struggle to maintain our numbers." Mercury gazed out to the moonset beyond his windows. "Nature does not care for souls. She seeks winners."

The void that separated Mercury and his brother reestablished itself. Harold, considered Mercury, had thrived within the safety and surety of the Glade of Silver Night. Now he was a monk confronting the irreligious world on the outside of the monastery.

"So, we destroy Lassiter," said Harold. The temperature of a freshly dug grave accompanied the words.

"No," said Mercury, choosing his words with precision, "we, or rather Mitch, saves Kenzie. His plan is well thought out and relies on simple deceptions. Lassiter is undoubtedly aware of Mitch's uncertain status. For the boy to reach out for help from Graham privately is risky but the safest route for Kenzie." He paused to think. "The technocrats and their machines will want to control her or kill her. Killing Lassiter but losing Kenzie will signal the final days of magic, and the opening epoch of the soulless. Saving her leaves our path to the future open. Mitch is the one person who has proven he would sacrifice himself for her. Still, he plays it cautiously regarding her safety."

Harold nodded. "Then my task is clear. Teach her to control her power and keep her safe in the realm of magic until she can defend herself." Sorrow filled his next words. "Your path is more difficult."

Mercury dipped his chin in acknowledgment. "To help Mitch and Kenzie stop Lassiter. Nature has pitted the two champions against each other. Lassiter must not get control of the Arts, or we might as well surrender our humanity now."

"I can stall Raymond about approaching the Rubieras."

"Good," said Mercury.

The brothers sat in the quiet of the library, each lost to his own thoughts and calculations. Mercury's mind drifted to the problem of the Spanish wizards, the *hechiceros*. *One battle at a time,* he thought. Submitting to their authority would rob them of their humanity as much as losing to Lassiter, just differently. Instead of becoming cyborgs plugged into the electronic universe, they'd be slaves and chattel.

It was easy to talk about trusting the grandeur of the magic to guide him, but relying on a sixteen-year-old boy to play the part of hero made his nerves tingle with apprehension, and his knees wanted to buckle.

For Kenzie's sake, he hoped that Mitch could be trusted to answer the call.

CHAPTER FORTY-FOUR

Kenzie woke to fog outside the curtains, but felt clear-headed for what felt like the first time in a year. She extended her arms above her head in a languorous stretch that finished with her rolling the kinks out of her shoulders. She came fully awake with a stark realization that time was her enemy, and her arms snapped down.

It was Sunday. Unless her parents went shopping, they'd be home all day.

She propped herself up against her pillows and pulled her knees up. A yawn forced its way out, and she took a deep breath following it. The reticence she had felt yesterday was gone, replaced by curiosity to see what her parents were hiding. Still, searching for the combination with them in the way struck her as a rotten idea.

She reached over to her nightstand. A fast check on her phone showed no calls, no messages, no nothing from Mitch since yesterday. Her cheeks warmed as she recalled his hot temper after she had slapped him, but the picture of taut and defined muscles and hard jaw stood out more. She waffled, then her thumbs darted across the screen. *Good Morning* glowed briefly as the message launched to the ether.

A second later, she second-guessed herself. She knew that he didn't trust the phones and had told her not to use them, but it seemed silly to stop altogether, since that would send up an alarm, too. She parsed Mitch's instructions, reasoning that he had meant not to trust the phones.

Reassured, she checked the screen. No reply.

Kenzie flipped the covers back and slipped on her bathrobe, cinching it tight at the waist. She tucked her phone into the capacious pocket.

Downstairs, her parents sat in relative inactivity, her father reading the Sunday paper, her mother checking messages on her tablet. Both glanced at her as she went to the coffee machine. Her father met her with a tired face. Her mother's face held a noncommittal expression, but Kenzie read her mood from the angry flicking motion that dismissed message after message.

Great. They're fighting.

Odds were that it was about her. She faced away from them and let her lips compress to a pained line. She poured milk into her mug and added two teaspoons of sugar before adding the hot coffee. The clink of her spoon against the side of the cup seemed disproportionately loud in the early-morning gloom.

Her father folded the paper down onto the table next to his half-full cup of black coffee when she turned. "I have to go out later this morning," he said. "I have some things I need to chase down at work. While I'm gone, practice setting wards."

Kenzie took her directions in with a silent and perplexed nod of confirmation.

Her mother spoke next, residual anger showing in the set of her jaw. "I have to head into the office. Your father feels that there exists the barest possibility of a breach in our security, so I need to access the logs and video." Her fingernails clicked on the glass surface of the tablet as three more e-mails were kicked to oblivion.

Yes! They both were leaving.

"It's not very fair to call Jackson out again," she ventured in a timid voice. She felt guilty about taking the bodyguard away from his family the day before.

Her parents exchanged glances that set her to worrying.

"We discussed that, along with the way you violated our judgment by dismissing him yesterday before one of us arrived," answered her father. His eyes twitched to the side as if looking for support, or at least, no vocal opposition to his speech. "Our thinking is that the threat is . . . perhaps overblown on the personal injury side—"

Wrong, she thought, but kept the disagreement from her face.

"—while the other existent threats pose a greater risk specific to you," he finished. "My feeling is that as long as you are inside the house, you enjoy a relative degree of safety. This assumes that you will agree to abide by our decision and not leave while we are gone."

Kenzie started as she realized that he was asking more than telling. It felt weird, and she looked at him with her head tilted over like she was trying to recognize something both familiar and brand-new at the same time. Puzzled, she said with a shrug, "Yeah . . . okay."

Her phone vibrated in silent mode against her hip, tickling. *Bad timing.* The thickness of the robe absorbed the telltale buzz. It took all her willpower not to reach for it.

"So you'll stay inside?" her father pushed.

"Can the wards be set on a wall without a roof?" she temporized. "I mean, can I set it on the wall outside so I can at least go in the backyard?" She set her gaze on him, striving for an earnest look. "Please?"

Indecision appeared on his face.

Her mother shook her head and answered into the breach of the negotiation, "Absolutely not."

"They can," said her father. "The wards have their limitations, and I think that is what concerns your mother."

"What concerns me," said Sasha, her head shifting side to side while her face contorted into a sneer, "is the presumption that Kenzie will govern herself in a responsible manner when she's been openly hostile to the point of insulting a wizard to his face when he was a guest."

Kenzie spoke before she had chance to restrain her own anger. "You mean Aric, the loser that was banging Belinda in the bushes at the Gathering last night? I was right about him, and you should have seen it, too. He's a jerk." Her voice went shrill with mockery. "*Here, have my daughter.* We must make sure the magic survives, after all. Too bad he's busy having someone else."

Her mother's mouth opened once, twice, but no words came out, though bright blossoms lit on pale cheekbones.

Her father responded first. His demeanor changed in an instant, the relaxed Sunday-morning man replaced with the Monday-morning police interrogator. "How do you know this?"

His voice chilled her. She recounted surprising the pair as she ran back from the lagoon. He probed for additional details and sounded exasperated at the paucity of her memory.

"I don't remember anything else. I . . . they . . . I wanted to get away from them," she exclaimed with a shudder.

Raymond glared at Sasha. "When you get the logs, make sure to bring everything that Aric has been associated with. I want his timesheets, security logins, keyloggers, any video of him. If you have a piece of data on him, I want it."

"Aric would never betray—"

Her father interrupted, cold and precise in his mannerisms, the consummate cop. "I don't know that, and I certainly don't know that of a Wilder who's been covering up her level of skill." He faced Kenzie.

"She was the only other one that showed any mastery in the class yesterday, correct?"

"Harold told you," she said. Followed with, "You were checking up on me."

"I was checking up on you because the range and power of the magic that you are exhibiting can be dangerous. I need to know where you're at if I am to provide the proper guidance; not as your father, but as a wizard. Why else do you think I offered to teach you about the wards? You are ready, even if your control is highly suspect."

Kenzie saw the truth in the words, along with something else he did not mention. He hadn't sought to teach her any exotic incantations. Wards were steady, unspectacular, and, for wizards in jeopardy, essential to continued health.

"Wards require precision," she said, understanding that the practice held a dual purpose of protection and training. "And I now have another means of self-defense. That's why, isn't it."

"Yes," he said, holding his gaze steady on her. "On both counts. I want you safe."

He turned back to Sasha.

Kenzie saw a fleeting moment of cunning expose itself before her mother could cover it with outrage. "I would think that you would have higher priorities than bothering Aric, considering our daughter is threatened by criminals you *still* have not caught." Her protests held an accusation but possessed a forced quality.

"Every scrap of data," the cop said, discounting her deflection. "Today."

Curiosity almost made her stay. But common sense told Kenzie to get the hell away from what was going to be a major fight, so she fled, coffee in hand, back to her room. The voices below escalated. Through her closed door, she could hear them tearing into each other. Back pressed against the door, she gathered her wits. At least she didn't have to figure out how to get them both out of the house, she thought with a twist to her lips. She pulled her phone from the bathrobe pocket.

Mitch had texted not once, but twice. She must have missed the second buzz when her parents opened up on each other. The format lent itself to terseness. In the first message, Mitch had conveyed the fact that the weather had returned to a normal Seattle gloom. She smiled. The second text simply said *Good morning*. The smile faded. He had said at the yogurt shop to give him thirty minutes after his text, and he'd meet her at the back of the garage. He was probably on his way.

He could not get here that soon. An image of Mitch in the backyard, both parents confronting him, alarmed her. A couple of hours, she thought, at least. It would take that long for the fight to wind up, plus her parents would have to get ready to leave the house. She tapped in a hasty response she'd be busy until noon.

Phone clenched in her hand, she listened to the controlled yelling downstairs. She discovered with some surprise that she sympathized with her father. He kept showing flashes of humanity, that he cared about her. She wasn't so sure the same was true of her mother, who seemed more concerned about the enchantress that Kenzie was becoming than the girl she was.

The cell vibrated. He'd gotten the message.

She set a protective web, analyzed it, and released it. Each iteration came a smidge faster, the web a small measure tighter. She also found that it centered on her. When she moved, it moved with her.

She had wheedled her father to set his barrier at the edge of the property so she could go outside. Unlike her drifting hemispheric domes, his clung to the perimeter wall like a floating curtain, following the contours around the home. It created a cool effect in the magic like that of an aurora borealis that only a few could see. He had tied a capture function to the webbings, combined with an alert.

The totality of the weave was far superior to the limited ward she had brushed aside on Friday night. More than anything he said, the upgrade in the protection told her how concerned he really was. She expanded hers until it touched his. A tingle touched her fingertips. She withdrew, noticing the quiver in both webs.

Can magic interact with other magic? she wondered.

A branch lifted up on the hillside, distracting her.

Kenzie saw Mitch clambering down through the stout vegetation, taking a direct route instead of the deer trail she had followed. His torso was turned so he could use the sides of his shoes for purchase against the leaf-covered slope. He glanced in her direction, bobbed his head.

He'd seen her. Good. Kenzie went to the protected point in the wall. She called out when he was still twenty feet away. "Hi. Be careful. Don't touch the wall. My dad has some warnings set up that will trip if you try to climb over."

Only after she finished did she realize that she'd used "dad" instead of "father."

"Well, how do we talk then?" came Mitch's annoyed reply, followed by a prompt, "Never mind, got an idea."

He slid the rest of the way down the hill, disappearing behind the wall. A second later, a lanky leg snaked up and over a branch of a tree that overlooked the rear of her house. The rest of him swung around the pivot point.

"There," he said, scanning the surrounding area. He appeared satisfied that they were alone as he kept speaking, though he kept the volume down. "Next problem is yours. How do I get a phone to you without tripping off the whatever doohickey your dad has set up?"

"Toss it, I guess." Kenzie moved away from the hard surface of the garage wall and stood on the grass.

"Why won't that set it off?"

"Do you always ask so many questions," asked Kenzie, glaring at him. Her lips twitched, though, and she snorted. "It only seems to work on living things."

"What about birds? Or squirrels?"

"Would you toss me the phone," said Kenzie. "There's a minimum threshold, I think." She closed her eyes. "Yeah, I can change it to respond differently depending on the sensitivity limits."

"Shame it doesn't work on inanimate objects," Mitch said. "Be nice to have a force field." He held the phone, with a hard case to protect it, in his hand. "Catch."

She did.

"I think I found where my mother hid the memory storage," she said.

Mitch nodded. "Good. I got Lassiter to agree to let us set up the meeting point." He said it nonchalantly and wouldn't meet her eyes. "How soon until you can actually get it? We need to verify the data, and we should copy it. It might be a handy insurance policy for us. I'm assuming that your mother has it backed up, too, but no sense in taking chances."

Kenzie's eyes narrowed. How had he . . . ? She wasn't sure she wanted to know.

"Where did you set it up for?" she asked.

"I didn't specify," said Mitch, perched in the crook of the branch, leaves fluttering around him. He looked like a delinquent Peter Pan. "But I was thinking that we should keep it close, so Seward Park again. This time we should be up at the picnic area. You know it, right?"

"Yeah," she said. "It's awfully open. And crowded this time of year."

"I expect Lassiter to do the exchange at night. It's easier to cover your tracks." Mitch glanced down at her. "How soon can you get it?"

A jot of worry made her shake her head. "I don't know. It's in a safe."

"So jigger the tumblers," said Mitch.

Kenzie started in surprise. "Do you have any idea how much control fine actions like that take? No, I'll have to figure out the combination."

Mitch pursed his lips like he was ready to say something, and then seemed to think better of it. "Your mother the kind of person to write the combination down?"

With a shrug, Kenzie answered, "I don't know. I didn't even know they had a safe until yesterday."

Mitch adjusted his position, the springy foliage bouncing around him.

Kenzie moved closer to the wall until ten feet separated them. Mitch looked worn at the edges despite the lightness of his voice. He lifted his left shoulder in a self-deprecating gesture. A small smile showed for a moment.

Kenzie crossed her hands at her waist. "I wish you could come down here," said Kenzie, her shoulders undulating with the words.

The smile flashed and vanished. "You could come up."

They sighed at the same time.

"You're not wearing that necklace." Mitch made a circular motion with his finger at the base of his throat. "It's . . . I like it."

Kenzie's fingertips pressed into the notch at the base of her throat. "I can't wear it here," she said. She hurried on because Mitch was sure to ask anyway. "It came from . . . someplace else." She widened her eyes to keep him from pursuing it further. He got the hint.

"It looks good on you" was all he said. He did another survey.

Kenzie shuffled her feet. Looking over her shoulder, she said, "I should go. I need to figure out the safe while they're gone."

That earned her a nod.

"Yeah, I should get busy, too." His gaze hardened and the lines on his face sharpened as his attention drifted inward. "We need to meet someplace where we can talk without the whole world listening in. No offense, but this is not safe. I don't think Lassiter is the only problem you have."

His sudden divergence confused her.

"What else?" she asked. "It's not like it can get any worse."

"I think Hunter's family is looking for you."

CHAPTER FORTY-FIVE

Mitch made the final adjustments to the bot. He had already switched the power supply from the base AC they used in the lab for a DC battery. This was a planned modification since they would run on battery power for competition anyway.

Test time. He placed the compromised cell phone into a holder on the bot and hit the button to initiate the series of movements programmed for the pincher fingers. Like a metallic mother caressing an electronic baby, one finger ran a tip down the side of the phone, pausing at the power button. The screen came to life in a splash of color. The vibration of the phone starting altered its position in the grip of the pinchers. Mitch squinted. Should be okay, he thought, but decided he should add a bushing to alleviate the motion.

The next programmed function was the tricky one. His phone was built with a capacitive touch screen. Since the human body possessed an electromagnetic field of its own, his finger would distort the field of the screen whenever he wanted to call or surf. The robot finger was electronically inert, so Mitch got creative. Emulating the more expensive capacitive styluses on the market, he jury-rigged one of Alice's fingers to be reactive to the phone.

Mitch held his breath as the digit extended and tapped at the screen. If his measurements were accurate, the first tap would bring the phone to life, and the second would start the sequence to dial a preprogrammed number.

The second motion missed the target. He groaned but made another minute adjustment. Before testing again, he scrounged and found a piece of rubber thin enough to work as a shock absorber. Powering down the phone, he restarted the test from the beginning.

This time everything worked to perfection as the house phone started ringing. He heard his uncle answer it, mutter, "Stupid telemarketers," and hang up.

Alice was ready.

Time to make the thermite.

The pointer on the old-fashioned balance scale wavered with each added spoonful of iron oxide to the reddish mound. Mitch held his breath as the pointer settled on zero. One hundred grams. Perfect. He lifted the sample pan from the scale. With a smooth motion, he shook the powder into a glass jar. Using a fine-bristled brush, he swept any remaining particles from the pan to the floor to avoid contaminating the batch. The pan went back onto the scale, and Mitch reset the balance to a mass of thirty-seven grams.

Mitch worked with greater care with the finely powdered aluminum. If the particles became airborne in the garage's atmosphere and there was a spark, the metal had a fair chance of igniting. Using a wooden spatula to minimize the risk of setting off an unplanned and unpleasant reaction, he deftly piled up the flat gray reactive metal. The scale teetered until he had the correct amount on the pan. This was added to the jar.

Tipped to a forty-five-degree angle, the powders lay in the jar like a sedimentary rock, or a crude sand glass decoration. Mitch turned the jar around its axis, the metals mixing in the bottom as they flowed over each other. When the mixture was thoroughly combined, he poured out the cementlike result into a glass custard bowl. He pulled out some homemade play dough that he'd made earlier and tested it for set. It was pliable and firm. He nodded. He measured out thirty-four grams. Into the bowl went the binder.

Latex gloves stretched onto his hands and snapped at the wrist. Mitch kneaded the components of the thermite into his dough until he achieved a uniform texture and appearance. Then, he picked it up and rolled it until it resembled a large meatball. He wrapped it in plastic wrap and put it into the Camaro.

The whole thing weighed about six ounces and would burn through a half an inch of solid aluminum plate in seconds. He'd place it in Seward Park tomorrow, if Hunter came through with the initiator by then.

He could have used a standard magnesium fuse, but the burn time for the strip of flammable metal to start the oxidation reaction of the thermite was slow.

He put the robot into the trunk and slammed it with finality.

Everything was ready for a bigger, quicker bang.

Mitch took a last look around. He still had extra materials for more thermite. He stored them at the back of a base cabinet where no one was likely to look. He wiped some sweat off his brow and clicked the light off. He entered the house to meet "jolly" Uncle Henry.

Lassiter wasn't the only one who could use minions and the promise of violence. Mitch would be ready for him this time.

CHAPTER FORTY-SIX

Kenzie inspected the dial. Minute lines with numbers marked by the tens. She couldn't even figure out the odds of hitting the combo by accident—she didn't know how many numbers were needed, or which way to turn the dial.

It was hopeless.

On a lark, she tried to "see" inside the lock. With a lot of effort, she built a feel for the mechanism. Moving it, on the other hand, proved impossible. She growled with frustration. Briefly, she considered using brute force to break the safe, but the repercussions might wreck the rest of the room. Maybe even the house.

Sorry, Mother, it got away from me. She giggled. *A bit.* She giggled again.

Lips still twitchy, she looked at the gray face. She spun the dial with a quick twist of her wrist. Smoothly, it whirled clockwise with the faintest of clicks and glided to a stop. The effect was mesmerizing: blurring, slowing, settling to a fixed number. She spun it again. It stopped at thirty-two. Two to the fifth power. Whir, blur, sixteen. Two to the fourth power. Intrigued, she gave the dial another ride, this time counterclockwise. Thirteen. The unlucky prime. One more time, to get rid of the bad-luck thirteen. Twenty-nine, prime.

Quit wasting time, she thought.

Where would her mother write down a combination?

Would she be that dumb?

The second question made her waver. As chilly as they were to each other, her mother exhibited both extraordinary intelligence and drive. To be a CEO in a hyper-competitive industry like tech required more than a pleasant smile and a short skirt. Her mother had made a name for herself by being right more often than her competitors, smart and competent men mostly. She also waged business as war, ruthless in executing innovations.

Still, inside the safe confines of the house, her mother might. Unless it was easily memorized. Like a birthday? She tried her mother's birthday, followed by her father's, and her own. None of them.

Anniversary?

Nope.

She couldn't think of any more numbers that might be important. She snorted.

It wouldn't be that easy. The safe combination might be preset by the manufacturer and bear no relation to her mother. Seizing on that hope, Kenzie quickly tapped the name of the company into her phone. The web page came up, and she selected the product support tab. The corner of her mouth puckered in as the very first piece of advice she saw suggested changing the combination when the safe was set up.

She glanced at the time. Maybe another thirty minutes until someone came home. She couldn't plan for more than that.

Kenzie meandered out of the closet and gazed around the bedroom, feeling overwhelmed. She tried to put herself in her mother's position. Where would she hide a combo? Her eyes strayed to the bedside table. Someplace close. The pad of paper, two dates written on it. Hope blossomed with a smile. Her mother *had* written it down. She pulled the drawer open. The pad was on top. The months were written out in full, which wouldn't work. She memorized the dates, converting the months to numbers. She discarded the years—both were for the current year. That left her four numbers: 4, 18, 9, 30. Assuming that none of the numbers repeated, that left her with twenty-four possible permutations.

Back to the website. The very helpful guide to amateur safecrackers indicated that the first turn should be to the right, four revolutions, then left for three, right for two, and left to the last digit.

Ten minutes later, the safe sat impassively closed as the last option failed to work.

"*Dang it,*" said Kenzie aloud. She breathed out heavily. She had been so sure. . . .

She went back to the pad. She had the numbers right. It dawned on her and made her feel stupid. Her mother had complained enough that Kenzie was tired of it. The dates, she realized, were for tax filings for the company. Not an elaborate code. She slipped the drawer closed, resisting the urge to slam it.

She had searched the compartment in the room that belonged to her mother. If the combination was here, she couldn't see it. It wouldn't be down in her office. That was too far away. The master bath was a dumb place to hide anything, but it was about the only place she hadn't already investigated.

She curled around the end of the bed, shooting a sideways glance at the titles on the spines of the stack of books on her father's night table. She paused, half-turned.

She hadn't searched everything. She had skipped her father's drawers, assuming the safe was business-related.

What if it wasn't?

She hurried to that side of the bed. She braced the tabletop to keep it stable as she opened the drawer. If the stack of books avalanched, she'd never get it put back correctly.

The interior of the drawer was sparse of possessions, but her eyes were drawn to a scrap of paper torn from the flap of an envelope. Four digits.

Nooo, she thought. *That's too easy.*

She guided the dial around the sequence. A delicate click resonated through the tips of her fingers. The irony of her father, security maniac that he was, leaving the combination for her to find made her shake her head.

She went from stooped over the safe to her haunches. Now that it was unlocked, a powerful reluctance to open the heavy-seeming door overtook her. Screwing up her courage, she reached and twisted the handle. The dull thud of the retracting bolts echoed. Taking a breath, she stood and pulled.

She almost dropped it, the unexpected weight of the door catching her off guard. Grunting, she levered it up. When it crossed the vertical plane, the mass pushed the handle toward the wall. Minding her fingers, she rested it in a divot in the wall. It had probably slipped from her father's hands and crunched into it.

Inside the recesses of the safe sat stacked manila folders closed with brown string wrapped around yellowing once-white buttons. Kenzie recognized the firm indentations of her father's handwriting on the label of the top folder. A name she didn't know. *Matthias.* She lifted it out. The next one, much thicker, read *Harold.*

With a chill coursing along her spine, she saw the files as they were, dossiers on the Family. One by one, she removed them, already certain that she would not find a memory stick or card or drive in the confines of the metal box. She had mistaken the safe for her mother's; it was her father's. Out came *Belinda, Aric.* Belinda's file was the most slender in the stack. Every name except for the enigmatic Matthias related directly to her, right now.

Her hand frozen in midair, she exposed the next file before she put down Aric's. The tag read *McKenzie*. Her face went numb, and she swallowed. Hand trembling to the thumping of her heart, she put Aric's file on the stack with the others. Her fingers shook as she pulled her file from the safe. She settled to a kneeling position, the file laid against the corner of the wooden enclosure. She fumbled at the twine, unwound it in jerks. The flap quivered as she opened it.

The inch-thick stack to the right seemed to be updates on her. The page facing from that side covered the fallout of the kidnapping and the progress of the investigation. A growing sense of repugnance built as she scanned the details. She flipped up the page. A terse account of the attempted abduction. The next page recapped her school records for the year. Feeling defiled, she shifted her gaze away from the pages proving she had no privacy that her parents would not violate to the other side of the packet. Her birth certificate—it read "Certificate of Live Birth" and had her name and birthday visible above the edge of the flap of the pouch—sat to the left.

Kenzie had never actually seen her birth certificate. She drew the stiff paper out with a rasping sound, feeling a moment of resistance as though the folder was reluctant to let her see the document. She gave it a tug. The folder surrendered up the page.

She noted the embossed seal, read through the data fields. All the print was in capitals. The top line had the certificate number and an issue date—which didn't match her birthday, earning a frown. Next was her given name, McKenzie (with no middle name), and last name, Graham. Then came her actual birthday, correcting the record. The issue date must refer to when the document had been created, she thought. Then, place of birth, *Seattle, King County, Washington*, and sex, *Female*.

Her gaze dropped to the next line. Her mouth dropped open, and with an explosive push, her breath forced itself out as though someone had punched her in the gut.

Blinking, she looked again. Read *Mother's Maiden Name: Elowyn Graham. Place of birth, Seattle. Age, 23.*

Her mother, Sasha Graham, the one she called Mother, wasn't. Her chest filled with ice and a tremor trickled down her spine, and back up her neck to the nape. Thoughts floated amorphously through her mind, unanchored to any sense of reality.

She glanced to the certificate again, a tangible reminder that something could exist amidst the lies all around her.

No information regarding her father was recorded.

The import of "Maiden" finally registered.

Elowyn Graham was her mother. *Maiden* name, Graham. The same as hers, given from her father.

Unless her father engaged in incest, Raymond Graham wasn't her father, any more than Sasha was her mother.

Her stomach surged like it wanted to disgorge the disgust with her lunch. She clamped her lips closed. She hurriedly put the file back together and shoved it into the safe. The others went back in order, the enigmatic *Matthias* on top.

Kenzie closed the heavy door with a clang, uncaring if someone might hear. With a violent motion, she twisted the dial to reset the locks. The bench seat went back into its protective position, hiding the secrets her father kept. A single glance confirmed that everything appeared the same as when she entered.

She fled to her room. The door slammed with a loud bang and a shudder in the floorboards. Kenzie lifted her arms, tilted her head back, and screamed her pain. She did it again. Rawness grasped at her vocal cords, made her stop.

Sight rimmed with red, Kenzie called on her powers to complete a vision of the house turned to matchsticks, all the lies exposed, all the truths bleeding in the light. The magic blocked her, retreated like a scared animal, wouldn't let her touch it. Kenzie redoubled her efforts, panting with her exertions, to no avail.

The more she tried to destroy the house, the further power stepped back. Straining eyes rolled back into the top of their sockets took note of an emerald glow overtaking the red cast of her fury. Lucent and intense, the living color crept across the floor and flowed up the walls. Startled, Kenzie dropped her gaze down to observe the expanding rays. The glow touched her like a salve. A consciousness of her attempt to destroy the house around her, and immolate herself in the process, led her to lower her arms.

The gemlike light receded like a tide. Kenzie tracked it, saw that it emanated from her closet.

Her breath stuck in her throat. She rushed to the door, opening it with a snatch.

Hidden at the back of the closet, below her dresses and behind the shoe rack, was the necklace from the Glade. Between her pair of white pumps and calf-tall brown leather boots, she could see the residual gleam within the gem. She removed the necklace from its hiding place. The stone weighed heavy in her hand, warm to the touch. The gleam disappeared.

Kenzie turned it in her hand to catch the light. It sparkled as it always did. Normal, except missing a stone.

Not normal, thought Kenzie. *Magical, from the Glade.*

Her next thought was *How dangerous is the necklace?* and she wished she had never removed it from the Glade. She turned it again. It glittered.

Mitch likes it.

She closed her eyes. Like a bath, there was a flow of magic around her. Now that she had lost her fury, she could access it. She threaded a tendril of the energy into the gem, which she could "see" with her eyes closed. The crystal resonated in her hand. Her eyes snapped open to see a spark in the depths of the jewel.

So what do you do, exactly?

She was staring into the clarity of the gem, seeking its secrets, when the thought struck her that nearly everything she knew was a lie, especially everything about her parents. Simultaneously with the thought came the realization that she knew where her mot— where Sasha had hidden the damn data.

CHAPTER FORTY-SEVEN

Hunter met Mitch in the garage, walking in with a small plastic bag in his hand.

"Hey, yo," he said, stepping around the various parts of the car strewn on the concrete floor. "I thought you had her running."

"She is, doing a little fine-tuning." Mitch spied the bag. "That the gear?"

"As requested. Are you going to let me in on all the details or what?" He held the bag out. "I tuned the initiator to the RFID. Will that work?"

Nodding, Mitch took the sack from his friend. The initiator for the thermite was the biggest piece of equipment, about the size of his hand, mostly for the battery. The relay was the size of a deck of cards, and the RFID chip was in a small box, so it didn't get lost. A remote control for the initiator, as mundane-appearing as a garage door opener, completed the set.

Pulling the trigger out, he glanced at Hunter. "How hot?" The trigger was a boxy rectangle of metal. Two leads of black, insulated wire led to copper-tipped probes. A rubber band kept them from getting damaged by strapping them to the case.

"Should hit six thousand degrees in less than a second. Going to make noise, though, when it jumps the gap."

"How long?"

"It can sustain the drain for two seconds. If you don't have the thermite set right or gap it wrong, you won't get ignition." Hunter eyed his friend. "So why electronic? A mag strip would be easier."

"Magnesium is too slow. I don't want to give him any advanced warning."

Mitch walked to the workbench. He put the trigger down and, stooping, removed the ball of thermite from its hiding place. He undid the plastic wrap. Dragging over a dead piston that he'd replaced a month ago, he put it flat side down. He'd already pulled the wrist pin that connected the piston to the connecting rod. The open space resembled an open bowl with one edge of the arc cut down into half the depth.

Mitch could feel Hunter staring over his shoulder. Using his fingertips, he molded the ball along the higher wall of the piston, creating a diagonal slope facing the open edge.

"A shaped charge?"

Mitch responded without looking up. "Not exactly, since the putty isn't an explosive. Shaping it this way exposes a lot of surface area that will radiate at once. More flash than bang."

He poked his pinkie finger into the base of the putty, making a cavity. Onto either side of the cavity, he embedded an electrode, aligned so the tips pointed to each other with a millimeter of gap separating them. Some thermite pinched over them secured them into position. Mitch shuffled the tools on the bench and found a piece of thin cardboard. He tore a piece and placed it between the points.

"Just in case," he said.

"Not sure that will stop it." Hunter sounded dubious.

Mitch grunted and said, "Pretty sure I don't want to find out." Using an entire roll of electrical tape, he attached the larger unit to the piston. He stood up straight and rolled his shoulders to work out the kinks. "Let's see the rest of it."

The RFID chip was bigger than Mitch expected. He knew size-wise they could range from the diameter of a pepper flake to a system as big as a phone. He turned to Hunter. "Pretty big."

"Yeah, had to find a balance between size and function. I figured you wanted an internal power supply and a decent antenna. Both take up space. This gives you a hundred yards' range to the relay. The relay can transmit burst signals up to two miles. The RFID activates on the first query it receives from the relay, so don't turn on the relay until you're ready to roll. After that, it will ping until the internal battery dies."

"That will work. What's the freq and data identifier?"

Hunter grinned. "I knew you were going to ask that." He fished out a thumb drive. "The tech data is on there, including the broadcast frequency, the modulations, and coded nonsense into the data. You didn't specify, but I got it built for ultrahigh frequencies to maximize range. That's another reason it's bigger than you expected."

"You didn't hand-build it?"

"Hell, no. Why should I when the stuff is available off the shelf?"

Mitch fumed. "Because commercial stuff is traceable."

"This isn't commercial, it's military grade, and the person who tries to backtrack it to my Family will discover the same big blank you did." Hunter's surety annoyed Mitch, but the Rubieras obviously had serious resources. He dropped it and dipped his head to inspect the chip. The slender piece of sophisticated electronics had a switch built into the edge to turn it on and a slide switch on the opposite edge for the delay. He squinted while he thought, and moved the indicator down to fifteen seconds.

That ought to be enough. Lassiter would want to verify the authenticity of the data as soon as he could, but short of bringing a computer into the meeting, he'd have to trust them. With, of course, his usual promise of blasting one or the other of them. Worse, Lassiter might try to take Kenzie hostage—not too outlandish a thought, since they'd already tried abducting her once.

He asked idly, putting the chip down and picking up the relay, "So what does your dad do, anyway?"

Silence greeted his question. Mitch glanced at Hunter, who met his stare with one of his own.

"Let me guess," said Mitch, "you'd tell me but then have to kill me."

"Not exactly." Hunter twitched a couple of fingers on his right hand, and Mitch tensed. "But you can't shoot your mouth off without thinking." He paused to make sure his meaning was clear.

Mitch gave a hard nod to acknowledge the warning. "I get it."

Hunter waited another second, and said, "My father owns banks."

"One isn't enough?" joked Mitch, the words slipping out before his brain could issue a cautionary thought against flippancy.

A frown creased Hunter's brow. "Yes, more than one, private banks, that make the types of investments that are very profitable to preferred investors."

Mitch held his tongue this time, but inside the privacy of his mind, he recognized the distinction that his friend had drawn. The Rubieras were not interested in community banking and personal checking accounts. They were banksters, hidden from sight and, Mitch was willing to bet, from investigation. A wave of a hand and bank examiners would smile and issue a report of full compliance. A gesture to an investor and the family would have access to enormous assets, both monetary and intellectual.

"Venture capital, too?"

"Under the right circumstances, yes."

"So that's why you're in a school that focuses on tech instead of a fancy school that leads to Harvard and an MBA."

"It took a bit of arguing, but my father saw the value in having a person fully versed in both."

Mitch reassessed his friend. He looked the part of a son to a business scion, with the dark looks and preppy clothes. His demeanor conveyed the same, as though he were meant to lead. Still, there was an undercurrent of excitement that came out in the lab. Mitch faced Hunter. "You'd make a lousy accountant."

Annoyance showed in the folds at the corners of Hunter's eyes. "Accountants work their little sums for others, people that are better at making the judgments to manage large enterprises. My father is one of those, but he's like everyone else that didn't come of age with tech. He doesn't understand the full ramifications of the tools we have today or the measure of control that can be exerted, but when I laid out the methods that we could utilize, he saw the potential."

"I'm not building stuff to control people," argued Mitch. "There's plenty that needs to be done to help people. Those tools for control should belong to the people using them, not some corporate tech company or their *bank*"—he used the first two fingers on each hand to add scare quotes—"act like kings in a castle ruling over them."

"That would be great, except the vast majority of people can't fart without someone telling them what to do. Look around you. You see them, practically all of them are mouth-breathers and knuckle-draggers. Even in school, with a supposedly high-performing student body, we have our fair share of stupid kids. Probably three-quarters of the regular population could disappear, and the world wouldn't notice."

"I told you that you are an asset. Your ability to identify patterns on limited data is special. If you had any sort of magical ability at all, I'd guess you were a Wilder. How many can process information like you and I do? With my Family, everyone operates at a high level of precision. In your family, what's left of it—"

Blood boiling, Mitch raised his fist. Hunter stepped back and put a hand out in front, tensing the fingers into a claw until the tendons popped out. Mitch's shoulder and arm convulsed with cramped muscles. Grinding his teeth, he strove to drive the arm forward.

"Stop acting like a fool," Hunter said, sounding contemptuous toward Mitch's straining effort. "You've seen enough by now to know what we can do. Or did you think that only your Kenzie girl was special."

The frozen muscles shrieked along nerve endings. Mitch ignored the signals. "She . . . is . . .special." He forced the words out past the pain.

"Maybe, but her Family isn't any different than mine. The only thing the Families disagree over is when to implement a plan to put us in our rightful position. Or did you think that developing a means of increasing the power output of wizards was for some other benefit." Hunter shook his head. "No, they plan for the same future. But they do so in bad faith, forgetting to include all the Families." He scowled. "Not for the first time, either. They are very creative, even if undisciplined." Hunter dropped his hand.

The spasming agony of Mitch's seized muscles disappeared, replaced by a trembling exhaustion. Still gasping, he stepped forward, chin jutted out and pointed. "You don't mess with Kenzie. You might be right about everything else, I don't care. You do not mess with her."

"I don't intend to, or I wouldn't be helping you, though she's bad for you. You go stupid like the rest of them when she's part of your equations."

Mitch clamped down on his teeth to stifle his words, but the thought remained, exactly as he'd told Jackson; Kenzie was the best thing to ever happen to him.

Hunter misconstrued silence for agreement. "Good. Now can we complete the project?"

Mitch nodded, still not trusting himself to speak. The "project" had just gotten way more complicated.

Mitch left his phone in the car before he sauntered over to the edge of the clearing and checked to make sure nobody was watching him. He didn't know how accurately his location could be pinpointed, and revealing a lot of back-and-forth activity would heighten suspicions. He looked again. All clear, as he expected for a Monday morning. It wouldn't stay that way for long since it was spring break. Time to get busy.

Below him on the hillside sat the amphitheater like the skull of a flat fish, the concrete benches acting as the ribs as they radiated out from the center line. He had abandoned the first location by the picnic area after walking the grounds. The sightlines were so constricted that Lassiter's gunmen would be right on top of Kenzie. For his plan to work, more separation needed to be created, hence the relocation. This laid out much better.

The stage of the amphitheater was raised about five feet from the ground and curved in an arc of about fifteen degrees. On either side, steps rose to the stage, with bushes hiding the treads from the front. Mitch approached the steps on the left. Kenzie would enter stage right, following a thin ribbon of wooded trail from the paved running path below.

Mitch was tall enough to see over the stage. Kenzie would not be, so he'd have to give her directions. Lassiter would stay away from her. He had already seen how effective she could be in close range. He'd end up about right where Mitch was standing—any farther back, and he'd be into the bushes.

Lassiter, paranoid that he was, expected a trap.

Mitch grinned without showing teeth or a hint of warmth. His penetrating search of the nearby vegetation revealed the perfect spot for the thermite. Close enough to cause confusion without a risk of injury to Kenzie.

The robot could be situated anywhere close. The only purpose it served was to dial the burner phone to summon help and act as a distraction.

The woods, he decided, on the side opposite the trail Kenzie would be on. The security goons for Lassiter would scan for threats. He already knew that they monitored electronics. They could detect Kenzie doing her thing, which still bugged him. He shrugged it off. *Worry later,* he thought.

Infrared. He could screen the bot for that. Hiding it now gave the metal time to achieve temperature equilibrium with the surrounding growth.

Metal detector? Probably not.

All in all, he considered, this would work.

Mitch carried the robot down, along with a cardboard box and a flat sheet of plastic. The forecast was for sunny skies, making this about the nicest spring he had ever had in Seattle. Normally, the gloom sat on everything, sucking energy out of him until at least June. He basked in the warmth for a minute.

He found a protected spot next to a towering lodgepole pine surrounded by leafy underbrush. With the sole of his shoe, Mitch cleared the leaves. An earthy scent wafted up to him. Into the cleared area went the robot. Mitch checked the balance and ran a test sequence to ensure it would work. The arm moved smoothly to the phone. Mitch jabbed the controls and interrupted the program before the phone could be powered up. Satisfied, he put the robot into hibernation mode.

He tied a line to the actuator arm and threaded it through the branches of the bush. He wouldn't need a big distraction, just enough to get the man to look over his shoulder. Mitch walked the line twenty yards to the left side of the amphitheater. He stuck the heavy plastic into a bush and tied the fishing line to a prepunched hole he had made. He gave a gentle tug. The bush made a satisfying rustle.

Lifting the box over the shrubs, he finagled the cardboard through the clingy branches. He pressed it down, listening to the scratch of the plants against the side of the box. The flaps hit the soil first, and Mitch bent at the waist to adjust them so they folded out.

"Hey, mister!"

Startled, Mitch cut his forearm as he spun to face the direction of the shout.

Standing up the hillside was a boy, maybe eight or nine, staring at him with curiosity. Mitch cursed under his breath. It could have been worse than a noisy kid.

"What's up, man?" Mitch hollered, putting a smile on his face. He wiped his hands on the front of his jeans.

"Whacha doing?" The kid cocked his head over.

Mitch forced a laugh. "Just setting some stuff up for a new show next weekend." He inclined his head at the stage of the amphitheater. "I need to get some equipment in. Want to see?" He gestured with his hand, simultaneously hoping the stupid kid would remember not to come near strangers. Didn't the little dweeb have a mother somewhere?

The kid eyed Mitch, a battle between his curiosity and caution showing. Caution won.

"I got to find my mom." He backpedaled.

"It's cool," said Mitch. "Tell her the gig is next Saturday, eight o'clock. We'll have this place rocking, for sure."

"Un-huh." The kid gathered steam and turned his back to Mitch.

Sixteen and gonna die of a heart attack, thought Mitch. Quickly, he took tent stakes out of his hip pockets and impaled the flaps of the box to the ground. He adjusted the foliage and added some downed twigs to cover up the box. Stepping back, he inspected his handiwork. *Not too bad,* he thought. If you didn't know it was there, you'd walk right past.

Mitch hid the thermite in the bushes, covering the old piston with a paper bag. He frowned, worried that he was going to do irreparable damage to the foliage, then shrugged. Added it to the "worry later" list.

Standing, Mitch eyeballed the angles, squinting into the sun. *Lassiter would stand about there, and I'll steer Kenzie to that spot.* That put riflemen at the corners by the parking lot. They'd need to establish the proper angles for firing without endangering their boss. He'd insert himself between Kenzie and Lassiter.

Last step. He walked down the path at the rear of the stage. It led to the asphalt path that ringed the island. In a quick jog, he went back to the kids' play park with the swing. Before it was a patch of poison oak, which park managers had helpfully marked as such with a wooden sign. Careful not to touch the leaves, he winnowed his way up the hillside. Using another stretch of the transparent fishing line, he lashed it into a high crook of an oak tree, where it would stay hidden. He tapped the activation button, and the relay went live. If Lassiter's men were scanning for the frequency, he was toast, but it was a risk he had to take. The ultrahigh range of the relay probably would be outside their detection parameters. That part was good thinking by Hunter.

His jaw set hard as he thought about his former friend. The changes taking place in the dude were stunning. Always cocky, new Hunter had gone from exuding arrogance toward everyone to outright contempt, with a strong sense of totalitarianism for humanity as a whole.

He wondered what Lassiter would think of the activity at Seward. Did he suspect that Mitch knew about the compromised phones, or did he think that he still held that advantage? Mitch knew that the man examined every possibility. Chances of the crook leaving via the parking lot approached zero. The island was an isolated system with a single road. Lassiter would opt for a water extraction where he could flee faster and in more directions. Mitch discounted the possibility of a helicopter. They were noisy and too easy to track on radar.

He could add explosives to the list of things that Lassiter's crew would search for. The lines of a hard grin compressed his lips. Explosives almost always used nitrogen. They would look, but not find his explosives. They'd also know he'd planted a tracker, discouraging them from opening the Faraday bag until they obtained the security of a shielded room. He planned to announce the tracker during the handover. Lassiter was sure to threaten him again, but Mitch suspected that Lassiter wanted to use Kenzie more than he wanted to snuff a teenage boy. *I hope. . . .*

Mitch strode back to the Camaro. The easy part was done. Time to make one more stop, to drop off the thumb drive that Hunter gave him, along with instructions for Raymond Graham.

Mitch fingered the envelope in his pocket as he replaced the phone. Kenzie would kick his ass if she knew about it. It contained a letter with everything he knew for a fact, most of what he suspected, and a request for assistance. More like begging for help, since he was acutely aware of how limited their resources were against someone like Lassiter. It would be convenient if Kenzie could wave a wand and turn the man into a slug they could squish under a heel, he mused, but that was wishful thinking. Pretending two teenagers could take out a well-organized crook with a full team behind him wasn't any more realistic.

He punched the accelerator a couple of times as he turned the key, enjoying the throaty response, the heavy vibration muting the disquieting tenseness in his stomach. He backed out and looped back to the park entrance.

He drove slowly along Lake Washington Boulevard, scanning in front and behind for traffic. As he approached the Grahams' mailbox, he slowed further.

Now, he thought, hitting the brakes and stopping the car dead in the middle of the road. He launched from the driver's seat like a pilot ejected from a burning plane, and sprinted across the road. A second later, the envelope was in the mailbox. He was back in the car and pulling away in less than ten seconds.

Ten minutes later he parked the Camaro in his garage and breathed a sigh of relief. Mitch clambered from the car, went inside, and headed directly to his room.

As he opened the door, the other phone, Kenzie's private line, went off. He reached for it.

I need a ride, read the message.

His thumbs twitched across the screen. *Say please.*

The reply came in seconds. *Please.*

The second one came seconds later. *Butthead.*

CHAPTER FORTY-EIGHT

"How long until Jackson, uh . . . recovers?" asked Mitch in the silence that followed him killing the engine.

Kenzie shrugged, ignoring Mitch's agitation. "A couple of hours, at least, but if we get done fast, I can bring him back up in a sec." The barrel roof of the church stood stark against the sky while the closed-up front gave the impression of slumbering until the next Gathering. "You can't stay here in front. Someone will see you. Pull down one street and make a right. I'll text you from inside when I'm done."

"I can come in with you. As a precaution?"

"No, you can't," Kenzie said with a definitive shake of her head. "I'm not sure I can get myself around the security without alerting my dad. It'll be double bad if I get caught bringing you in, too." *And I have no idea what the Glade will do to a mundane boy, either,* she thought. One of those things she should keep to herself. How the whole thing hadn't blown Mitch's mind astounded her, but she felt a thrill that he hadn't abandoned her.

She put her left hand lightly on his forearm. "I'll be fine," she said, meeting his eyes. Mitch's irises held a violet blue, deeper in color to go along with the pinched forehead. "Wait for me, okay?"

"Forever," he blurted, then blushed at his naked impulsiveness.

In response, Kenzie leaned close and gave him a peck on the cheek and, as her insides went wobbly, she wondered which of them was more shocked.

"I'll be right back."

She slid out of the car and heard Mitch start the big engine that vibrated the air. The pent-up power of the sports car was crazy different than her parents' more sedate sedans. Mitch revved the motor, shattering the normal busyness of the street. Kenzie loved that sound, fraught with wildness.

Mitch up-ticked his chin, then pulled away from the curb as though he were holding a race horse that desperately wanted to hurtle into a sprint closely in check until the time was right.

Kenzie mounted the steps, absorbing deep soothing breaths with each riser. When she reached the broad oak doors, she reached for the handle with both her hand and her every sense. Safe, so far. She entered the code and heard the click of the lock releasing. Her palm slick against the weighty handle, she pulled. The door squealed. The noise paralyzed her in place while she waited for a reaction. One second, two, and she let out the pent-up air and took a single pace into the dim foyer.

A peculiar spell swirled around her. The *Linius* spell floated in front of her, waiting to capture her again, but this other spell didn't seem to do anything. Tentatively, she relaxed, letting the force of her magic drift from her. A feeling of revulsion grew at the back of her throat, bilious and bitter, and for an instant, she contemplated fleeing the building. Swiftly, she reasserted control. The feeling disappeared.

Interesting, she thought, hands trembling. That's how the Family kept out random strangers who might, through luck, find their way past the locked doors. For a moment, she pitied the stray drunk seeking solace and shelter in the church during Seattle's incessant rains, only to be driven away. She swallowed, but the nastiness remained.

Kenzie gave a hard shake of her head and her right eye narrowed at the corner. The *Linius* was nearly identical to the spell of Sasha's she had broken. Instead of breaking it, though, she needed to bypass it.

Like . . . this?

Her right hand, of its own accord, turned palm up. With a push, the whole fabric of the spell rose like a curtain to the ceiling, leaving an open space below.

Kenzie took one step, searched for another spell. She repeated the exercise four more times. With each step, the inlaid stars at the door gained in brightness, until she thought she could feel the pressure of the cleansing light.

What the hell is this? The last spell was tied to the doors to the interior, wrapped around the handles like woven snakes. A primal quaking shuddered through her body. She placed a hand out, palm forward and fingertips up, to gauge the nature of the spell.

The spell reacted instantly, forming a head that extended toward the proffered hand. Kenzie snatched it back, folding it up under her breasts.

The venomous-looking head returned to its position as sentry.

She studied the trap. As near as she could tell, magic wasn't directly involved.

That made these quasi-real, imbued with special properties, like scaring little girls. It was working.

She put up a quivering hand, well out of striking range. The head rose to meet it. She exerted some sideways pressure with magic. The serpent went from relatively benign to hostile, jaws opening to release a vicious hiss, tongue flicking toward her.

Kenzie hurriedly dropped the spell. The snake resettled around the handles.

No magic, then.

That left mundane answers, like snake charming—or snake handling.

Her teeth chattering, Kenzie lifted her hand again. Battling muscles that fought to keep her from touching the sentry, she forced a violently trembling hand under the head of the snake.

"Come," she whispered, and the reptilian shape unwound and slithered onto her arm. Every muscle went rigid to prevent her from flinging the serpent off. The heft of the dense muscular body pressed against her flesh as the snake traversed her arm, before winding itself around her shoulders.

"Enter," came a disembodied voice.

Trembling, she reached for the handle and pulled it open to see the ranks of pews lined up in front of her. Kenzie stepped through the doorway, and the snake shifted, sliding back to the door. Kenzie turned to see it disappear through the crack of the closing door, getting impossibly thin to fit.

She was in. Still shaking, she proceeded down the length of the aisle between pews, releasing a sigh of relief as the comfortable change into her robe took place, the walls receding as the Glade came to vivid life, the moon brighter than ever. She paused at the base of the grotto, head turning right and left.

Now what? she thought. A brief moment of panic froze her lungs, and Kenzie consciously forced herself to relax. She let the Glade soak into her senses. The stars were scattered across the sky like a jeweled necklace, their glitters accenting the lunar light. Darkness sat below the silent, still trees, deep shadows cast from above. Impulsively, she lifted her hand, and a hint of a zephyr rose to touch her skin. Her robe captured the breeze and flowed against her body in a gentle caress. The air reached the trees, and broad leaves turned to silver as they rustled and reflected silver rays to where she stood.

A peaty scent pervaded the air and carried with it a smoky taste, far from the usual flowery sweetness of the Glade. Not unpleasant, it conjured a feeling of lying near a fire, listening to the crackle.

Kenzie drew in a deep breath as though she could inhale the Glade and its wonder, then let it sigh out past open lips.

She could search for hours and days without finding the object her mother hid. The Glade, with its natural magic, would adapt to her activities and change shape and size to accommodate her.

The Glade isn't really real.

It was a dumb thought, and probably not quite right, but, in it, Kenzie saw a way forward. She allowed her eyelids to drop. Chest rising and falling in steady rhythm, she brought calm to her center. In her mind's eye, she saw the Glade, down to the ribbing on the leaves. Into this, she injected a request bearing a feather of magic.

She sought a sign to lead her to the device and called on the Glade to provide it. A heat grew on her skin, but she kept her eyes sealed. Pulling more magic to her will, she declared in a whisper, "I need to find the object that Lassiter seeks."

The untruthfulness behind her words agitated the magic. Kenzie fought for control and her center. Water formed behind her eyelids, and she resorted to honesty.

"I need to save Mitch."

Instantly, a vortex in the magic swirled into being, the terminus at her chest, pulling and lifting her. Her back arched as her feet left the ground, the inexorable force seizing her. After a first, frantic flinging of arms and legs from surprise, Kenzie surrendered to the forces, arms extended and toes pointed to the ground below.

Chest heaving with tremulous breaths, she tried to open her eyes and found that she could not. There was no pain, or even strain as she tried harder. Despite her inability to observe all that was happening, she could feel herself transported through little clues: the swing of her hair, the shifting of her robe, chill wind raising goose bumps on the skin as it blew past.

Kenzie held one thought tight and bright in her mind, repeating it as a mantra or a prayer, *"save Mitch."*

The tops of her toes brushed against grass, and Kenzie tipped her toes skyward. She landed lightly on the balls of her feet, as carefully as a delicate piece of porcelain was set away into the china cabinet. The pressure of the vortex, having borne her, dissipated into nothingness.

Testing, Kenzie opened her eyes, looking heavenward. The stars filled the sky, more numerous than before, but the moon didn't reside in its customary position. She dropped her gaze, saw the moon on the low horizon, backlighting the white marble altar with *The Incantaraus* and casting a long shadow toward her. Kenzie could make out the shape of something that used the darkness for concealment. When she peered into the darkness more closely, a huge head rotated to face her, and Kenzie lurched back a step.

A gytrash lay on its haunches in front of her, the glow from the eyes spooky red. Its length blocked the altar. Kenzie stared, tension at the sides of her eyes. The gytrash dropped his lower jaw and exposed canine teeth like small daggers.

Kenzie's gaze flitted to the sides, up to the ancient leather-bound book on the surface of the marble, back to the gytrash.

"Are you here to destroy me or to guide me?" She couldn't keep the fear out of her voice.

The gytrash rose. Its head reached Kenzie's shoulders, and its elongated body, higher in front than its hips at the rear, rippled with muscle. Its coat glistened, unlike that of the beast that Harold had conjured. A tail half the length of the body swished in the air. The creature turned to face her and took one step in Kenzie's direction.

Kenzie sought magic to ward off the gytrash, then stopped. The Glade had brought her here, and the gytrash, too. Deep inside her, she looked for trust.

The beast took another step, and the peaty smell of the Glade took on a bitter tang of animal sweat. Its eyes burned and never left her. The huge head dropped as though the animal were shifting into stalking behavior.

Kenzie held her ground. *I handled a snake.*

Two more steps brought the gytrash to Kenzie. The eyes bored into hers, and the black snout lifted, scenting the air.

The smell from the beast was pervasive, not foul, nor clean, but sharp and real. Terror pressed against her heart as though it would crush it as the snout continued toward her face. Violent tremors rattled her bones.

"Will you help me?"

The snout touched her nose, gently, and sniffed. The soft black skin was cool but the panted air exhaled from the beast was hot and damp.

Kenzie didn't breathe during the intimate inspection.

The massive forehead turned to an angle, in the manner of a puppy who sees a cat for the first time and is unsure what to do about it. He backed up a step, then a second, then turned and padded to the side, leaving her a clear path to the altar.

"Thank you," Kenzie said in a hoarse whisper.

She staggered forward and rested her weight against the cold stone. *The Incantaraus* sat closed in front of her. The script curlicued across the cover, glowing with a starry sheen. Hesitantly, she reached and turned the cover, opening the volume. The title repeated on a ivory-colored page, rough cut at the edges. With the title came a warning in a scrolling hand. *Be warned, Wizard, that the Magic serves Itself.*

It sure wasn't serving her, thought Kenzie. She lifted the edge of the page—or tried to, as the paper did not move. Flummoxed, she used her thumb at the corner to rifle through the book, but the sensation was more like running her fingers on the edge of a sculpture of a book than touching an actual tome.

So how the heck do you get anything out of it? Kenzie strained in concentration for a clue, a guide. She was getting a little tired of puzzle-solving, between opening the safe, getting into the Glade, and now finding the memory storage for Lassiter. . . .

The last part of that thought brought her up short. The marble was bare except for the book of spells, but the magic had delivered her here first. True, she planned to swipe a spell (or two or three) to deal with that cold-hearted creep, Lassiter, but until she had the secrets in hand, she couldn't initiate her scheme.

A small tinge of guilt pressed her at holding out on Mitch, but it was for his own good.

"So where is the damn memory?" she asked aloud.

The ground under her shook, rattling the leaves in the Glade, and the air in front her shimmered.

Earthquake?

Gasping in disbelief, she gripped the edge of the white altar for support. The Glade should have been immune to events outside, even one of the small earthquakes that periodically shook Seattle. Blinking rapidly, she looked around. The gytrash met her gaze with a languorous loll of its long tongue but seemed otherwise unconcerned. The shaking tapered away. Kenzie let go and scanned the area, worried that the Glade might have sustained damage. It looked normal, other than the moon on the horizon. Glancing in front of her, she froze. *The*

Incantaraus lay open to the middle pages. Sitting incongruously on the right-hand side was an SD card, black against the buff paper, with its distinctive snipped corner. The label faced her, announcing the brand and capacity, a whopping sixty-four gigabytes.

Well, okay.

She picked up the card and set it off to the side, pushing it away from the magical book. Kenzie went to flip through the pages again to peruse the incantations, but the book had resumed its stubborn refusal to move.

"So I have to ask?"

The beast to the side snorted as though mocking her ineptness. In front of her, the pages shimmered, which she took as an affirmative. Magic sometimes was a total pain in the butt.

"What incantation can I use to neutralize Lassiter?"

The book did the shimmy-shake routine again, but produced another blank page.

"What, do I have to say please?"

Another affirmative.

Kenzie wondered who had created *The Incantaraus,* because whoever it was deserved a talking-to. Magic should perform according to set principles and actions, not on a whim or a "please." She sighed, and asked, "Please give me a spell to zap Lassiter?" It came out more flippant than she intended, but the book reacted with alacrity, the page blurring before letters popped into bold text, *How to Tune a Ward to an Individual,* across the top.

She had never heard of a tunable spell. Intrigued, she read the directions, noting the actions were very similar to what her father had shown her, with an additional step at the end and one extra component. That one, she saw, would be a big problem. She needed to get a piece of Lassiter. The directions suggested a hair or piece of fingernail.

How the heck . . . ? She couldn't walk up to him and say, "Excuse me, sir, could I have a hair or two?"

Reading the directions a second time for more clues on how to pull off the spell, she noted that the quantity necessary to activate the magic was not specified.

"Does that mean that any amount, no matter how minuscule, will work?"

The words blurred, sharpened. She reread for the third time. The instructions had changed, adding a single clause. *Thou shalt secure some small sliver of thy intended victim, of any size, ere thee attempt the final binding.*

Kenzie nodded in grim satisfaction. She could manage that. Once she had Lassiter targeted, she would use the *Linius* spell to hold him. . . .

The Glade convulsed again, and Kenzie cried out, "I didn't ask anything." The violence made her lose her balance, and she had to use the altar again to remain upright. The SD card jumped on the surface, and a sickening odor of charred meat filled the air.

When it stopped, finally, Kenzie stared down at *The Incantaraus.*

She felt the blood drain from her face and her scalp crawled as though insects had infested her hair. The tome rejected her idea of lashing Lassiter in a web of magic until someone else took care of him. With mounting revulsion, she understood the obligation that magic was placing on her, to defend and protect. No mere binding spell this, but a powerful and deadly incantation.

A Fire spell.

CHAPTER FORTY-NINE

Mitch pulled his Camaro to the curb to wait for Kenzie. He shot a glance up to the door of the church, but she wasn't in sight yet. A fast check of the mirrors didn't reveal anything suspicious, so he popped the stick into neutral and held his foot on the brake. He wasn't parking in an illegal zone, he was only stopping.

Come on.

The huge oak door swung open, easily twice the height of Kenzie, and she stepped into the daylight. Mitch leaned forward to take a quick gander at the interior, but the darkness was impenetrable. Mitch took in the grim expression that Kenzie wore, and his optimism sank like the sun setting, not a fast *kerplunk,* but a slow descent to night's bleakness.

The door moved ponderously to close, but before the gap pinched completely, a dog, the tallest and lankiest that Mitch had ever seen, slithered through, and trotted to the shadows under the trees, disappearing like a phantom. Mitch pulled his shoulders back to ward off the feeling at the base of his neck.

A grim-faced Kenzie yanked on the door latch and climbed in.

He was about to ask her where the dog came from when she spoke.

"I got it, let's go," she said, her words as hard as the set to her jaw.

"You got it?" he asked. At the surprise in his voice, she turned to face him. "I mean, you . . ." He gestured toward his face. "You don't seem, uh, excited." Sensing the inanity in his words, he shut his mouth, though his brain went racing ahead.

What's the right word for stealing data? he wondered. *"Excited" ain't it.* "Guilty" would fit, but Kenzie didn't appear guilty. Or scared. Or happy or anything else he expected. Instead, she seemed more like *burdened.*

"Let's go," Kenzie repeated, avoiding his eyes. She slouched in her seat. "Can we be ready tonight?"

Nodding, Mitch put the car into first gear. "We can. I dunno about Lassiter. I'm guessing he'll want this resolved as quickly as possible, so probably." He checked the mirrors—then checked over his shoulder to the church. For an instant, he thought he'd seen a face at a window, but now it was blank, reflecting the trees and sky. "I'll call him after I drop you off."

Place was creepy, he decided.

Mitch barged into Mercury's study without knocking. The wizard sat in a chair reading, legs crossed at the ankles.

"Do you ever do anything?" asked Mitch.

"Other than deal with intemperate youths?" replied Mercury, putting the book down on his lap. "Of course I do. I study my Art. Wizards don't pop out, able to turn brash teenagers into frogs from the get-go. It takes practice."

Mitch paced the length of the room, ignoring the rebuke. "It's time to do something about Jackson. We're moving tonight."

"Are you sure that you want to continue along this path?" Mitch stared at him, so Mercury continued, "As you will. I can start the process now. I will have his family to safety by six this evening. Is that sufficiently prompt?"

"Yeah, that should work. Lassiter will want to work in the dark, when there are fewer people to notice what's going down."

"And if he doesn't?"

Mitch felt his gut tighten and he stopped pacing to meet Mercury's stare. "Then I'm more screwed than I thought." He scanned the room, impatient at the delay. "Will Kenzie's dad do his part? If he doesn't show up, the whole thing comes apart."

"I think that is the last of your worries. A greater one is if Lassiter refuses to play along with your plan."

"He's not going to. As soon as he knows the location, he's going to take control back. For starters, he's not going to let himself be limited to a single road off the island that's less than a half mile from Kenzie's house. I'd be really surprised if he didn't plan for a boat to pick him up. But he'll show up at the amphitheater, because that's where the data card will be."

Mercury's left eyebrow raised, but the wizard didn't say anything.

Mitch resumed pacing. "You sure you can handle Jackson?"

"Do you wish to be a frog?"

Anger roiled in his blood, and Mitch glared at Mercury. "I think I'm the toad. Or sacrificial goat." He inhaled. "Okay, let me call Lassiter."

A voice with a curt *"Leave your message"* answered the phone on the other end. Likely a bounce to another phone through a network to prevent tracing, thought Mitch. The man was not dumb.

At the beep, he simply said, "We have it. Seward Park Amphitheater."

And the waiting began.

CHAPTER FIFTY

The smoke from a neighbor's grill, heavy with the odor of meat cooking, made Kenzie's stomach turn. In her hand, Kenzie held the choker, the gem hanging off the edge of her palm, quiescent at the moment. Testing it with magic had produced no notable result. She'd been able to light a spark in it yesterday, yet today she couldn't replicate the glow. The gem had blocked her from giving in to her anger and destroying the house. That part was okay, but it kept magic out of reach. That made it more than a curiosity and something pretty to wear for Mitch. It was dangerous, and treacherous, too. And a welcome distraction, something to focus on instead of perfecting the Fire spell.

She questioned the missing setting. A second stone, for a second purpose.

Kenzie turned the amulet—it had to be an amulet, a powerful one—over. No marks were visible in the silver etchings. Turning it back gem side up, she studied the broken mount in the heart of the piece. The ends were twisted as though whatever stone had been set there had been removed by force. It added to the queasy sensation in her stomach. A battle. Whoever had worn the amulet had probably lost, else it would still be intact.

She took a deep breath. Tonight loomed. Getting out of the house was going to be a problem. Sneaking out her window might work again, but with the upgrades to the wards, trying to bypass them while jumping off the roof of the garage bordered on reckless. She dismissed the worry. She'd think of something.

Do I have the courage? she thought. *Can I be a full-fledged enchantress?*

The amulet's single gem swayed with the trembling of her hand, and Kenzie clenched hard around the broken setting, the sharp points impaling her palm. Sighing, she went to the closet and rehid it next to the data card. When Mitch got the time from Lassiter, she'd be able to get to it quickly, but no one else would tumble to its presence.

Tasks such as putting an end to the threats and to Lassiter didn't fall to children. That was the message that *The Incantaraus* had delivered, but she didn't feel ready.

I don't want to be ready, not for this.

Tears threatened. She closed her eyes and breathed deep. With the rest of the world cut off, she calmed herself.

The odious task sickened her, but the Magic, for whatever reason, had placed a responsibility upon her. She held on to that logic, sought comfort in its righteousness. Lassiter threatened her world, magical and Mitch. She could make him pay the price for his evil.

Eyes still shut tight, Kenzie promised herself that she would be the obedient servant. She would incinerate Lassiter.

With a shudder, she went over the Fire spell again and again to dispel the doubts she had.

The text from Mitch arrived at a quarter after eight, right after sunset.

10pm. i'll meet you across the street @ 9:30

Kenzie's breath caught. She was curled into a recliner in the living room alone with a book, turning unread pages while she waited. In her pocket was the data card and the pebble she'd turned into an on-demand light.

She had suffered through dinner, avoiding conversation by the simple expedient of keeping her head down. She caught Sasha shooting frowns in her direction, but an air of satisfaction perversely accompanied them. Kenzie felt too stretched to worry about Sasha's machinations. Her father ate efficiently and excused himself from the table early, barely acknowledging her.

When it pushed close to nine thirty, Kenzie unfolded and stood, listening to assess any reaction. Clacking from the keyboard in the den told her Sasha was preoccupied. Her dad was nowhere in sight.

"I'm going to bed," she announced. A barest of hesitations in the clicking keys signified Sasha heard her. Heart bruising her ribs, she walked to the front door instead of the stairwell, eased open the heavy door, and slipped into the night. She held the latch open until the door was seated against the weather stripping to mute the noise of the mechanism.

She waited, ears straining to hear any indication over the rush of pounding blood that she was busted. With a start, she realized that standing on the front porch under a light was profoundly irrational if she was trying to avoid detection. Three quick strides took her to the steps. She descended into the dark and went looking for Mitch.

The sulphur glow cast by the streetlights cut an amber cone in the mist of the drifting fog. Teeth chattering, Kenzie hurried across the street, peeking over her shoulder to make sure that no one chased her from the house.

"Avoid the light," came Mitch's disembodied voice from her right.

Peering into the darkness, she made out a dark outline and headed for it. Approaching, she saw he was dressed in black, head to foot. His eyes were active, quartering their perimeter, while he stood tense and ready. He pulled the Faraday bag from the front pouch of his hoodie and opened it.

Without speaking, Kenzie removed the SD card from the back pocket of her jeans and handed it to Mitch. His long fingers curled around it and dropped it into the bag. A second later, Mitch had the bag sealed. He let out a long, slow breath.

"You ready?"

Kenzie put her hand on his arm, feeling the dampness. She looked up at him. "How long have you been out here?"

"A while. I left my car at the park and walked back. Quieter."

She tried one more time to deflect him, willing him to see reason and avoid the sights of Lassiter. "You don't need to go."

Mitch's gaze was steady, yet tender behind the hard ice in his eyes. "Yeah, I do."

She blinked back tears, angry at herself for being such a pile of pudding all day. She couldn't order him not to come with her; he'd blow her off. Still, she didn't want him there to watch her . . . *deal* with Lassiter.

"Okay, then."

She had planned for this. She'd deal with the fallout from Mitch later.

He gave her a sharp stare, and she could see the calculations taking place behind his eyes, cyphers and tumblers clicking and clacking as he tried to put her into the pattern. She forced a smile and strode off, headed for the rendezvous a half mile distant. Mitch fell in beside her.

He fumbled for her hand, found it, and entwined his long fingers with hers. She could feel his pulse racing and hoped that he could not feel hers galloping, too. She suppressed a shudder and leaned into his shoulder.

"Next time we go out, let's make it a date instead," Mitch said, trying to sound lighthearted, but carrying an edge. He glanced over his shoulder, and Kenzie squeezed his hand.

"Is there someone there?" she asked, envisioning her father stalking them in the fog. *Did he see me sneak out the front door?* She looked back.

Mitch shook his head with enough vigor to make his shoulders move. "No, it's all good."

"It will be soon," she assured him. *I hope.*

They were fifteen minutes early, and the parking lot was empty. Mitch took her by the elbow and guided her into the play area. The swing moved forlornly on the hint of a breeze.

"Okay, the path is up there," Mitch said, words coming rapid-fire and taut. "That'll take us up to the amphitheater for the meeting. His men are almost certainly here by now, even if we can't see them. When we're five minutes out, I'll go up the trail with you behind me, okay? As much as possible, keep me between you and him."

Kenzie touched the pebble in her pocket. *Keep him talking,* she thought, stomach tight. "What about light?" She made herself relax.

Mitch reached to his back pocket and pulled out a pair of small flashlights. "They're pretty bright; LEDs with about four hundred lumens each." He clicked a button, and a circle of white light exposed the leaves and wood chips in stark contrast to the night. In the reflected glow, she saw him push a button on the barrel, and the beam intensified. He hit a rubber-gasketed switch on the base and blackness swarmed in.

"Here," he said, handing her one. His eyes swept the parking lot again as a Lexus SUV cruised past the entrance.

"What are you looking for?"

His gaze twitched in her direction and back out to the open space. "Nothing. Everything."

Kenzie nodded, understanding. She pointed at a picnic table twenty-five yards away, in the direction of the path. "I'm going to sit down." She walked away, keeping an ear cocked to see if Mitch would follow. He did, grumbling something about not being able to keep watch.

She sat, but Mitch stood, head on a swivel.

Kenzie patted the bench next to her. "Sit?"

Mitch glanced at her face. Indecision was etched into his.

"Please?"

He settled onto the bench, and Kenzie felt a tremor of trepidation. She turned her back to him and leaned into his body, sensing Mitch's startlement as he shifted to accommodate her. She laid her head back against the muscles in his chest and reached for his hands, pulling them around her.

"It'll be over soon," she said, stroking the skin on the back of his hand. It was soothing, and his embrace engulfed her.

"Not soon enough," said Mitch in a whisper.

I could stay here forever, she told herself, but trembling revealed her lie. Five minutes. For now, this was heaven. She pursed her lips, wanting more: more time, more peace, more Mitch.

The pressure mounted in her chest, squeezing tighter. She took a deep breath, feeling Mitch's arms tightening as well. She hummed, barely audibly, as she touched him.

"We have to go soon," said Mitch. He yawned and abruptly stiffened. "Stop!"

"*Katheudos,*" Kenzie murmured, ignoring Mitch's growing agitation. She added a touch of magic to the word. She could feel Mitch battle the sleeping spell, so she repeated it again, soft as a mother coaxing a child to slumber. A shudder went through his body, and then a wave of relaxation as his hands fell away from her. Kenzie grabbed them, leaning forward to keep Mitch from toppling.

She stood and faced him, supporting his torso. His chin drooped against his chest, and his breath came in a deep, steady rhythm. Straining, Kenzie got him turned to the table top. She folded his arms in front of him on the wood planks and used them to cradle his head.

When he woke up, he was going to be crazy mad, she thought, but this was better than letting Lassiter kill him.

Kenzie bent down. *Don't be too mad,* she thought. She gave him a peck on the cheek as a hot tear fell into his hair. Her voice shook as she whispered, "*I love you.*" He'd never hear it, but it was enough to say it. For now. Then she stood and, with a final blurry glance at Mitch, stood tall and went to meet her duty.

Kenzie took the pebble from her pocket, willing it to illuminate the root-strewn dirt. It took only the tiniest bit of magic to generate the glow. She held it between the first and second fingers of her left hand, palm flat, like a piece of brilliant jewelry. From there, the rays reached the ground, the path in front, and the trees above. To preserve her night vision, Kenzie fixed her eyes ahead and kept her hand low to her waist. The Faraday bag was pinned to her side by her left bicep, leaving her fight hand free.

At the same time, she cast her ward as wide as the island and as light as gossamer. If Lassiter called her on the use of magic, she'd explain it with the amulet of light. She'd know soon if the detector they had could tell the difference between the magnitude of the energy field of the amulet and the Fire spell. Her stomach twisted tighter. Hopefully not the magnitude of power she planned to pull, or she was thoroughly screwed.

The path ended more quickly than she expected, opening to the broad expanse of the amphitheater. She turned her hand to shine light around the open space. It was vacant. Up the hillside, the silhouettes of two vehicles perched along the ridge that marked the road boundary. One, low-slung, looked like Mitch's Camaro. The other glistened, shiny and new. The passenger-side door popped open, the latch loud in the night, and slammed shut as Lassiter exited to meet her. She heard a click, and a flashlight sprang to life.

Stepping into the hollow at the front of the stage, Kenzie remembered Mitch's directions to avoid the side away from the path. He hadn't told her why, but she carefully set herself as though she were prepared to flee back the way she came. It didn't take much salesmanship—*Saleswomanship?* she thought irrelevantly. Her knees were practically knocking, and the jerky effect of the light from her shaking hands announced her trepidation better than if she'd posted a notice.

Lassiter spoke while still ten yards away. "Miss Graham, you are violating the terms of this meeting and trying my patience."

"I have what you asked for—"

"And where is Mr. Merriwether? He has a habit of acting on impulse, and I would prefer that he be where I can watch him."

I bet, thought Kenzie. Easier to shoot him that way. Aloud, she said, "He is indisposed and will be for some time. I placed him under a spell that renders him asleep." She stepped forward, extending her hand to shake as the man approached.

Lassiter turned his chin sideways and looked at her with a suspicious air. "And why would you do that?"

"He is unnecessary to this transaction and, as you mentioned, tends to act on instinct. That is a poor basis for conducting business." She lifted her right hand an inch higher.

Lassiter took the proffered hand in a limp grasp. "Indeed," he said, without releasing her.

Kenzie pulled, turning her fingernails into his palm. She couldn't hide the look of distaste from her face, and anger showed in Lassiter's gaze.

Kenzie extemporized. "You requested a specific item, Mr. Lassiter. I acquired it as per your instructions. There is no tracking device attached to it"—though she didn't know if Mitch had planted anything in the bag, which was another reason to keep him far from Lassiter—"and it is packed in the manner you prescribed."

He weighed her words, and his hostility retreated for the moment. "Dowse your light and hand me the package, Miss Graham."

Kenzie reached for the bag with her right hand to distract him while she touched the web of magic. The skin cells under her fingernails, acquired when she scraped his palm, might be enough to tie the ward to Lassiter. She closed her eyes for a moment, envisioned the signs, *saw* a tendril connect the two.

"I prefer to keep my own light." Kenzie shoved the bag at him, forcing him to take it.

He appraised her with black eyes, his fingers clutching his prize. He switched hands, freeing his right hand. "I believe that you should come with me," he said. His right hand reached into his jacket and emerged with a weapon. Unlike her herky-jerky hands, his could have been carved from ancient petrified wood.

"That was not part of our deal," said Kenzie, mustering her courage to appear calm and in control. The light betrayed her, though. *Now,* she thought, recalling the steps to the Fire spell. Her right hand rose and inscribed a symbol of a flame. *He won't shoot me.* It was as much a prayer as a thought.

Lassiter's head turned again, a predator evaluating his prey. "That is quite enough, Miss Graham."

Kenzie tied together the last part of the spell, reached for the huge amount of energy necessary to combust a body—

The world turned a ferocious white, a spluttering noise behind Lassiter growing to a blinding roar, breaking her concentration as she went to incinerate Lassiter. The Fire spell broke free of her control, potent and dangerous and unconstrained.

Simultaneously, the gun in Lassiter's hand fired, and Kenzie felt a hard jolt to her chest, high on the left side, above her armpit in the space between breast and shoulder. The impact on her body and the shock to her senses caused her to spasm. The pebble sailed into the air, burning brighter and brighter as it absorbed the Fire spell, flying over Lassiter's head.

I was wrong, she thought as consciousness faded. *He would shoot.*

The pebble landed in the white fire behind Lassiter. Kenzie felt the impact of the amulet releasing all its magic like a grenade, an explosive wave that battered her senseless. It flipped her orientation such that she seemed to see the world from Mitch's eyes. Instinctively, she knew Mitch was awake and coming for her. Kenzie willed him to stay away, stay alive, but her last memory was from his eyes, his perspective, as he ran through the parking lot, filled with dread at a pursuing gytrash, and possessed by all-consuming worry for her.

CHAPTER FIFTY-ONE

The nightmare skulked into Mitch's mind, intent on swallowing him whole. Red eyes glared at him, and the foul breath of the creature brought bile to the base of his throat. He tried to backpedal, to assess the menace, but his body refused all his commands. Caught in the boundary between full sleep and wakefulness, he was aware that it was a horrid dream that held power only as long as his eyes were closed.

Spittle dripped from his open mouth, and he swallowed the ugly taste, his body reacting with a shudder.

Kenzie!

Her soft voice, whispering a spell, had done this to him. To protect him. The nightmare was a side effect.

Who was protecting her?

Panic took the place of the nightmare, though the red eyes still haunted the inside of his eyelids. He fought the soporific effects that she'd laid upon him. Moaning gave him something to focus on. Huffing, Mitch willed his eyes to open. They quivered, and a glimmer of dim light showed in a thin line at the lower edge of his vision. He redoubled his efforts, his chin rising off his crossed arms.

The spell broke, and his eyes flew wide.

"SON OF A—"

Mitch hurtled backward off the bench, falling on his ass, and scrambling away.

Standing across the table was a huge supernatural wolf with baleful red eyes like coals from hell, the same creature from his nightmare. Lanky, it leaned forward toward him, like a hunter stalking prey. Its mouth dropped open, and a long black tongue lolled out. Mitch would have sworn it was licking its chops at dinner.

Mitch searched for a rock or a big fricking stick, but only blades of grass and some dead leaves met his frantically grasping hands.

His position of helplessness on the ground sank in, and he exploded to his feet in one convulsive motion.

"Get out of here!" he shouted, waving his arms and trying to be big and terrifying.

The beast didn't move but cocked its head to one side as though amused.

Mitch glanced at the path. How long had he been asleep? He needed to get to Kenzie. . . .

Maybe the damn thing would stay put if he treated it like a bear. He had practice with that, in Idaho before everything went to shit. *Talk softly and walk away at an oblique angle.*

"Hey, puppy," he said, the incongruity of calling a five-foot-tall wolflike apparition a puppy striking him as he sidled sideways, toward the amphitheater.

A short growl met his words, and the beast stepped to block him.

Mitch shook his head in anger. "I'm going to head that-away and leave you alone, how's that sound?" He tested another step.

The reaction was immediate and frightening as the wolf-thing leapt from the table to the path. Its front haunch dropped, and it took a step in Mitch's direction, a rumble emanating from its throat that turned Mitch's insides to liquid.

Mitch retreated.

The creature watched.

Looking around, Mitch evaluated his options. The thing was blocking the path, but he could get to Kenzie by following the road up. Well, kind of to Kenzie, and right on top of where he expected to find the shooters.

Graham!

He hadn't sent the signal for Kenzie's dad to ride to the rescue. Cursing himself, he reached into his pocket. Separating the trigger for the thermite from the remote for the robot, he hit the button to activate Alice as he backed up. Without breaking eye contact with the red orbs that reminded him of hell, he steered a course to the parking lot. Walking backward, he eased away, an occasional low growl setting the hairs on his arms on end.

His feet hit asphalt. He turned his back to the huge beast and started to run while a voice in his head warned him not to act like prey. He glanced over his shoulder, expecting to see the canine closing in a predatory chase, but the creature stood unmoving.

Mitch shifted gears from a lope to a flat-out run. It was about a third of a mile on the road to get up to the car and the top of the open field. Call it two minutes. He willed his legs to turn faster, adrenaline from the confrontation lending him false speed. His lungs burned, and his fingers tingled from a lack of oxygen, but he bore down. As long as his legs kept moving, he could endure the agony.

Gasping, he slowed on the uphill section and cursed mentally. Seconds ticked away in his head.

He glanced back again. Thirty yards behind him and trotting comfortably was the damn animal. Pressure inside, a foreboding, made him reach for the thermite trigger. How far away did Hunter say it would work? He couldn't breathe, couldn't remember, but he had to do something.

Stumbling into the parking lot, he tried to shout, but he had no air to form words. He broke to the stage and tripped, falling on the ground and sliding. The back of his mind, always operating to fit the patterns, recognized he had tripped on a body and, by the angle of the head to the neck, a dead one. Someone had taken out Lassiter's shooters.

He ignited the thermite. Stark shadows reached for him as the electric white light burned into the night air. He saw Lassiter lift a gun toward Kenzie, just as a star, so intense it had to be magic on her part, rose above the two at the stage, and then arced back to earth as gravity asserted itself.

The flaming star of Kenzie's landed, and a shock wave engulfed him. He saw the gun in Lassiter's hand jump but *felt* the impact in his shoulder, the same spot where a feathery red dart blossomed on Kenzie. Like he was in Kenzie's skin, he experienced the unbelievability of being shot.

A split second later, there was a gunshot from his right, and Lassiter lurched and fell. Mitch spun on his stomach. Between his car and the other one, he saw the barrel of a rifle. He heard the bolt get pulled to eject a shell casing, and the rack close again.

Down by the stage, Mitch saw Raymond Graham speeding to Kenzie. A glance to the rifleman showed the rifle barrel steadying, taking careful aim.

"Hell, no!" Mitch shouted, and scrambled to his feet. The barrel wavered and began to lift and turn to face Mitch.

I'm going to get shot, thought Mitch, and perversely, the thought calmed him. He sprinted as the man went from a kneeling shooter's stance to upright.

He's right-handed, Mitch saw. *He'll be slower turning and targeting.*

Mitch sped across the gap, saw the gun coming around. Ten feet out, he jumped into the air, feetfirst, aiming for the hood of the Camaro. He landed on his hip, the metal buckling beneath him. He slid across the hood on a downward angle as he aimed his kick.

Too late, though. He was looking at the barrel, saw a flash as his foot missed the torso and connected with the man's chin. Instantaneous pain exploded in his head and blinded him as he fell off the car and crumpled to the ground.

CHAPTER FIFTY-TWO

Mercury saw the gytrash pursuing Mitch up the road and followed, chest heaving. *Old wizards are no match for a fit teenager,* he thought. The crack of a gunshot galvanized him to greater exertions, though. Wheezing, he caught sight of Mitch sliding off the hood of his car, arms and legs limp. Between the vehicles, the gunman stood impossibly tall, rifle clasped in his hand. As Mercury procured a spell to remove the man as a threat, the gunman reached an apex and started a final fall to earth.

A glance toward the amphitheater was all that he required to absorb the grisly demise of the man next to the prone body of McKenzie. Graham was crouched over the girl, examining her. Another man unfamiliar to Mercury, but wearing robes, joined him. Graham pulled something from his daughter's shoulder and stood shaking his head, relief evident on his face. Mercury matched the emotion as he recognized the tranquilizer dart.

More people, all Family from the looks of them, gathered to care for Kenzie and cleanse the site of any evidence that might implicate the collective members. Mercury turned his back on them, a contemptuous twist of his lips marring his features.

He reached the crumpled shape of the boy and checked for a pulse at the carotid. Rapid, but strong.

He stood at the sound of footfalls. Graham approached toward the vehicles.

"He is mine, Raymond," Mercury said across the intervening distance. "You cannot have him."

Raymond Graham halted.

"Matthias." Graham's voice carried the whiff of an accusation attached to the name. He glanced to the young man. "So you finally found your hero?"

"I don't use that name anymore. I use Mercury now." He hesitated. "He's not my hero, Raymond, and magic found him and delivered him to McKenzie. I had nothing to do with that."

"Delivered him to *you*." The response was emphatic. "Kenzie had nothing to do with this."

"You owe him your life. Who do you think was next in the sights? And he trusted you to do the right thing for your niece."

Graham glared at him. "She is my daughter."

"Is she Sasha's daughter?"

The question opened a wound, and Graham's eyes hated him for it. He raised his hand, forefinger up, scrolled a quick character in the air, and flung a spell at Mercury.

Mercury waved a hand as though fanning flies from his face, and the spell dissipated in the space between the men.

"You were not my equal before, Raymond, so stop with the silliness." He peered at the other man, and a speculative thought crossed his mind.

Mercury indicated the body at the base of the tires with a shift of his chin, careful not to take his eyes from Graham. "You reached out to the *hechiceros,* did you now?"

"They contacted us."

"As did the boy. He trusted you."

"He's *Meat!*" The tone was vicious. "He interfered where he had no right, as you did, and—"

"And no responsibility, yet twice he came to McKenzie's aid. Don't be a blind fool. You stood next to me when Elowyn passed, heard her prophecy."

"She was aflame. The magic had already consumed her. Her prophecy means nothing." Graham shifted the argument. "You encouraged Elowyn to evade her marriage to the Rubieras, and she left the Family for Meat, and the magic of the Families splintered apart."

"She left for love, I should think," said Mercury, shaking his head as if correcting the record. He changed the subject. "McKenzie is very like her mother: terrific power without full control. The skills that she has learned in her martial arts—"

Graham started at the revelation that Mercury knew this detail.

"—as Mitchell has mentioned to me, have been a great assistance," he finished smoothly, to provide cover for Harold. "She has the power to unite us again, but not without Mitch."

"That was never part of the prophecy," Graham said.

Mercury quoted: "'A hero will come to save her—and us. Trust his heart.'" He shrugged. "It's not quite as clear as 'Bet on the number seven horse at Emerald Downs,' but it's pretty close."

"You always were an irreverent jackass." Graham looked down to the boy. "You can have him. Keep him away from my daughter."

"What should we do with the other?" asked Mercury.

"Whatever you wish." Graham looked at the body. "Your boy broke his neck." Graham took three fast strides in the direction of the stage, stopped, and turned back. "You are still banished. You will not contact anyone in the Family. I may not be able to stop you by myself, but you can't stand against us collectively."

With a final flat stare filled with a desire to see Mercury face a rougher justice, Graham nodded and went to his daughter.

Mercury knelt at Mitch's side. The boy's face was bloody from a wound that creased the middle of his forehead under the hairline. Mitch's chest rose and fell with regularity. Mercury placed his right thumb along the jawline, first two fingers splayed, the pointed finger on the temple and the middle on the boy's forehead over the left eye. He muttered *"Æsculapium"* and lifted his hand.

The boy would sleep for a bit, so Mercury investigated the two cars.

The second one, presumably belonging to the man that Mitch had defeated, held the most interesting surprise: a cell phone jammer. *Now, why would . . . ?* With a rush of insight, Mercury saw the truth. The jammer had smothered the signal that Mitch sent to alert Graham. Raymond's response had been on intuition, and he'd arrived too late.

How much to tell Mitch? he wondered. A groan brought urgency to the question. The deaths of the two sharpshooters and Lassiter would be laid to this nondescript, yet apparently lethal, young man. Mitch made a perfect fall guy.

He walked back to Mitch.

The boy's blue eyes were open, twitching to the sides. Awareness returned to his face. In a spasmodic tightening of all his muscles, Mitch tried to practically hurl himself from a supine position to his feet.

"One step at a time, Mitch."

"Kenzie? Where is she? She got shot. Is she okay?"

Mercury glanced at the stage. "She's in the care of the Family and safe, thanks to you."

Mitch's hand darted to his head. The blood had already begun to congeal and black flakes stuck to his hand. "I was shot."

"Not fatally," said Mercury.

"I need to see Kenzie." Mitch struggled to his feet, with more success this time. His gaze went to the stage. A cringe crossed his face at the bustle of eerily quiet activity.

"As I said, her father is with her. I would strongly suggest that you do not try to contact her for a bit, as Raymond is most upset with you." Mercury searched the boy's face to see if the message registered. Stubbornness glared back. "If it's any consolation, I'm not welcome at the Graham household, either."

"It isn't."

"Can you walk?" An inane question for the youngster, who a moment ago was ready to rush to Kenzie's side, but Mitch had more motivation, then.

"Yeah." Mitch staggered to the side. "Mostly. I'm a little light-headed."

"Not bad for a man who was shot," said Mercury, taking Mitch's elbow. "I left a scar for you."

Puzzlement greeted the statement. "What?"

"Your wound. I left a scar. It adds a dashing air."

Mitch saw the killer in the shadows between cars. "What about him?"

"Graham will dispatch people to handle this," said Mercury, "and I ensured that he would stay asleep for a while." He delivered the lie smoothly and pulled the boy along. "We'll come back for the car in the morning. Graham won't tow it because it would create questions in the record."

"It was like I could see through her eyes for a minute there, when everything went crazy; like I was inside her skin and she was inside mine." Mitch's voice sounded disjointed.

Mercury tugged. "Come now, your part tonight is done."

Mitch hesitated, turning to search once more for Kenzie, and then, disappointed, followed.

CHAPTER FIFTY-THREE

How empty can someone get? Kenzie didn't know, but could feel the void inside her. The shoulder that had taken the dart still ached, but worse, her head wanted to split. She squinted to limit the glare of the day.

It should be raining, she thought.

She'd failed. She had started the spell, felt the magic. Then had come the brilliant white light, the gun in Lassiter's hand, and before she slid to oblivion, panic at a vision of Mitch flying through the air, getting shot.

She touched magic and sought Mitch, found him, seething, but understood it was magic. It lied. It wasn't really Mitch, but something her mind created to fill the painful hole left by him. She released the beguiling magic.

Kenzie heard unfamiliar voices downstairs. She ignored them, as she had ignored Sasha and Raymond when they lit into her about her "adventure." She clenched her teeth, remembering the interrogation by Raymond. She got a measure of revenge, though, pointing out it was Sasha who had put them all at risk and nearly gotten her killed. Sasha, who had kept the full import of MAGE from everyone, including Raymond. Aric had known, was a willing accomplice, because he wanted to be powerful. Now the dumbass was dead, per Raymond, and Belinda the Witch was missing.

A shout from Sasha interrupted her ruminations. "McKenzie, come downstairs, please."

More like "by imperial decree," she thought, but roused herself. She checked her hair in the mirror. She was presentable. She practiced a smile. *Ugh.*

The living room held her parents and two new people, shuffling their feet in tension and talking in monosyllables. The one she could see clearly was an older man. First impressions revealed a tall man, ridiculously handsome, with graying hair at the temples and an olive complexion. A man very much in control of himself—and everyone else. The suit he wore must have cost thousands to look casual, and she could picture him in a tuxedo, opening a gala. And he was a wizard. Lines of force flowed from him. She recognized the pattern. A personal ward.

The other person stood in the shadow of the first, obscured.

"Mr. Rubiera, may I introduce my daughter, McKenzie Graham," said Sasha, her tone faintly anxious.

Kenzie's eyes narrowed at the tone and the formal speech.

Rubiera faced her and inclined his head. "A pleasure, Miss Graham." A cultured voice with a hint of steel; the voice of one used to obedience.

"The pleasure is mine," Kenzie replied, glancing to his eyes as she extended her hand. The smile froze on her face as she saw his onyx orbs, lacking any warmth or humanity. The smile that came to his lips at her reaction twisted them in a cruel line. Unbidden, her hand dropped to her side.

A teenage boy, her age or close, stepped out from behind Rubiera. He stood an inch taller than his father but shared his looks. Instead of a suit, he wore chinos, a button-up shirt, and polished black shoes. And he, too, was a wizard, but blazing like a nova to everyone else's pinprick of stars. No constructed wards or spells, yet he radiated sheer power.

"I'm Hunter," said the youth.

He made no move toward her, and she stood her ground, mind racing.

How many wizards were named Hunter? Kenzie knew of one, Mitch's friend. There couldn't possibly be two.

She looked to Sasha, saw the triumphant gleam that she wore, and instantly realized that this was not a chance or friendly meeting. This was a formal visit.

The Magic must survive.

Kenzie glanced back to the Rubieras. An open pit formed in Kenzie's heart. Sasha would have her will done, but the naked ambition of the woman left Kenzie dismayed. Not only would she force Kenzie to marry but, in the process, seek to unite the two Families. Undoubtedly, she expected to be the matriarch of both. Kenzie wondered if Rubiera understood Sasha's scheming for what it was.

Kenzie's stomach lurched, and she closed her eyes. If she put out a hand, she thought she'd be able to touch Mitch, wanted to touch Mitch. If the Families suspected that she loved Mitch, they would kill him.

The Magic must survive.

No, she thought. *Mitch must survive.* To save Mitch, she had to betray him.

She opened tear-filled eyes. Hunter's expectant gaze met hers, and she surrendered.

"Hello, Hunter."

CHAPTER FIFTY-FOUR

"There's a cop here to see you," Uncle Henry yelled down the hall, triggering a sense of *déjà vu* in Mitch. He rubbed the left side of his chest in a hard circular motion, below the collarbone. Must have hurt it when he hit the ground. Weary, he got off his bed to see what Mercury wanted now.

He made it to the living room, turned to the door, and froze. It was Kenzie's father who stood in the doorway wearing a cop face, not Mercury. He wore a pea coat to ward off the weather, which had reverted to Seattle drab.

What now? thought Mitch.

"Why don't we talk outside," Graham suggested. He directed his next comment to Mitch's uncle. "Sir, any problem if I talk with your nephew in private for a few moments? It's nothing serious, just getting a few points clarified."

"Whatever," Uncle Henry said. The mellowing effect that Hunter had laid on Henry was fading, and the old disagreeableness showed at the edges. Mitch gave it another week before he returned to his full-jerk self.

Graham indicated the open door with a sideways nod of his head, and Mitch followed him into a drizzly gray afternoon. The police lieutenant led him away from the door to the middle of the driveway, out of earshot from the house. Next to the garage, Mitch's robot sat in a cardboard box. The cop looked weary, with furrowed worry lines at the corners of his eyes. Mitch waited.

"What am I going to do with you, Mitch?"

The rhetorical question rankled him, and he bit down on his initial intent to respond flippantly. Mitch said nothing, letting the cop lay out the agenda; though, based on the tone, he was certain to not like it. It must have showed on his face.

"I'm not here to be your friend. Probably the opposite. But I owe you some order of gratitude for the way in which you helped McKenzie.

First"—he nodded across the street—"when they tried to kidnap her, and then again with Lassiter. It took some intestinal fortitude to reach out to me as you did."

"You were late!" Mitch scowled at Graham. "I had it set up, all you had to do was be there on time, and everyone would still be okay."

"I was late because the second group that crashed your party brought a jammer to make sure that you couldn't get a signal out." Graham sighed. "That's not relevant now. You're lucky that the *hechiceros'* hired man didn't kill you on the spot."

Mitch filed the term "*hechiceros*" away to look up later and fingered the scar. "He tried."

"And he will pay the appropriate price," said Graham, his eyes evasive. He reached into an inside pocket of his voluminous coat, pulling out a picture. He held it out.

Reluctantly, Mitch took it from Graham. It took a second for him to recognize the setting: a dim hallway, and a teenage boy in a hoodie sneaking in a door. It was the charter school, obviously. Him in the hoodie. Hunter, though, was missing from the picture, airbrushed right out.

"I have you for breaking, entering, and theft of chemicals, with intent to make an explosive device," said Graham. "Because of your age, I might be able to get the DA to try you as an adult, meaning a minimum sentence of ten years."

Mitch fought his face, strained to keep the anger off it. If Graham had wanted to arrest him, he'd already be in a holding cell. "What's the condition?" he asked, knowing already.

With a hot stare, Graham said, "You stay away from my daughter. You don't try to see her, you don't call her, you don't even think of her. She's not meant for someone like you. If I find out that you are still trying to corrupt her and lead her away from her rightful place in our world, I will have the charges brought. They will stick, and you will go to jail. Am I clear?"

"Yes, sir." *Don't show it, let him think he won.*

They held a long stare-down, neither willing to concede to the other.

Graham looked away first. "I'll hold you to that." He pivoted to leave.

"Have you told Kenzie the same thing?" Mitch called after him.

The man stopped, facing Mitch. "McKenzie knows her duty," he said with finality.

Mitch gave a fast, angry nod. Graham searched his face for another second and walked to his car. In seconds, he was gone.

Mitch walked to the park. He shouldn't have expected anything less from Graham, he fumed. Cover up all the traces of Kenzie and Hunter's family, but keep leverage over Mitch with evidence of felony theft and any other crap charge that Graham could drum up.

Scary as hell that a cop could—*would!*—cover up the dead bodies of Lassiter and his men.

Mitch counted steps to block out the image of the dead men. The steady cadence of his steps soothed him. Taking his phone out, he looked up "*hechiceros.*" Spanish wizards.

Natch.

Hunter's people. So they were behind the second shooter at the park. A shudder ran up his spine as the image of the gaping barrel flashed before his eyes, followed by the crunching memory of his foot connecting with the assailant. He suppressed it by tightening all the muscles in his back and chest, clenching until the fear-filled spasm passed.

Hunter, or his dad, had tracked him, stayed a step ahead of him. He puzzled over it, and the only answer that made a modicum of sense was they already knew who Lassiter's boss was. If they didn't, they would have tried capturing him so they could get information. By implication, they knew about the SD card, and the schematics stored on it. Mitch had palmed the original, put a fake into the bag. Right now, the real card was stashed at the bottom of his computer desk drawer. He wondered how long it would be before someone came looking for it. How many someones? Hunter's family, probably. And whoever hired Lassiter. Kenzie's mother.

His thoughts shifted tracks.

He reached the amphitheater from the path that Kenzie had followed. He glanced up at his car. As Mercury had promised, nobody had towed it. A fluttering piece of white was stuck on the windshield. Mercury hadn't said they wouldn't ticket him. The slight grade felt like Everest as he trudged upward.

McKenzie knows her duty. The words burned, and now he let his emotions show, hands clenching into fists. Like she was chattel, and that left him royally pissed off. *Kenzie can make up her own mind,* he thought, offended at the most instinctive of levels. The rest of them could go to hell.

He glanced over his shoulder, to where he had set up the thermite. The bushes showed scorches but otherwise looked okay. As he was turning back, a glitter caught his eye, arresting his movement. Head cocked at an angle, Mitch retraced his steps. Cautiously, he made his way to the bushes, noting the new turf installed to disguise the location of Lassiter's demise.

Whatever had captured his eye disappeared when he approached, so he dropped to his knees to look under the bushes. He took a deep, quaky breath and pushed the singed branches out of the way.

He shook his head. The remains of the thermite and piston lay concealed. A surge of adrenaline sent Mitch's pulse racing. Graham and his people were too efficient. No way their cleanup crew would have missed collecting all the evidence.

A blue sparkle of light leapt to his attention, defying the shadow cast by the vegetation. Mitch gathered the piston and slag, dragging them out of the way. A blue gemstone, seemingly burning with an interior fire, remained. Mitch felt his eyes widen when he saw the square-cut, polished facets. Fingers trembling, he plucked the crystal from its hiding place and turned it in his hand. The spark disappeared but the light of the day refracted from the cut faces. *A blue sapphire,* he thought in wonder. *Pure aluminum oxide. Purely impossible.*

He closed his fist around the stone, and wobbled, almost falling. Kenzie's presence leapt close to him, and his shoulder hurt worse than ever.

Despair gathered around him, and resignation.

Shivering, he pocketed the sapphire.

The sun, seemingly absent a moment ago, warmed his back.

Mitch took a deep breath. He was going to have to get better at the hero business. Fast.

Kenzie still wasn't safe.

OTHER NOVELS BY PAUL DUFFAU

A<small>CCIDENTAL</small> H<small>ERO</small> S<small>ERIES</small>
G<small>OT</small> T<small>O</small> B<small>E</small> A H<small>ERO</small>
S<small>TAND</small> Y<small>OUR</small> G<small>ROUND</small>, H<small>ERO</small>
(coming December 2017)

Y<small>OUNG</small> A<small>DULT</small>
T<small>RAIL OF</small> S<small>ECOND</small> C<small>HANCES</small>
F<small>INISHING</small> K<small>ICK</small>

THANK YOU!

Writers don't say that often enough. I wanted to make sure I didn't forget. I hope that you enjoyed reading *Got To Be A Hero*. If you did, please do me the kindness of leaving a review at the retailer that you purchased it from and let your friends know about *Hero*, too.

I'm going to get back to writing and get the next book done. Again, my thanks!

Paul Duffau

MORE ABOUT PAUL DUFFAU

By day, Paul gets to play with spider-infested crawlspaces, walk on roofs, and narrowly avoid electrocution while he checks out houses. For fun, he trail runs in the Pacific Northwest with the deer, elk, an occasional moose, and panic-inducing rattlesnakes. Bears he avoids, mostly.

You can follow Paul on Twitter and Facebook. To sign up for his non-spammy newsletter, visit his website at www.paulduffau.com.